THE BARENTS INCIDENT

John A. C. Kiff

Published by

**MELROSE
BOOKS**

An Imprint of Melrose Press Limited
St Thomas Place, Ely
Cambridgeshire
CB7 4GG, UK
www.melrosebooks.com

FIRST EDITION

Cover designed by Hannah Belcher

ISBN 978 1 907732 33 1

Printed and bound in Great Britain by:
CPI Group (UK) Ltd, Croydon, CR0 4YY

FSC
www.fsc.org
MIX
Paper from
responsible sources
FSC® C013604

DEDICATIONS

To my dear wife, Joyce, for her continued patience, support and tolerance during the production of this book.

To my very good friend, Dick Lloyd-Williams, without whose constant advice and encouragement this book may never have been completed.

Lastly, but certainly not least, this book is dedicated with my deepest respect and thanks to all those diesel-boat submariners who took part in covert patrols in the earlier years of the Cold War but who, in accordance with the Official Secrets Act, received no recognition for this.

PROLOGUE

Early December 1945. The Soviet submarine *Shtshuka* is on a covert surveillance patrol in the North Sea, and is now stationed forty miles due east of the Moray Firth.

The lights of the fishing fleet, still flickering wetly in the darkness, were again the first thing that Kapitan Lieutenant Uri Molenov saw as his periscope broke surface. He had known they would be there. It was midnight, and *Shtshuka* had been in close contact with this approaching fishing fleet for the past two hours, listening to them on her ASDICs and occasionally coming to periscope depth for a visual sighting. A frown now furrowed Molenov's brow as he carefully studied this fleet of six British trawlers. They were too near for comfort. They were becoming more than a nuisance; they were now a potential danger.

Commencing yet another all-round periscope sweep, Molenov again meticulously searched the full 360 degrees of horizon. It was a clear night – exceptionally clear for this time of year – and it was very cold. A myriad of stars glinted brightly from the cloudless skies, as if competing with the lights of the nearby fishing fleet; while a primrose-coloured crescent moon cast its pale glow over the dark heaving surface of the sea, highlighting the profusion of white horses that danced ceaselessly on the crest of each short wave in a tide that was running south by south-east. This was good submarine periscope weather.

His search completed, Molenov again trained his periscope back towards the fishing fleet. He estimated the nearest approaching trawler to be about 1000 metres to his north, bearing fine off his starboard bow and steering steadily south, towards him. If she continued on this course she could soon become a problem. The second trawler was no more than 100 metres off the starboard beam of the first, almost parallel and steering an identical course. Molenov guessed they were pair fishing. The lights of four other vessels comprising this small fleet were in a fairly tight cluster, still some 2000 metres distant as far as he could tell, and roughly on the same bearing. He would go deep and let them pass, and then he would steer north and put himself well behind them, where he would surface and recharge his batteries uninterrupted. *Shtsthuka* had been dived for almost twelve hours. Her air was becoming increasingly foul and her batteries were low, but with luck she should manage a full battery charge before daylight.

Thirty minutes later, at 00.35, Molenov's ASDICs told him that the fishermen were now to his south, but only just, and they appeared to have stopped. So he again brought *Shtshuka* cautiously to periscope depth. The nearest two boats were stopped less than 200 metres off his stern, but at least they were clear of him. He would dive again and continue on a northerly course to put at least four kilometres between himself and this fleet before surfacing. Then, after fully recharging his batteries, he would again turn south, skirt around the fishermen, and take up station off the Firth of Forth, the most southerly point of his designated patrol area.

Then without warning *Shtshuka* shuddered violently and jarred to a stop. The surprised curse from Molenov as the periscope lens assembly buried itself painfully into his right eye socket was completely obliterated by the harsh shriek of metal grinding against metal somewhere above him. He realised immediately what had happened. It was a situation ranking high in every submarine commander's order of nightmares. *Shtshuka* had run into the trawl of the fishing fleet – probably the pair of fishers nearest to him now. Still cursing, but now more quietly, he ordered the periscope to be lowered and stopped his drive motors. Without propulsion *Shtshuka* slowly began to sink. Praying that they were not yet too badly entangled, Molenov ordered both her motors to slow astern. A wire grated noisily across the casing above him, warning that further movement was risky, too risky, but he knew that he must keep these nets clear of his propellers at all costs, and to do this he must surface and cut her free. There was no other option!

Molenov then ordered his first officer to muster a party of three seamen to stand by in the control room, each armed with various types of wire-cutting tools. This party would be headed by the young fourth officer, Lieutenant Alexci Portrova, not yet turned nineteen years and the youngest officer aboard. When they were mustered and ready, Molenov brought *Shtshuka* gently to the surface.

Now on the surface and trimmed down with her casing barely clear of the water, *Shtshuka* still rolled in the heavy swell. Portrova and his men, using shielded lighting from their torches, climbed carefully down from the bridge to the sea-swept casing.

They soon found that the situation was not as drastic as it might have been – at least not yet. A wire, some five centimetres thick – probably a main trawl wire – was snagged firmly around the forward end of *Shtshuka*'s bridge, almost at casing level. Straining bar taut in the darkness, this thick woven steel line had already cut deeply into the metal of the bridge structure. In order to release *Shtshuka*, this wire would have to be cut.

A bitterly cold wind of about force four was blowing from the north. This would not make their job any easier, but more important was the fact that in the relative still of this night, a wind such as this would almost certainly carry any sound southward, easily as far as the fishing fleet. An axe would be quicker, but too noisy. He would try first with a hacksaw.

One of his men began to saw with a slow deliberate motion, while the other two, using bundles of wet cotton rags tried, but with little success, to muffle the sound of this hacksaw. It had been slow and difficult work, with the rags repeatedly fouling the hacksaw blade and the men cursing continuously at the icy drenching spume now breaking over them.

Portrova knew that this was taking far too long. At any moment the trailing wire could slacken and drop down to foul *Shtshuka*'s propellers. Now impatient, he grabbed the saw and, discarding the cotton waste, began cutting frantically, using long rapid strokes. In spite of the bitter cold and the freezing wetness he was soon sweating profusely and stopped momentarily to throw off his lifejacket.

Then, when almost two thirds cut through, the wire suddenly parted. Hissing viciously, it snaked back around the front of the bridge, flaying hard against Portrova's waist, spinning him around, knocking the wind from his body. Then he was falling, bouncing off the steep saddle tanks, his skull striking hard against unyielding metal as he slid helplessly into the sea.

Alexci Portrova sank like a stone into that icy black water. The weight of his weatherproof clothing, combined with his heavy leather sea boots, dragged him under the surface even before the bitter cold of the North Sea had begun to lance into his body. Now he struggled, gasping and gagging, to the surface, his already leaden arms flailing wildly and bitter sea water spewing from his burning lungs. His eyes strained into what seemed to him a stygian blackness as he searched desperately for help. But there was no help! Again he became blinded with the icy salt water. He tried to call out, but no sound came from his mouth. Spitting sea water, he gulped in a deep breath as the sea again closed over his head. He was sinking, and there was nothing he could do to help himself.

Then quite suddenly there was quiet. The roaring noise in his ears had stopped and the panic had left him even though he knew he was still sinking. Sharp stabbing pains in his chest reminded him to release his breath. He released his breath, slowly, controlling it through pursed lips, as they had taught him in the submarine school. The pain in his chest began to ease and he was again moving upward, slowly at first, then faster, until he was once more on the surface, where, spluttering and gasping and with salt-filled eyes stinging mercilessly, he again strained into the darkness for signs of help.

Then at last he saw what he was searching for: a long dark shape just to the north of him, low in the water, almost invisible. *Shtshuka*! It could only be *Shtshuka*... no more than ten metres distant, but for the most part hidden behind the swell. He began to shout, his first attempt no more than a series of rasping croaks. Then at last he managed a full-blooded yell.

Something hit him hard on his left shoulder. Summoning all his strength, he reached out and grabbed the hard cork ring that was now bouncing against his head. Clutching this lifebuoy, he struggled to make himself secure. It wasn't easy but finally, with his head and one arm lodged through the ring, his strength again left him and he lay floating half submerged, exhausted and helpless, too weak even to call out. His frozen fingers began searching for the line. But where was the line? It should have been attached to the lifebuoy, with the other end aboard *Shtshuka*. They should be pulling him in by now. But this lifebuoy was not attached to anything!

As he topped each successive swell he continued to search desperately for his submarine. Yes – she was still there, but now she seemed further away. He called out repeatedly, trying to ignore successive mouthfuls of bitter freezing water. Then his throat began to close over and his cries became weaker until finally he could call out no more. He could see that *Shtshuka* was getting smaller. He was drifting away from her. He knew they would be searching for him, but he also knew that his captain would not risk detection and for this reason he would not search for too long. If they failed to pick him up soon they would simply write him off as lost – another regrettable accident at sea. They could do no other. Alexci Portrova suddenly felt very alone.

Then from somewhere behind him he heard splashing and heavy grunting. Someone else was in the water. An arm struck his upturned face, and another grabbed his shoulder. 'I have you, Alexci. Hold on, my friend.' The voice was strained and choking, but Portrova recognised it immediately. It was the voice of Kapitan Leitenant Gregori Lenkov, *Shtshuka*'s first officer.

Lenkov had been watching from *Shtshuka*'s bridge when Portrova went into the sea, and without hesitation had pulled off his sea boots and, stripping off his leather watch-coat, had dived into the sea from the bridge. He was a strong swimmer. He would find Portrova.

Together they lay on their backs, treading water, Portrova still with his head and one arm through the lifebuoy, but now with Lenkov supporting him. They both searched for *Shtshuka* as each swell lifted them, but she was no longer there. The lights of the fishing fleet seemed much nearer now and both men knew that they were drifting rapidly towards this fleet. Lenkov gasped, 'Hold on, my young friend. Together we will swim to the fishermen. They will give us safety.' On their backs, they kicked with their feet. Portrova was exhausted and Lenkov's legs now provided most of their propulsion. He seemed to have strength for both of them. Every few minutes he would turn his head to look for the nearest fishing vessel.

Portrova began to drift in and out of consciousness. The bitter cold was taking its effect and he'd lost track of the time he'd been in the water. Summoning the last of his strength, he too now raised his head to look for the fishing fleet, and in the pale light of the moon he could just make out the dark shape of the nearest trawler. Instinctively he began to kick out more strongly, helping the now-struggling Lenkov.

Both men had been barely conscious when the trawler's stern had loomed over them like a huge black shadow. But even in the pale light of that winter moon, the rust-smeared white lettering on the blunt stern bore a name that Portrova would remember for the rest of his life. *Ocean Harvester*, Lowestoft. She was moving forward very slowly, carrying Portrova and Lenkov down her port side. The two Russians had expended the last of their strength in a series of loud hoarse yells. Even so, they were rapidly approaching the trawler's bows before the fishermen finally heard them. Then, amidst a sudden profusion of dazzling lamp- and torchlight, the trawler's crew threw lines.

Lenkov grabbed a line and secured it around Portrova's waist as quickly as his frozen hands would allow, and the fishermen pulled Portrova aboard. Lenkov then looked up for a second line and a grappling hook hit him full in the face. For a brief moment he lost consciousness, but then he had recovered sufficiently to feed a hook through his belt. With numbed hands and eyes filled with blood this had been difficult, but it was this same cold that mercifully numbed the pain from the huge open gash in his head. Gregori Lenkov would not have known that his skull was broken, and that even now he was a dead man.

They hauled Lenkov aboard, dragging him unceremoniously up the ship's side and onto the fo'c'sle. Carrying him aft to the sparsely lit upper deck, they threw him face down on the cold steel deck next to Portrova, also face down and still gagging uncontrollably.

Someone knelt beside Portrova and turned him over. Still choking and coughing up water, Portrova stared up at the ring of faces looking down on him. Blinking wildly, he tried to focus his salt-filled eyes past the glare of torches and lanterns and at the men who held them, but he was still completely incapable of speech. Now another figure moved forward to lean over him, shining his torch directly into his face. He muttered to the group standing behind him, 'Who the hell are they?'

'Well, they ain't Brits, that's for sure,' growled one of the standing figures.

'No – they're friggin' Jerries, I'll bet,' muttered another. 'Wot you two doin' out 'ere all on yer own then, Fritz?' He was looking down at Portrova.

'Nah, he ain't no Jerry,' said another voice. 'You can tell that by the gear 'e's wearin'. No, I reckon he's a bleedin' Ruskie!'

Now the kneeling man turned his attention towards Lenkov. 'This one's in a bad way; 'e's bleedin' badly. Looks like 'e's bumped 'is 'ead. Could be serious.'

'He come up on an iron,' said one of the group. 'Looks like 'e caught it wiv 'is 'ead!'

'So, which one of you stupid sods threw an iron over the side?' The kneeling man looked up at the surrounding faces. No one answered his question.

Then a large oilskin-clad figure emerged from the bridge. Clutching unsteadily at the bridge rail, he directed a handheld searchlight at the group of men on the deck below him, and bellowed in a heavily nasal Liverpudlian accent, 'I ain't payin' you friggin lot to stand about gawpin'. We got a lot of fucked-up nets to sort out, you know that.' The skipper lowered his six-foot-plus frame unsteadily down the bridge ladder and lurched across the deck, barging his way through the half-circle of men, to where Portrova and Lenkov lay.

'We just pulled 'em aboard, Skip!' The man kneeling beside Portrova stood up.

'Aye, so you 'ave. So you 'ave!' The skipper knelt and stared intently at the prostrate Portrova. 'Who are you, fella?'

Portrova had managed to stop coughing, and returned the stare. But even in the darkness which now disguised those dull, sullen and bloodshot eyes, it didn't need instinct to tell him that this man was not a friend. He was glad that he had picked up more than a rudiment of the English language while at officers' training school, and had tried to improve on this since. Even so, his

English was still very limited. Painfully he pulled himself up to rest on one elbow, knowing that he must speak, even if just to tell this man who they were.

'I am Lieutenant Alexci Portrova, of the Soviet submarine *Shtshuka*, and this is Kapitan Leitenant Gregori Lenkov, also of *Shtshuka*. We are lost overboard.' He spoke carefully, with all the dignity he could muster, but with a hint of defiance he could not hide. The effort to produce just these few words now sent him into a further paroxysm of coughing, sea water and bile pouring uncontrollably from his mouth and nose.

Ignoring this, the skipper grabbed Portrova's coat and, standing up, effortlessly pulled the still-choking Russian to his feet. 'So, you're a bloody Ruskie, eh?' Now those bloodshot eyes were filled with hate. 'An' you went an' fell off yer friggin' submarine?' He shook Portrova like a rag doll. 'Well now, ain't that a bit of 'ard luck!'

'Easy, Skip,' muttered one of the men stood behind. 'He's done nowt to us an' the bloody war's over now, anyway.'

'Done nowt to us, you say?' The skipper started to shake Portrova even harder. 'Done nowt? Who do you think just fucked up a perfectly good set of nets, eh? I'll tell you who. It was these two bastards an' their oppo's out there in their frigging submarine. That's who it was! And they've cost me an' you bastards a lot of time and a hell of a lot of money! So don't let me be 'earing you say they ain't done nowt to us!' With that he let go Portrova's coat while at the same time balling his right hand into a huge fist and punching him hard in the stomach.

Portrova dropped like a stone, writhing, gasping, and spewing up even more sea water. Another of the crew stepped forward. 'Steady, Skip; you'll bloody kill 'im.' Turning to the others, he mouthed silently from behind his hand, ''E's pissed again!'

Now the skipper rounded on the group of men standing behind him, his eyes blazing with fury. 'Kill 'im, you say? That's what I ought to fuckin' well do. Ruskies, Jerries. Frenchies, bloody Eyeties – they're all the fuckin' same! Can't stand the bastards, and neither would you lot if you'd seen as much of 'em as I 'ave over the past five years!'

Then he stepped over Portrova's still-writhing body to where Lenkov was lying, now semi-conscious, groaning softly.

'An' wot about this bastard, then? What's 'e got to say for 'imself? Fuck all, I shouldn't wonder. Looks like you got an 'ell of an 'eadache though, fella!' Bending, he grabbed the back of Lenkov's collar and hauled him roughly to his feet. 'Wot you got to say fer yourself then, Ivan?' But Gregori Lenkov wasn't hearing or saying anything. He was unconscious, just seconds from death. The skipper grunted, releasing his grip on Lenkov's collar and letting him fall heavily back to the deck. Now glaring down at the prone figure at his feet, he uttered a snarl of contempt and drove his heavy sea boot hard into the Russian's defenceless head. Lenkov jerked violently, coughing a thick stream of bile and blood, and then lay still, with dark red trickles of blood seeping from his ears and nose mingling with the black congealing blood crust already covering his head and face.

'Christ, Skip, you 'ave killed 'im!' The men stepped back as one, horrified.

'Killed 'im, 'ave I?' snarled the skipper. 'Well, in that case 'e might as well go back to where 'e bloody well come from, eh? P'r'aps 'e may like to 'ave a word wiv Davy Jones.' Grinning savagely, he turned back to the now-dead Lenkov and placed a foot under his body, pushing him effortlessly towards to the ship's side. Then bending, he grasped the Russian's body with both hands and rolled him under the guardrails, back down into the freezing dark waters of the North Sea.

The dazed and totally confused Portrova had witnessed this. Now filled with an uncontrollable rage, he struggled painfully to his feet and lurched towards the skipper with both arms raised in a feeble gesture of attack. The skipper turned. Eying Portrova drunkenly, he reached out with both arms to grab the staggering Russian's shoulders, swinging him roughly around to face the crewmen. 'So, what was you lot thinkin' then? Maybe I'll let this bastard go. Wos that it? Well 'e really ain't any use to me, or to any other bastard, come to think of it, and 'e's cost me a lot of money tonight.' He swung the Russian around to again stare into his face, at the same time gripping Portrova's lower jaw with his right hand and squeezing hard. Portrova groaned with pain. Oblivious to the groans, the skipper squeezed even harder, cruelly, viciously, as though trying to force his fingers through Portrova's cheeks. 'An' you just a young whippersnapper not even dry behind yer ears yet. Well, there's a thing! But I think we'll put you back from where you come from as well.' Releasing his grip on Portrova's face, he balled his fist and punched him hard in the mouth. Then grabbing the Russian's sagging shoulders to hold him upright, he pushed him against the guardrail and, with another snarl, toppled him back into the sea.

Now he turned to glare at the horrified faces of his watching men. 'All right, lads, show's over. Get yerselves back to work.' He lurched towards the bridge ladder and, stopping half way up the ladder, he turned towards them. 'An' you lot better remember this as well. You ain't none of you seen nothin' tonight! This never 'appened, all right? I don't want nobody gabbin' off about this when we gets back alongside, or they'll be joinin' our friends down there, an' you better believe that!'

The men shuffled uneasily, but said nothing. They knew their skipper was a bad man to cross. 'Scouse' Dennehy was never a pleasant man, especially when he was in drink, and he was in drink more often than not these days. But tonight, as hard and rough as these men were, Dennehy had turned their stomachs. They watched him slowly haul his heavy frame up the ladder to the bridge and to his waiting bottle, knowing that he would have no regrets, no remorse for his brutal actions, not even in the cold light of day.

A born-and-bred Liverpudlian, Dennehy, like many of his peers, had been raised in a hard school. His war, too, had been a particularly hard one. During two years as first mate in tankers shipping fuel to Russia he had twice been torpedoed, miraculously surviving both sinkings virtually unharmed. He had also survived the sinking of his freighter in the south Atlantic in 1943, spending eighteen days in an open boat with little food or fresh water before being picked up. That war had turned him into an even harder and more bitter man, trusting no one, not even himself.

He had spent the last two months of 1944 between ships, and while on leave in his home town of Liverpool he had taken up what he liked to call his 'rest and relaxation' period, consisting of one long round of drinking, whoring and gambling down to his last penny. Then he met Sylvia. But Sylvia was not just another woman; even in his semi-permanent state of drunken confusion he could tell that she was different from all the others. Sylvia was special, a haven from the hell that he had lived through for the past five years. They melded from day one. Dennehy had never before felt love for any woman, or indeed any other thing, but for this love of Sylvia he sobered up and had gradually pulled himself together. They rented a flat on the outskirts of Liverpool, and together they made a solemn pact that they would marry as soon as the war was over. Sober now, Dennehy pawned his pocket watch to buy Sylvia an engagement ring. They were happy together; the happiest he could ever remember being.

Then at the February of 1945, with the war in Europe coming to an end, Dennehy signed as first mate on an auxiliary minesweeper. He saw no action aboard this sweeper and she had docked in Liverpool on the eve of the VE celebrations. He had played a full part in these celebrations. He couldn't help himself; he felt it was his due. But, when twenty-four hours later he turned up at the flat looking for Sylvia, she wasn't there. The flat was empty. Neither Sylvia nor her clothes were to be found. For four weeks he had searched for her or for any news of her. Finally it transpired that she had run off to the States with a GI, just before he had been paid off in Liverpool to join the victory celebrations.

Dennehy had never recovered from this cruel situation, and after wrecking the flat he'd spent the next three months in a drunken stupor, drinking, brawling, and sleeping rough on the few nights that he was not confined to a police cell. But finally he had accepted that Sylvia was never coming back to him; she had gone from his life for ever. By the time he had accepted this, through sheer willpower and the knowledge that he was well on the road to self-destruction, he had managed to face up to his life again, but by now as a full-blown alcoholic. In spite of this he had made his way across country to Lowestoft, where he found work on the trawlers.

Now here aboard *Harvester*, Dennehy was master – albeit a hard and embittered master with no friends except his whisky bottle. But he knew his job, and in spite of the drink and his unforgiving attitude, he caught fish. He was one of the most successful skippers working out of Lowestoft. His crew knew who buttered their bread; they would say nothing more of this night.

Because of Dennehy's success in fish finding, the skippers of the other five vessels had come to regard him as their leader. They were known as the 'Scouse Dennehy Squadron' and wherever he went, they followed. Now, with his nets finally repaired, Dennehy leaned over the microphone of his short wave radio and bellowed to the rest of the fleet, 'D'you hear there? This is *Ocean Harvester*. I'm carryin' on up north to look for some fish off Norway, where we shoulda been in the first place! You lot comin'?' Without waiting for any replies, he swung the wheel hard to port and came around to steer north, setting a speed of ten knots. The rest of the fleet followed.

★ ★ ★ ★ ★

Alexci Portrova would never know how he survived the next hour. His abrupt return to the icy water had shocked him back to full consciousness and he had struck out to force himself clear of *Ocean Harvester* with all the strength that remained in his body. Away from this fleet and these British madmen, he was once again swimming for his life. The wind had now dropped considerably, and although he didn't know it, he was nearing the waiting *Shtshuka*.

Portrova had no fear of dying; he felt only a soul-consuming hatred, and this was the hatred that would keep him alive, would succour him. It was this hatred that banished the effect of the icy cold of the water from his exhausted body and fuelled him with the will to live, giving him the strength to keep swimming no matter what. He would live, and one day he would take his revenge on those Britishers. No matter how long it took, sooner or later that day would come. They would pay dearly for the murder of his friend Gregori.

When they had pulled him from the sea, Portrova had been more dead than alive. Molenov had said that it was truly a miracle that they had found him at all – a chance in a million. The fishing fleet was on the move again, now heading north, and Molenov had circled *Shtshuka* around the fleet on a south-easterly course before surfacing and again looking for Portrova and Lenkov. The time was approaching 01.50 and although he knew that it was a forlorn hope, he had decided to wait that little bit longer, to give both

Lenkov and Portrova every chance. That decision had saved Portrova's life. Delaying the battery charge, Molenkov had trimmed *Shtshuka* low in the water and had watched as the fishermen disappeared over the horizon to the north. He then filled the bridge with lookouts and, together with further lookouts on the partly submerged casing, she had cruised slowly and quietly on one motor, searching and listening for any sign of her missing crewmen. Molenov had decided that they would wait for a further thirty minutes. Who knows, he thought, perhaps they had been picked up by one of the fishing boats. That was a consoling thought, but his orders overrode all other things. He was to avoid detection at all costs.

Aboard *Shtshuka,* they had been hearing Portrova for some time before they saw him, a dark shapeless form, tired limbs thrashing through the swell, choked gasps and hoarse cries now carrying clearly through the still night. Grabbing a line, one of the seamen had scrambled down from the bridge and had thrown himself into the sea, striking out strongly towards those cries.

Portrova had still been swimming as they heaved him on to *Shtshuka's* casing. But before he had blacked out he managed to gasp out the news that Lenkov was dead. They had hustled him below to his bunk, while *Shtshuka* began her much-needed battery charge before heading cautiously northward in the wake of the fishing fleet to continue her patrol off the Firth of Forth.

★　★　★　★　★

Portrova slept solidly for more than ten hours, finally awaking to a body racked with pain. He was bruised from head to foot, his nose was broken, four of his ribs were cracked, and three of his front teeth were missing. This he accepted. He was young and he was strong; he would soon recover. But mentally he was deeply scarred. He had never met an enemy in action. He'd been at sea for four months only, and a full naval career lay ahead of him. But he would never forget the events of these last hours; they were branded indelibly into his soul. In his mind his survival had been no miracle. It was neither *his* efforts nor the flow of the tide that had saved him; it was fate – his destiny. He knew now that his life had been preserved in order that one day he might sit in judgement over these British heathens who called themselves seamen.

Now pulling himself up in the bunk, gritting his teeth against the excruciating pain that tormented his whole body, he rolled his feet onto the deck and sat up. Shadows in the darkened bunk space began to swim before his eyes. He gripped the bunk rail to steady himself. Ignoring his pain-racked body, he sat for a moment in silence, waiting for his head to clear. Then suddenly, and almost without sound, he began to sob, his whole body shaking in violent jerks, streams of silent tears running uncontrollably down his cheeks.

Gregori Lenkov had been Portrova's one true friend aboard this boat – possibly the only true friend he had ever had. By nature Portrova was very much a loner – a quiet, pensive and melancholy young man whose manner was often mistaken for sullen moodiness – a mistake that he made no effort to correct. His upbringing had been harsh. Never knowing his parents, his boyhood years had been spent in a state-run orphanage. At the age of fifteen he was sent from the orphanage to a naval training school, where life for him was even harder. Although not excelling in any particular field, by the age of eighteen he had demonstrated sufficient of the required qualities to become an officer cadet. It had not been easy for him. Because of his background and his coarse appearance he had never really fitted in, and his peers regarded him as little more than a peasant. He was secretly talked about as a peasant, and these whispers, as time went by, became increasingly less covert, until the time came when his peers openly demonstrated their scorn towards him.

★ ★ ★ ★ ★

He had been glad when his time at the training school was finally over, and had immediately volunteered to join the submarine service, though he didn't know why exactly. On completion of his submarine training he had been appointed to *Shtshuka* as her fourth officer. It was not long before Gregori Lenkov, *Shtshuka*'s first officer, had seen something different in this dark swarthy youngster and had taken him under his wing. Portrova blossomed under Lenkov's guidance, and quickly turned from novice to professional. The two men formed a friendship born of mutual respect.

Portrova's sobbing had ceased as suddenly as it had started. Now his thoughts concentrated on just one thing – revenge. Then, alone in the silence of the darkened bunk space, he called aloud, 'This is my pledge – to my honour and to you, my good friend Gregori. There is an account to be settled and I will not rest until I have settled this account in full.' Then, utterly exhausted, he again fell back on his pillow and lapsed into deep sleep.

★　★　★　★　★

In the April of 1946, during a fierce spring gale in the North Sea, Dennehy, again in one of his bouts of drunkenness, fell from the bridge rail of *Ocean Harvester*, landing head first on the main deck just fifteen feet below. Breaking his neck, he died instantly.

CHAPTER ONE

07.50 Tuesday, 1st September 1959

'Bloody weather!'

Lieutenant Commander Nigel Bradley, commanding officer of Her Majesty's Submarine *Spearfish*, stood on his bridge and hunched his shoulders against the rain squall now sweeping across the choppy grey waters of Portsmouth Harbour. He reached up to pull his cap more firmly down on his head, before dragging up the hood of his oilskin to cover the cap completely.

It was not yet 08.00. *Spearfish* was making an early start. Slipping from her pierside berth at HMS *Dolphin* just ten minutes earlier, she was now stopped in mid-harbour, paying cautious deference to an incoming Isle of Wight ferry.

Lieutenant Oliver Strong, *Spearfish*'s first lieutenant, stood beside Bradley and again wiped the lenses of his binoculars with a saturated handkerchief – a futile and useless gesture in this weather. He too, was dressed in full oilskins, with only his face exposed to the elements. Now this late-summer combination of driving rain and wind chill had changed his normally pallid features into a plum-like glow under his dripping hood. In front and slightly above them, on a raised platform at the front of her cramped bridge, *Spearfish*'s navigating officer Lieutenant Tim Bishop crouched intently over the compass repeater, busily taking bearings. Bishop had a bad head cold, and was frequently pausing in his work to sneeze heavily into a soggy white handkerchief now

1

tightly balled into his left fist. Behind this trio of officers, squeezed into opposite corners at the back of the bridge, huddled the oilskinned figures of the bridge lookout, with Leading Signalman Sam Conroy, signal lantern as always, at the ready.

'Shouldn't be too long now, Sir.' Strong sounded almost apologetic as again through his binoculars, he carefully studied the ferry *Shanklin*, which was now ploughing steadily through the narrow harbour entrance, butting her blunt bows into the outgoing tide.

'Take her back a bit, Oliver,' grunted Bradley. 'We'll keep well clear.'

Strong leaned forward and called down the voice pipe to the control room, 'Group down. Wheel amidships. Slow astern together.'

Below, in *Spearfish's* control room and now at the helm, the cox'n, Chief Petty Officer Harvey Greene, repeated the order into the voice pipe while the seaman standing at his side rotated the telegraph handles to convey this order to the motor room. Almost immediately Strong could feel the increasing vibration running through *Spearfish* as she moved slowly astern. Looking back along her after casing he could see the white foam building up over her twin propellers.

'Give her plenty of room, Oliver,' muttered Bradley.

Again Strong called down the voice pipe, 'Half astern together.' Now the vibration increased, as did the white waters over *Spearfish's* twin propellers. Then, when he was satisfied that the ferry would cross *Spearfish's* bow at a distance of at least sixty yards, Strong again leaned towards the voice pipe. 'Stop together.' The vibrations ceased and the water around *Spearfish's* stern returned to an oily black swell.

Without making it too obvious, Bradley had been watching Strong closely, finding difficulty in resisting the temptation to compare him with Mike Fallon, his previous first lieutenant. To Bradley, Fallon had been an excellent number one, a complete extension of himself. But now Fallon had got his well-deserved first command, and here in his place was this as yet untested 'new boy'.

This was Strong's first trip to sea in *Spearfish*, having joined her just ten days earlier. *Spearfish* was his first boat as first lieutenant and although

2

already he seemed to be fitting in well and taking everything in his stride, Bradley knew that it was still too soon to judge. As far as he was concerned, Strong was still very much an unknown quantity.

Just twenty-six years old, Strong seemed to be typical of his kind: eager to learn and even more eager to please. Thin-framed and of medium height, his pallid features were invariably partially masked by strands of lank black hair which seemed to have a constant tendency to fall forward over his face. He had certainly appeared capable in his duties alongside the wall, but Bradley knew that Strong's real trial was yet to come. From now on would be his real testing time, the beginning of his real learning, and even though Bradley knew that, given time, Strong would probably be all right, maybe even better than all right, his predecessor Fallon would be a hard act to follow. This coming patrol was neither the time nor the place for a brand new first lieutenant and Bradley knew that he was going to miss Fallon during the coming weeks. As *Spearfish* had cast off, Bradley had turned to Strong and said, 'OK, Oliver, she's all yours. Take her out!' Strong had looked faintly surprised, but up to now he hadn't put a foot wrong.

Shanklin was now droning noisily across *Spearfish*'s bows, gradually reducing speed while aiming her cumbersome bulk towards the ferry berth at the foot of Portsmouth Harbour station. Strong trained his binoculars on the shadowy figures inside her rain-streaked bridge windows. Panning aft, he could see that even now there was very little sign of activity within her white-painted slab-sided upper works. He checked his watch – 08.02. Then, waiting until the first wave of the ferry's wake slapped into *Spearfish*'s bow, he again leaned towards the voice pipe. 'Starboard ten – slow ahead together.'

Spearfish nosed slowly forward. Below him Bradley listened to the voice of his casing officer, Torpedo Officer Lieutenant Ross Murray, whose clear, polished tones contrasted sharply with the rough bark of the second cox'n.

Strong called down the voice pipe. 'Slow ahead port – starboard fifteen.' *Spearfish*'s bow swung slowly around to line up with the harbour entrance. 'Wheel amidships. Both main motors to group up.'

Bishop sneezed again suddenly, almost missing his soggy handkerchief. 'Heavy cold?' thought Bradley, 'I hope that's all it is.' He knew well that just one man with a dose of flu could spread it to everyone else aboard within weeks, days even. He could still remember the effect of 'Asian flu' a couple of years back. At that time the boat he'd been on then had been virtually put out of action. Then, as though sensing the thoughts of his captain, Bishop turned and said, 'Sorry, Sir. Just a summer cold, maybe with a touch of hay fever and a very late night.'

Bradley grunted but said nothing.

Now *Spearfish* was directly in the middle of the narrow harbour entrance, with the early morning lighting of Fort Blockhouse wardroom broad on their starboard beam and the grey and forbidding granite bastions of the sallyport to their port. Bradley called to the signalman standing behind him, 'Pipe.' All hands, both on the bridge and the casing, stood to attention, with the officers saluting. A shrill wail of acknowledgement from a bosun's call carried in the wind from HMS *Dolphin*. Bradley dropped his right arm from the salute and, turning to Strong, said, 'Right, Oliver, let's get on with it.'

Strong leaned towards the voice pipe. 'Half ahead together. Start both main engines.'

Cox'n Greene's voice came back up immediately. 'Half ahead together. Start both engines. Both telegraphs are at half ahead together. Wheel is amidships.'

'Thank you, Cox'n. Steer one-four-zero and float the load when ready.' Helped by the now-racing ebb tide, *Spearfish* was making rapid progress through the narrows, with Bishop still busy with his bearings and still periodically sniffing and sneezing into his sodden handkerchief.

Bradley trained his glasses to the port bow, scanning the almost deserted rain-swept Southsea esplanade. No waving holiday makers out there this morning, but somewhere over behind those closely huddled rooftops Sue would have already started counting the days to his return.

Then the main engines clattered into life – first the port, then the starboard – both racing at first before settling down into a steady throb as they took the load of the generators. Strong looked astern to see the first black gouts of diesel smoke billow from the exhausts on either side of the after casing, before the spray from the exhaust mufflers beat it down to a watery blue grey haze.

Greene's voice echoed up through the voice pipe. 'Bridge – Helm. Course one-four-zero. Both telegraphs set to half ahead together group up, revolutions two-three-zero. Floating the load both sides.'

From Strong, 'Very good, Cox'n.' Now the power from *Spearfish*'s main batteries to drive her propulsion motors was being replaced by an equal amount of power from her main generators. She was 'floating the load'.

Beneath him, Strong could hear the casing party manhandling casing gear that could not be left inboard through the fin door and down through the conning tower, where these items would be securely stowed in the forward tube space. The noise of the air being drawn down the tower by the main engines increased to a roar as each man made his way below to the control room. The second cox'n, together with a leading hand, then completed a final check under the casing to ensure everything was properly secured: a loose item rattling about under the casing could easily put the forthcoming patrol at grave risk. Finally satisfied, they emerged back onto the casing and checked that all the access plates were screwed down securely before they, too, made their way below.

Now *Spearfish* was through the narrows and into the dredged channel. Bradley kept his back to the strengthening south-westerly and continued to survey Southsea. He had left home at six o'clock this morning, hugging Sue and little Jamie, who would have his first birthday in just three days from now. Saying goodbye was always a wrench but, for some reason, this time it felt more painful than usual. This was going to be a long patrol – ten weeks at least – and now he felt acutely conscious that he had not made the most of their last evening together. Instead, he had spent a large part of it here on *Spearfish*; he had agreed to come back aboard on the previous evening for drinks in the wardroom – a traditional pre-patrol evening. Strong had invited several officers from inboard and from the boats alongside, and had especially asked Bradley if he could join them for an hour or so. It was a male-only do and, in any case, Sue would have been hard pressed to organise a sitter for Jamie at such short notice. He had been loath to accept, but under the circumstances he had felt that it might seem churlish to refuse. So he had dutifully appeared in *Spearfish*'s wardroom at the appointed time of 20.30, and had not left until well past 22.00.

It had been a pleasant evening, much more so than he had anticipated. By the time he had arrived there were fourteen officers spread between the wardroom and the control room, and as the evening had progressed this had increased to more than twenty. For the officers of *Spearfish* this would be their last social event for many weeks. Goodwill and spirits were flowing profusely in equal measure. Strong had proved to be an excellent host, a fact which had somewhat surprised Bradley. Then just before he had been about to take his leave, an officer from Northwood, the Naval Intelligence base in London, had arrived in the control room completely unannounced. Although Bradley had been expecting Lieutenant Commander Toby Cannings, he didn't think he would see him until shortly before they sailed the next morning. He knew Toby very well; they had worked together before.

Cannings was just eight months senior to Bradley in age, but looked much older. Short, balding and stocky to the point of being obese, Toby had not changed since the last time Bradley had seen him. What remained of his prematurely white hair was set in a thin ring around the base of his skull. This, together with his cherubic features, sparkling blue eyes and ready smile, gave him the appearance of an ageing monk. But Toby Cannings was certainly no monk, and it would come as a surprise to many seeing him now, that in his day he had been a swimming champion for the Navy. But now he was an expert in this special field of work, which was, basically, intelligence gathering.

Bradley had been glad when he heard that Cannings had been seconded to *Spearfish* for this patrol. Greeting each other with a genuine affection, Bradley had introduced Cannings to Strong and the rest of his own officers. 'Sorry to barge in like this, chaps,' Cannings had said, beaming, looking anything but apologetic while reaching for a proffered "horse's neck". 'Got all sorts of boxes on the jetty, you know, trappings of the trade – need bringing aboard. More importantly, I see that it's party time. Once again, perfect timing – even though I say it myself. By the way, have my three chaps turned up yet?'

Bradley had confirmed that three special telegraphists – Tel S's – had reported on board that afternoon and were now billeted in the fore-ends, using camp beds. They would be Cannings's right-hand men. Split into three watches; they would operate all the specialised equipment contained in these "trappings", that would be set up in the fore-ends, sonar room and the W/T office during the journey north. These were the tools of his trade and would be absolutely essential for effective intelligence gathering during the coming patrol. But for now they must be cleared from the jetty – a job for the duty watch. Bradley turned to Murray, who was the duty officer. 'Would you get that sorted, Ross? Get it aboard as quickly as you can!'

'And get my three chaps to give 'em a hand,' said Cannings.

Bradley had stayed for one more drink and a further chat with Cannings before making his way inboard to arrange for a taxi. He had stayed much longer than he had intended, but he was glad that he had taken the time to be on *Spearfish* that evening.

Bishop's voice snapped Bradley out of his thought pattern. 'Come five degrees to port, Sir.' Bishop had taken a bearing on the Spit Sand fort. Now he straightened up, grabbing the hood of his oilskin as a sudden gust tried to peel it from his head.

Strong called down the voice pipe, 'Helm – Bridge. Steer one-three-five.' Then lifting his binoculars he squinted south-west, directly into the rain squall, again muttering his annoyance at the liquid film forming on the lenses, obscuring even more the faint grey blur which was the Isle of Wight. To the south, the division between the slate grey sea and the sky was barely distinguishable. The sea now coming up fine on *Spearfish*'s starboard bow was short and choppy and the heavy driving rain completely failed to quell the feathery spume flying from the wave crests. Now *Spearfish*'s bow began to lift and fall. Strong could plainly hear the sea slapping against her black shining flanks, occasionally breaking over the top of her casing to race away in foaming streams down across her ballast tanks.

Spit Sand fort was now falling astern on the starboard quarter, and Bishop was busy lining up on the "No Man's Land" and the 'Horse Sand forts'. He called to Strong, 'Steer south.'

Strong again called down the voice pipe, 'Steer one-eight-zero.' *Spearfish* would pass centrally between these forts.

Bradley turned to look westward over Strong's shoulder down the Solent.

Squinting against the rain, he rubbed the water from his eyes with the back of his hand and looked at his wristwatch. It was just coming up to 08.25. 'Well done, Oliver. Go to passage routine when you're ready. Keep "special sea duty men" closed up, till you're happy, that is. I'm going below now. We'll do a briefing in the wardroom at 14.00. Perhaps you would arrange that – just a quick run-down on our programme. Then perhaps you can brief the troops later this evening.' He glanced down at his watch again. 'We'll do a trim dive tomorrow forenoon once we've cleared the Thames estuary. In the meanwhile, adjust your speed to keep a full battery.'

Without waiting for a reply Bradley turned and made his way down the fin ladder towards the conning tower. Strong watched him disappear through the hatch, and then turned back to the voice pipe. 'Helm – Bridge. Captain coming below. Go to "passage routine". Stand fast, special sea duty men.' He listened to the increased air-rush through the tower as Bradley made his way down, and he heard Greene calling over the tannoy for white watch to close up in "passage routine".

CHAPTER TWO

At last it was Saturday, 10th October, the final day of *Spearfish's* patrol, a day which Bradley was beginning to think would never come. He was leaning over the chart table in the dimly lit control room, unmoving, elbows resting on the thick glass table top, cupped hands supporting his chin, seemingly completely oblivious to all and everything about him. To an observer he would be dozing but, in truth, he had never been more awake.

Only his eyes moved and even this was only a mere hint of movement, a barely perceptible flicker as he studied the two clocks flushed side by side into the white-painted panel above the chart table. The clocks were identical in size and design: brass rimmed with bold black Roman numerals standing out trim and neat against their clear white faces, the only recognisable difference between the two being that the one on the right was set to GMT, or "Zulu" time, with its hands now partially obscured by a large letter Z scrawled roughly in red crayon across its polished glass face, whereas its partner to the left was set to local time.

His eyes continued to flick from one to the other of these clocks, intense, calculating, as though mentally gauging this perpetual movement of time, appearing mesmerised by the smooth sweep of the slender second hands as they alternately lagged then led the progression of the larger minute hands, which were moving in a series of half-minute jerks, each jerk accompanied by a barely audible tick.

It was now 08.00 local time. He grunted and straightened. He had made up his mind – he would bring *Spearfish* to periscope depth in two hours from now, at 10.00 hours. Early Arctic winter time had made the days shorter, and they would get shorter yet. But by 10.00 the darkness above them now should have eased sufficiently to give them enough light to be useful, while it would hopefully be still dark enough to provide some protection from prying eyes.

After an eleven-day transit from Portsmouth, *Spearfish* had taken up her appointed position off the entrance to the White Sea on Saturday, 12th September, where she had stationed herself off the Kola Inlet, carrying out covert surveillance of traffic passing into and out of the White Sea. The hours of daylight were longer then, and it had been a busy time: traffic had been heavy and there had certainly been much more Soviet naval movement than was the norm for this time of the year. They had gathered much intelligence during that period: Russian naval ship movements, photographs, propeller signatures and much more. Both Bradley and Cannings had been more than happy with their activities during this period. But there had been little or no respite during those first weeks and Bradley had needed all the guile and cunning developed during his years "in the trade" to get the results he wanted without being detected. It had been a long and wearing time, a time of great strain for all on board, but then that was the nature of this type of work – days and nights for the most part indistinguishable, where time merged into one long round of watching, listening, tracking and recording, with individual sequences of activity often culminating in a call to "attack teams", which, from the rules of this type of patrol, could be nothing more than anticlimatic gestures.

At this stage of the patrol, perhaps the one man still revelling in his work was Bradley's old friend Toby Cannings. Cannings liked to be kept busy, his zest for the job never diminishing. Oddly, perhaps, this professional zeal was totally counterbalanced by his easygoing nature. His instant wit and often outrageous sense of humour had quickly endeared him to the crew. Rather like a ship's padre, he was all things to all men, but still a firm favourite among all on board. Cannings was the ultimate professional, whether in the sound room surrounded by his mysterious grey boxes, up in the seamen's mess playing cribbage or pontoon with the lads, or making up a foursome for bridge in the wardroom. He brightened any company and even in this humdrum world of alternating tedium and tension, he still made men smile.

Tedium among his crew had become an increasing concern for Bradley. Although he knew from previous experience that it was largely inevitable at this stage of the patrol, it could, if allowed, give rise to a variety of problems. Those members at the "sharp end", who were directly involved in the surveillance work, were perhaps the lucky ones, since even though often subjected to protracted, and in many cases pointless, periods of tracking and recording activity, they at least were aware of what was happening around them; whereas for others, like the tubes crews, the engine room and motor room staff and all those not directly involved in surveillance, this type of patrol often meant prolonged stages of boredom. For this reason all of *Spearfish*'s crew were constantly kept informed of what was going on with a daily update from either Bradley or Strong.

Then, at last, those four weeks were over and, in accordance with her orders, *Spearfish* had headed north-east on a four-day dived transit towards the second phase of her patrol.

The forced lull in activity during this transit had brought a measure of relief to all on board, but this had been a very temporary relief. Arriving at her new position at midday on 14th October, *Spearfish* stationed herself at a position some 120 miles north-west of the northernmost tip of the island of Novaya Zemla, at a latitude of seventy-eight degrees north and a longitude of sixty-two degrees east. She was back on the job, painstakingly patrolling these cold and hostile waters, with just the grey desolation of Novaya to her east and little, if anything, to her north except the barren islands of Franz Josef Land and the freezing wastes of the arctic ice pack. Her orders were to remain here for seven days, which would bring her to the end of this patrol.

At first there had been very little surface activity in this new area, but Bradley was certain that this situation wouldn't last. *Spearfish* had been sent up here to this exact position and at this time for a reason, even though he as yet didn't know this reason. But he would be patient, and for whatever reason he was here, when that reason became clear both he and *Spearfish* would be ready.

But all was not well with Bradley. For the past forty-eight hours or so a nagging sense of concern had been building inside him, niggling at first, but growing stronger as each hour had passed. This had now reached a stage where it had become more than apprehension; now it was a definite feeling of foreboding, a feeling which he could neither explain nor ignore. Apprehension and uncertainty were a part of life up here and this he accepted, but now there was something like a heavy invisible cloak hanging over his shoulders which, try as he might, he couldn't shake off. His last patrol up here in the spring of this year had been relatively incident-free and disappointingly uneventful. The main problem then was the daylight: there was far too much of it − not good for covert operations of any kind but, although reaping very little in the form of intelligence, that patrol had provided very valuable experience for him and his crew. This time he had been warned before leaving base that there was every chance that this patrol could be a lot more fruitful. Intelligence sources back in the UK had told him to be prepared for something "a little more interesting during the final week". They had strongly hinted of a Soviet nuclear submarine missile test launching, and this hint was repeated in his patrol orders. But he had been under no illusions from day one of this patrol about what the coming weeks might throw at them. The timing for this patrol had been carefully chosen, and he knew that it could reap some special rewards − but only if he played the game properly.

Up here you were on your own. You received what you could, when you could, on the radio, and you transmitted nothing. The sole objective of the patrol was to gather intelligence, and this they had done. Already they had gathered intelligence by the sackful and a lot of this intelligence was good − Cannings had assured him of that. But the patrol wasn't over yet, and he would keep up the pressure right to the end. Then he would get *Spearfish* home, and leave it to the experts back there assess her achievements. Until that time he would switch off to everything except the job in hand.

An ability to completely ignore all else but the job in hand was something that he had worked on over the years. He had become expert at developing a concentration which, like a protective shell, obscured everything but his end objective. He had never been able to decide whether this was a gift or a curse, but it was *his* shell and he couldn't and wouldn't change it now. From the moment *Spearfish* had dived off the east coast of Norfolk to catch her trim, he had banished all other thoughts from his mind except those relating to *Spearfish* and her patrol. Even Sue and Jamie were pushed into the background; he was not proud of this. But still this feeling of foreboding hung over him and, try as he might, he couldn't switch that off.

But now, here in his dimly lit control room, Bradley had other things on his mind. Surface activity had started to escalate during the late afternoon of the previous day. A rash of new contacts had appeared on his sonar: all warships, and all apparently going nowhere. This activity had continued to build all night. It was becoming increasingly obvious that something special was on, and since this was the last day of his patrol, whatever he had been waiting for had been left to the last minute. He felt a strong sense of relief at having brought *Spearfish* to the right place at the right time. For whatever reason this surface activity was building up, it was fast becoming apparent that a major portion of the Russian Northern Fleet had been turned out to witness it.

He quietly suppressed a yawn; it had been a long night with no time for sleep. With the control room "attack team" closed up since midnight he, comfortable in his brown leather slippers, an old pair of khaki corduroys and a dark cotton shirt, had repeatedly prowled the few short steps between his cabin, the sonar room and the control room, thinking, listening, evaluating, guessing. He had kept *Spearfish* at 150 feet all night, alternating her drive between port and starboard motors, slow group down, conserving her battery power and providing her propellers with the barest amount of forward motion needed to keep her on depth. At 01.30 he had called for restricted movement within the boat, with all unnecessary lighting and machinery switched off in order to reduce noise and to conserve electrical power. Then, at 02.30, with the surface activity still escalating, he had ordered the boat into the "ultra-quiet" state, with all but essential machinery switched off and all hands not required for duty to lie on their bunks, thus minimising the risk of possible detection even further.

Again he scrutinised the chart spread in front of him on the chart table, studying the scribbled notes and figures he and his officers had inserted during the course of the night. He wondered fleetingly why he kept doing this. He knew *Spearfish*'s position and the exact positions of key elements of the fleet above him. Nothing had changed significantly since his last scrutiny, less than five minutes ago.

Now rubbing achingly tired eyes with both hands, he sniffed appreciatively at the faint aroma drifting forward from the small galley aft of the control room. Bacon! In spite of the need for quiet he had allowed the cook to prepare breakfast, and it smelled good. Somehow he knew that a good breakfast would be especially important this morning, and it dawned on him that he too was very hungry.

'Coffee, Sir?' Able Seaman Nobby Hall, the control room messenger, appeared at his elbow, bearing a tin tray upon which sat seven large mugs of steaming coffee.

'Well done. Thank you, Hall.' Bradley reached out and took the nearest mug. It was too hot to drink so he pushed it onto the shelf at the side of the chart table. He'd drunk at least a dozen mugs like this since midnight. Did he really want more coffee? He thought not, even though his mouth was tinder dry. And he still felt strangely uncomfortable, knowing that this wasn't because of his tiredness, his dry mouth or his growing hunger. The vague feeling of unease that now seemed to be with him constantly had increased as the night had worn on. He couldn't remember experiencing anything like it before. What the hell was it? A premonition, perhaps? No – he didn't have premonitions. But he definitely felt jittery, and he couldn't explain why. Now he wanted yet another pee. God, how many times had he gone since midnight? Was it his nerves, or was it just too much coffee?

'Shit!' The muffled curse came from the starboard for'd corner of the control room.

Bradley glared through the semi-darkness towards the large transparent perspex square of the contact evaluation plot, with its dim red shaded glow outlining the shadowy shape of the operator now crouched, groping awkwardly around in the darkness under the plot.

Another curse. 'Ah, gotcha, yuh bastard!' The plot operator straightened up and looked apologetically across at Bradley. 'Sorry, Sir. Dropped me pencil.'

Now back in his seat, the CEP operator resumed his task of updating the plot with his recovered red chinagraph pencil, listening through earphones to an almost non-stop stream of sonar reports. Bradley shook his head, controlling his annoyance and the urge to snap at the operator. What the hell's the matter with them? They all seem a bit jittery this morning. Or was it him? Could it be that the nervousness he felt was catching? He eyed the miscellany of lines, squares, circles, and crosses that were now rapidly filling the plot, reflecting the constantly changing scene up there on the surface. *Spearfish* was using passive sonar only, and even though he had ordered the sound room team to restrict their reports to new contacts and any surface movement within a range of 1500 yards, these reports still came through, thick and fast, and he knew now that it would get even busier.

CHAPTER THREE

S tanding over the stainless steel basin in the tiny Formica-panelled washroom, Bradley stared at his reflection in the smeary mirror in front of him. The normally sallow features staring back at him now looked positively haggard. Weeks of interrupted sleep, irregular meals and constant strain had taken their toll. He pushed lank strands of straw-coloured hair back from his dark-rimmed eyes and stuck out his tongue. It was heavily furred and streaked with yellow, swollen and rough – a hangover tongue!

'Christ,' he muttered to himself, 'it's about time you gave this silly bloody game up.' Pressing down on the blue knob of the cold tap, he watched the water-trickle gradually fill the basin, then, bending and using both hands, he sluiced the cold water over his face. It felt good. Rubbing his eyes, he again stared into the mirror. Thank God this one was nearly over, and at midnight tonight they would be leaving the area, moving out to the south-west and starting their long journey homeward. On reaching the North Cape he would send his surfacing signal, and the remainder of the passage back to Portsmouth would be completed on the surface.

This would be his last trip with *Spearfish*; he was due to be relieved early in the New Year. He knew that he would have regrets when that time came. *Spearfish* had been good for him in so many ways. It had been almost two years now, but he remembered the day he joined her at the Vickers shipyard in Barrow-in Furness as though it were yesterday. Then, she was barely recognisable as a submarine – little more than a partially painted steel cylinder propped up in a dry dock, for the most part obscured by an intricate network of scaffolding and adorned in a tangled mass of pipes, wires, airlines, electric cables and temporary lighting. Brown-and-white boiler-suited figures had swarmed over this confused mass, and streams of workers flowed in and out of the many dark orifices in her unfinished hull like an army of ants. And the noise! The deafening cacophony of pneumatic hammers and caulking guns, accompanied by the constant shrill scream of escaping high-pressure air and steam. The chaos was even worse inside her pressure hull, and the noise was even more unbearable.

He had stayed well clear of *Spearfish* during dockyard working hours in those first few months, restricting himself to the comparative comfort of the Group Building Offices, spending his days poring over an apparently inexhaustible supply of technical drawings and books, learning and digesting every detail of *Spearfish*'s construction and operating systems. For most of this time Lieutenant Eric Crane, his engineer officer, had been with him. Crane had joined *Spearfish* long before Bradley, before even the sections of her pressure hull had been welded together, and what Crane didn't know about *Spearfish* just wasn't worth knowing.

After long days together in the office, and when the builders on night shift came in, he and Crane would venture down into the boat, where with Crane's help Bradley would tie up the theoretical knowledge acquired that day with the real thing on board. He prided himself that he had been there at *Spearfish*'s birth, and he felt privileged. Even now he remembered how he had marvelled at the finished product. She was the first of the new "S" class. Truly a state-of-the-art submarine. Normally carrying a crew of about seventy-eight men, she was powered with the latest type of diesel/electric drive system and was designed to be very fast, both on the surface and under water. When dived she was very quiet – the quietest class of British submarine ever built. During her service to date, *Spearfish* had more than justified that proud claim.

Bradley's appointment to command *Spearfish* had been a bit of a feather in his cap, as well as something of a surprise. He knew that he had been given this command over the heads of several more senior colleagues. Never one to suffer fools gladly, he had been a hard and unforgiving taskmaster, especially during the first months after *Spearfish*'s commissioning. Nothing but the best was good enough for him. He had made that very plain from the start. But he set himself the same high standards that he expected from his crew and, together with his first lieutenant Fallon, had gradually trained them to reach his own levels of expectation. Those that failed his requirements found themselves inboard; there was no place for slackers or troublemakers on *his* boat. By the end of *Spearfish*'s sea trials and work-up, his people had come to respect him, but it was a grudging respect. Although they trusted him completely, they didn't like him. He was not a popular captain – he knew that, and it didn't bother him at all. Now, still only in his thirtieth year, his sights were firmly set on the nuclear submarine programme. He knew that this was where his future lay, and he wanted to be in at the beginning. It was now being said that sooner or later all submarines would be nuclear propelled, and he for one, was convinced that this would surely happen.

He looked at his watch: 08.55. It would still be dark up there on the surface. He pulled the plug from the basin and, letting the water dry on his face, walked back into the control room, where he picked up his mug and took a large swallow from the now-cooled coffee before turning to Oliver Strong, who was standing behind the hydroplane operators. 'Go to full red lighting at 09.30, Oliver, and we'll go to diving stations at 09.45 and come to periscope depth at 10.00. Probably won't be able to see much up there, but we'll have a look anyway.'

At exactly 09.55 Bradley stood waiting behind the attack periscope, his eyes fully adjusted to the full red lighting that now cast a warm but almost eerie glow over the control room. Men moved in the dark shadows, quietly, purposefully, each knowing his role intimately and each going about his individual task with the surety and slick precision of long practice. It was quiet now, except for the muted murmur of voices between the sound room and the CEP, and the occasional soft hiss of pressurised hydraulic oil as the planesmen, under the watchful eye of Strong, gradually brought *Spearfish* towards her ordered depth.

Now they were ready, expectant and waiting. Bradley peered over Strong's shoulder at the large circular depth gauge between the hydroplane controls.

The needle was moving slowly counterclockwise, providing the only indication of *Spearfish*'s gradual upward movement. On the after planes the Cox'n began to call out the depth in a low voice, his eyes flickering between the depth gauge and the small bubble set in the green liquid of the curved clinometer in front of him.

'Eighty-five feet, Sir… eighty-two feet… eighty feet… seventy-eight feet, Sir.' Greene nursed the after hydroplane control with a skill born of long experience. 'Seventy-five feet… seventy-one feet… seventy feet… sixty-eight feet… sixty-five feet, Sir.' Now *Spearfish* was coming up rapidly, perhaps a little *too* rapidly.

With his eyes still on the depth gauge Bradley snapped, 'Up attack.'

In the dark shadows at the after end of the control room the panel watch keeper, his eyes fixed on the shape that was Bradley's back, lifted the periscope control lever and the dark tube of the attack periscope, glistening dully with a mixture of water and grease, slithered upward with a soft slushy hiss. Bradley, on bended knees, grabbed the periscope handles immediately they cleared the rim of the well. Rising up with the periscope he snapped the handles down and pulled the crosshead around to face its single lens forward. Now with his left eye glued firmly into the eyepiece, he continued to rise as one with the periscope until its head broke surface, immediately commencing a 360-degree all-round look.

From the after planes Greene's voice continued in a low monotone. 'Depth fifty-eight feet… fifty-five feet… fifty-six feet… fifty-four feet… fifty-two feet.' The periscope head had now dipped under the surface. 'Fifty-eight feet… fifty-five feet… fifty-four feet.' Now the periscope head was well clear of the water even in the peaks of the swell, and *Spearfish* was rolling heavily as the surface sea bore against the slab sides of her fin.

Bradley felt the annoyance surging up inside him. 'For Christ's sake, Oliver,' his tone sharp, without tolerance, 'sort this bloody depth out. Keep fifty-eight feet. It's just as bloody well it's dark up there!'

'Keep fifty-eight feet, Sir.' Strong coughed nervously and leaned forward to busy himself with the ballast pump telegraph. He knew that *Spearfish*'s trim was not good, and that this was mainly his fault.

Bradley grunted, immediately regretting his outburst. Steady, Bradley, get a grip. He completed the first all-round look – no problems. His sweat-dampened palms relaxed on the periscope handles. It was quite dark up there, and for this he was thankful. The sea, a rolling, almost oily dark mass, with its surface completely void of white caps. This did not make for good periscope weather, but at least in this light there should be little chance of visual detection. The lack of light made it difficult to determine a clear horizon, but now, as his eyes became accustomed to the darkness, he could just determine the streaks of a lighter grey now appearing in the sky towards the east, and between the sloshes of water over the periscope head he could just make out flickering pinpoints of light grouped together down to his south, on that barely distinguishable horizon.

'Aha! There they are, and just where they should be!' Now he started to hum quietly to himself, just as he always did when concentrating. The periscope dipped again and stayed dipped. He shot an angry glare towards Strong. 'Depth now?'

'Sixty-nine feet, Sir.' It was the cox'n who answered.

'Very good, Cox'n. Come up to fifty-eight feet, Number One, and see if you can do something with this bloody trim! Speed up a bit if you have to.' Bradley's tone was controlled, although he was fighting his annoyance. The periscope head again cleared water and he completed another all-round look. Now the lens was becoming blurred. He knew it would be starting to freeze. He stepped back from the periscope. 'Dip and raise.'

Almost before Bradley had spoken, the periscope was hissing swiftly down into the dark well at his feet, and then it was on its way up again. Again he caught the handles as they cleared the well. 'Now let's see.' He squinted through the eyepiece, fingers fiddling with the prism adjusting knob.

'There's one or two "bergy bits" floating around. Nothing too big though.' Ice was a constant hazard up here at any time of the year. Smaller pieces, known as 'bergy bits', that had broken away from the fringes of the main ice pack during the summer melt had drifted slowly southward, and with the onset of winter with its rapidly decreasing temperatures, many of these were gelling together, some of them becoming a considerable size, easily big enough to puncture a ballast tank or bend a periscope – definitely something to be avoided.

The leading telegraphist now stood immediately behind Bradley. He would be the periscope bearing reader, and now directed the red beam of his torch up towards the periscope bearing ring above Bradley's head, ready to call out bearings for input information to the torpedo control calculator, or "fruit machine", as it was more often called. Bradley ignored the telegraphist, concentrating only on what he could see through his eyepiece. Around again, another all-round look. He started to hum again quietly, tunelessly, then in a low voice and to no one in particular he muttered, 'Nothing very close, but there are a lot of busy boys down south.' He continued muttering to himself very quietly, then in a louder voice, 'Sea state – not more than two I should think, possibly three. A long swell though, coming down from the north-east, and it looks bloody cold up there!'

Pulling his head back from the eyepiece, he knuckled tired eyes, then went back to the eyepiece, where he muttered, 'I can't see much through this bloody thing: keeps icing over.' Again he was talking aloud to no one in particular. 'Right, now I want to get a bit closer!' He stepped back and snapped up the handles, and the periscope immediately slithered down into its well.

'Group down. Slow ahead together. Come around to one-two-five, Oliver, and go to 150 feet. Stay in red lighting and sort your trim. I'll be in the sound room if you need me.'

At 10.35 Bradley was back in the control room, his slippered feet scuffing over the deck. 'Christ, it's hot in here,' he muttered to himself. Already he could feel his shirt clinging to his back and he knew that the heat wasn't the only reason for this. If only he could shake off this bloody awful feeling. He brushed back strands of hair that had fallen over his eyes. His stomach felt hollow and his legs leaden. He also knew now that this wasn't simply tiredness. No, it was bloody nerves! That heavy cloak was still hanging over him and, if anything, feeling even heavier. 'This hasn't been an easy trip,' he reasoned to himself. 'Perhaps I've been pushing it a bit too hard lately.' He took a deep breath, and frowned. The air in the control room was heavy, thick, and stale. Even though they'd been running oxygen generators and CO_2 absorption units whenever the opportunity permitted, the atmosphere in the boat was still thick enough to taste. They had managed to get in four hours of unbroken snorting the night before last, recharging the batteries and dragging in some very welcome fresh air, but that was over twenty-eight hours ago. Then, during the night before that, they had actually surfaced, though this was from necessity rather than choice. They had stayed on the surface for just long enough to ditch the garbage which had been piling up in the fore-ends. The garbage ejector, or "gash gun", as it was more popularly known, was a convenience introduced with this class of boat, its purpose being to eject bags of garbage through the pressure hull while the boat was dived, rather like discharging a mini torpedo. This "gash gun" was generally regarded as a bit of a "fancy waistcoat", and in *Spearfish*, had never worked properly since leaving the builder's yard, and so more often than not they were forced to get rid of the garbage by the time-honoured method of bagging and weighting it and then forming a chain of men to haul it up the conning tower and heave it through the fin door. Normally this practice would be regarded as nothing more than a necessary nuisance, but on this type of patrol things were very different: the need to surface the boat in order to ditch gash was more than just a nuisance; it could possibly put the whole patrol at risk. Because of this faulty gash gun, the fore-ends now housed more than two days' accumulated garbage, which did nothing to improve the quality of life aboard *Spearfish*.

Fifteen minutes earlier, in spite of the bad air, Bradley had given permission to smoke – 'One all round' while dived. This permission was always well received by the smokers. Most on board were smokers, and those who weren't didn't seem to mind. Even after almost five years there were still times when Bradley regretted having given up the habit, and this morning was definitely one of them. But it was still his belief that with these smokers, permission given for one all round helped to reduce tension and sharpen concentration. It had been a very long night, and even though there was hardly enough oxygen in the boat to support the flame on a match for long enough to light up, he knew that to be given the opportunity for a "quick burn" would be well appreciated. But now, as he took a deep breath of stale fetid air, he regretted giving his permission to smoke. Bloody cigarettes! He moved across to the chart table and spoke quietly to Bishop.

'Tim, as soon as we get up there I'll do a quick all-round look, and if there's anything worth looking at we'll get the search periscope up and you can do your bit, but I don't want to leave either periscope up for longer than necessary, not in this sea.'

Bishop nodded in the darkness. 'Yes, of course, Sir. Ready when you are.' During this patrol, periscope photography had been used whenever possible, by means of an infrared camera rigged to the search periscope. Although a bit of a "lash up" and still in its experimental stage, a high level of success had been achieved with this camera up to now, and Bishop, who initially had been very reluctant to accept the role of photography officer, or "snaps" as he had now become known, had spent hours operating this camera during the past six weeks and had become very proficient in its use. Indeed he now considered himself to be an expert. What had started out as a bit of a chore had now become quite an enjoyable part of his job.

It was slightly lighter now and whatever was going to happen up there this morning, Bradley was determined to get the best possible record, both on sonar recording tapes, the camera film and on Cannings's surveillance equipment. After this he would pull back and go deep. There was no point in taking chances. He knew that he would have to be especially careful with the periscopes this morning. Leaving them up for too long, even in this sea and dim light, could prove disastrous – an instant giveaway to an even half-alert surface lookout. After one more careful scrutiny of the CEP and a further report from the sound room, Bradley called across to Strong.

'OK, Oliver? Come up to fifty-eight feet. Call out the depth after eighty.'

'Come to fifty-eight feet, Sir.' Strong ordered both telegraphs to half ahead. Now *Spearfish* seemed to be better trimmed, and just minimal movement of the hydroplane controls was all that was needed to bring the depth off. Slowly, almost imperceptibly, she began to creep upward.

Then from Greene, 'Depth eighty feet... seventy-eight feet... seventy feet... sixty-five feet.' *Spearfish's* rate of ascent was quickening.

'Up attack.' Bradley again straightened with the upward moving periscope. *Spearfish's* fin, although well under the surface, was now almost at right angles to the swell coming from the north-east, and she began to roll heavily.

'Sixty feet... fifty-eight feet... fifty-five feet... fifty-three feet.'

Spearfish was now rolling even more heavily. Bradley cast a withering glance towards Strong. 'Come on, Oliver! What's the problem now? If you take me up much further I'll be able to shake hands with our friends out there! We must be too bloody light, for Christ's sake!'

Strong looked uncertain, nervous. Leaning across the planesmen, he set the ballast pump telegraph to flood and ordered into his microphone, 'Engine room, flood 200 gallons from sea to M starboard.'

Bradley hadn't missed that slight crack, that hesitation in his first lieutenant's voice and he knew that his outburst had made Strong even more nervous. 'And another 200,' he growled, immediately feeling a sharp twinge of guilt. He knew that he wasn't helping Strong, but the boat was too light – that much was obvious – and Strong shouldn't have to be told, so sod his feelings!

'Fifty-eight feet, Sir... fifty-nine... sixty feet... fifty-nine feet... fifty-eight feet... fifty-eight... fifty-eight feet... fifty-eight feet.'

'That's more like it,' Bradley grunted, already into his all-round sweep. Now he could clearly see the lights of the surface fleet deployed in a wide, almost unbroken semicircle, stretching from fine on his starboard bow right around to his starboard quarter, flickering and dancing in the sombre gloom of what passed for daylight – a myriad of pale "Will o' the wisps". The nearest vessel was about 2000 yards off his starboard beam.

Bradley continued his sweep, slowly – carefully. 'Let's ease this roll a bit. Come around to zero-two-zero. 'Bloody hell!' He stopped his sweep, concentrating on his starboard beam. 'That one is close. Too bloody close! Destroyer... Very close... Looks like one of their "O" class. Bearing is that?' Bradley's tone was clipped, terse, as he adjusted the periscope ranging mechanism.

'Relative bearing is now zero-five-five.' The telegraphist squinted to read the bearing ring, his voice slightly high pitched, nervous, tense, reflecting his captain's mood.

Bradley held the periscope on the destroyer. 'Plot, have you got her?'

'Negative, Sir,' from the CEP.

'Course zero-two-zero, Sir,' reported the helmsman.

'She's stopped.' No wonder the sound room hadn't picked her up. Bradley adjusted the ranging controls, again humming quietly to himself. 'Range 1300 yards. Close… Far too bloody close for comfort!' He knew that he should pull back now, put more distance between himself and this destroyer. Sod him! Bloody nuisance! This could spoil everything. He swung the periscope around, completing the sweep. All clear to port anyway. 'Damn this bloody ice!' He stepped back, snapping up the periscope handles. 'Dip and raise.'

Rising up with the periscope, Bradley again felt the excitement surging through him, but again his excitement was tempered by that cloak of acute unease. Another all-round sweep. The destroyer off his starboard beam was still stationary. All of his senses, his judgement, his years of learning and experience were telling him that he should pull back and go deep. She was too close – well inside his "safety go deep" circle. He studied her for a moment, then, grunting under his breath, swung around and began to inspect the more distant semicircle. *Spearfish* was now exactly where he had wanted her to be. Everything looked good – except for that damned destroyer. Ah well, he would just have to watch her, and if she moved he would go deep right away. Now he was concentrating on the semicircle of the other surface ships. 'Stand by bearings.'

The periscope reader again took up his position, hovering behind Bradley's shoulder, directing the red beam of his torch upward at the dull orange glow of the periscope-bearing ring.

His vision again began to cloud. 'Sod this bloody ice,' he snapped. 'Dip and raise.' It was slightly lighter up there now and as the periscope came up he again studied the area around each distant bobbing light. Now he could make out the grey shapes of even more distant ships smudged into the darkness of the sea and the slightly lighter-streaked horizon beyond. He was humming, again something without a tune. Now he was talking to himself. 'Right, what's this? Ah, yes! By God, it looks like a "Romeo" class. Bearing is that?'

Again the periscope reader strained to read the bearing ring while Bradley, without taking his eye from the attack periscope, called out, 'Raise the search periscope', then to Bishop, 'Pilot, try green four-zero, 2000 yards. I think it's a "Romeo" class; in fact I'm bloody sure it is! See if you can get a shot or two.' Behind him he could hear the slush of the search periscope emerging from its well, and he resumed his slow sweeping search on the attack periscope. 'Aha! What's this?' The excitement was clear in his voice. 'Where the hell did that come from? Bearing is that?'

'Zero-seven-zero,' from the periscope bearing reader.

Ignoring the destroyer still stopped directly off his starboard beam, Bradley held his periscope on the newly acquired target. He called to Bishop, who was now training the search periscope, while setting the controls of the camera. 'Tim, never mind the *Romeo*; go to green seven-zero.' Adjusting his ranging control, he called out, 'Range is 1700 yards. She's just surfaced. Christ, it's a bloody BN! One of their "Hotel" class, I think. She's stopped and very low in the water. Messenger, get Lieutenant Commander Cannings to the control room. He'll want an eyeful of this bugger!'

There was real excitement in Bradley's voice. 'Now, let's have another look. She's trimmed right down but I'm sure she's a "Hotel". Stay on her, Tim; she may be going to do a surface firing, or she might dive to do it, but whatever, I shall want some good pictures, so stay with her.' He looked back to Bishop. 'She'll probably dive, but I'm sure she's going to do a missile firing of some sort. Get everything you can, anyway.'

He fell silent, realising that he was talking too much and too loudly, but his mind continued to race. So this is what they had been waiting for; this was obviously meant to be the highlight of his patrol. So they had been right, back there at *Dolphin*. They had told him to expect a sighting of one of these new "Hotel" class ballistic nuclear submarines, and yes, by God they were right! Sure enough, here she was, and here he was! Good intelligence? Bloody marvellous intelligence! This would be the grand finale to their past weeks of toil and hardship – a finale that would *really* make it all worthwhile. Now it was up to him to make it happen.

'Come along, my beauty.' Again he was murmuring to himself. 'Do a turn for your uncle Nigel. Show us your fireworks, Duckie!' Then louder, 'Have you got her yet, Tim? Stay with her. By the size of her entourage she could well be about to do a missile firing. We don't want to miss anything now.'

'Affirmative, Sir. I'm on her and I've got some shots already.' Bishop, too, sounded excited.

'Good show! Now if we—' Bradley was cut off by the call from the sound room.

'Captain, Sir. Sound Room!' The voice of Leading Seaman Willy Kinross came over loud on the action intercom, his normally soft Scottish burr now high pitched with urgency. 'New contact, Sir, bearing green five-five. One thousand yards and closing fast!'

'Sod it!' Bradley immediately swung his periscope towards his starboard beam. Kinross's voice was there again, loudly, now even higher pitched, urgent, almost frantic.

'Sound Room, Captain. The contact has split. First contact still bears green nine-five, with identical contact bearing green one hundred. Range of both contacts now 500 yards and closing fast!'

Bradley pulled his periscope around towards the first bearing. 'Where the hell did they come from?' Then for just one fleeting moment he saw it – the dark-grey flare of a destroyer's bow, slicing vertically up through his field of vision, scything through the water towards them, sheets of white spray arcing away high to either side. Port and starboard searchlights trained forward to probe the dark waters directly ahead of them. Bradley gasped in shocked disbelief; it was almost on top of them. 'Oh, my God! The bastard's going to ram us!' He flung himself back from the periscope. 'Down all masts! Group up, full ahead together! Flood "Q"… Stand by for collision! Go to 120 feet! Come on, Oliver; get some bloody dive on those planes!'

His orders came in a solid unbroken stream. He had recited this drill so many times in the past, but now it was real, and already he knew that it was too late – far too late. Even before he had finished mouthing his orders, *Spearfish* heeled violently to port as, with a jarring, tearing crunch the destroyer's knife-like keel ploughed into the top of her fin. Now she was being dragged, tilting, helpless, thirty degrees bow down. The noise was deafening, and still she went over, bumping and twisting, tossing cursing men and loose equipment into tangled heaps to the port side of the control room. The whole contents of the chart table slid and fell with a crash about Bradley's ankles and he groaned in agony as the corner of a heavy volume of *Jane's Fighting Ships* landed on his slippered right foot. Grabbing the edge of the chart table, he struggled to stay on his feet. *Spearfish* was now heeled at forty degrees to port.

And still the noise went on. A loud crack came from the search periscope. At the moment of impact this periscope had still been coming down, but now, with the crosshead just entering the well, the long dull grey tube started to vibrate, setting up a hum like a giant tuning fork as jets of sea water spurted in freezing lances from around its straining hull gland. The gyrocompass in the machinery space below the control room had toppled, the harsh urgent jangle of its alarm bell providing yet another input to the already cacophonous orchestra of sound that now penetrated every nerve, every sinew, paralysing the mind and beggaring coherent thought.

Then, with a sudden vicious lurch, *Spearfish* finally righted herself. Above them the noise of tearing metal abruptly ceased. The destroyer had passed, the deep rhythmic beat of its propellers now fading like a receding express train, leaving only the hysterical clamour of the gyro alarm bell to stir the stunned and dazed control room crew from their state of shock. *Spearfish* was passing ninety feet with full dive still on the hydroplanes and now heeling sharply to starboard. Bradley stood, splay-legged and ashen-faced, still tightly gripping the edge of the chart table. 'Wheel amidships! Full astern together. Get the white lighting on, and for Christ's sake someone stop that bloody bell.' His voice, forced through a dry throat, was no more than a hoarse croak.

Someone switched over to the white lighting, the sudden harsh light vividly revealing the shambles wrought within the control room during the last two minutes. The two planesmen and the helmsman had struggled back into their seats and with the wheel now at amidships, the list had started to come off, but *Spearfish* was still plunging downward, now passing 130 feet.

Strong had been thrown forward on top of the autopilot between the planesmen, cracking his head sharply on its steel case. Now trying to extract himself from the autopilot casing while bleeding profusely from open gashes on his forehead and left cheek, he was stunned, dazed and confused. Through the red haze of blood covering his eyes he could see the plummeting needle on the depth gauge and instinctively reached across to the ballast pump telegraph, setting it to the pump position.

Bradley's legs felt like jelly. It was difficult to stand and he badly needed to sit. *Spearfish* was still angled steeply down by the bows, and was now passing 250 feet. 'Blow "Q"… Get that bubble off, Cox'n; she's going down too damn fast… Come on, Number One, reverse your planes, dammit. Get that dive off now!' his forced words still no more than a croak.

The needle on the deep depth gauge was now passing 280 feet and was not slowing. Both planesmen had reversed their planes without waiting for the order from Strong, who was still visibly shaking, half blinded by blood, and as yet unable to speak.

Chief ERA Jones, who had been walking forward from the engine room at the time of the impact, had staggered into the control room, almost falling over the panel watch keeper stretched out on the deck, who was nursing his arm and moaning with pain. Jones grabbed for the "Q" tank blow valve. 'Blow "Q", Sir!' he shouted, and spun open the valve. Now Bradley heard the dull thud from up for'd, as high-pressure air was released into "Q" tank – the "quick diving tank" in the bow – blowing 400 gallons of water to sea almost instantaneously. *Spearfish,* suddenly lighter by these 400 gallons in her bows, faltered in her downward plunge and her bow started to rise. She was still heavy but she *was* levelling, slowly, oh so slowly, but with the deep depth gauge now reading 350 feet, she was still sinking bodily.

'Stop blowing "Q". Full ahead together. Keep pumping, Oliver, and keep that rise on your planes.' Bradley's mind was beginning to clear. He again glanced at the clinometer. *Spearfish* was level now, and the depth gauge needle had finally stopped at 380 feet. For a few moments it had remained motionless, as if purposely teasing them, and then it moved – just a tiny movement, a mere flicker – but they *were* going up, and Bradley felt the relief flood through him. He had regained control. He was able to think again.

But now the awful realisation of the situation was dawning on him, and he suddenly felt sick with guilt. He'd nearly lost *Spearfish*. God, but he'd been lucky to get away with that one. He'd known that that he was far too close to that destroyer, but he'd ignored all the rules and just pressed on. That was unforgivable: you just didn't take chances like that. And it wasn't just the one destroyer; it was two of the buggers. One must have been hidden behind the other, and he hadn't seen it because he hadn't taken the time to look properly. In his eagerness to get some decent pictures of that SSBN he'd broken just about every rule in the book. He'd put *Spearfish* and all of her people at a risk that should never have been taken. He should have gone deep immediately at that first report; he should not even have waited to look. How could he have been so utterly stupid? And only a few moments before all of this, he thought he was being lucky!

At the back of the control room, Bishop had picked himself up and now stood ashen faced, with both hands pressed tightly against his forehead, blood seeping through his fingers and running thick and black down the back of his hands. The panel watch keeper, now squatting white faced in the swilling black mixture of oil and water at the foot of the diving panel, clutched his right arm and continued to curse softly to himself. The gyro alarm bell suddenly went silent.

Strong now lifted his microphone, his voice consciously controlled. 'Engine room, report the ballast pump.'

From the engine room, 'Five hundred and fifty gallons pumped from "M"'s to sea.'

'Very good. Stop pumping.' Now *Spearfish* was rising steadily.

Bradley surveyed the chaos that surrounded him. He too spoke with a forced calm. 'Well, it certainly looks like we could do with a bit of a tidy up in here. What about the rest of the boat?' He reached up unsteadily for the main broadcast microphone. 'All compartments report damage. Torpedo officer required in the control room. Christ!' He jerked violently, almost dropping the microphone as a shock of freezing spray from the search periscope hull gland hit him full in the back of his neck. 'Shit!' He again lifted the microphone. 'Outside ERA to the control room at the rush!'

The tall slim figure of Murray the torpedo officer now appeared at the forward end of the control room, as always, unhurried, unruffled and immaculate in a dark blue long sleeved shirt complete with silver cufflinks and a navy cravat. Affectionately known as "The Dude", the easygoing attitude of Murray had made him a firm favourite of the crew. 'Got a problem up in the fore-ends, Sir. There's no damage as such, but poor old Toby was pitched head first into the bilge when we went down. He's conscious, but only just. Taken a terrible whack on the head. Lots of blood, and it looks like either his arm or his shoulder is broken. We've laid him out on the deck plates. I don't think he should be moved too much.' Murray shot a quick glance around the control room, then continued in the usual lazy, almost indolent drawl, a drawl that had at times irritated Bradley almost to distraction. 'Looks like you've been having some fun and games. So what the hell happened, Sir?'

'We've had a slight altercation with one or two of the Reds upstairs. I think the bastard that run us down has wrecked the bloody fin. All I hope is that he's taken his own bottom out at the same time.' Bradley paused, realising that he was again talking too quickly and too loudly. Then he resumed in a quieter voice. 'Oliver's had a bit of a shake-up. Take over the trim, Ross, it's bloody awful. Keep 350 feet while we get ourselves sorted.' He nodded towards Strong, 'Off you go, Number One. Get something done about that head.' He again lifted his microphone, and called over to Greene, 'Cox'n, get a relief on the wheel and go for'd to see what you can do for Lieutenant Commander Cannings. It sounds like he could be in a bad way.' Now he again surveyed the control room. 'Is everyone else OK? Billings…? Dunn…? Forrester…? Hall…? Any more injuries?'

One by one they answered, loudly, firmly, some perhaps a little too firmly and a little too loudly. But now their confidence was returning. It was over. They were safe now, and it seemed that things were fast returning to normality. The panel watch keeper, now relieved by the Chief ERA, had stumbled for'd, favouring what was almost certainly a broken arm. Strong and Bishop had also made their way into the wardroom for some first aid.

Then the reports began coming over the main intercom. 'After ends, no damage… Fore-ends, checked correct… Engine room, no dam—'

Bradley suddenly realised the extent of the noise all around him – the main broadcast reports, the banging and hammering, everyone talking excitedly.

'Christ,' he muttered to himself, 'it's like bloody Fred Karno's in here. They'll be hearing us back at Gosport.' Lifting his microphone again, he spoke in a deliberately low voice. 'D'you hear there? This is the captain speaking. All compartments cease reporting. Maintain the ultra-quiet state.' Then to the control room crew in general, 'Right, that's enough. Keep the noise down. No more unnecessary talk.'

He moved towards the sound room, where Kinross had just reseated himself on his stool and was now replacing his headset. 'You all right, Kinross?'

White faced, Kinross turned to Bradley, obviously very shaken, and when he spoke his tone was apologetic. 'It wasnae just the one, Sir; it was two o' them! An' ah didnae detect that till they started to move.'

'It wasn't your fault.' Bradley instinctively patted Kinross's shoulder. 'Keep a good ear out; they may be back.' He made his way back to the control room, where the bulky figure of Crane, together with the outside ERA, was straining down on the bolts around the search periscope pressure hull gland, at last reducing the scything jets of icy water to mere trickles.

'Essential repairs only, Eric; for the time being anyway.'

Crane grunted and continued with his efforts.

'Course to steer, Sir?' It was the helmsman, Able Seaman "Ginger" Dunn. Usually loud and brash, one of Spearfish's many self-styled comedians, Dunn now spoke in barely more than a whisper. 'Gyro's down, Sir, an' me magnetic compass is all over the place.' He sounded almost apologetic

'Keep your wheel amidships. Is the EA working on the gyrocompass?'

'Yes, Sir.' It was Murray who answered.

Bradley turned to Murray. 'What's the trim like, Ross?'

'It's OK at the moment, Sir. We're under control.'

Then from the sound room came the voice of Kinross. 'Captain, Sir. Two contacts, loud surface HE bearing 210 and 280, coming in fast!' Again the urgency in Kinross's voice triggered panic signals in Bradley's brain. The bastards were coming back!

Spearfish had settled at 300 feet when the first destroyer again passed directly over her. Even at this depth they could clearly hear the thrashing of her twin screws, sending shivers down Bradley's spine. He looked around him, seeing all eyes staring upward at the pressure hull, silent, waiting, and he could almost smell the apprehension, the fear that now pervaded the control room as the thrashing screws eclipsed all other sound. Then she had passed; her propellers receding rapidly towards *Spearfish*'s starboard quarter. It was quiet again.

'Thank God!' Bradley continued to look upward, feeling an intense relief. 'They've done their job, and given us more than a good bollocking. Now they've got that off their chests they'll be on their way. They probably didn't even realise they'd hit us.' He turned and looked into the ruddy features of Crane, whose six foot of burly Yorkshire brawn had been largely responsible for the successful sealing of the periscope hull gland.

'I'm afraid the fin's taken a bit of a hammering, Eric, but we'll have to wait...' He paused and looked upward, wincing as a second set of propellers approached from their port side.

Then the second destroyer thrashed by overhead, this time fading off to their starboard bow. Turning back to Crane, who was also staring upward with obvious apprehension, Bradley continued talking as though nothing had happened. 'Perhaps you would take a scout back aft, Eric, just to confirm there's no other prob—'

BAROOOOM!

He never finished his sentence. The explosion immediately above him would have completely blotted out his words anyway. A giant hammer had smashed into *Spearfish*'s pressure hull, flinging her hard over to starboard.

Bradley had listened to many personal experiences of depth charging, and had read a great deal more. He had often wondered what the real thing would be like and how he would react. But he was in no way prepared for a shock like this. It was staggering, unbelievable. Shock waves ripped up through the deck beneath his feet and down from the pressure hull above his head, striking simultaneously at the back of his neck and the soles of his feet before stabbing through his body to meet with a sickening thud somewhere in his stomach. He felt his muscles suddenly relax all control over his body. Now led only by instinct, he was shouting loudly into the microphone still clutched in his hand. 'Shut all watertight doors. Shut off from depth charging.'

Then all the lights went out, and for an instant they were in total blackness before the automatic emergency lanterns flickered on just as *Spearfish* righted herself. Bradley gulped and swallowed. His eardrums were popping loudly and he realised as he opened his mouth to speak that he was completely deaf. God, that was close! How could *Spearfish* survive a shock like that? Had she survived it?

BAROOOOM! The second explosion came just fractions of a second after the first. This one was even closer and the shock drove Bradley to his knees. This time *Spearfish* was sent heeling madly to port, and this time it seemed that she wasn't going to stop. 'Oh, my Christ! She's going over! She won't stop now!' He reached out, clutching for the periscope support, pulling himself to his feet, stunned, dazed, and still totally deaf. 'Group down... Half ahead together... Port twenty. Go to 400 feet.' He couldn't hear his voice. Jesus Christ! They've got us – spot on, position and depth. There was no doubt in his mind now. These bastards were out for blood!

Again his ears popped. Now he could hear the voice of Crane, who had been knocked flat on the deck by the last explosion but had now climbed to his hands and knees and was shouting with uncontrolled rage. 'Ee! Don't those bastards up there know that t' bloody war were over fifteen year ago? We were on their bloody side, anyway!'

Now the realisation was beginning to dawn upon Bradley. Now he knew what those feelings of apprehension had been about. His mind was racing. Had these bastards known we were here all the time? Was their intelligence as good as the British system? Had they been up there waiting for us, playing a "cat and mouse" game with us? But what the hell are they trying to do now? Surely depth charging was taking things a bit too far. Boats had been caught out up here before, but usually a couple of small warning charges providing an invitation to surface, followed by a polite request on a signal lamp to "Foxtrot Oscar", had always been considered quite adequate to get the message across. But not this time. It seemed that this time these guys were serious. They want to punish us, and it looks like they're playing for keeps. Why?

The confused rush of thought through Bradley's mind now gave way to the sound of water under pressure, jetting into the boat through what he guessed would be scores of fractured pipes and sprung hull glands. He closed his eyes tightly, hearing the shouts and curses of shocked men struggling to shut down valves on various sea water, hydraulic and high-pressure air systems, calling urgently to one another for tools and assistance as they battled in semi-darkness to control lances of freezing water and invisible jets of shrieking air. He felt his stomach start to curdle. Oh, my Christ; this is it then. Game over!

But wait. Where was all the flooding? Where was all the excess pressure? He swallowed and opened his eyes. He swallowed again, feeling both ears pop yet again. He knew that each of *Spearfish*'s five compartments would by now be isolated into self-contained pressure-tight boxes, and he knew that at this moment in time he didn't have a clue what was going on in any of those boxes apart from the one that he was in, and that any one of these boxes would be capable of sinking *Spearfish* if it flooded.

BAROOOOM!

A third charge exploded somewhere ahead and above *Spearfish*'s bow – further away this time, but still pushing her bow sharply downward. There were sounds of smashing glass from the wardroom, and Bradley could imagine the chaos on the other side of the watertight bulkheads. They would be busy, they would be swearing and sweating, and there would be fear, real fear. Despite all their training, they would never be prepared for this. This was something completely new to them – as it was to him.

Spearfish had now passed the ordered 400 feet and was still driving downward. She was very heavy. 'Stop together... Group up... Full astern together... Trim from for'd to aft... Pump from "M" starboard to sea.' Overriding Murray, these orders came from Bradley's lips automatically, without thinking. He knew now that he was fighting for *Spearfish*'s life, for all their lives.

Then came the fourth explosion. This time it was aft, and this one was the closest yet. BAROOOOM!

Spearfish writhed in agony. Her stern corkscrewed madly as she shuddered and groaned along the whole of her 290-foot length. Bradley squirmed. How much more of this could she take? As if to indicate the answer to his question, the emergency lanterns flickered twice then went out. Again, they were in total darkness.

'Blast!' Murray snarled as he lurched forward into the automatic pilot gear, falling heavily to his knees between the planesmen's seats.

'All right, Ivan, all fuckin' right! We can take a friggin' 'int so sod off; we know where we ain't wanted.' It was Dunn on the helm. Gone now was the whisper; he was shouting with rage.

Still on his knees, Murray rebuked Dunn sharply, his voice no longer a laconic drawl. 'That's enough, Dunn. Keep the noise down. Bellowing like that won't help. They can't hear you.' Then, almost under his breath, he added, 'At least I bloody well hope they can't.'

The emergency lighting flickered uncertainly and came back on again. Bradley breathed a sigh of relief.

Now came a new voice, this time from the overhead loudspeaker, hollow and muffled, but so calm that in the current circumstances it sounded completely out of place, almost ludicrous. 'Control, this is the after ends. Serious flooding in the shaft space! The port stern gland has blown. Major flood in the after ends!'

Bradley groaned loudly. 'Stop trimming. Stop port. Full ahead starboard.' Then into his microphone, 'Motor room, evacuate the after ends and open the salvage blow.' Already he could feel *Spearfish*'s stern getting heavy. Christ, he really was losing her now.

A muffled roar came from aft as the salvage blow valve was opened, releasing compressed air at 4000 pounds per square inch into the after ends. Back there in the motor room the noise of this air would be deafening.

But *Spearfish* was still dropping by the stern. Bradley knew that they were now in a desperate situation. 'Trim from aft to for'd, Ross.' He stared at the depth gauge, every fibre in his body willing the needle to stop its steady clockwise rotation. Looking across to the panel he called to the chief ERA, 'Keep your eye on the bottle group pressures, Chief, and let me know immediately they drop below 3000.' He must keep a good reserve of compressed air at all costs, but he also knew that if he could get enough air into the after ends to check that flooding, then hopefully he could regain control.

But there was no salvation. In spite of the drive from the starboard motor, *Spearfish* was still sliding astern. She was sinking. Now with a 25-degree stern down angle on the clinometers, the deep-water depth gauge was reading 500 feet.

Bradley shut his eyes tightly, his thoughts in a turmoil. He knew that there couldn't be much more than 100 feet of water below them now. Should he run the port motor to give himself some extra thrust, taking the risk of tearing out the stern gland packing altogether and increasing the rate of flooding? Or should he simply blow all main ballast? If he blew at this depth, *Spearfish* would go up like a cork. There would be little, if any, control over her; and God only knows what would happen when she broke surface, right in the middle of the fleet that he had been inspecting with such relish just a few minutes earlier. To come up in the middle of them would be bad, but an even worse scenario was just as likely, and that was to come up right under one of them. No; he would wait. There was no danger of crushing yet. *Spearfish* could withstand much deeper depths than this.

He shuddered and opened his eyes. There had been no more charges. Again he looked at the depth gauge. It was slowing down. Yes, thank God, it was slowing down. He looked again at the clinometers – 530 feet. The stern down angle was coming off but she was still just under thirty-five degrees stern down and listing slightly to starboard. He started to breathe again, mentally praising the skills and professionalism of those men back at Cammel Lairds, who had built *Spearfish* so well. Yes, he would wait. There was still a chance they could recover from this.

Then came the crunch! The sickening grinding crunch of metal tearing into stone. The depth of water had been even less than he had thought. *Spearfish's* stern had hit the bottom, and it was rocky. The deck beneath his feet started to bounce viciously and the harsh scraping of steel on stone now blanked out all other sound. 'Stop starboard!' he barked.

But it was too late. In the seconds before the starboard motor could be stopped, the still-thrashing starboard propeller was beating into the rocky seabed, the deafening vibration and noise drowning out even the shrieking of the keel as it slid across bare rock. *Spearfish* was tearing herself to pieces. Then mercifully the noise stopped. Unable to take this punishment any longer, the starboard propeller had disintegrated, and as the starboard shaft finally came to a stop it carried only the shattered remains of the propeller.

Now there was a silence, so sudden and so absolute that it was startling. *Spearfish* lay still, the spirit knocked completely from her battered body. She had taken a terrible beating. Now on an even keel, her bows started to dip slowly as she settled herself on the rocky seabed, gently, almost daintily, with just one or two sharp cracks and graunches as her keel bit deeply into rock. Then, at last, she was still again, finally coming to rest. Bradley could have sworn that he'd heard her groan, a long deep sighing groan, as if expelling her final breath.

Meanwhile, at some 570 feet above *Spearfish*'s crippled body, the commander of a "Hotel" class ballistic nuclear submarine, the latest addition to the Russian Northern Fleet, prepared to dive in readiness for a missile test fire, completely oblivious of *Spearfish* and the man who less than six minutes earlier had been happily anticipating a ringside seat at this firing, but was now squatting, head in hands, amid the chaos of his crippled submarine.

Was she really gone? Had he really lost her? For the first time in his life Nigel Bradley realised utter despair and, even worse, complete inadequacy. His testing time had come and he had failed miserably. He watched a saturated Murray climb slowly to his feet. Now, seemingly as cool as ever, Murray had removed his cravat and was using it to carefully wipe the water and oil splashes from his face and neck. Bradley stared up at him, his stomach still a knotted ball. 'My God, Ross,' he croaked, 'what a bloody mess! What an absolute bloody shambles!'

CHAPTER FOUR

The Russian destroyer *Otvashni* had now lost speed and had finally come to a stop. Kapitan 11 Ranga Alexci Portrova stepped back from the bridge screen, lowered his binoculars to his chest, and loosed a loud sigh – a mixture of weariness and perplexity.

Portrova was puzzled, frowning, his heavy brows now knitting together to become almost indistinguishable from the black fur of the ushanka pulled low over his forehead. Tugging the thick leather mitten from his right hand, he reached up to unclip the protective strip of collar covering the lower half of his face, revealing a thick black moustache which almost obscured his wide full-lipped mouth. The trapped breath, now released, instantly formed a thick dense cloud in the bitterly cold air.

He was by any standards a big man – square shouldered and barrel chested, and with coarse weather-seasoned features from which sloe-black eyes set deep beneath those heavy brows glinted with a piercing brightness, displaying an astuteness and intelligence completely contradicting his peasant-like visage. The heavily padded black leather coat with its upturned collar now lost in the shaggy blackness of the ushanka, served to accentuate his bulk. Portrova had the distinct appearance of a large black bear.

Groping into the side pocket of his coat, he withdrew a large nickel-plated cigarette case. Flicking it open, he briefly surveyed its contents: two neat rows of Black Sobranie. Carefully selecting one, he placed it between his lips and immediately felt the heat of a flame from the lighter now held in front of his face by the gloved hand of Starsh 1 Lieutenant Bassisty, his watch officer.

He grunted, eying Bassisty thoughtfully as he drew heavily on his cigarette before blowing out a thick dark stream of smoke to mingle with the breath still hanging in a white cloud in front of him. Then he turned and looked to starboard, where some 300 metres distant the destroyer *Osornoi* had also come to a stop, a signal lantern on her bridge now blinking urgently through the greyness of the morning, 'Contact lost.' Portrova checked the time on the bridge clock: exactly 10.42

'Ah yes, my friend,' Portrova muttered. 'Contact lost. Now we hear it, now we don't.' He turned to Bassisty. 'Have we a report on the damage yet, Comrad Lieutenant?'

Bassisty, barely twenty-two years old, stared straight ahead, uncertain of his captain's mood, but fearing the worst. Portrova didn't just look like a bear; at times he took on the personality of a bear, and this, as far as Bassisty was concerned this morning, could well be one of those times. 'Not yet, Comrad Kapitan. Kapitan Lieutenant Carlov is still below with the engineers.'

Portrova grunted and again drew heavily on his cigarette. There had been something there, he was sure of that. But whatever it was he had lost it. He was annoyed and he was worried. The admiral would not thank him for any damage to *Otvashni*, especially when caused for no visible reason.

Exhaling another dense cloud of smoke, he flipped his half-smoked cigarette over the side of the bridge. Now he gazed forward over *Otvashni*'s bows, as if expecting the answers to his questions to appear out of the dark rolling water in front of him. He turned to Bassisty, 'Make to *Osornoi*: "Continue the search".' Again raising his binoculars, Portrova scanned through 360 degrees, picking up the flickering lights of the Northern Fleet as its vessels waited in silent smudges some two kilometres south.

Had he been too hasty? No, it had been a firm contact, a definite contact. *Osornoi* had picked it up at the same time. It was a submarine, and it should not have been there. It was not one of theirs. He had, of course, reported this contact to the flagship, and had been mildly surprised at the response: 'Locate, intercept and hold for interrogation.'

He smiled to himself, tight-lipped. By the gods, but it must have given them a shock. *Otvashni* had been pushing twenty-five knots and still not up to her full speed as he had driven her directly over the contact. He had clearly felt the sudden judder in her bow, which had then travelled back to the deck of the bridge beneath his feet, and he knew then that he had hit something. He had leaned over the bridge to peer down into the foaming wash of *Otvashni's* bow wave and in the powerful beam of the searchlight he could have sworn that he had seen the glint of glass. He had seen a periscope! He was sure of it. But now they had lost the contact. Then he had doubled back on a reciprocal course and, knowing that the target would have gone deep, he had dropped two depth charges set to eighty metres. Under his orders, *Osornoi* had followed him in, and had dropped two more charges, set at ninety metres. Using active sonar he had dropped these charges with precision accuracy, as had *Osornoi*. They had been told not to destroy, but to hold any intruders for interrogation.

'Comrad Kapitan.'

Portrova turned as his second-in-command, Kapitan Lieutenant Sergei Carlov stepped onto the bridge. Over six feet five inches tall, with a lean build and sallow, aquiline features, Carlov was in appearance the exact opposite of his captain. Carlov spoke in a firm steady tone, looking over the head of his captain, almost disdainfully. 'There is damage, Kapitan, but this is not serious. Some flooding in the forward bilges and in number one boiler room, but this has been contained.'

'That is good.' Portrova displayed no sign of the relief that he felt. 'We, too, shall now continue the search.' He raised his glasses, again looking back towards the fleet, then, swinging over to *Otvashni's* port quarter, he focused on the dark-grey shape of the "Hotel" class submarine, now trimmed low in the water at a distance of some 600 metres. Without taking his eyes from her, he called over his shoulder to Bassisty, 'Slow ahead both engines.'

★ ★ ★ ★ ★

At last Bradley had found the strength and the will to force himself to his feet. Slowly, painfully and with his senses still numb, he finally stood upright, staggering momentarily and reaching out to the chart table for support. For no other reason than habit, his eyes went to the two clocks over the chart table and saw immediately that something was different. The clocks had somehow changed. What the hell was it…? Ah yes, there was no Z on the face of the one on the right. Where had it gone? He wondered briefly why he was thinking of such trivia and then he saw that the glass from the clock face had fallen out and was lying on the chart table in front of him, miraculously still intact, the red Z now plain against the white of the chart. For a reason certainly unexplainable to himself, he felt a sharp sense of relief. Both clocks were still working. Local time was 10.48 – exactly sixteen minutes since the moment of impact with the Russian destroyer had set this nightmare into motion.

Now there were voices, distant, floating. He shook his head, knowing that he was still concussed and partially deaf. Pinching his nostrils, he blew hard. His ears popped and his hearing was better. Then, from somewhere behind him, he heard movement, and a low moan followed by a sharp curse.

'Fuckin' 'ell!'

Bradley recognised the voice, and looked across at the shadowy form of Dunn, now back on his feet beside the wheel. 'Are you all right, Dunn?'

'Fink so,' mumbled Dunn. 'Wot the 'ell 'appened, Sir?'

'I think the world just fell in on us, that's what happened.' Bradley continued to look about him, seeing other shapes moving around the control room, silent, almost ghostly in the meagre yellow light of the emergency lanterns. He turned to Murray, who was still standing between the planesmen. 'Can we get some more light, Ross?' He realised that he was whispering. It seemed the natural thing to be doing: everything was so quiet, so peaceful.

Then he heard footsteps, heavy, loud, amplified by the quiet. A large shadowy figure approached from aft, and Crane spoke to him in a low voice.

'Pressure seems to be holding the water down in the after ends, Sir. I should say it's about up to deck level, but the flooding's stopped. Everything seems OK in the engine room, apart from a few leaks. Superficial damage, of course, but no major problems and nobody's seriously hurt. I can't tell you much more 'til we try to start the diesels.'

Bradley nodded. 'What about for'd?'

'I'll go and have a look now.'

Bradley blinked, startled, as the first of the white fluorescent lights flickered uncertainly, and then stayed on. He turned back to Murray. 'Right, Ross, revert the hands to watch diving and get any walking wounded for'd to the cox'n. Then get some people in to sort this place out. Oh, and pass the word through the boat, I want absolute quiet from now on.' He looked across to the second cox'n, who was trying to retrieve a parallel rule from behind the autopilot box. 'No point in you being here at the moment, Second Cox'n; we're not going anywhere just yet. Go for'd and help the cox'n with any casualties.' The second cox'n straightened and walked for'd. 'In fact, I'll come with you,' Bradley added. He had suddenly remembered Toby Cannings. 'Look after things here, Ross. I'll be up in the fore-ends, and if you can find the steward, get him to rustle up some coffee for the wardroom, will you?'

Reaching the torpedo space, Bradley joined the cox'n and the second cox'n, who were kneeling beside the prone figure of Cannings, now laid out on the centre plates and still unconscious. They had covered him with a sleeping bag and pushed a pillow beneath his head. Bradley could see immediately that Cannings was in a serious way. His normally jovial features were now fixed, unmoving, chalk white in stark contrast to the dark congealing blood now matting into the fringes of his sparse white hair.

Greene looked up. 'It's pretty bad, Sir. I wouldn't be surprised if his skull is broken. He must have taken a hell of a fall. I reckon his shoulder's broken as well. Good job he's out of it: at least he isn't feeling anything. Apparently he was up here getting some spare gear out of one of his boxes and was caught off balance. We're going to have to see to him properly and then get him turned in somewhere. He can't stay here.' Greene stood up to allow Bradley to kneel and feel for the pulse in Cannings's neck.

'Pulse is very weak.' He leaned over, his ear closing on Cannings's chest. 'And his breathing's very shallow.' He stood up. 'Yes, you're right; he *is* in a bad way. We'll get him down to the wardroom while he's still out. Lay him out on the wardroom table. We might be able to do something with the shoulder, but I don't know about the head wound. Organise a few hands to carry him aft. Stay with them. Make sure they don't shake him up too much – you know what to do. I'd better get back to the control room.'

Lieutenant Bill Morris, *Spearfish*'s weapons electrical officer was waiting for Bradley in the control room. 'Both battery breakers tripped out during the attack, Sir. Number two battery is back on again, and we've got essential power services back on line. The EA has gone up for'd to look at number one battery breaker now. Oh, and both battery sumps are dry, Sir, so I shouldn't think we've got any leaks down there.'

'Thank God for that at least. Well done, Bill, keep me in the picture.' Bradley turned to Murray. 'Toby's in a bad way, Ross. They're bringing him back to the wardroom. I'd better get in there and see what can be done for him. You stay here and look after things. Call me if there's any more panic.'

They had now laid the unconscious Cannings on the wardroom table, where Strong and Bishop sat, still nursing bloodstained heads. At Bradley's request they both moved into his cabin. The steward had made coffee and had passed in a cup for each of them. 'We've got to see to Toby first,' Bradley explained, 'then we'll get the cox'n to check you two out.'

Greene had raised Cannings's head and had wedged a pillow under his neck. He looked up at Bradley. 'It looks like it's his upper arm that's broken, Sir, not his shoulder.'

'Do what you can for that first,' said Bradley. Then bending, he again checked Cannings's breathing and pulse. The breathing was still very shallow, and now a pulse was hardly recognisable.

'I'll reset the arm as best I can, Sir.' Greene had shredded Cannings's right shirtsleeve up to the armpit, revealing an upper arm which had now swollen to twice its normal size and was almost black in colour. Even through the swelling, the arm was plainly bent. Greene ran both his hands gently around the arm, stroking and gently manipulating it until it was straight. He looked up at Bradley. 'It's definitely broken, Sir. Difficult to locate the break with all this swelling but I can feel something there that's not as it should be.' He continued to manipulate the arm, stroking, squeezing. 'Ah, that's it, I think.

44

That's more or less back in line.' He stood up and wiped sweat off his brow with the back of his hand. 'Thank God he's still unconscious; this is going to take more than a couple of painkillers to put right. I'll immobilise the arm as best I can – some sort of splint strapped to his body. There'll be a splint in my first aid kit in the store. I'll go down and fetch it, and we're going to need a lot of bandage as well.' Greene paused, grim faced, and looked directly at Bradley. 'Of course they'll probably have to break it again and reset it when we get back.' With that he turned and made his way for'd.

Bradley stood, looking down at the unconscious Cannings. 'When we get back,' he muttered to himself. 'Nothing like a bit of optimism, I suppose. God, I'm so sorry, Toby. This is my bloody fault, all of it!' He turned and leaned through the wardroom door, calling to the messenger standing beside the wheel, 'Organise a large bowl of warm water, and bring it here as quick as you can, and get the steward in here.'

The steward appeared immediately. 'Yes, Sir?'

'The bottom bunk in the passageway outside the wardroom – get it cleared out and put Lieutenant Commander Cannings's sleeping bag in there. He'll be less disturbed out there than in here. And when you've done that, fetch me a cup of coffee, if you would.'

'Ay ay, Sir.' The steward disappeared.

Greene returned with a splint and an armful of bandages. Without further ado he secured a splint to the injured arm before dexterously applying sufficient bandage to strap it firmly in place against Cannings's inert body.

Bradley was genuinely impressed with Greene's expertise. 'Well done, Cox'n. That looks a pretty good job.'

Greene stood up. 'All in the training, Sir. I just wish we could deal with his head in the same way though. We've got plenty of bandages, so all we can do is clean him up and dress the wounds. I'm getting a bit worried that he's still out cold though. He should be showing some signs of coming around by now.' Bradley was about to agree when the messenger arrived with a large aluminium pot filled almost to the brim with tepid water.

'Hope this is all right, Sir. How is he?' The messenger sounded genuinely concerned.

'I'm afraid he's not very well,' replied Bradley, cautiously dipping his fingertips into the water. 'Yes, that'll be fine.' He took the pot and set it down on the deck, then, using pieces of bandage soaked in the warm water, both he and Greene began to gently remove the congealed blood on Cannings's head. They could now see the wounds – one gash about two inches long and obviously very deep, with two smaller gashes beside it. Bradley was sure that the deeper gash had penetrated Toby's skull.

Greene muttered, 'This is a bad one, Sir, very bad. If you want my opinion, he's gone into a coma. He needs expert medical treatment, and he needs it bloody urgently!'

Now the blood was again starting to ooze through the open gash, thick and red. Bradley held a piece of dry sheeting over the wound. 'Fat chance of that at the moment,' he muttered. 'I think you're right, though. He could well be comatose.' He lifted the sheeting. 'Let's get him bandaged up and turned in. I'm afraid there's little else we can do for him now.'

Together they carefully lifted Cannings, and gently placed him on the bunk outside the wardroom, where Greene again checked that the injured arm was in the right position before strapping him securely into the bunk.

'We'll need someone here to watch him all the time,' said Bradley. 'I want to know immediately he wakes up. The steward is probably the best man for the job at the moment, but you may have to organise a roster.'

'That's if he *does* wake up, Sir.' Greene looked apologetic. 'I'm sorry, but we have to face it, what with all that's going on at the moment.'

Bradley purposely ignored Greene's last words and said, 'You'd better take a look at the rest of the wounded. The first lieutenant and the navigating officer are in my cabin and I believe the panel watch keeper has gone for'd with a damaged arm.'

Returning to the now-empty wardroom, Bradley slumped onto a seat locker, drinking the remains of his coffee while trying to collect his thoughts. It was obvious that Cannings needed urgent medical attention, and if he couldn't get that attention very soon, then he would surely die. And if he died, then it was he, Bradley, who would have been his executioner – it was as simple as that! But he knew the only place he could expect to get any expert medical attention for Toby. 'For just once today, do something right and get Toby the help he needs!' He muttered to himself, rising wearily to his feet, almost overburdened by his debt to Toby and to the whole crew to get this sorry business sorted. He could, of course, simply stay down here and hope that the Russians would refrain from further offensive action and move from the area – unlikely – or he could attempt to move *Spearfish*, but again it was likely that the Russians would then resume their attack, perhaps fatal this time. Lost at sea through unknown causes. But in any case neither of these options would help Toby, and was he going to be responsible for a submarine loss which would blemish the current eight-year safety record for British submarines? No, not if he could help it! A wartime encounter or even an accident would be acceptable, but not this situation! He straightened up and made his way back into the control room, knowing now what he had to do.

'How's things, Ross?'

'Nothing much to report, Sir.' Murray was back to usual casual flippancy. 'At least my feet are still dry, though it is getting pretty hard to breathe in here.'

Now, for the first time since all this had begun, Bradley again noticed the atmosphere in the boat. The air was so thick that he felt he could almost bite on it. It was really becoming difficult to breathe. He knew that they needed some air purification now, so sod the noise! It wouldn't really matter anyway. He said to Murray, 'Run the CO_2 absorption units forward and aft, and make sure that the oxygen generators are kept going. Then I want you in the wardroom, Ross. Turn the control room over to the PO of the watch.' Picking up the main broadcast microphone, he requested all officers to come to the wardroom.

★ ★ ★ ★ ★

'Well, gentlemen, we nearly lost her, didn't we?' Bradley looked around the table at the tense faces, and immediately regretted his opening statement. There was no response; he didn't think there would be. Why should there be? He was only stating the obvious. I bet they're wondering why I used the word "we"; they know that it was me who nearly lost the bloody boat, not them. He realised that they were still stunned. The situation was as unreal to them as it was to him, and still hadn't yet fully sunk in. At least he would have expected some comment from Murray, even if this were only some inconsequential quip or wisecrack. But no, they all looked tired, haggard, especially Strong and Bishop. Sitting there pan faced, both with heavily bandaged heads, they looked odd, comical even. But there was no humour around this table.

Bradley continued, allowing his tight features to relax momentarily into a wry grin. 'I know that some of you are suffering from headaches and aftershock right now, and you will know that poor old Toby's in a very bad way and needs urgent medical help. But, putting all that to one side, we have other problems, and these may well be serious considering the beating we've taken, so before we do anything else we need a detailed assessment of the shape we're in.'

He looked around at all their faces, ignoring the lack of response. 'As I see it, the position is this. We're on the bottom in just under 600 feet of water. It's a rocky bottom, so we're not likely to be stuck. The after ends are flooded through the port stern gland, but as far as we know the air from the salvage blow seems to be holding things for the moment.' He paused, again looking around the table. 'So now it seems that as long as our air purification stays working, we've got some breathing space. The rest of the boat is dry, and there's no need for any panic action. The other problems we know about are, firstly, the fin: it's taken a hell of a bashing, though as yet we don't know how bad things are up there, but the search periscope has been written off for a start, and probably a damned sight more as well. Next, and possibly more importantly, we've buggered up the starboard screw, so with that and the blown stern gland on the port side, we've effectively got no propulsion. In fact we'll be lucky if we haven't done damage to the rudder and possibly the after planes as well.' He paused briefly, eying their faces. 'Lastly, but by no means least, as far as we know the whole damned surface up there could be littered with Reds. They're using active sonar. They know that we're down here somewhere, and sooner or later they'll find us. They've already made it more than clear to us that we're not exactly welcome. Furthermore, there's every chance they'll want to have another crack at us. But never mind. The important thing now is: what are we going to do about it?'

He wanted to sound confident, and to inspire their confidence, but already he knew that he sounded shallow and unconvincing. Well, what the hell else could he say? He waited, studying faces. Then there came a rap on the wardroom door and the curtain opened to reveal Cox'n Greene.

Greene spoke directly to Bradley. 'Captain, Sir, you asked me to report on the casualties. Well, the damage, apart from to Lieutenant Commander Cannings, who you already know about, is two dented heads – that's the first lieutenant and the navigator, Sir.' Then, grinning mischievously as he eyed the bandaged heads of Strong and Bishop, he said, 'But they're OK now by the look of things. Looks like Nesbitt, who was on the panel, got a broken wrist; and one of the engine room boys has a crushed hand, not serious though. I've seen to 'em both. They'll live. Kinross has got problems with his ears. As you know, he was on watch in the sonar room when the bombs dropped. Seems he didn't get his headset off in time. Apart from a few other minor cuts and bruises, that's about it.'

'Thanks, Cox'n.' Bradley turned back to his officers. Now he needed to calm things down, to get these men back into a thinking team again.

Bradley turned towards Crane. 'Eric, organise a complete set of readings from all internal tanks. I want to know exactly what weight we've got and where it is.'

Crane lumbered to his feet, but Bradley raised his hand. 'No – wait for a minute. What's left in the battery, Bill?'

'The last dip was taken a few minutes ago, Sir,' replied Morris, 'and that gave us about thirty per cent working capacity.'

'OK, not good but could be a lot worse! No more electrical load than necessary from now on, but keep the air purification working. I also need to know what's still working in the fin. Eric, perhaps you and Bill could get a team together and do some checks.' He stood up, thankful that he could do no more at this time. 'Right, gentlemen, are there any questions?' There were no questions, but this didn't fool him. 'Good.' Now he spoke with a forced briskness. 'I want your reports as soon as possible. In the meanwhile I want to stress the need for quiet throughout the boat, apart from the air purification, that is. Get that around by word of mouth.' He looked around at still-tense faces of his officers. 'But, first things first, where's that bloody steward got to? I could murder another cup of coffee.'

★ ★ ★ ★ ★

At 12.45 Bradley again met with his officers in the wardroom, who pushed together around the already cramped table to make room for him to sit. He then listened carefully to all the situation reports, which were, in the main, very favourable. Then he said, 'Right, gentlemen, first of all I must tell you that Toby is still asleep. It's obvious now that he's gone into a deep coma and needs help urgently. It must be our first priority to get him that help, though sadly the only way we can get it is from the Russians, and that'll mean deliberately putting ourselves in their hands. We can't just let Toby die! From your reports, thank God, our overall situation isn't as bad as it might have been. With some luck and a positive attitude from the Reds, this shambles can still be redeemable.'

Now he felt back in control. The various situation reports he had received had worked wonders for him. 'May I?' He reached over and poured himself yet another coffee from the jug on the table before continuing. 'There's no other major flooding but we're obviously heavy aft. However, we should be able to compensate for that. We now know exactly what's in our tanks and we'll need to do a bit of trimming to spread the weight. The ballast pump is still in working order and so is the trim pump. So we can pump, flood, and trim as necessary. Also, the hydraulic systems seem to be intact and we've got a reasonable amount of air left in the bottle groups, as well as a few amps left in the battery. So, all things being equal, we're not too badly off.' Taking a sip of his coffee, he glanced quickly around the table before continuing, 'When the time is right we'll attempt to blow ourselves to the surface!' Another pause, not for effect, but to study their faces. He wondered what they were really thinking. He knew that he'd let them down when it had really counted – there was no getting away from that – but they must believe that he was still capable of getting them out of this mess. He mustn't lose their confidence now. 'After careful consideration I've decided that our first priority must be to get help for Toby. We'll see how things go after that.'

Each face was now turned towards him and he knew he had their undivided attention. He said, 'We don't want to add to the damage already done to the screws, so we'll see if we can lift the stern off the bottom by pumping from aft to sea, and trimming for'd before we blow. Our main problem is that once we start blowing we don't know how she'll react. Even just a short puff could send her up like a bloody cork. We'll have no propulsion and possibly no after planes. Quite possibly there won't be time for any further trim adjustment once we start to move, and once we start going up the chances are there'll be no stopping her.' Bradley looked around the table again. Still getting no response, he continued, 'This is not a bad thing under the circumstances, I suppose, as long as we don't come up directly under one of the Reds! We've still got quite a bit of fuel left in three and five main ballast tanks so we'll keep them locked off – we'll need that for going home.' He looked around the table, again briefly studying each face in turn before continuing, 'With no immediate means of propulsion, and without knowing the extent of any other damage, if the Reds are still up there, and I think they will be, then it's them who'll be calling the shots, not us. But for the time being we'll just concentrate on getting to the surface in one piece. We should lose a lot of the water from the after ends as the sea pressure comes off on the way up, and if that stern gland has moved under shock it may well start to hold as we lose depth. Then hopefully we can get someone in there to fix it.' He looked at Crane. 'Right, Eric?'

'Right, Sir.' Crane nodded his head. 'One thing, though. I hate to throw cold water on your plans, but you're obviously assuming we've not damaged the main ballast tanks.'

Cheers, Eric, thought Bradley, always the bloody optimist! But he still forced a fleeting grin. 'Yes, I'm assuming that the ballast tanks are still intact, but if we have holed them, we'll just have to hope that any damage should be on their bottoms, so they should hold enough air to get us up there.' He paused, again looking around the table before continuing, 'And so, on the assumption that everything goes to plan, we will reach the surface. I think we can forget the starboard screw for the time being, but if we can do something with the port stern gland then we'll have propulsion on that side and hopefully we can start to make our way out. This is all assuming that the Reds permit us to go, of course.'

'What about the fin damage, Sir?' It was Strong who spoke.

'Not good,' replied Bradley. 'Bill and Eric have checked as far as they can, and it looks like everything is down, apart from the attack periscope.'

'So we've got no radar, or W/T?'

'That's right, although we should have the whip aerial. But we're obviously going to miss the wireless mast if and when we get further down south. Communications, or rather the lack of them, are going to be a bloody nuisance. But then again, I think that we can take it as read that the balloon will go up as soon as our surfacing signal becomes overdue at noon on the 22nd.' Bradley now rose to his feet, glad to have finished this briefing. 'Right, gentlemen, that's about it then. I want you all to continue with your checks. Oliver, perhaps you could brief the men. I think most of them have a fair idea of what's going on but you can update them, anyway. I want to go to full diving stations at 13.45, when we should be ready to make our move. We'll surface at 14.00!'

Murray stood up. 'Before you go, Sir, what do you think started this lot off? I mean, they were pretty bloody persistent, weren't they? They really meant business up there this morning.'

'Your guess is as good as mine,' replied Bradley. 'They were on some pretty sensitive business though, and I'd say we certainly touched a nerve. Naturally they wouldn't take kindly to anyone nosing in on their missile firing, but I'm surprised that they reacted with quite such force, which also makes me wonder why they stopped when they did. They had us bang to rights, you know. They had us straddled, and I'm pretty sure that they could have finished us with just a little more persistence.'

'And for that we should be grateful?' muttered Murray.

'Under the circumstances, it's for being here now that you should be grateful,' Bradley retorted sharply, and immediately wished he hadn't.

★ ★ ★ ★ ★

At exactly 13.55 Bradley stepped through the curtained doorway of his cabin into the control room. *Spearfish* had gone to diving stations ten minutes earlier. The control room was in dark red lighting. He closed his eyes tightly for a few seconds and then slowly opened them. Although the wardroom and his cabin had been automatically switched to red lighting at the same time as the control room, the darkness in the control room was at first total. Pausing, he watched the sharp pinpoints of red, green and orange lights on the various control panels, which merged with the dull red blobs of the larger lighting to splash the shadows with a dull red tinge, and cast an eerie crimson-tinted glow to both machinery and men.

Gradually his vision adjusted. Now he could separate the brighter glow of the instruments around the hydroplane and steering controls from the glow of the "fruit machine" with its myriad bright red and orange pinpricks illuminating a cluttered mass of dials and controls. It was still very hot, and the red lighting seemed to make it even hotter. Even though the air purification systems had been running continuously, he had a dull headache. They hadn't breathed fresh air for almost forty-three hours, and now the air in the boat was almost unbreathable. He knew he wouldn't be the only one with a headache.

He felt calmer now, but it was an uneasy calm. The guilt of this morning would not go away. Neither would the feeling of complete inadequacy that he had carried with him since *Spearfish* had grounded this morning. It would break him eventually – he knew that. But for now he must brush these feelings aside and concentrate on getting his boat and his crew to the surface. That should be all that mattered now. He was completely resigned to whatever might happen during the next few minutes, and he knew that he was as ready as he would ever be. *Spearfish* was ready too. They had done all that they could. She would get them to the surface, he was sure of that.

But what then? No surface contacts had been reported on what was left of his passive sonar, so it should be clear. But what if it wasn't? What if… Oh, to hell with 'what if'; he could do no more. He took up his position behind the attack periscope. Bishop moved back towards the chart table to give him more room, and Bradley looked towards Strong, who was leaning intently over the planesmen. 'You ready, Oliver?'

'Ready to surface, Sir. Sound room reports no contacts, and we are shut off for collision.' Strong's voice was calm, measured, a completely different Strong from this morning. Bradley felt relieved: he knew now that Strong was ready. He looked behind him towards the huge shadowy bulk of Crane, who had stationed himself at the diving control panel together with the outside ERA.

'Everything all right on the panel?'

'Aye, Sir, all ready,' Crane answered quietly.

Murray was for'd in the fore-ends, and Morris was aft in the motor room. They would look after any emergencies at either end of the boat. Bradley squeezed his eyelids together once more, then blinked, satisfied that he was now fully adjusted to the red lighting. He looked at the clock. The time was 14.00 exactly. Bradley's voice was sharp. 'Right then, gentlemen, let's get the show on the road! Stand by to surface, Number One.'

Strong lifted his microphone. Holding it close to his mouth, he spoke softly and deliberately quietly. 'All compartments stand by to surface! Report main vents!' They waited for the completion of the incoming reports on the main vents. Then Strong turned to Bradley, 'All main vents checked shut, Sir. Ready to surface.'

'Very good. Surface the submarine.'

Strong looked over to the diving panel, his voice now crisp, almost a bark. 'Surface the submarine! Blow one, two, four, six, and seven main ballast!'

CHAPTER FIVE

Portrova lay on the bunk in his sea cabin immediately below the bridge. He had lain like this for almost two hours, stretched flat on his back, fully clothed down to his heavy sea boots, lulled by the movement of *Otvashni* as she drifted restlessly on the gently rolling swell.

For a little of this time he had been sleeping, but this was a brief, shallow sleep that brought no relief to his troubled mind. For the most part he had been thinking, contemplating the events of this morning, his thoughts interrupted only by the brief snatches of conversation coming from the ladder outside his cabin as men made their way to and from the bridge, or else from his own occasional need to clutch wildly for the rail of his bunk as *Otvashni* encountered a sudden extra-high swell.

He had lighted yet another of the black cigarettes, which he now held loosely between the thick fingers of his right hand, periodically raising it to his mouth to draw heavily before exhaling dense yellow smoke which curled lazily upward to pollute even more the already stifling atmosphere of the tiny cabin and add a further layer of colour to the tobacco-stained deck-head above him.

Now he studied the toecaps of his sea boots through half-closed eyes. It had been a submarine! A definite contact, he was sure of it. It certainly wasn't ice that had ripped through *Otvashni's* keel this morning. But then he reflected, 'Perhaps I should have waited just a little longer, and really established that contact.'

After her initial impetuous dash towards this apparently phantom contact, and the subsequent release of her depth charges, *Otvashni*, together with *Osornoi*, had continued to search the area, but had found no wreckage and had raised no further contacts. Portrova had informed the flagship accordingly. Then at 11.00 hours precisely, the submarine missile test launch had been made.

Portrova had watched the launch from his bridge. He had clearly seen the white-and-black painted 'Sark' missile rise up through the surface amidst a torrent of spume and fumes. For a brief moment it appeared to hang suspended over the boiling turbulence it had created, then, belching a combination of fierce yellow flame and black smoke, it had accelerated upward in a tight spiral, chased by a small ball of orange flame, before disappearing into the low cloud away to the north-east. He knew from the many visual signals between the fleet and the wireless transmissions immediately following the launch, that it had been a complete success. They would be congratulating themselves now, both there among the fleet and back at the Kremlin.

At midday the fleet had dispersed, disappearing into the cold grey haze down to the south-west. Portrova had been ordered to keep *Otvashni* on station. Together with *Osornoi*, he was to remain in the area for a further twenty-four hours, just in case his mystery contact decided to reappear. After carrying out a further intensive search of the area and raising no further contacts, Portrova had ordered *Otvashni*'s engines to be stopped. Signalling *Osornoi* to stop and maintain station at four kilometres to port of him, he had retired to his cabin. Both ships would now keep a listening watch.

He reached up and stubbed his cigarette into the ashtray on the shelf beside his bunk, his eyes clouding as they rested on the face of the dark-haired woman in the large wood-framed black-and-white photograph fastened to the bulkhead above the shelf. Now he raised himself up onto one elbow, his eyes on the photograph.

She sat upright in her chair, arms folded across a full matronly figure dressed in a white high-collared blouse over a long dark skirt, dark hair combed high above her plain, sharp-featured pale face. Anna would then have been in her mid-thirties. But even this scratched and faded photograph could not hide the profound sadness in those eyes, and to Portrova it seemed that those sad eyes now followed him everywhere. It had been almost one year since Anna's death. Married for twelve years, it had not been a contented marriage even though he had loved her and she had loved him. For most of those twelve married years they had been apart. His job had been his first priority, as it had always been. Now his thoughts strayed back over the years. *Shtshuka* had been his first and only submarine, but he had felt no regrets when he was returned to general duties after his experiences in 1945. Not long after this he had met and married Anna. It was a rushed marriage, scheduled to fit in with his ship's operational requirements. They had had so little time together. Even when their twin daughters became ill and died at the age of four, he was away at sea. He had never been there for Anna, or his family. Then Anna was run over and killed by a tram on a freezing Moscow street. Again he had been at sea when he was given this news. They had buried her three weeks before he returned.

Now he was a lonely, bitter and guilt-ridden man, hating the service which had kept him from his Anna. Neither wanting, or indeed knowing any other way of life, he shunned the thought of a proper home, preferring to live either here on board his ship, or in the naval base at Polyarnyy, where he drank, mostly alone, and far too heavily.

'Ah, my Anna, do you watch me?' His voice a low murmur, hardly audible. 'There is still a great sadness in my heart for you, my love, and my life is nothing since you have left me. I grieve for you still.' He flopped back on his bunk and closed his eyes, feeling the hot tears welling beneath the lids. 'Well, who knows? If there is a foreign submarine out there, she may yet put a torpedo through us, and maybe we could then be together again.' Letting out a long sigh, he folded both arms under his head and resumed the fixed scrutiny of his toecaps.

Initially, certainly for the first two years after his encounter with *Ocean Harvester*, he had thought of little else other than taking his revenge on Dennehy, but then Russian agents had reported back through the intelligence grapevine that Dennehy was dead. Sorely disappointed at this news, he felt angry – cheated. But over the ensuing years he had, of necessity, applied himself to his career. Although his intense hatred of the British had remained as fierce as ever, it had become more dormant as the years went by.

Knowing even now that he could be waiting here for the reappearance of this mystery submarine, he began to doubt himself even more. But then, he reasoned to himself, *Osornoi* had picked up the same contact at exactly the same time, so could they both have been wrong? Not likely. In any case, if not a submarine, then what had he hit? No, it had been a submarine, and *Otvashni* had just scraped over the head of her periscope – a near miss. Any nearer and the damage to *Otvashni*'s hull would have been much more serious. Maybe those depth charges had done the job too effectively. She could be sunk, and that as well could mean trouble for him since the Kremlin had specifically ordered that his contact should be forced to the surface and arrested. But she could now be down there on the seabed, crippled, unable to surface. What was she doing now, this phantom submarine? Maybe even at this moment she was preparing a counter-attack.

He grunted, groping for yet another cigarette. So what if he had sunk this submarine? She was intruding, obviously spying, and so they deserved his attack. He had acted under orders, and in defence of his country. Her sinking would have been declared as accidental, but what would be the political ramifications? Russia was not at war with Britain, so what reason could there be for sinking one of their submarines? The reasons for any foreign submarine being up here at this time would be questionable. But to sink her? No, to chase her off would have been the normal action. They had done that before on several similar occasions, so why not this time? Surely a delay in the test firing would not have mattered that much. He exhaled another dense cloud of smoke and sighed deeply. Ah well, these are strange times: no war, but no peace.

The loudspeaker over his head suddenly erupted into life, bringing his thoughts to an abrupt end. 'Kapitan, to the bridge!' The urgency in that crackling voice energised him, and despite his massive bulk he was off his bunk and through the cabin door in one bound. Leaping up the iron stairs leading up to the bridge, he cursed roundly as he collided with Bassisty.

'Ah, Kapitan, we have a contact on red nine-zero.' Bassisty had turned on the narrow steps to make way for Portrova, who pushed past him with a grunt.

The time was just after 14.02. The afternoon was dark and with little or no wind. Carlov was leaning over the port side of the bridge, gazing intently into the darkness through his binoculars. Portrova positioned himself beside Carlov, raising his own glasses.

Without moving Carlov said, 'A contact, Kapitan. Sonar reports heavy water turbulence and noise, which they think is air. But no propeller noise.' His usually passive voice was now shaking slightly with a building excitement.

Now, in the darkness, Portrova smiled to himself. At last! I knew I could not be wrong. 'It is a surfacing submarine that you hear, my friend,' he answered quietly. 'She is blowing main ballast but is using no propulsion. Possibly she will be crippled. Train your searchlight to the port beam.'

★　★　★　★　★

Spearfish was not moving. Seemingly reluctant to leave her resting place, she lay still, heavy, dead. Bradley shot a quick glance towards the clock. For over a minute they had been blowing on main ballast tanks with 3500 pounds per square inch of compressed air, and still no movement. All eyes were on the depth gauges, anxious eyes, tense with expectation as precious high-pressure air continued to explode relentlessly into *Spearfish*'s ballast tanks, purging them of cold black water and imparting a new life force into her steel flanks, a renewed will to live, a buoyancy that would lift them from this lonely watery crypt back into the living world.

But did *Spearfish* have that will? Bradley's mind was racing as his eyes darted continuously between the depth gauges and the high-pressure air bottle group pressure indicators. The noise of the blowing air was deafening. The high-pressure air bottle group was now down to 2000 psi, and yet still the depth gauge needle remained static. Were those bloody ballast tanks all right, or was he just blowing all this precious air to sea? No, he reasoned. All the main ballast tanks wouldn't have been damaged anyway. But surely something should be happening by now!

Then, suddenly she stirred. At first just a slight tremble, hardly noticeable, but now there was a definite movement. He could feel it, yes, she was lifting. Now her keel grated harshly on the sharp rocks beneath her, the noise mingling with the roar of the air. At last, the depth gauge needles were moving, very slowly, but they *were* moving. *Spearfish* was rising by the bows. She was alive again!

Strong, standing behind the planesmen, called to the panel watch keeper without taking his eyes off the depth gauge, 'Trim from aft to for'd.' Now *Spearfish's* stern was beginning to lift. The harsh sound of metal on rock became even louder and then suddenly stopped. She was clear!

Bradley felt an almost overpowering sense of relief. He wanted to shout, to laugh, to slap someone on the back. They were off the bottom. Now the depth gauge needle was moving steadily. 550 feet… 530… 480… 400 feet… Spearfish was coming up very rapidly.

'Stop blowing,' Bradley shouted above the noise of the air, and immediately the outside ERA on the diving panel spun the blow control valves shut. Still *Spearfish* accelerated upward. She was on a level trim. Strong had stopped the trim pump and was now flooding through the ballast line in a vain attempt to slow their ascent.

The scream of high-pressure air was now replaced by a host of other noises. The loud groaning and creaking along the length of *Spearfish's* hull was as intrusive as, and certainly more frightening than the noise of the high-pressure air. Now they were passing 200 feet, and still hurtling upward. Bradley's eyes were glued to the needle on the depth gauge. Oh, my God! he winced. She was coming up far too fast.

Strong shot an anxious glance over his shoulder towards Bradley, and Bradley nodded as if to reassure him, while gritting his teeth and muttering to himself, 'God, I just hope we've got a clear pitch up there.' He knew now that they had overdone the blowing. *Spearfish* had been lighter than he had reckoned. Strong was flooding water into her at full rate, but she wasn't going to stop now. She wasn't even slowing down.

'A hundered and seventy feet, Sir.' Strong was calling out the depth. 'A hundred feet… eighty-five feet… seventy feet…'

From the sound room, 'Control room. Passive sonar, no contacts.'

'Just as well,' muttered Bradley under his breath.

From Strong, 'Sixty-five feet. She's slowing, Sir.'

'Too bloody late now,' Bradley muttered, now on his knees behind the attack periscope. 'Up attack periscope.'

★　★　★　★　★

From where they stood on the bridge of the destroyer *Otvashni*, Portrova and Carlov could now hear *Spearfish*. They stared intently downward along the yellow beam of the port searchlight to the point where it formed a large ragged glow of light on the oily surface of the heaving black water. First there was a rumble, a deep hollow rumble: the unrestrained turbulence of thousands of gallons of water violently displaced by an undersea express train. Now the rumble became louder, reinforced by an increasingly high-pitched whine which then stopped abruptly, to be replaced by an almost musical staccato produced by the creaks and groans of expanding metal. Then came the phosphorescence – a pale white cloud spreading upward through the water like a huge jellyfish, expanding upward and outward until it finally burst through the surface in a deafening explosion of huge bubbles, with gouts of air exploding into white froth and churning the surface into a seething, boiling cauldron of foam.

Spearfish broke surface just over one kilometre to port of *Otvashni*. She rose like a huge black whale, right in the centre of the floodlit pool. First came her fin, its huge slab sides gleaming black in the stark glare of the Russian searchlights, and shedding streams of roaring white water which flowed in torrents down her sides. Then, with an even louder roar, came the casing, bows first but almost perfectly trimmed for'd and aft, streaming off even greater torrents of water. Still she came roaring upward, until finally almost clear of the water, where she hung in momentary suspension as though supported by a giant hand, and her ballast tanks now gleaming black with white water cascading from every orifice, the whole length of her sleek body bared almost down to her keel. Then she plummeted downward, back into the raging white spume, heeling violently, first to port then to starboard, before coming to rest with her casing just awash, the combined beams from the two destroyers' searchlights leaving her starkly outlined, naked and utterly vulnerable – trapped.

Portrova and Carlov continued to stare as though transfixed at the now silent, gently rolling shape in front of them. 'So, Comrad,' muttered Portrova, patting his jacket pocket in search of his cigarette case, 'we have caught a big fish this time. Now, what are we to do with it, eh?'

★ ★ ★ ★ ★

Bradley had started his "all-round sweep" even before the attack periscope had broken surface. Split seconds later, *Spearfish* was fully on the surface. The fierce dazzle of white light from the searchlights of the two destroyers had instantly blinded him. Jerking his head back from the eyepiece, he cursed sharply and rubbed his eyes. Then, pulling the periscope around so that the single eyepiece faced directly forward, he again trained it through a full circle. *Spearfish* was rolling now, long slow rolls that sent anything not tied down careering noisily across her decks.

In the red-tinged shadows of the control room his team watched him expectantly, eager for a sign that would tell them that all was well. But now his complete silence said it all. Steadying himself on the heaving deck, he turned, tight-lipped, to face these shadows. His stomach knotted; his mouth again became very dry. 'Just as I thought,' he muttered. Without waiting for a response, he reached up for the main broadcast microphone and, holding it close to his mouth, spoke slowly, deliberately. 'Do you hear there? All compartments, this is the captain speaking. We are now on the surface. Open up bulkhead doors and ventilation. We are not alone; we have Soviet destroyers on either side of us! Under the circumstances we have little option other than to liaise with them and to comply with any directive they may give. However, my prime concern at this time is to get medical treatment for Lieutenant Commander Cannings. After that, what happens will be entirely up to the Russians. I will keep you informed. That is all.'

Now completely drained, Bradley replaced the microphone and looked across to the clock. The time was 14.05 – just three minutes since they had started blowing main ballast. 'Officer of the watch, take the periscope.' He left the periscope and walked slowly to his cabin.

In the privacy of his cabin Bradley looked into the small mirror, hardly recognising the gaunt features that stared back at him. Grunting in complete disgust at what he saw, he turned to his narrow wardrobe and yanked out a thick woollen submarine sweater and his naval uniform jacket. Hastily pulling them on, he groped into the back of the wardrobe for his cap. Finding it, he pulled it firmly down on his head, glancing again into the mirror as he did so. This was the first time he had worn his hat since leaving Portsmouth. It felt tight, uncomfortable, and he knew that he looked even more incongruous with his corduroys completing his ensemble, but at least this hat gave him some sense of authority. Then he remembered he was still wearing slippers. He kicked them off and searched in the cupboard for his shoes. Finally he pulled on a heavy biscuit-coloured duffel coat. He felt strangely calm now. Although he knew that he had many new problems to face, at least *Spearfish* was on the surface and all his men were alive.

Strong had been relieved in the control room by Murray, and was now standing under the conning tower hatch waiting to give the word to open up. He too was now wearing warm clothing, but instead of his cap a parka hood favoured his bandaged head. The signalman, similarly clothed, was standing beside him. They would accompany Bradley to the bridge.

Now Bradley was back in the control room. He looked towards Strong. 'How are we doing, Oliver?'

'Ready to go up, Sir,' replied Strong.

Bradley checked his red torch, and pulled his cap down more firmly.

'Pressure in the boat, Sir,' warned Murray.

'Roger,' replied Strong. 'Start the LP blower. Helm, drain down and open up the voice pipe cock.'

Below them, in the auxiliary machinery space, the "blower" rumbled noisily into life, pumping low-pressure air into the main ballast tanks, evacuating the remaining water and giving *Spearfish* increased buoyancy but, more importantly for now, soaking up the excess air pressure in the boat.

Bradley was watching the barometer. Now the "low-pressure blower" was drawing air from the boat and the pressure was falling steadily. He turned to Strong, forcing a briskness that he didn't feel. 'Right then, Oliver, I suppose we had better get up there and do some talking. Open the lower hatch.'

Strong was already three rungs up the ladder, his slight frame straining on the locking lever of the lower hatch. The hatch sprang suddenly and he dropped back off the ladder to make way for Bradley, who now climbed up through the tower to wrestle with the upper hatch, with Strong directly underneath him clutching his captain's legs tightly in case any sudden release of air pressure from within the boat tried to lift him. Now, as the hatch was unclipped, the small pressure still within the boat took charge and the upper hatch flew open with a force that bounced it heavily against its stops, almost dragging Bradley with it. Climbing through, he made his way up the steep ladder towards the top of the fin, closely followed by Strong and the signalman, who was bearing his signal lantern.

Bradley, hampered by his heavy clothing, could feel the thick clammy mist that was now filling the fin, and he was acutely aware of the intense cold. His eyes started to water uncontrollably and he felt dizzy. The air he was breathing was sweet, sickly. He could taste it and he wanted to vomit. It was always like this. After weeks of breathing stale second-hand air the sudden change to fresh air was a shock to the system, but he knew that this would soon pass. He paused on the ladder, taking another deep breath of this sweet air while the intake of freezing cold made his teeth ache and his windpipe and lungs raw. Finally he pulled himself up through the narrow hatchway onto the bridge. Strong and the signalman clambered up behind him. Bradley straightened and blinked in the blinding white glare of the searchlights that were now trained directly upon *Spearfish*'s bridge.

'Hello, the submarine.' The strident bellow, amplified by a megaphone, came from the bridge of the vessel on *Spearfish*'s starboard side. It was not a pleasant voice – guttural, slightly nasal, and heavy with Russian, but its message was very clear.

'You will please pay full attention. You will remain where you are and make no attempt to get underway, or to dive. You will await further instructions.'

'Ah well, that's telling us,' breathed Bradley, his eyes now making full use of the searchlights to carry out a hasty survey across the top of the fin behind him. His worst fears were confirmed. The upper section of the fin from the search periscope aft was a total wreck, absolute devastation. The search periscope, caught halfway down at the moment of impact, now pointed lopsidedly to port, its top completely missing, the jagged twisted end of the metal tube glinting dully in the glare of the searchlights. He let out a low slow whistle, and muttered to Strong, 'Well, that answers at least one of our questions; we're not going to get much joy out of anything up here.'

'Looks like they've got their firepower trained on us, Sir,' said Strong.

Bradley shaded his eyes against the glare with his hands and studied the dark shapes of the destroyers on either side of *Spearfish*. He could see that the two forward turrets of each vessel were trained directly on them.

'What are they, Sir? Do you know?' asked Strong.

'"O" class,' replied Bradley. 'About eight years old. Three twin 5.7 turrets and quite a lot of secondary stuff. Yes, I think we might as well accept their invitation to stay awhile!'

Now the megaphone on the ship to starboard barked again, 'Hello, the submarine.' It was the same unpleasant voice. 'You will stand by to receive one of our boats… We wish to talk with you… Your commander and one officer are invited for a meeting… Your visit will be short.'

'And there's another invitation that could be hard to turn down,' muttered Bradley.

'You're going over, Sir?' Strong asked.

'Can't really do anything else under the circumstances,' replied Bradley. 'We might as well get this business sorted, see where the land lies. They can't really hold us for ever but at least they can look after Toby, and anyway, you never know, they might want to give us some help, get us on our way.' Even as he spoke he knew that he was being wildly optimistic. *Spearfish* was in a lot of trouble and so was he; he was sure of that.

Strong looked dubious. He seemed to be reading Bradley's thoughts. 'It's my guess they're going to be awkward, Sir. We're well outside of their territorial line but I suppose, technically speaking, we *have* been intruding on them.'

Bradley shrugged. 'A subtle choice of words, Oliver, and yes, technically speaking I suppose you're right.' He paused, knowing that Strong was absolutely right. 'But there's not a lot that we can do about it now. We'll just have to wait and see what Mr Khrushchev's standing orders are with regard to this sort of situation.'

'Who will you take with you, Sir?' Strong asked.

'Tim Bishop, I think. He's got a smattering of Russian, and I want you to stay here on the bridge, Oliver. Keep station as best you can and keep the signalman up here with you, as well as two lookouts. We shouldn't be too long but do nothing unless it's to maintain the direct safety of the boat or unless you hear from me. I'll go down to tell the others what's going on, and collect Tim.'

Arriving back down in the control room, Bradley called across to Bishop, 'Get your gear on, Tim. You're coming with me. We've been invited to pay a courtesy visit on our Russian friends.' He then called the rest of the officers together in the wardroom, quickly briefing them on the general situation, of the visible damage to the fin, and of his impending visit to the Russian destroyer.

They listened in grim silence as Bradley spoke. 'While I'm over there Number One has the boat, of course. But I want everyone and everything to carry on as normal. We might as well use whatever time we have to get ourselves straight. How's that port stern gland, Eric?'

'We're working on it now, Sir. I think we may be able to do something with it.'

'Good! You and Bill get the main engines and main motors checked out, and then we ought to get a charge on as soon as possible.' He now turned to Morris. 'Bill, one other thing – and this really is top priority – bag up all our records, tapes, film, all the documentation, the bloody lot, and that includes Toby's records. Seal the bags, weight them, and load them into five tube. If I'm not back within two hours, or if any Russians try to come aboard, then fire five tube. We'll get rid of everything rather than let the Russians find it!'

'Captain, Sir.' The control room messenger's head appeared through the curtained doorway. 'Message from the first lieutenant on the bridge. He says to tell you there's a boat comin' across from the Russian on our starboard side.'

Bradley immediately made for the conning tower ladder, followed closely by Bishop. Even now as he climbed the ladder, his doubts and fears again began to run riot. Was he doing the right thing? Should he really be leaving *Spearfish* at this time? What if these Russians did turn really awkward? Had he really thought this through properly? He knew that he probably hadn't. Since the sighting of that first destroyer he'd been thinking on his feet, but had he been thinking logically? Had he been making the right moves? But then, what real choice did he have now? There certainly wasn't a manual of instruction on the correct procedure for this situation, so where was the logic in upsetting the Russians at this point? They were holding all the good cards, so why risk turning an awkward situation into a disastrous one? No, what the hell, let's get on with it; let's find out what the bastards want.

CHAPTER SIX

The time was 14.35. Bradley and Bishop now sat huddled together in the bouncing stern sheets of the Russian motor boat as it made its way across the heaving black water towards the waiting *Otvashni*. Getting into a small boat from the casing of a submarine while at sea was never an easy job, and this transfer had been no exception. Bradley had clung to a rope tied to the casing and half slid, half fell down *Spearfish's* steep tank sides to stumble awkwardly into the arms of two Russian seamen in the waiting boat. Bishop had followed him with an equal lack of grace. Having replaced the bandage around his head with a large plaster, Bishop's hat still sat very precariously on his head and, perhaps inevitably, he lost it while jumping down into the boat. Bradley shuddered. Even with all his extra clothing he felt bitterly cold.

Behind them, in the stern sheets of the boat, stood a Russian officer – young with boyish features now pinched and pale in the glow from the searchlights, the single small star on his plain shoulder epaulette pronouncing him a sublieutenant. He had made none of the customary show towards senior ranking officers – no salute, no spoken word, just a brief hand motion to indicate where they should sit. Now he stood silently behind them, ignoring them, staring fixedly towards the increasingly large grey shape of the destroyer *Otvashni*.

Then they were alongside, the boat nudging carefully towards the waiting ladder at the destroyer's waist. Both Bradley and Bishop ducked instinctively as a shower of freezing spray from the compressed swell broke over them. Apparently impervious to this, the sublieutenant motioned towards the ladder. *Otvashni*'s upper deck lighting had now been switched on, its cold yellow glare bathing Bradley and Bishop, who were exposed, uncertain, dripping icy water and feeling utterly wretched. Bradley cast a quick backward glance towards the still floodlit *Spearfish*, again feeling doubt. Should he be here? Should he have left his boat?

A tall figure stepped forward from the shadows. Bradley had read up on the books relating to the Russian navy and he recognised the three stars of a kapitan lieutenant on the shoulder tabs of the man in the long black watch-coat. A lieutenant commander. But again there were none of the usual welcoming formalities, no exchange of salutes – just a quick hand gesture pointing for'd. 'You will come!'

They followed the tall officer forward along the upper deck. Bradley could not fail to note the shining black leather holster strapped high on the left side of his waist. He heard the sound of footsteps close behind and, shooting a glance over his shoulder, he saw that they had an escort of two seamen, both armed with submachine-guns.

Climbing a steep steel ladder from the upper deck to the fo'c'sle deck, the small entourage stepped through open watertight doors into a dark passageway. Five steps along, the Russian officer stopped in front of a grey steel door, banging on it twice with his gloved hand.

'Come.' The invitation was a bellowed order. The tall officer pushed the door open wide and stepped through, turning to beckon Bradley and Bishop, who were followed by their escort standing motionless behind them, eyes staring implacably to the front.

Bradley looked about him. It was a large, brightly lit cabin, but he was immediately struck by the sparseness of the furnishings, the complete austerity. Four bunks indicated that it was a cabin meant to accommodate four people, probably officers. The whole place had an unpleasant aura, utterly cheerless. So this is how they live, he thought to himself. Ah well, it figures. The bunks were fitted athwart ships, one above the other, on either forward and after bulkhead. The dark-grey curtains of each bunk were drawn. Directly opposite him, below the square scuttle, the deadlight of which was clipped shut, was a stainless steel hand washbasin mounted into a grey metal chest of drawers. This in turn was flanked on either side by twin full-length lockers of a similar colour, matching the worn dull grey linoleum that covered the deck. In the centre of the cabin, about six foot from where Bradley now stood, was a plastic-topped table, behind which three men were seated on straight-backed chairs.

Even when sitting down, it was clear that the central figure was a big man – dark, swarthy features with a heavy petulant mouth almost hidden behind a thick black moustache. This fellow, thought Bradley, studying the bear-like figure, must be of Russian peasant stock. The bear-like man was dressed in a heavy black leather coat topped with a black fur ushanka boasting a single large silver coloured star set into the fur at its front. A broad gold stripe on each of his shoulder epaulettes carried the same star. Bradley knew that this signified the rank of commander. Ah well, perhaps looks can be deceiving. The bear cupped a half-smoked black cigarette in his right hand. Wisps of smoke curled lazily upward through his fat, hairy fingers.

The man sitting to the bear's right was in appearance his exact opposite. Small and dapper, he wore no topcoat, and his impeccable uniform fitted glove-like to his slight frame. Heavily ornate gold epaulettes bearing the three silver stars of a rear admiral gleamed in the bright lights of the cabin. His hat and black leather gloves were laid neatly on the table top in front of him. Coughing quietly, as though clearing his throat, the admiral studiously flicked some imaginary object from his sleeve with finely manicured fingers. Certainly the admiral's appearance gave no indication that only some ten minutes earlier he had completed a three-mile motor boat journey from his flagship to *Otvashni*.

The admiral pointedly ignored the new arrivals. Now he made a show of carefully selecting a cigarette from the open packet of Phillip Morris that lay on the table top in front of him, his movements and body language obviously effeminate. After leisurely applying a flame from a gold cigarette lighter, he drew deeply on the cigarette before finally raising his eyes to view the two British officers. There was no warmth in his eyes, just a cold disdain as he studied the faces of the two men in front of him. His eyes lingered momentarily on the plastered head of Bishop before lowering to concentrate once more on his smoking cigarette.

The man sitting on the bear's left was dressed in plain clothing, and even smaller in stature than the admiral. He too, had made the motor boat journey from the flagship. Scruffy and thin almost to the point of emaciation, the skin stretched over his pinched features resembled dull yellow parchment. But the most noticeable feature about this man was his skull, completely bald, with a prominent oversized forehead set into a grotesquely oversized head. Clearly a deformity. The shabby dark-grey leather coat that enveloped his emaciated frame was also oversize, his scraggy yellow-skinned neck protruding through the buttoned collar like an ancient turkey, hardly looking capable of bearing that massive head. Bradley's thoughts reached back to his younger days. This man reminded him of something, someone. It was a character from his boyhood. A boys' comic? Was it the Eagle? That had been his favourite. Now what was that little bastard called? Ah, yes – the Mekon! This man seated in front of him was the Mekon reincarnate. Even in his present circumstances, Bradley almost wanted to laugh aloud. Yes, that's it, this guy's the bloody Mekon! Christ! thought Bradley. Is this what we're up against? A peasant, a queer, and the bloody Mekon!

The Mekon's arms rested on the table in front of him, bony fingers barely emerging from his sleeve cuffs, constantly, nervously, picking at the brim of a stained grey trilby. He was a figure of complete ridicule, but as he gazed up at Bradley and Bishop through unblinking pale-yellow reptilian eyes, it was clear that this was also a figure of intense evil. He exuded evil. Bradley could smell it, almost taste it. This, he thought, is the dangerous one!

The trio eyed Bradley and Bishop for a full two minutes, saying nothing. Bradley eyed them back, expectantly, defiantly. The silence was becoming embarrassing. Beside him he heard Bishop cough nervously.

At last the Mekon spoke. Raising his expressionless yellow eyes, he looked directly into Bradley's face.

His English was good. 'Who are you? Why are you here?'

Oh well, there's nothing like coming straight to the point, thought Bradley.

Ignoring the Mekon, he fixed his gaze on the bear.

'I am Lieutenant Commander Nigel Bradley, Royal Navy, commanding officer of Her Majesty's Submarine *Spearfish*, and this,' he indicated towards Bishop, 'is Lieutenant Bishop, my navigating officer.' Suddenly he felt very foolish. This was fast becoming completely unreal. Where was the bloody manual now? Was there a procedure for dealing with situations like this? Like hell there was!

The bear had now turned to the admiral and was speaking quietly in Russian. The admiral listened intently, then nodded, and the bear turned back to stare at Bradley.

'Ah yes. We have been aware of your presence for the last four days.' Without the megaphone his voice was still guttural, but perhaps not quite so harsh. His black sloe-like eyes were now fixed intently on Bradley's face. 'Commander Bradley of Her Majesty's Submarine *Spearfish*.' His tone was lazy, indolent almost to the point of disinterest, but Bradley knew that this was an act, a game. The bear now leaned forward to stub out his cigarette in the ashtray. 'Tell me, Commander. To what do we owe the pleasure of your company?'

'We are carrying out independent cold water trials and exercises.' Bradley was now staring over the heads of these three Russians, towards the scuttle. This story was something that he'd rehearsed while waiting to surface *Spearfish*. He had felt then that it sounded completely plausible, but now, as he stood in front of this table in the harsh light of this sparsely furnished cabin, looking down at these three Russians, it sounded completely pathetic. Nevertheless he continued. 'We developed serious mechanical problems last night and my compass is down as well. It seems that we are—'

The Mekon suddenly grunted, jerked upright in his seat and slapped the table in front of him. The voice that came from his small mean mouth was shrill, high pitched, and vicious. 'Enough! Now, tell us what you are *really* doing here, Commander.'

Bradley looked down at the pinched features, making no effort to disguise his scorn. Little bastard, he thought, so you want to be stroppy, eh! Now speaking even more slowly and deliberately, he again addressed the bear. 'I repeat, we are operating independently, and we have developed mechanical problems. As a matter of fact we were rather hoping that you might be able to give us some assistance. Furthermore, as a result of your uncalled-for attack, one of my officers has very serious head injuries and needs urgent medical attention.'

'Pah!' The Mekon's yellow features contorted into a sneer. 'I put it to you, Commander, that your mechanical problems began just this morning, when you were run down by this very vessel.'

Again Bradley ignored the Mekon and looked towards the bear, who was talking in low tones, again in Russian, to the admiral. The admiral nodded and shot a quick, almost furtive glance towards Bradley before turning back to the bear and nodding his head in the affirmative. '*Da.*'

Beside him, Bishop nervously cleared his throat, and Bradley wondered whether he'd been able to make any sense out of the bear's conversation. It was obvious now that this admiral could not speak English. So it *was* this one that ran us down, he thought, and they're still afloat with no obvious signs of damage. That's a pity! Looks like poor old *Spearfish* got the worst of the encounter after all.

Now the Mekon was speaking again. 'We know that you have been in this area for at least four days, Commander. Kapitan Portrova has been tracking you.'

Bradley replied in a controlled tone, 'We have indeed been in the area; I do not deny that. As I have told you, we have been carrying out cold water equipment trials, but we didn't realise that we were this far to the east. Our gyrocompass is out of action and we've been relying on our magnetic.'

Bradley knew that he sounded pathetic now. Grasping for excuses, but knowing that there were none, he felt like the child caught with its fingers in the biscuit barrel. But one thing that he couldn't believe was that *Spearfish* had been tracked for the past four days. That bit was utter bullshit!

'You were spying, Commander!' the Mekon snapped. 'And now you are lying.' His wizened features exuded even more malevolence. He was on to his own ground now – no more polite pussyfooting, just plain nastiness.

Bradley lunged forward, overcome with a sudden and overwhelming desire to grab this little runt by the throat and shake him. The tall officer beside

Bradley stepped forward and reached out to restrain him, and Bradley didn't miss the fact that this officer's other hand was groping at his holster cover, or that the two escorts had quickly moved forward to hover threateningly at his shoulders.

Seemingly oblivious to this sudden flurry of movement, the Mekon leaned across in front of the bear and was now talking in a low whisper to the admiral. Although they spoke in Russian, Bradley could tell that their conversation was becoming heated, with the Mekon flashing vitriolic glances towards Bradley and Bishop while drumming the clawlike fingers of his left hand hard on the table top. Bradley dearly wished that he knew what was being said.

The admiral now seemed unsure as he looked up at Bradley. Finally he nodded in the affirmative towards the Mekon, who, leering with obvious satisfaction, nudged the bear's left arm and nodded towards Bradley.

The bear spoke again. 'I am sorry, Commander, but I have to tell you that you must now place yourselves and your vessel under our care. We will hold you until we receive further directions, but that should not be for too long. Your injured officer will get the help he needs aboard this ship.' He stood up, and then as an obvious afterthought and with an almost comic display of politeness, he continued, 'But you must forgive my manners, gentlemen; I have as yet made no introductions.' He motioned towards the admiral, who was now carefully extinguishing his cigarette. 'May I present Kontre Admiral Anton Malkov of the Northern Fleet. The admiral speaks no English.' The admiral remained pointedly seated, not even bothering to look up.

'And this,' the bear motioned towards the Mekon, who had also remained seated, 'is Comrad Dimitry Borstoy, of the KGB. Both Comrad Borstoy and the admiral joined us a short while ago from the flagship of the Northern Fleet. And I,' he continued, now puffing out his chest even more and dragging his feet together in a half-hearted attempt to come to the position of attention, 'am Kapitan Alexci Portrova, commander of this ship.'

Bradley deliberately resisted the impulse to come to attention and Portrova openly smirked, sensing his discomfort. 'You have caused us many problems on this day, Commander. But now, gentlemen, perhaps you would be kind enough to wait in a spare cabin while we find a solution to our problem.' Portrova motioned towards the tall officer. 'Kapitan Lieutenant Carlov will show you the way.'

★   ★   ★   ★   ★

Carlov pulled open the heavy steel door and ushered Bradley and Bishop into the spare cabin, which was identical to the one they had just left, and equally inhospitable. The steel door slammed shut behind them, and they heard the clips being pulled into place. The two guards would be taking up their positions outside.

Bradley took off his cap and duffel coat and then slumped into a chair, suddenly conscious of a throbbing headache. 'Well, Tim, this'll be a day to remember, and that's for sure.'

'What do you think will happen now, Sir?' Bishop sat down. He, too, looked very tired.

'That, my friend, is the million dollar question and I'm sorry, but right now I haven't got a bloody clue. I suppose everything will depend on the directions that come back from Moscow, but I've got a horrible feeling that we're going to be seeing a lot more of those chaps. Sorry, old son, but we've been bloody well hijacked. It looks very much like we're now prisoners of the Soviet Navy, and so, I am afraid, is *Spearfish*!' He stood up and walked across to the closed scuttle. 'In fact, I strongly suspect that *Spearfish*, and all of us, are intended to be an early Christmas box for Nikita Khrushchev.' Returning to his chair, he picked up his cap. He held it out in front of him, carefully studying the faded gold cap badge. 'Did you manage to pick up any of that private conversation in there?'

Bishop sighed and shook his head. 'Not really, Sir. Afraid my Russian is more than a bit rusty, though I did get the impression that the admiral chappie wants to be rid of us, send us on our way and let us fend for ourselves. But the KGB man wants to take you back to Russia and put you on trial for spying. He wants to throw the book at us. The big fellow, what's he called? Portrova, wasn't it? He seemed to be backing the KGB man all the way, suggesting to the admiral that they should take *Spearfish* and all the rest of us back to Russia and put you on trial. Anyway, it seems the admiral is going to leave the decision up to Moscow.' Then he added, 'I don't want to appear pessimistic, Sir, but I reckon the KGB will have a pretty powerful say in the matter.'

'Yes, I thought as much,' Bradley scowled. 'I didn't like the look of that little bastard either. I think he would be happy to have us shot on the quarterdeck!'

'I rather got that impression as well,' replied Bishop. 'First time I've met a KGB type.' Now they lapsed into silence, each busy with their own thoughts.

Bradley leaned back in his chair and looked at his watch – just after 15.10. He closed his eyes and stretched his legs, trying to ignore his throbbing head. He'd been putting on a brave face, but his stomach was in knots. It was difficult to accept that he was in so much trouble, but accept it he must. An involuntary shudder spread through his slouched frame as here, in the silence of this cheerless cabin, the self-recrimination that had haunted him relentlessly since the sinking returned, and again the waves of undiluted anguish flooded over him. Could he have avoided all this? Yes, of course he bloody well could have! And he would have if only he'd reacted differently to that first destroyer. Why hadn't he? He'd known that he was far too close to it, and he'd been careless. No, not careless, more like bloody incompetence, criminal bloody incompetence. And why? Simply because he'd been so hell-bent on getting in close. Completely ignoring the basic rules, he'd pushed his luck and it hadn't come off – it was simple as that. Now they would all suffer for his stupidity. Yes, it was his fault. The blame was entirely his; no excuses. This whole situation could have been avoided.

He leaned forward, his aching head in his hands. Christ, he hadn't even seen the second destroyer. The first one must have been stopped, with the second one lying directly behind it, and he'd missed it! Again, because he hadn't taken the time to look properly. But why hadn't passive sonar picked up their movement sooner? The bastards must have left it right until the last minute before they rushed in on him. Had they really been up there waiting for him? And what about those charges? What had he really done to take evasive action after that first charge? Nothing! He, like everyone else, had been taken completely by surprise, and done absolutely bloody nothing. And now, to top it all off, he'd literally given *Spearfish* to the Russians. By God, they were going to take a dim view of all this back in Gosport.

Now Bishop's voice aroused him from his misery. '*Seal*, wasn't it, Sir?'

'Wasn't what?' Bradley's tone was terse.

'The last British boat to be actually captured – during the last war, 1940, I believe, in the Kategatt. She hit a mine, then got strafed by the Luftwaffe. She was so badly damaged that they thought she was about to sink, so in order to save life, her captain surrendered. Trouble was, she didn't sink. The Germans took her and all her crew ended up as prisoners of war.'

Bradley quietly groaned to himself. He really didn't want to hear this. 'Yes, yes, I know all about *Seal*, but what's your point, Tim? There's no parallel between the *Seal* incident and our situation. For a start, we were at war then.'

'Of course, Sir,' Bishop muttered hurriedly. 'I wasn't suggesting that there was any similarity; it was just that when you mentioned the word *captured*, the *Seal* incident came to mind.'

Bradley grunted and said nothing. His mind was working overtime. Tim knows what I've been thinking, and he's thinking the same. So will the others back in *Spearfish*.

Then, from outside, they heard the door clips being noisily pulled back. The door swung open to again reveal the tall figure of Carlov, who beckoned to Bradley. 'You will come, the two of you.' The time was 16.00 exactly.

Now they were back in the first cabin. The admiral was no longer there – just Portrova and Borstoy, both again seated at the plastic-topped table.

Portrova slouched carelessly in his chair, still in his fur hat and the same heavy coat, looking rumpled, overclothed, more like a bear than ever. He looked up as Bradley and Bishop entered, still with that indolent half-grin, seemingly looking right through them, his black eyes completely expressionless. He tapped repeatedly on the table top with a pencil he held in his right hand.

Borstoy, on the other hand, was eying them with an even greater malevolence than before. Clearly excited, small bubbles of white saliva forming at each side of his pinched mouth, he still played with the brim of his dirty grey trilby.

Portrova laid the pencil on the table top and focussed his gaze on the two British officers, as if seeing them for the first time.

'Ah, gentlemen, my sincere apologies for keeping you waiting, but you know how it is.' He shrugged his massive shoulders and shook his head in an exaggerated gesture of apology. 'Modern communications, *da*?'

The bastard's playing with us again, thought Bradley. He opened his mouth to speak but was cut short by Portrova.

'Contact has at last been made with Moscow, and the Kremlin has been acquainted with your problem, Commander.' Portrova paused, seemingly awaiting something from Bradley. Bradley started to speak but was again cut short by Portrova who, ignoring Bradley's obvious frustration, continued, 'We now have instructions regarding yourself and your vessel.' Again he paused, studying the two men standing in front of him.

Bradley again tried to speak. 'Yes, well I—' Once again he was interrupted by Portrova.

'Our instructions are, Commander, to escort you and your vessel to our base at Polyarnyy. where your vessel will be repaired, and you, together with your crew, may be accommodated in comfort and safety.'

Bradley felt the knot in his stomach tighten. This was exactly what he had not wanted to hear. This was the next step in his nightmare, his worst nightmare ever. He closed his eyes and swallowed, his mind racing. He knew now that he would have to play the part, go along with this pointless charade, but he would wait for his chance. After all, there was always a chance.

He spoke with difficulty through dry lips, 'Yes, well, thank you, Captain Portrova, but I think that we can manage without that. My engineers will be working on our faulty equipment even as we speak.' He paused, looking at Portrova and knowing that he was wasting his breath. Portrova was listening intently, but Bradley had not missed the mocking glint in those cold black eyes.

'Nonsense, Commander.' Portrova had now hauled himself to his feet, and stood glaring directly at Bradley, with only the table separating them. 'Our prime consideration is the safety of your crew and your vessel. Our instructions are clear. You *will* accompany us to Polyarnyy!'

Bradley's shoulders slumped, but he stood his ground and spoke in controlled, level tones. 'Are you telling me, Captain Portrova, that we are under arrest? Because if so, I would advise you that neither you nor your government has the right to do this.' He paused, drawing a deep breath before continuing, 'I have to tell you, Captain, that as the lawful commanding officer of Her Majesty's Submarine *Spearfish*, I alone take responsibility for the safety of my ship and my crew, and you, Captain, have no right to detain us against our will. In doing so you are in breach of international law. Now, Sir, with your permission, Lieutenant Bishop and I would like to return to our ship.'

Portrova continued to glare into Bradley's face. He said nothing but the mocking glint was still there, plainer than ever.

Now Borstoy was on his feet, and Bradley could see that his head barely reached Portrova's chest. My God, he's a bloody dwarf! Borstoy seemed to be having difficulty in hiding the grin, or was it a sneer, that now split his wizened features. He had been waiting eagerly for the chance to have his say and now he was going to enjoy himself. Puffing out his scrawny chest under the shabby leather coat, he glared up at Bradley.

'Commander Bradley.' Again the voice was high-pitched, squeaky. 'You may place whatever interpretation you will upon our offer, but you *will* do as you are told.' Now he was losing his battle with the sneer and stopped trying to hide it; he was enjoying himself too much. 'You have been caught spying within Soviet territorial waters. You have no rights! You will—'

'Enough, Comrad Borstoy,' Portrova barked, cutting Borstoy off in mid-flow. 'That is enough!' Portrova had lifted an arm and placed his hand directly in front of Borstoy's gloating face. Borstoy scowled and sat down.

Bradley turned slightly as he heard the door behind them open, and from the corner of his eye he saw Carlov beckoning three more people into the room. The newcomers entered, and Carlov indicated that they should move across and stand by the side of the table.

Bradley saw that the first of the three was an officer, with the same rank as Carlov, but with narrow stripes of red around his shoulder straps. This was not a young man. Even though he stood to attention his stoop was pronounced. His immaculately trimmed white beard added to this impression of age, but the piercing deep blue eyes, now fixed steadily upon Bradley and Bishop, radiated an energy and an alertness that contradicted these years. The other two men were dressed as seamen, the chevrons on their sleeves suggesting some form of seniority. Bradley guessed that they would be petty officers of some sort. The officer carried a side arm at his waist, and the other two men shouldered submachine-guns.

Portrova waved a hand casually towards the three newcomers, but his eyes remained on Bradley and Bishop. 'Now, gentlemen, I would like you to meet Kapitan Lieutenant Viktor Ravoski.' Ravoski straightened slightly and nodded, before relaxing once more into his stoop, but Bradley could have sworn that, just for a brief moment, he saw a twinkle in those blue eyes. Portrova continued, 'Viktor is one of my engineers and, like myself, is a submariner. Also like myself, Viktor speaks excellent English and is expert in submarine electrical and mechanical engineering.' Bradley nodded briefly towards Ravoski, and began to wonder what the hell this was all about.

Now Portrova was speaking again. 'Soon, Commander, you will return to your ship. Lieutenant Ravoski and four assistants, who are also engineers, will accompany you. They will give you any help that you may require on passage to Polyarnyy.' Then he added, apparently as an afterthought, 'Oh, by the way, we shall, of course, be taking your vessel in tow.'

Bradley's patience was running out. This was becoming too much. The knowledge that he was completely powerless was fast beginning to tip him over the edge, but he remained calm. He knew that this large, supercilious Russian standing in front of him held all the cards.

'I repeat, Captain Portrova.' Bradley's tone completely masked the frustration boiling inside him. 'What you propose is against international law. You have no right to detain either my ship or my crew, and I submit to your actions only because I have no option. But you should know that I do so only under strong protest.'

'You were spying, Commander…' Borstoy was on his feet again, like some grotesque prehistoric bird. Determined to have his say, his squeaky voice became even shriller. '…And it is *you* who have broken international law. Therefore, *you* have no rights! You should consider yourself fortunate that we permit you to remain with your vessel.' He sat down, breathing heavily, his bony yellow fingers shaking visibly as they clutched for the brim of the dirty grey trilby.

'We have broken no laws,' said Bradley, his voice still level, cool, in marked contrast to Borstoy's hysterical outburst. 'We were engaged in our lawful business when we were attacked, and your intended course of action can only be described as piracy!'

'Yes, yes, Commander, of course.' Portrova's tone was plainly patronising now. 'I note what you say, but come, we have our orders and these orders are fully for the benefit of yourself and your crew, so let us waste no further time. I am anxious to be underway as early as possible tomorrow. There is a forecast of heavy weather from the south and your vessel will no doubt require some preparation. Now, perhaps you would again care to wait in the next cabin for a short time, while I make the necessary arrangements for your return to your vessel. Your injured officer will be brought aboard for medical care as soon as possible.'

Back once more in the sparsely furnished cabin, which was now to all intents and purposes their prison cell, Bradley and Bishop sat in silence, each again lost in his own thoughts. Bradley was fighting the depression that now threatened to overpower him. The time was now 15.25 and the events of the last hours were churning repeatedly over and over in his mind until his mind felt numb. Struggling under this overwhelming weight of self-doubt, he was living a nightmare, a personal hell which was becoming worse by the minute. But he knew that he couldn't give in. He must not give in. He had to stay on top of this for all their sakes. There must be something that he could do. Surely it couldn't all end like this. He looked up, startled at the sound of Bishop's voice.

'Blast! My bloody head's starting to bleed again.' Bishop had straightened up in his chair, and was fishing a handkerchief from his pocket. He gingerly dabbed the blood now seeping from under the plaster on his bruised forehead, then looking towards Bradley. Almost as though he had been reading his captain's thoughts, he asked, 'Well, what do we do now, Sir?'

Again Bradley forced that brave face. 'Well, Tim, my old son: as the actress said to the bishop when confronted with the inevitable, why not lie back and enjoy it?' Then realising what he had said, he added, 'Nothing personal, by the way.'

Bishop didn't even smile, 'Well, those bastards in there seem to be enjoying it, especially that poisonous little KGB shit.'

Seeing Bishop's empty look, Bradley replied quickly, 'No, seriously, Tim, I'm afraid we're going to have to accept the situation as it is for the time being. At the moment it certainly looks as though we *shall* be detained – there's no question about that – but as for how long, well, your guess is as good as mine.' He paused, yawned and rubbed his eyes. 'We'll get back on board and give the others the bad news, and then I suppose we'll have to let these bloody Reds drag us back to their den. With those two destroyers sitting on top of us, it'll be difficult to make a break, and that's assuming *Spearfish* is still in any condition to try such a thing.' He stopped and gave a wry smile. 'It's bad enough that I've lost the bloody boat; I don't want to lose the crew as well.'

'No, Sir, quite.' Bishop was yawning as well now. Then he asked, 'What about those people they're going to put aboard us?'

'I think this Viktor character may well be an engineer, as Portrova has said, but it's my guess that the others will just be armed guards. We'll just have to go along with the situation and see what happens, but I'm fairly sure now that the Reds anticipate a lot of political mileage out of this situation, and they'll milk it to the full. Oh, they'll let us go in the end, but not before the shit has well and truly hit the fan!' He stretched and stood up. 'I'm not so sure what they'll have lined up for me though: probably the bloody salt mines!' He looked at his watch. 'Right, it's nearly twenty past four!' He walked across to the cabin and banged on the steel with both fists, in total frustration and impatience. 'We've been here long enough. Where are these bloody guards? It's time you and I were back on board, Tim.' The door finally opened at 16.40.

CHAPTER SEVEN

It was after 17.10 before Bradley and Bishop finally arrived back aboard *Spearfish*. Now seated in the wardroom, surrounded by his officers and gazing thoughtfully into a steaming cup of coffee, Bradley began to feel slightly better.

Some minutes earlier he had clambered down the conning tower ladder into *Spearfish's* control room, closely followed by Ravoski and the four guards, with Bishop bringing up the rear. Strong had been the first to greet him.

'Welcome back aboard, Sir. Glad to have you back.' Looking at Strong's anxious face, Bradley could see that he meant every word of it.

'How's Toby?' asked Bradley.

'I'm afraid there's no change, Sir,' replied Strong. 'He's still unconscious.'

The Russian motor boat had waited alongside to receive Cannings. Cox'n Greene, with a couple of helpers, had placed the still-unconscious officer into a Neil Robertson stretcher, with Greene personally supervising his conveyance up through the tower and onto the boat, which had then set off back towards *Otvashni*.

'God, I hope he's going to be all right,' muttered Strong.

'Amen to that,' Bradley replied fervently. Then he greeted each of his officers in turn. They had all turned out to welcome him and Bishop after Murray had called down from the bridge that the boat was on its way across, and now they all looked relieved to see him. Bradley had managed a cheerful wave up to Murray, who was leaning over the top of the fin as he had climbed back onto *Spearfish*'s casing. The drone of her diesels, together with the fierce downdraught in the conning tower, had told him that they were still charging the main batteries. Excellent.

On reaching the control room Bradley, with tongue in cheek, introduced Ravoski and the four guards to his officers, who looked quizzically at the light machine guns the guards carried. Then he turned to Crane with a request that he give the Russians a quick guided tour of the boat

Crane had headed aft, with the five Russians following him. Bradley then quickly ushered his officers into the wardroom, which was relatively warm compared to the bitter cold of the control room, in which the main engines were still dragging an arctic wind down through the tower. After divesting himself of his duffel coat and cap, which he threw through his cabin doorway onto his bunk, he followed them into the wardroom, eager to relate the events of the past hours.

By the time he had finished talking, his small audience looked thoroughly despondent. He knew he would have to snap them out of this, get them thinking positively again. He rubbed his hands together vigorously. 'Now, over to you people. Oliver, give me a run-down on the general state of the boat.'

Strong's pallid features brightened just a little. 'Well, Sir, all things considered she's not in bad shape, except for the top of the fin, that is. You've seen that so you'll know there's not a lot that we can do about it. But Bill here...' – he motioned to Morris – '...reckons that he may be able to rig some sort of jury aerial to give us a transmit-and-receive capability, albeit limited. I'm afraid the rest of the stuff up there is a complete write-off. All the masts except the attack periscope are too badly damaged to do anything with, and that includes the snort induction.' Strong paused, watching Bradley's tired face closely. 'On a more positive note the situation in the after ends appears to be under control. We've pumped the water down to two feet, and the black gang have managed to beef up the packing in the port stern gland. Eric estimates that it should hold at least down to 200 feet – even deeper at a push. We've already been using the port screw as required to keep station with those buggers up top and there's no sign of any problems with it or the main motors or engines, though the starboard side is, of course, a write-off as far as propulsion is concerned. We still don't know whether we did any damage to the after planes when we grounded, though the signs are they're still OK. All other compartments are dry, including the main battery sumps. A lot of the minor damage has been taken care of, and we've had a standing charge on both sides for the last three hours, so both main batteries are almost fully charged. Oh – and the gyrocompass is back on line.' Strong paused, looking expectantly at Bradley. He then said, 'The bad news is, Sir, that we carried out your your instructions and fired number five tube. It's all gone! Not long since. The bloody lot. Everything we've worked for.'

'Well, it had to be done; we couldn't afford to let the Reds get their hands on it. It's a great shame, but at least there should be nothing left as reason for them for treating us as spies. Well done, Oliver! In fact, well done all of you! How about the men? How are they taking things?'

'Oh, they're cheerful enough, Sir,' replied Strong, 'though, of course, they don't know the full story yet, do they?'

There was a sharp knock on the panelling outside the door, and the heavy blue curtain scraped back to reveal the head of Steward Johnson. 'More coffee, Sir?' He was looking at Bradley.

'Yes please, Johnson, and as quick as you like.' Bradley was recovering his vitality rapidly. Forgetting his tiredness and other worries, his mind was beginning to buzz again, and *Spearfish* was in far better fettle than he had dared to expect. There may be some sort of chance for them yet. He turned back to his officers. 'Now listen carefully…' He paused, listening for any sign of movement outside the door curtain, then went on in a low voice, 'I'll tell you now what's on my mind, and you people can spread the good word as and when the chance occurs. Now that the Reds have got Toby in their care, if the opportunity presents itself I intend to slip their bloody tow and make a dash for it, but it's got to be at the right time – we mustn't jump the gun because I doubt we'll get more than one chance, even if we get that. I'll try to put some sort of plan together and we'll talk again later, but in the meantime we'll go along with anything they want, and do anything they say, within reason of course. And on no account give them any information!'

The officers nodded. Saying nothing, they got up and departed the wardroom, leaving just Bradley and Strong sitting there. Johnson reappeared with another steaming pot of coffee. Looking at the first lieutenant, he said, 'Where are we goin' to bunk the Russians, Sir?'

'Ah yes.' Strong thought for a moment. 'The officer had better use the bunk that Lieutenant Commander Cannings was in, and the other four can use camp beds, for'd and aft. Fix that with the cox'n, will you, Johnson?'

Bradley poured two more cups of coffee, and together they sat there, sipping in silence. Then Bradley said, 'What's your trim like, Oliver?'

'I've done nothing to it since we surfaced, Sir,' replied Strong.

'Then see to it. I want us to be as heavy as possible. When you've done that, make sure that we maintain the status quo by keeping a running check on any trim alterations from then on. If and when we have to dive suddenly, I don't want any hiccups.'

Strong nodded, and Bradley finishing his coffee with a gulp and stood up. 'Right, I'm off to get an hour's shuteye and I suggest that you do the same. Today could be a very busy day. Oh, by the way, this fellow Ravoski – make sure they're all civil to him. I don't know why, but I have a feeling about that gentleman.'

'Yes, of course, Sir, if that's what you want,' replied Strong.

★　★　★　★　★

'It's just coming up to 20.00, Sir, and your coffee's on your desk. I'll put the lights on.'

Bradley forced open his eyes and immediately closed them again as he was dazzled by the fierce glare as the white fluorescent lights in his cabin flashed on. 'Thank you, Johnson,' he mumbled at the hazy shape of the steward now disappearing through the curtained doorway. Groaning to himself he sat up, swinging his legs off the bunk and reaching for the coffee. He felt groggy and thick-headed; the hour of sleep had done little to refresh him. If anything, he felt worse. Carefully sipping the piping hot coffee, he let his mind ease slowly back into gear. He could hear movement, footsteps in the passageway outside his cabin. People were up and about. Yes, of course, they would be: they were still in sea watches. He sensed a quiet within the boat, and realised that the engines had stopped. They must have finished charging the batteries. Well, at least they would have a fully charged battery, if or when it was needed.

There was another light tap on the panel outside his cabin. The curtain was pulled back, and Crane stepped inside, his large frame sagging with tiredness and his normally ruddy features now drawn and haggard. 'Evening, Sir.'

'Good evening, Eric.' Bradley looked at Crane closely for a few seconds, and then said. 'Christ, you look just how I feel! How goes the battle?'

Crane forced a grin, and answered in a low voice, almost a whisper, 'In answer to your observation, Sir, I am bloody well knackered, and in answer to your question: not too badly, or perhaps let's just say things could be a damn sight worse. They got their towline aboard us about thirty minutes since, and want to be underway in half an hour.'

'What have you done with Ravoski and his strikers?'

'Two of the guards are turned in now: one up for'd and one back aft. The other two are wandering around getting in everyone's way. It looks like they've put themselves into two watches. Viktor's drinking coffee in the wardroom at the moment.' Crane paused for a moment, listening for any movement in the passageway outside the cabin. Satisfied, he continued, 'This Viktor chap, he seems to know what he's talking about. Apparently he's a submarine engineer. Seems a nice bloke as well.' Then he frowned. 'But as for those other sods…' – he shook his head and pulled a face – '…absolute bloody zombies! Nasty pieces of work as far as I can see, and I don't think they'd need much persuading to use those ruddy guns either. Oh, yes, by the way, that's something you should know, Sir. Viktor wanted the keys to the small arms lockers. I cleared it with Oliver and handed 'em over. Bit of a joke, really, because we've got the two spare sets. I'm sure he'll know that, but I don't think he's too worried about it; it seems almost as though he's putting on an act for the benefit of those goons with him. He's had all the main vents cottered and locked and he's carried out a search of the boat as well. That too was a bit of a hit-and-miss exercise. He got the two on-watch

87

guards to help him, but as far as I could see he was simply going through the motions. There's something about that fellow. Can't make my mind up yet exactly what it is, but he's certainly not acting as I would have expected, and that's for sure.'

Bradley scowled. 'But only five of them! Christ, that Portrova character must think he's really got us over a barrel, so bloody confident that we're not going to put up any resistance. But don't try anything with them, Eric. As you've just said, they might be only too happy to use those guns they're carrying, and Viktor could just be playing a game with us. Personally I don't doubt that that Portrova character would be only too pleased to hand us another hammering, given half a chance. Make sure the rest of our people know that as well.' Now he, too, lowered his voice. 'As I said earlier, if we get the chance we'll make a break for it. I don't know when. It's a long way between here and mainland Russia, but the time has to be right. I don't want anyone jumping the gun. I'll try to give you all good warning before we make any attempt at breaking loose. Now, who's up on the bridge?'

'Bill Morris, Sir.' replied Crane.

'Right, I'll wander up and have a word with him, but first, where's that bloody steward? I'm starving.' Bradley suddenly realised that he'd eaten nothing since very early this morning; he'd not even thought about food.

Some twenty minutes later, his appetite satisfied by a plate of scrambled eggs and four rounds of toast followed by more coffee, Bradley made his way up to the bridge, into pitch darkness. *Spearfish* was still fully lit by a searchlight from *Otvashni*, now stationed about one cable to starboard. The other destroyer had turned off her searchlights and was now lying in complete darkness off their port beam. It was very cold.

'Evening, Bill,' called Bradley as he pulled himself up the fin ladder and onto the bridge. 'How goes the battle?'

'Quiet and very cold, Sir!' Morris was wearing a thickly padded parka, with the hood pulled down over his head and a thick scarf covering his mouth. The only visible part of his face was his eyes.

Bradley bent over the voice pipe. 'Helm – Bridge, get three cups of coffee up to the bridge please.'

'Thanks,' mumbled Morris. 'The feet are suffering the most. Can't seem to get 'em warm. Got no feeling in them at all.' Then, to emphasise this fact, he began to stamp hard on the steel deck. 'Should've thought that a southerly wind would make it a little warmer, but it isn't.'

Bradley turned to look back at the lookout, who was also wrapped up like a mummy, and completely unrecognisable. 'Who's that?'

'Able Seaman Clements, Sir,' came the muffled reply.

'Everything OK with you, Clements?'

'Yes, thank you, Sir.' Clements muttered something more under his breath, which Bradley couldn't quite make out. Probably just as well, he thought.

Morris completed an all-round sweep with his binoculars, and turned to look at Bradley. 'There's quite a swell building up from the south, Sir. I'm having to use the port motor quite often in order to keep us roughly positioned between the two destroyers.'

Bradley studied both destroyers in turn through his binoculars. He could see no movement on either of them but he knew that they, too, would be watching. He also saw that all their heavy armament was still aimed directly at *Spearfish*. He leaned closer to Morris. 'As I said to you all in the wardroom this morning, if we get half a chance we'll be making a break for it. I don't know how or when a chance will occur, or even if it will, but if it does then we've got to be ready to take it. In the meantime, just keep things on a low profile. We don't antagonise the bastards, and we don't do anything until I give the word. Oh, and another thing: we need to conserve all the power we can. No unnecessary lights or machinery. You'll see to that, won't you?'

From below came the sound of someone struggling up the fin ladder, and the head of Johnson emerged from the hole in the deck, bearing a large flask and three mugs. 'Coffee for three, Sir.'

'Thanks, Johnson,' said Bradley. 'Bit out of your territory up here, aren't you? What's wrong with the watch messenger?'

'Oh, that's all right, Sir,' mumbled Johnson. 'Got the decent china 'ere, anyway. Can't trust them bastards to come up 'ere with the decent china.' He sniffed loudly and briefly studied each of the two destroyers, then said, 'Christ, it's parky up 'ere. Too bleedin' cold for me. I'm off below.'

Bradley smiled to himself. Bending down, he picked up two of the thick white mugs. 'Best bloody china indeed! Here, hold these, Bill.' He poured the steaming coffee, and Bill Morris passed one mug back to Clements, while Bradley picked up the third and poured his own.

'Something else you should know about, Sir,' said Morris. 'We seem to be losing fuel oil on the starboard side. Look.' He pointed a handheld lamp down to where the dark waters were surging against Spearfish's starboard ballast tanks. Bradley peered with him, at an even darker stain which was lying like a widening blanket, flattening the choppy surface for three or four yards out to the edge of the lamplit patch. Morris took a grateful gulp from his coffee mug and said, 'I don't think it's a bad leak, Sir, but what's it going to look like in daylight?'

Bradley scowled to himself. He sipped his hot coffee and tried to appear unconcerned. Then he said, 'You're right, Bill. It won't be very visible up here in this light, but it could cause us some problems later. Luckily though, we won't see much proper daylight for quite a while.'

Then Bradley was back down in the control room, talking to a tousle-haired and bleary-eyed Strong. He said, 'You look bloody awful, Oliver. How much sleep did you get?'

'Thanks for the compliment, Sir,' replied Strong, now attempting to smooth back his lank black hair with both hands. 'I've managed an hour and that'll do me for now. A quick rinse and I'll be fine, but—'

'Helm – Bridge.' Both Bradley and Strong looked towards the helmsman's voice pipe, where they could clearly hear Morris's voice calling from the bridge. 'Tell the captain: a boat from one of the destroyers is approaching on our starboard side.'

Bradley called across to the helmsman, 'OK, I've got that! Tell the officer of the watch I will meet the boat on the casing.' Then, turning back to Strong, he said, 'Stand fast that rinse, Oliver. You'd better get your coat and come up with me.'

It was exactly 20.50 as Bradley, closely followed by Strong, stepped out of the fin door and down onto the casing. The motor boat from Otvashni was already bumping alongside Spearfish's starboard ballast tanks, with Carlov standing upright in its stern sheets, seemingly oblivious to the violent motion of the small boat.

Even as the line was thrown across and caught by one of *Spearfish's* waiting casing party, Carlov leapt nimbly onto the ballast tank and quickly pulled himself up onto the casing, to stand before Bradley. Tall, lean and very erect, his height and slim build were again accentuated by the long black leather overcoat pulled in at the waist by a shining black belt which carried a holstered pistol. His face, under the black ushanka was, as usual, completely impassive. Again he made no attempt to observe the courtesies of rank, merely bringing the heels of his gleaming black boots sharply together and giving Bradley the briefest of nods.

Returning the nod, Bradley felt a surge of annoyance. 'Good evening, Commander. I trust your visit will be a short one.'

The Russian either didn't catch, or deliberately chose to ignore this jibe. 'We will commence your tow in fifteen minutes from this time. You will be ready in all respects. Now I will speak with Kapitan Lieutenant Ravoski.'

Bradley shouted up to Morris, who was now leaning over the top of the fin. 'Get the Russian officer up here, will you, Bill.' Ignoring Carlov, Bradley now turned away and, followed by Strong, walked back to the fin door to speak to the second cox'n.

'I expect you heard that, didn't you, "Scratcher?" We'll be under a tow in fifteen minutes from now. Make sure that everything's ready up here'

'Yes, Sir.' The second cox'n moved forward to talk to one of the leading hands of the casing party. Everyone ignored Carlov. Bradley looked up to where Bishop's head was now peering down on him from the bridge. 'Is everything OK up there, Tim?'

'Yes, Sir, though a bit of sunshine wouldn't come amiss! I've just relieved Bill.'

Ravoski finally emerged from the fin door. Carlov watched him climb down onto the casing, then he turned sharply and walked for'd. Stopping by the fore planes, he waited for Ravoski.

Bradley watched from a distance as Carlov and Ravoski conferred, with Carlov doing most of the talking and shooting occasional rapid glances towards

Bradley and frequently gesticulating with his hands as though reinforcing his point. Ravoski responded with periodic shakes of his head. After ten minutes they were finished, and Ravoski made his way aft towards the fin door while Carlov, without a further glance at Bradley, jumped down onto the ballast tank and back into the motor boat, which had kept its engine running. Its bow line retrieved, the small boat spluttered away in a cloud of smoke and spray, making its way back towards *Otvashni*. Carlov, again standing erect in the stern sheets, did not look back.

★　★　★　★　★

The local time clock over the chart table read 21.00 exactly. *Otvashni* had now moved forward to a position directly ahead of *Spearfish* at about 100 yards distant, and *Spearfish*'s crew had closed up at their stations for "special sea dutymen". On the bridge Bradley was directing his binoculars at *Otvashni*. Because of the way she was lying he couldn't see her bridge. Instead he focussed his glasses directly on her stern. Again he was waiting, but he didn't have to wait long. At exactly 18.04 he saw the telltale white froth building up under the Russian's stern as one of her twin screws began to bite into the black water and she started to move slowly forward.

'Wait for it,' he muttered, 'wait for it... and there it is now!' With a deep hiss, the 300 feet of two-inch diameter wire rose up from the surface of the sea like a huge grey snake, vibrating, humming, bar taut and dripping water. *Spearfish* jerked forward, and then slowed, almost stopping as the wire slackened and dropped back into the sea only to reappear seconds later, again jerking bar taut. Now, albeit reluctantly, *Spearfish* was moving steadily, but she *was* moving. *Otvashni*'s other screw started to turn and she gradually increased speed to four knots. They were on their way. Bradley lowered his binoculars, again feeling an overpowering wretchedness welling up inside him. Suddenly he wanted to be sick. He turned to Strong, who was standing at his side. 'Who's got the watch, Oliver?'

'Tim, Sir,' replied Strong.

'OK, I'm going below. Make sure that a good eye is kept on that bloody tow, and call me if there are any doubts. At least this southerly wind won't be helping the Russians.'

Now back in the solitude of his cabin, Bradley lay on his bunk, listening to the voices and the footsteps of his people moving to and fro in the narrow passageway outside. Hearing this made things seem almost normal. He could also hear the sound of the sea outside the pressure hull. Just inches from his head the waves were slapping along the tanks and the wind was starting to increase. *Spearfish* was moving, but apart from a slight roll there was no sense of movement within her, no throaty hum from her diesels, no vibration, no urgency, no purpose.

Even here in the comparative quiet of his cabin he still felt no peace. His mind was in turmoil. Plagued by the events of the day, he lay with his eyes clamped tightly shut, fighting back tears of frustration and anger. As tired as he was he knew that sleep was not an option, not now, not when there were so many questions to be answered, so many plans to be made. He opened his eyes and looked at his watch: 22.10. He'd been lying here for over an hour. It wasn't warm in the cabin, but his back was wet with sweat. He groaned quietly to himself and sat up, swinging his legs down to the deck. He must start thinking positively. 'Come on, Bradley,' he mumbled to himself, 'enough of this bloody moping. What the hell's the matter with you? Pull yourself together, man, and bloody well take charge. You got us into this bloody mess, and it's up to you to get us out.'

Now standing, he moved three short paces to the cabinet, which served as a desk. Opening the drawer, he pulled out his framed photograph of Sue and Jamie, and wondered when he would see them again, or even if he *would* see them again. He examined the photograph, his thoughts at this moment in a completely different world, miles away from *Spearfish*. Again he felt the hot tears welling up behind his eyes. 'God, how I miss you both,' he murmured.

There was a sharp rap on the panel outside his door, and the curtain slid back. It was Johnson. 'Ah, you're awake, Sir! There's a brew goin'; would you like a cup?'

Bradley blinked, startled at this interruption. 'Yes, yes, thank you, Johnson, I would.' Placing the photograph carefully back in the drawer, he rubbed his eyes and cheeks with the back of his hand. He was back in *Spearfish* again, but it wasn't his *Spearfish*. He was no longer in charge of her. She had been stolen from him, and someone else was calling the tune now. He knew that *Spearfish's* surfacing signal was due to be sent by 12.00 on the 22nd, and he wondered how long it would be before his masters back there in the UK would set up a search for her. He also knew that because of the type of work she was on, they wouldn't be in any rush to send out a "sub-miss" alarm.

Again the desperation welled up inside him. Now this was mixed with a hot anger, but this time his anger wasn't directed at himself. 'Those Russian bastards have got us well and truly by the short and curlies!' he muttered, closing his eyes and gripping the edge of the cabinet with both hands until his knuckles went white. Completely oblivious of Steward Johnson now standing at the doorway with a tray of tea and biscuits, he hissed aloud through clenched teeth. 'But not for much longer, old girl, not if I have anything to do with it.' Suddenly he realised that at this moment in time he had never felt closer to *Spearfish*, or to his crew. He knew now that he would get her back, get her home, or he would die in the attempt.

CHAPTER EIGHT

At 09.45 on the forenoon of 22nd November, Osborne Wilfred Jackson, better known as "Big Ozzie", or "Skip" to the more respectful of his fourteen-member crew, sat in his high chair on the bridge of the trawler *Imogen*, gazing for'd through the rain-smeared glass of her bridge screen, watching her high fo'c'sle lifting, falling, and gently seesawing on the heavy restless swell.

Now that the heavy southerly gales over the past three days had finally abated, this was peace indeed, but it was an uncomfortable peace and Jackson knew that this peace wouldn't last for much longer. This was just a lull. There was more to come. Even now, the glass was again falling. Overhead the sky was an unbroken canopy of watery parchment, without strength or depth, drained almost to transparency, contrasting starkly against the brooding dark of the heaving black sea, and in this less than half-light, almost eerie. It would be fully dark again by three o'clock this afternoon. They had completed their three weeks of concentrated fishing, and would soon be heading homeward. Now Jackson was impatient to start this journey back down south, where he would see proper daylight again, perhaps even the sun.

Except for the helmsman, Jackson was alone in the wheelhouse. *Imogen* was idling now, with just enough assistance from her single screw to hold a heading in a sea that still came from the south. This in itself was unusual, since at this time of the year the wind and sea came mainly from the north-east, and though it was already plenty cold enough, it would get much colder if the wind did swing around to come from the north-east.

Those of the fourteen crew who were not still turned in would be at late breakfast. Last night had been busy – an exhausting finale to three busy weeks. But in spite of the weather they had managed to keep the trawls out, and at nine o'clock this morning had hauled in for the last time this trip. Their work now done, a leisurely breakfast was the order of the day, after which they would secure *Imogen* for the long journey home. Jackson reckoned that barring mishaps they should be alongside at Hull inside of ten days from now. Despite the bad weather of the last week, it had been a good trip – so much so that they were able to be leaving the grounds almost a week earlier than planned. *Imogen's* refrigerated holds were full to the brim, mainly cod – a catch that should fetch a very fair price on the dockside markets back at Hull.

Jackson was a contented man this morning. Things had been going well lately. He had needed some luck and it now seemed that he was getting it, and in good measure. A few more trips like this would take a sizeable chunk off the loan he still owed on *Imogen* and he might even be able to settle the loan early. Who knows? At times it had seemed to him that he'd been paying forever. But this didn't worry him. Sooner or later the day would come when *Imogen* would be fully his. He had skippered her for just over five years now, and she was as much a part of him as his own two hands. Completed in 1951 and rigged as a stern trawler, *Imogen* displaced just over 700 tons, with a length overall of some 200 feet. Small, perhaps, when compared to many of the fishing vessels that worked this far north, but she was a good sea boat – the best. *Imogen* was all that Jackson had ever wanted; she was his world. The living she gave him and his crew was in many ways to him no more than incidental – a bonus.

He had been sitting here for less than half an hour, since he'd come up to relieve his first mate for breakfast. Now he felt distinctly drowsy. Like the rest of them on board, he hadn't got much sleep last night. Already he was uncomfortably warm. Even though the temperature outside was well below freezing, the atmosphere inside *Imogen's* enclosed bridge was stuffy, and the heat from three radiant electric heaters fitted to the bulkheads of the bridge was now sufficient to cause small beads of perspiration to break across his weathered forehead. Raising his large frame from the sticky warmth of the vinyl covered seat, he took his weight on each arm of his chair in turn, lifting his ponderous buttocks, first one cheek and then the other, before finally settling back down in the seat with a grunt of satisfaction, wiping the sweat from his forehead with the back of his hand.

Now he groped into the side pocket of the heavy leather jacket, which he hardly ever took off, and produced a large briar pipe, inspecting the pipe before tapping the blackened bowl hard against the rim of a purpose-built copper tray that he'd had fastened to the right arm of his chair.

The sudden noise of this tapping pipe caused the seaman leaning over the wheel over on the starboard side of the bridge to jump violently. Jackson grinned wickedly to himself before again delving into his right-hand pocket, this time producing a worn brown leather pouch and a box of Swan matches. Carefully filling the bowl with black tobacco from the pouch, he tamped it down with the knarled and blackened forefinger of his left hand – a finger that had so obviously been used for this purpose many times before. Picking up the box of matches that had been balanced on his knee, he then carefully lit the pipe. It took three matches to complete this operation, throughout which, seemingly oblivious to any pain, his left forefinger constantly prodded and poked the burning tobacco. At last, with the pipe properly lit, and now surrounded in a heavy cloud of rank-smelling blue smoke, he gave a loud sigh of contentment and settled back in his chair to again resume watch on Imogen's pitching fo'c'sle, eyes half closed, as though in private meditation. A sudden blast of cold air and the slamming of the bridge door on his right-hand side snapped him out of this meditation. He looked around to see his first mate, Joe Barnes, wrestling with the handle of the wooden door.

'Bloody door still sticks. Thought they'd fixed it,' Barnes muttered.

'Aye, well, lad, several 'ave 'ad a go at it, but 'appen it'll stay that way till we get back to warmer, dryer climes.'

Jackson's voice suited his appearance perfectly – big, loud, and booming. He eased himself off his chair and stood up. Removing his pipe, he opened his mouth in a cavernous yawn. He was a big man – a full six foot four inches tall. The mass of iron-grey curls now brushing against the deck-head hadn't seen a comb since leaving Hull, easily belittling several weeks' growth of the straggly grey beard now adorning his weatherworn face. He had a rugged face, coarse featured but not ugly, because Jackson smiled a lot. And he was fat, very fat. Even his height couldn't disguise that. This portly stature, together with his cheerful countenance, gave him the appearance of an oversize Mr Pickwick. Now in his mid-fifties, Jackson had been at sea for many years. The sea was his life. He was "a man of the sea".

'I were just wonderin' where the 'ell you'd got to, Joe. Bloody long breakfast, weren't it?'

Joe Barnes ignored his skipper's remark, and walked over to the small radar set on the port side of the bridge to study the darkened screen with its bright green cursor that traced a continuously rotating line across its radius. Barnes was a small man. His head barely reached Jackson's shoulders. A good ten years younger than Jackson, he was soft spoken and mild mannered. Although he too was a Yorkshireman, he was the opposite of his skipper in almost every way. But they had known each other for many years, and they understood one another perfectly. They had become a team, almost brotherly.

Barnes shot a quick glance towards Jackson. 'They're still there, Skip.' He moved his head closer to the screen, at the same time adjusting one of the knobs on the control panel and studying the two blips that came up on the screen with each 360-degree cycle. 'Range is about five miles now – almost dead on our starboard quarter. They're moving very slowly, though. On their present course they'll pass well astern of us.'

'Good.' Jackson moved across to join Barnes in front of the screen, sucking his pipe thoughtfully. These contacts had appeared just before 06.00 this morning. 'Nothing's changed,' Jackson grunted. 'There's a big bugger in front, and the littler one seems to be trailin' astern of 'er by about 150 feet, as far as I can see. If the weather were a bit clearer an' lighter we'd see 'em by now.' He walked back to his chair and tapped his pipe on the copper tray, then looked back at Barnes. 'Maybe the big one's got the little one in tow, eh? That's what it looks like to me.'

Barnes asked, 'Do you think we should go and have a look, Skip, in case they need any help?'

'Nay, we'll let 'em get on wi' it. They'll be all right. Looks like they're heading down towards the Kola. They should be all right now the weather's eased. Probably been a damn sight worse where they've come from though. It'll be bloody Ruskies anyway.' Jackson walked back towards the radar screen and again studied the contacts. 'We'll not interfere. We're up here for fish, not to look after them buggers. Not like some others that come up to these parts lately, pretendin' to fish, an' all they're really doin' is upsettin' the bloody Russians an' getting people like us a bad name. I've heard all about their bloody antics. Intelligence gathering, that's what they call it. What they're really doin' is shittin' all over blokes like us who come up here to try an' make an 'onest living.'

Barnes nodded but said nothing. This was one of Jackson's pet subjects. What he was saying was perfectly true, but Barnes had heard it all so many times before. Now he moved over to stand behind the helmsman. 'You want me to take over the watch now, Skip?'

'Yeh, sure. Thought you'd never ask,' grinned Jackson. 'How are things going below? Are we all secured yet?'

'About another hour, I reckon, and then we'll be on our way. I got a feeling we're in for more rough weather though.'

'Fair enough. Shouldn't be a problem if we're properly secured.' Jackson was yawning again. 'I'm going below to see if there's any bacon left. Let me know when we're cleared away and ready to go.'

Long before the hour was up, Barnes was on the bridge telephone down to the mess room. 'If you want to come up, Skip, the weather's still lifting and I can just about make out their lights. I reckon they've just altered course, towards us.'

Three minutes later Jackson was again standing beside Barnes. Reaching for his binoculars, he focused in the direction that Barnes was looking, fine off *Imogen*'s starboard bow.

'Looks like some sort of warship in front.' Jackson lowered his glasses and rubbed his eyes with the back of his hand, then raised the glasses again. 'Definitely coming this way though, an' she's definitely a warship – a Ruskie, I suppose. Can't really see what's behind her: too far off yet.'

The time was now almost 11.30. The skies had lightened, albeit very slightly, and the wind was still dropping. 'Weather's getting' better by the minute,' grunted Jackson.

'So it is,' replied Barnes, 'but the glass is still dropping as well, and it's still bloody freezing out there. I reckon it won't get any warmer until we get a good deal further south.'

'Well, ain't we the lucky ones then, because that's just where we're heading.' Now Jackson was smiling, thinking aloud as he concentrated on the distant ships. Then he asked, 'How much longer before we're ready to get cracking, Joe?'

'Should be about another twenty minutes, half hour at the most,' replied Barnes. 'Pity really. I'd have liked to have had a closer look at those two out there.'

Jackson raised his binoculars again. 'Yeh, well, they're less than three miles away now. The first one's a warship, I'm sure of it. Still, can't see what's behind her though. Must be something pretty small. You'd better keep an eye on 'em, Joe, but remember, they ain't anything to do with us!' He lowered his glasses and laid them on the seat of his chair. 'I'm goin' below again fer a few minutes. Aven't 'ad me "mornin' George" yet! Keep 'er 'ead where she is now. I'll be back up soon enough.'

Barnes nodded and continued to stare through his glasses. This was the first shipping they'd sighted for more than three weeks. He shivered at the icy blast of air as Jackson opened the bridge door, pulling it shut with a loud slam as he left, but still it didn't shut properly.

It was a good twenty minutes before Jackson returned to his bridge.

'It's a Russian all right, Skip. Not much more than a mile off now.' Barnes sounded more than a little excited. 'And that small thing she's towing looks very much like a submarine to me.'

'You said twenty minutes, Joe, an' we're still 'ere!' Jackson picked up his glasses and focused them again. The ships were less than a mile away now. 'Aye, she's a Russian all right, and I reckon you're right about the submarine as well. I suppose that's one of theirs. They're always breaking down, from what I 'ear.'

Jackson and Barnes continued to watch the slowly approaching vessels. It was clear to Jackson that if they stayed on their present course, the Russian would still pass well astern of *Imogen*. Now they could see figures on the upper deck of the warship.

Then Jackson said, 'There's something about that sub, Joe. It's not a bloody Ruskie and that's for sure. I've seen enough Russian subs in my time. They're more squat, if you know what I mean, an' they're more sort of rounded. Not like this one. She's low in the water but she's got a tall conning tower, you know? An' 'er bows are different.' He lowered his glasses and rubbed his eyes before raising them again. 'There's no markings on 'er. Look! You can just see people on her bridge. I can see four.'

'Yeh, I see them. She's under tow all right. Wonder what's wrong with her.'

'That's it!' muttered Jackson, lowering his glasses again. 'I've seen that type of sub before. I knew it! She's one of ours, Joe, I'm bloody certain of it. She's one of them new ones. I was down in Barrow when they sent the first one out on trials from Vickers. She's ours, Joe. She's one of ours!'

'So what the hell is she doing taking a tow from a bleedin' Ruskie?' Barnes lowered his glasses. 'D'you think we ought to speak to them, Skip? You know, see if there's anything we can do, like?'

'Yeh, I suppose maybe we ought to. No skin off our nose, an' another hour or so ain't goin' to make a lot of difference to us anyway. OK, let's go an' 'ave a look then.' Jackson put his hand on the helmsman's shoulder. 'Put some starboard wheel on, Barry, an' come around to zero-four-five, then give us 'alf ahead.'

★　★　★　★　★

Portrova leaned against the side of *Otvashni*'s open bridge and studied the approaching trawler through his binoculars. Since taking *Spearfish* in tow, his journey south had not been easy. *Otvashni* had covered less than 250 miles since commencing her tow. The weather had been brutal. The wind from the south-west had increased to storm force just hours after they had started out, and they had been driving straight into it. He had feared for the towline on more than one occasion, and with the sea that had been running it was indeed a miracle that it hadn't parted before now. He hoped that the British aboard *Spearfish* were suffering as a result of this weather; knowing from experience that a surfaced submarine can be a wretched place during a gale. This wind hadn't dropped below storm force until late last evening, and only then had he been able to increase *Otvashni's* speed to five knots.

This morning even he was feeling the cold, and he was tired, very tired. The lack of sleep brought about by the bad weather over the past days had taken a heavy toll on him. His eyes felt heavy and watered continuously, tiny icicles constantly forming around the lids, stinging, blurring his vision. Yes, he'd experienced all this before, it was not new to him, but this time it was different: this time he was doing something that he had been waiting to do for a very long time. He would see that this arrogant Bradley and his crew *really* suffered when they finally reached the Russian mainland, and that would be just a part of the debt he owed to Gregori Lenkov. He lowered his binoculars and drew the thick black fur of his cuff across his eyes in an effort to clear them, but the relief gained was very temporary; within half a minute they were icing up again.

Once his passage south had commenced, and in accordance with his orders, he had signalled *Osornoi* to break off and rejoin the fleet. He reckoned that if the weather didn't again deteriorate, another seven days or so should see him back inside national waters, and then he would make for Polyarnyy, where someone else could look after these damn Britishers. He raised his glasses again and turned aft to focus on the submarine wallowing under his tow. Now, although the forecast still wasn't good, he hoped that they had come through the worst of the weather, but he would never now make his target time to the Russian mainland. This thought brought him a measure of discomfort but also an increase in his determination. The Britisher was now really his; he would not lose her.

He turned his attention back to the trawler butting her way through the swell towards him and now less than half a kilometre off his starboard bow.

Now he turned to nudge Carlov, who was standing at his side. 'So, Sergei, we have another visitor. She too is British, is she not?'

'She is, Comrad Kapitan. As you know, she has been on our radar since yesterday. There are three similar contacts to the north-west, about twenty-five kilometres, but they are moving north.'

Portrova continued to train his glasses on *Imogen*. 'So this one is the loner, *da*? This one is British and she is here to fish, *da*? But is that all she does, Comrad?' Portrova was smiling but there was no humour in his smile. 'See, still she comes. She is very inquisitive, this Britisher!'

'The trawler is not here to fish, Comrad Kapitan. You know that as I do,' hissed the voice from behind them.

Portrova and Carlov turned to look down at the skeletal features of Borstoy. Borstoy was not a good sailor and the storms of the past days had not treated him kindly. Neither eating nor drinking, he had lain like a pile of discarded rags in his bunk, alternately vomiting and cursing. He had roundly cursed Admiral Anton Malkov for leaving him here on this godforsaken ship to endure this passage to Polyarnyy. He had cursed Portrova and his crew for making the passage possible, and he had cursed the sea, the wind, the ship, and all the gods in heaven, before finally even cursing himself for being so insistent that they take this Britisher in tow. But most of all, Borstoy had cursed Bradley and the crew of *Spearfish*, now trailing out there off *Otvashni*'s stern. Then, when at last there was nothing left to curse about and nothing left within him to vomit, the pitiful collection of bones that he called a body had finally fallen into a fretful but merciful sleep.

But now the weather had moderated and Borstoy was on his feet once more. He now stood scowling in front of Portrova and Carlov, who both looked down at him, hardly bothering to conceal the disdain and the disgust they felt for him.

'We should board them, search them.' Borstoy's voice was a hoarse whisper. He had still not eaten, and although he had poured several pints of water into his dehydrated frame he was still parched, and now he felt sick again. 'You hear me, Comrad Portrova? They must be stopped and searched.'

Portrova had no liking for the KGB and certainly none for Borstoy. But

Borstoy was a dangerous man, a man not to be ignored. He had the ear of people in high places, all of them Portrova's superiors. But it was Borstoy who had backed him in taking this British submarine back to the Russian mainland, and Portrova knew that the two of them had just one thing in common – a fanatical hatred of the British, even though Borstoy's reasons for this hatred were not for the same reasons as himself. Borstoy had long been indoctrinated with a political hatred of all things British. This had been with him since the days of Stalin. But though their aim was the same, Portrova's reason for dragging *Spearfish* back to Russia was not in the least politically motivated: he just wanted to see this arrogant British submarine commander and his crew suffer, and suffer for a very long time. He had waited many years for this chance and was determined not to let it go now. He would get them all back to Moscow to face whatever action the Kremlin deemed appropriate, and the harsher the better. He knew that things would certainly go hard for Bradley. A long internment in a Russian prison would surely knock the arrogance out of him, or a long spell in the salt mines would do the same; both probably worse for Bradley than being shot as a spy. No, he had decided that whatever happened, Bradley must suffer.

He nodded in reply to Borstoy's outburst, then turned back to study the trawler, which was now less than 200 metres distant and slowing. He could see shadowy figures through the glass of her covered bridge, and the men moving on her decks fore and aft. Still looking through his glasses, he shouted across to the watch officer, 'Stop engines.' Then, lowering his glasses and turning to Carlov, he said, 'Stand by to lower a boat, Comrad Carlov, and prepare Bassisty to take twelve men to board this Britisher. Perhaps she may have some fish to sell us, eh?'

*　*　*　*　*

Bradley lay flat on his bunk in his cabin. He had spent much of his time in this cabin during the past days, for the most part alone and seemingly oblivious to the mountainous seas coming up from the south-west, which had caused *Spearfish* to pitch and yaw unrelentingly under her tow, as well as subjecting all on board to abject misery and discomfort. But now this weather had eased. He had had very little sleep. Instead, he had spent long hours deep in thought. Much of this thinking had been dedicated to the usual self-recrimination. But then he had gradually managed to put this thinking to the back of his mind and concentrate more on *Spearfish's* present situation. He had by now examined every possible escape scenario. Over and over again he examined in his mind the role that each of his team would play in the event of an opportunity to escape arising, and how they would deal with these uninvited Russians they now carried aboard. But he knew that even if a chance did occur, then it would almost certainly be the only chance they would get, and if any attempt to break away failed, they would then end up having to take anything the Russians cared to throw at them.

But would such a chance ever come, or was he just clinging to slim strands of hope? On several occasions during the past hours, particularly when the storm was at its worst, he had been sorely tempted to make a break. Certainly the diabolical weather must be in his favour and would have given him the best possible chance, but how could he slip that tow in a sea like this? It would be virtually suicidal to send men for'd on the casing in this weather. Then the guards would have to be overpowered, preferably bloodlessly. No, it was too bloody risky, too dangerous. He couldn't forget the sight of those guns aimed directly at the defenceless *Spearfish*. Botching the job was one thing, but throwing away the lives of his men was another. Of course he could always force his way around to the destroyer's quarter and put a torpedo into her flank, but that even at this stage that was unthinkable. No, he would wait. The right time would come; he had to believe that.

He had used every opportunity to discuss these thoughts with his officers. These discussions were usually carried out on a one-to-one basis here in his cabin, but never with more than two at a time, and always when Ravoski was either turned in or known to be somewhere else in the boat. His own officers would be ready; he was confident of that. But what about Ravoski? Whatever or whoever he was, he was certainly no fool. Bradley had got to know him quite well during the past two days, though even now the

Russian still remained something of an enigma both to him and to all his officers. Ravoski had never ceased to surprise Bradley with his extraordinary un-Russian humour and friendliness but, perhaps more strikingly, with his seemingly infinite knowledge of the sea and of submarines, particularly of this submarine. Furthermore, he was to all intents and purposes now the captain of *Spearfish*, though he used little, if any, of the authority this situation gave him, except to converse occasionally with his four henchmen, none of whom could speak English and were by now treated with contempt by *Spearfish*'s crew.

But Ravoski had certainly demonstrated no animosity towards Bradley or to any of his crew – quite the reverse, in fact. With his ready smile and friendly manner he seemed pleased to be here in *Spearfish*, even to the point of enjoying the occasional game of bridge in the wardroom during the rare easing of the storms. He possessed an unflagging energy, being here, there and everywhere around the boat, friendly, asking questions, joking with the crew. It would be difficult for anyone to regard him as an enemy at this time. But Bradley reasoned that at the end of the day Ravoski was still a Russian officer, placed aboard *Spearfish* as a guard, and was still a very major question mark. Maybe he would not oppose any escape bid; at present various indications seemed to point that way. Maybe he even wanted them to escape. Maybe he himself wanted to escape – to defect, perhaps. All of this had gone through Bradley's mind time and time again. He badly wanted to believe the good parts, even though they seemed too good to contemplate. It was patently obvious that Ravoski was an experienced submariner and missed little, if anything, in the daily running of the boat. But Bradley was now beginning to wonder whether he was simply waiting for him to make a move, or just playing a game, a charade perhaps, designed to gain the acceptance and confidence of himself and his crew, just to make this transit back to Russia a little easier for all concerned. Naturally he would want to complete this transit as trouble free as possible. Or could there be other reasons for his friendly attitude?

He looked up as knuckles rapped sharply on the panelling outside the curtained doorway and Strong's head appeared. 'Captain, Sir, the trawler reported from the bridge earlier. It's clearly visible now. Definitely British, and it looks like she's coming over to investigate.'

'Thanks, Oliver.' Bradley was immediately on his feet and bounded past Strong, his haste taking Strong completely by surprise. It was an unnecessary haste but Bradley had to relieve the pent-up tension within him, and rapid movement was as good a way as any, whether necessary or otherwise. Grabbing his oilskin jacket and with Strong on his heels, he leapt for the conning tower ladder. Strong called out to the helmsman, 'Tell the bridge: Captain and first lieutenant coming up', before following Bradley up through the lower hatch.

Bradley cursed as the cold air in the tower penetrated his body. Apart from the oilskin jacket, he had not taken the time to put any protective top clothing on, and wore only a submarine jersey and his old pair of corduroy trousers. Pulling himself onto the bridge, he made room for Strong, who came up behind him, also unsuitably clad.

Murray was officer of the watch. *Spearfish*'s crew had been kept in full sea watches during the past transit, even though they had no control over her speed or direction. 'Looks like *Otvashni*'s stopping, Sir. So is the trawler. She's British!' Murray passed his binoculars to Bradley.

Otvashni had stopped. Bradley watched the foam at her stern subside and the long towline starting to slacken into the swell. He turned to look at the trawler, which had now also stopped. 'Looks like they're preparing for some sort of dialogue,' he muttered. 'Better go astern a touch, Ross; we don't want to run over that bloody towline. No. Belay that. Put some port wheel on and let our momentum take us around to her port side. Watch that bloody towline though!' *Otvashni* was drifting around to starboard. He could now see some activity on her upper deck.

Murray squinted into the half-light and called down the voice pipe, 'Steer Port five.' Turning to Bradley, he said, 'Looks like they may be getting ready to lower a boat, Sir.'

'Yes, I think you're right,' Bradley nodded.

'Bridge – Helm.'

'Bridge.' Murray was bending over the voice pipe.

'Permission for the Russian officer to come to the bridge, please?'

Murray looked enquiringly at Bradley, who frowned but nodded in the affirmative.

Murray bent to the voice pipe once more. 'Yes, please.'

Bradley continued to study the destroyer, which now lay about 300 yards off *Otvashni's* starboard beam and some 400 yards off *Spearfish's* starboard bow. With no way on her, *Spearfish* was pitching and wallowing in the swell, but she was slowly drifting towards *Otvashni's* port quarter.

The black-hooded figure of Ravoski pushed up onto the bridge to join them. As usual, he was smiling, his blue eyes twinkling. 'So, my friends, we have at last some excitement, *da?*'

The lookout had squeezed himself into the rear corner of the bridge to make way for the newcomer. Aft of where he stood was still a complete shambles, though the engineers *had* managed to tidy things up a bit. Over the past two days, in spite of the weather, they had cut away much of the masses of jagged metal that clung to the top and sides of the fin, including the top of the search periscope, but they couldn't do much to the other damaged masts.

'Looks like your guys and our guys are getting ready to have a powwow, Viktor.' Bradley was shivering with the cold now, again regretting that he had not taken the time to get suitably dressed. But already his mind had slipped into overdrive. Might this be the start of that chance he had been waiting for? *Otvashni's* motor boat was in the water now. He watched the small puff of smoke from her exhaust as she pulled away from the destroyer and headed for the trawler.

'Do you think they know we're British, Sir?' Strong asked. 'The trawler, I mean.'

'I don't know,' replied Bradley. 'They probably think that we're a broken-down Russian, but I suppose the bloody Reds will send them on their way with some cock and bull yarn...' Then he stopped talking. Lowering his glasses, he straightened up. This was it! This *was* the time! He knew now that this was his chance: probably the only one he would get. Again he felt his stomach knotting as he fixed his gaze on *Otvashni*. He turned to Strong. 'Come below now, Oliver. We need to talk. You too, Viktor. I'm not too happy about this bloody towline.'

Ravoski smiled and nodded, and Strong, sensing something in his captain's tone, was already on his way down the ladder, closely followed by Ravoski. As Bradley tuned to leave the bridge he nudged Murray. 'I want us around the Russian's port quarter. Get the signalman up here with an ensign – the biggest one we've got – and drape it over the starboard side of the fin. If we dive we'll dive stern first, but I want that trawler to see who we are.' He turned and quickly made his way below.

Once below, Bradley found Strong and Ravoski waiting at the door of his cabin. He motioned Viktor inside. 'I'll be with you in a moment, Viktor. Please go inside and wait for me. I need a quick word with the first lieutenant. That tow wire is worrying me.'

He knew that he sounded completely false. Surely Ravoski would be suspecting something by now, but he did just as Bradley had asked. Then, almost pushing Strong up the forward passageway, Bradley hissed. 'This is it, Oliver! Now is the time to make a break for it. That trawler is the distraction we've been waiting for! The Russians will all be watching that trawler. She'll be a complete distraction; at least that's what I'm banking on. Organise a couple of seamen with safety lines and some engineers up top at the rush with tools to get rid of the tow wire.' He paused, drawing a deep breath, realising that he was shaking almost uncontrollably. 'Organise it with Eric to get the main vents uncottered. He's got some keys. Don't on any account use the main broadcast system, but get that bloody tow cut pronto! Ross's going to put us off her port quarter, where we'll be least likely to be seen. If anyone wants to know what you're doing, you're just making sure we don't run over the tow wire. Keep as low a profile as possible. Tell 'em to use the sonar dome for cover. We'll dive immediately you're ready but we'll make ourselves fully visible to the trawler as we go down. Hopefully they'll see the ensign and know who we are.' He paused to draw another breath. Outside, the signalman hurried by clutching an ensign, and Crane walked through up the passageway.

'Ah, Eric, just the man.' Bradley was still whispering. 'Where are those four goons at the moment?'

'One's in the engine room, Sir, and I think one's up in the fore-ends.' Crane looked puzzled. 'The other two are turned in, as far as I know.'

Bradley nodded and pushed Crane aside. 'Sorry, Eric. Can't stop; got to go! Oliver will bring you up to speed.' He turned back to Strong, 'After you've briefed Eric, make sure the other officers know what's happening, and you'd better pop up to the bridge and put Ross in the picture as well. Remind him to keep us tucked in behind the Russian's port quarter and keep us there. Oh, and get word out to the cox'n and as many others as possible, but quietly. Tell 'em to stand by for anything, and I mean anything! And while you're spreading the good word, check the trim. Remember, we want to be heavy and I want everyone at diving stations as quickly as possible after I give the word. Let me know immediately we're ready to dive. I'll be chatting up Viktor. That's it then. I don't know how much time it will take you to get this sorted, but we need to be quick. I'm hoping they'll want to board the trawler. If so, we'll have the time we need. I'll leave all that in your hands, but for God's sake keep it casual; no need to alert our guests until the last minute.'

Strong nodded dumbly, trying desperately to keep up with the staccato stream of orders coming from his captain. He turned to explain the plan to Crane while Bradley walked aft to his cabin and the waiting Ravoski.

Suddenly Bradley felt very calm. The shaking had stopped and he knew now that he was back in control. Ravoski was sitting on his bunk and climbed to his feet as Bradley came in. Bradley motioned towards the bunk. 'Please sit down, Viktor. Sorry about that. Had to get some people up top to sort out that wire. Don't want any more problems, do we!' He slumped into his chair, knowing that Ravoski couldn't possibly believe what he was saying. Now casually gathering up some loose papers from the desktop, he opened the drawer and pushed them inside, at the same time locating the cold steel butt of his automatic pistol. It was a French 9mm Parabellum, which his father had brought home as a war trophy and had given to him shortly before he died just over three years ago. Bradley had no liking for this weapon, or any other type of handgun when it came down to it. He had only fired this gun twice and then only on the indoor range at Faslane. He was certainly no marksman and he'd kept the gun only because his father had treasured it. He had always kept it in his desk drawer while at sea, though he didn't quite know why.

He supposed that the real reason was that at least he knew where it was, but perhaps more importantly, it wasn't at home lying around the house. Now, as his sweating fingers closed around the tooled steel butt he thought, God, could I really use this thing on Viktor? There were just two dozen rounds of ammunition left for this gun, and these were normally locked in the ship's safe, but on returning from his recent visit to *Otvashni* he had taken them from the safe and had loaded fifteen rounds – a full magazine – into the Parabellum. The rest he left in his drawer just in case.

Aware now that he was beginning to sweat profusely, he grasped the weapon tightly inside the drawer. Now, Viktor, he thought, we'll find out on which side of the fence you really stand. Taking a deep breath he withdrew the weapon from the drawer and swung around to level it at Viktor's chest. He held that breath, surprised at the calm of his voice. 'Viktor, would you be kind enough to give me your gun?' He studied the Russian's face, waiting for a reaction, but there was no reaction, no sign of surprise from Ravoski, and certainly no signs of dismay.

'So, Commander, it is now the time, eh?'

Bradley fleetingly wondered whether this was a statement or a question. He looked at his watch; it was exactly 11.55. Viktor was still smiling even though the smile was confined to his eyes. Bradley felt a momentary confusion, a sudden near panic, almost a feeling of stupidity. This response was not what he had expected. He jerked the gun in a short motion, indicating Ravoski to stand. Clutching the butt of the pistol until the tooling dug painfully into his hot slippery palm, and with his forefinger arched on the trigger guard, he could feel the cold beads of sweat breaking on his brow. Wiping them away with his left sleeve, he said, 'Your gun, Viktor – if you please.'

Victor stood, his eyes still smiling. Slowly he unbuckled his thick black leather belt and passed it, complete with the holstered 9mm Makarov pistol, to Bradley, who motioned him to lay it on the desktop. Ravoski's tone showed no surprise. It was, if anything, complacent.

'Of course, my friend, just as as you wish.' He stepped back and Bradley motioned for him to reseat himself on the bunk.

'So, Commander.' The Russian settled himself. 'What now?'

'We wait here until we are ready.' Bradley was trying hard to conceal the relief in his voice.

'And if I do not wish this?'

'You have no choice, Viktor, and neither do I! I will shoot you if I must; it's you or us now. You know that.'

Again Viktor climbed to his feet. Ignoring the panic that flooded into Bradley's eyes, he calmly began to unbutton his black leather coat. Shrugging himself free of the heavy garment, he dropped it onto the bunk before again sitting down. 'So, Commander, now we are comfortable, eh? And now we will wait, but...' now he was grinning widely, 'if you are to shoot me, should you not first cock your weapon?'

Bradley felt the heat of sheer embarrassment mixing with the sweat already running down his cheeks. Christ, what a bloody idiot! He fumbled with the Parabellum, then looking up at Ravoski, who was still smiling broadly, he realised that he didn't need this damned gun anyway. Viktor was not going to be a problem; he was sure of that now. Well, almost sure. But still he carefully cocked his pistol and laid it on the desk at his side. Then, keeping a watchful eye on Ravoski, he reached for the discarded belt and took the Makarov from its holster. Fumbling for a good half a minute with the release catch at the base of the butt, he finally removed the magazine, complete with its eight rounds. Pushing the magazine into the drawer of his desk, he re-holstered the gun and passed the belt back to the Russian.

There was no need for words now; there was nothing to be said. Bradley and Ravoski sat in silence, listening to the footsteps now sounding on the casing above them and to the furtive voices of his people climbing up and down the tower. Now he could hear increasing activity in the control room – movement and subdued voices. He could hear the ballast pump telegraph bell, and the sound of the telemotor pumps cutting in at the demand for more hydraulic pressure. Clearly Strong was doing his job but how much longer would it be before Strong would call for him? He knew that the crew would be at "diving stations" by now and he prayed that they had managed to do this with great care. It had to be all so casual: everything depended on surprise, and the Russian guards must not suspect a thing. He looked across at Ravoski. It was almost three minutes since they had spoken and the silence was beginning to make him feel uncomfortable.

'You knew that I would try this, didn't you, Viktor?' Bradley spoke more to break the silence than for any other reason.

'Yes, Commander, I knew that you would do this… just as I would have.'

'And you make no attempt to stop me?'

'Stop you, Commander? How could I stop you? You have the gun!' Again, there was that enigmatic smile in his eyes.

Now came a loud metallic scraping from up for'd, and Bradley knew that they would be pulling in any slack on the tow. It shouldn't be long now. Then three sharp hammer blows, and silence. More movement in the tower, more bustle in the control room, then a sharp rap on his cabin door. He stood, his heart now pounding. This was it. Christ, I hope we're ready. He reached for his pistol and Ravoski, without being asked, stood up and buckled on his belt, complete with the holstered but now unloaded Makarov. Now it was obvious to Bradley that Ravoski intended to allay any suspicions that the guards might have until the last possible minute. He felt a surge of relief. Ravoski was going to be all right.

Bradley too, now stood, sliding his Parabellum into his right trouser pocket while keeping a firm grip on the butt. Then, in a voice that was little more than a croak, he said, 'Come on, Viktor, it's time to go.' Ravoski nodded and preceded him into the control room.

Bradley glanced quickly around the control room, seeing the cox'n and the PO of the watch seated at the hydroplane controls, with Strong standing directly behind them. Bishop was manning the attack periscope and Crane, together with the "outside wrecker", stood next to the diving panel, with one of the guards standing in the passageway just aft of them. This guard looked perplexed, jittery, as though he could sense that things were not quite as they should be. Crane caught Bradley's eye and gave him a sly but reassuring wink. Although they were closed up at diving stations, the men in the control room appeared to be going about their various tasks in a completely relaxed and casual way. Strong had briefed them well. In spite of this, Bradley could sense the inevitable air of expectancy. He could almost smell the underlying tension, which would soon become obvious to the guards, and knew that he must move quickly!

He walked across to the attack periscope and Bishop stood aside. 'Slow astern port.'

As *Spearfish* slowly emerged from the shelter of *Otvashni*'s port quarter there was complete silence in the control room, while Bradley studied the stern of the destroyer and the bridge of the trawler. Two men on the trawler's starboard wing bridge appeared to be having some sort of verbal communication with the men in the Russian destroyer's boat. He called across to the helm, 'Tell the bridge, from the captain: show the ensign as ordered, then clear the bridge.'

Bradley shot a further glance towards the guard in the after passageway – a big man, sullen, heavy featured, well into his thirties, the badges on his sleeve indicating age and experience. This guard had now unslung the submachine-gun from his shoulder and was looking enquiringly towards Ravoski, who still leaned casually against the chart table.

'Control – Bridge. Ensign in place. Clearing the bridge now.'

Spearfish was now a good ten yards astern of *Otvashni*. Bradley stepped back from the periscope. 'Full astern port. Port 30.' He reached for the overhead microphone. 'Do you hear there? All compartments – cut loose!' Then he called across to Strong. 'Dive the submarine, Number One.'

Strong responded, 'Open one, two, four, six and seven main vents.'

Spearfish shuddered as the air now rushed out of her ballast tanks, to be replaced by sea water. She began to settle in the water stern down. She was diving, and diving very quickly. Bradley breathed a murmur of silent thanks to Strong for preparing such a perfect trim to achieve this quick dive. It would not have been an easy task. Even before the attack periscope had bottomed in its well, the bridge crew came hurtling down the tower and Bradley heard the upper lid slamming shut. The signalman dropped through the lower hatch, throwing himself to one side to avoid the lookout, who landed almost on top of him. Then came Murray, who, pulling the lower lid shut, shouted, 'Bridge secured, Sir. Both tower hatches shut and clipped.'

'Very good. Wheel amidships. Full ahead port, port 30. Steer north.'

Now the guard standing nearest to the diving panel was totally confused.

He knew that something was wrong and looked across to Ravoski for support. But Ravoski, still leaning against the chart table, had now turned his back. Then the guard panicked and jabbed the muzzle of his machine gun into Crane's back. Without turning, Crane jabbed his right elbow into the guard's chest and, pivoting around with a speed and agility completely belying his age and weight, he landed a crushing blow to the Russian's jaw. The guard dropped to the deck and lay still. Crane rubbed his fist on his trousers and again winked mischievously towards Bradley.

The other on-watch guard had been in the engine room before Spearfish dived, and he too had looked puzzled when the engine room crew had unlocked and uncottered six main vents. But Leading Stoker "Geordie" Braithwaite slapped him on the shoulder in a gesture of friendly reassurance and then led him into the after-ends, where he uncottered seven main vent. Now turning to the still-puzzled guard, he gave him a broad friendly grin before decking him with a sharp blow to the skull from the trusty wheel spanner he always carried with him. Meanwhile, up in the fore-ends the two off-watch guards had been sitting with a couple of the seamen, who had for the last two days been trying to teach these two Russians the rules of cribbage. So engrossed were they with their cards that the fore-endsman on watch had had no difficulty in uncottering one and two main vents. When these vents opened and Spearfish started to dive, the crib students looked up in surprise, but their tutors were equally responsive. Still without realising what was happening, the two Russians were overpowered and firmly tied up.

Bradley ordered Spearfish to a depth of 120 feet before stopping to listen for any activity above them, but there was nothing. Still worried about that port stern gland, he gritted his teeth and ordered 200 feet. Setting a course north-west, directly away from Otvashni, Spearfish was free, but he still couldn't believe how easy it had been. Was this really true?

★　★　★　★　★

Imogen was stopped now, lying some 100 yards off *Otvashni*'s starboard beam. Barnes carefully studied the destroyer through his binoculars while Jackson concentrated on cleaning his pipe.

'Looks like they've put a boat over the side, Skip. Maybe they want to come aboard us.' Barnes counted the men in the motor boat now being lowered into the water from the destroyer's starboard davits. He could see that they were all armed. Turning to Jackson he said, 'I count thirteen of the buggers an' it looks like they've all got guns.'

Jackson stuffed his pipe into his pocket and, picking up his binoculars, moved across to join Barnes. He too now squinted into the half-light, watching the motor boat settle in the water and almost immediately pull away from the destroyer to make its way towards them. Away from the shelter of the destroyer, the small boat started to pitch and roll in the heavy swell, increasing speed, streams of sea water and spume flying back from its bows, drenching all on board.

'I should think they'll be looking to board us, Skip,' Barnes repeated, still studying the approaching boat, 'an' I just 'ope they get a bloody good wettin' for their trouble!'

'Nay, Joe, they've got no bloody right to board,' replied Jackson. 'We're in free waters, just doing our job, an' never mind the wetting, those bastards do not come aboard my ship. Not wi' out a fight from me!'

'Fight? fight? What the 'ell are we going to fight 'em with?' Barnes turned towards Jackson with a contemptuous snort. 'Three bloody signal pistols and a line-throwing rifle? Maybe we ought to get cookie up 'ere with a few pots an' pans to throw at 'em. That should frighten 'em off, eh? Anyway, what's the point of startin' a ruckus? They may be perfectly friendly.'

'Friendly my arse,' growled Jackson. 'Them bastards want to come aboard and check us out, make sure we're not one of them bloody spy ships, an' if we don't conform to their regulations for any reason then we'll be in deep shit! If they 'ad their way we wouldn't be allowed up 'ere at all. In fact, now that I come to think of it, that sub we saw with her — can't see it now but she was British, I'm sure of that, and I do remember that the top of bridge looked damaged, like she might 'ave been in some sort of an accident.'

'Well, we ain't a bloody spy ship, are we?' replied Barnes. 'So why not let the bastards come on board to see fer themselves? We got nowt to 'ide, 'ave we?'

Now Jackson's voice was raised. 'I already said: they ain't comin' aboard my ship, an'if they don't like it, then they can bloody well—'

His tirade was interrupted in full flow as the door on the starboard side of the wheelhouse swung open and Jimmy Frost, the radio operator, stepped inside, followed by the usual gust of freezing wind, and handed him a sheet of paper.

'Message from the Ruskie warship, Skip. *Otvashni*, she's called. She wants us to let her men in the boat come aboard.'

'OK, Jimmy, OK, I can bloody well read it for myself.' Jackson frowned as he studied the piece of paper before screwing it up into a tight ball and throwing it to the deck.

Frost stole a quick wink at Barnes before looking expectantly back at his skipper. 'Any reply, Skip?'

'No, there bloody well ain't no reply, an' you'd better get yourself back down to the radio shack, Jimmy, just in case there's something else those bastards want to talk about.' Jackson then turned to look out through the wheelhouse window at the Russian boat, which was now almost alongside. 'Well, I suppose we'd better see what the buggers want. You comin', Joe?' He followed Frost though the door, with Barnes close on his heels.

Jackson and Barnes now stood side by side, gloved hands clutching the rail of the open bridge wing as *Imogen* wallowed restlessly in the swell. The man in the stern sheets of the open boat was standing, bracing himself against the small wooden cuddy that covered the boat's engine. They could see him better now. He wore a black fur ushanka and a heavy black coat belted at the waist, which carried a holstered side arm. Jackson could see that in spite of the support this man was getting from the engine cuddy, he was still having great difficulty in staying on his feet. Now the Russian raised a loudhailer to his face.

'Attention, *Imogen*. We wish to board you.' He spoke very passable English.

Jackson cupped his hand around his mouth and shouted back, 'What for?'

'We wish to talk with you.'

'What about?'

Now the Russian was more hesitant. He appeared to be conferring with someone else in the boat. Then one of them passed him something which looked like a rucksack which, from the quivering whip aerial protruding from its top, obviously contained a radio. Jackson guessed that this man was now in conversation with the warship. After a few minutes he put the radio down and again raised his loudhailer.

'Attention, *Imogen*. We wish to board you. You will prepare to receive us.'

Again, through cupped hands Jackson bawled back, 'What submarine have you got in tow?'

There was no reply, so Jackson repeated his question. 'What submarine have you in tow? Do you need assistance?'

The Russian motor boat was now almost alongside, and even in the half-dark Jackson could see the man with the loudhailer much more clearly. He was obviously some sort of junior officer. This officer again raised his loudhailer. 'We need no assistance from you! I repeat, you will prepare to receive us on board.'

'And... why... would... I... do... that?' Jackson spoke slowly, deliberately pausing between each word.

'We wish to inspect your cargo.'

'We only carry fish.'

'I have orders to inspect your cargo!'

Jackson turned to Barnes, 'Persistent bastard, ain't he?'

But Barnes hadn't heard his skipper's last remark; he was staring across to the destroyer's stern and the submarine now emerging from behind her port quarter, moving slowly astern and trimmed low in the water. Now the large white ensign stretched over the starboard side of her fin was almost all that he could see of her, but it was all he needed to see. 'Bloody hell, Skip,' he shouted. 'You see that? There's your friggin' answer!'

Jackson swung around to look at the destroyer's stern and the now fast-disappearing submarine. He swore loudly. 'Ah, so she is one of ours! Didn't I tell you she were one of ours, Joe?' Turning again, he shouted down to the man now standing at the foot of the bridge ladder on the deck below. 'Colin, get all the men below now. I want no one on the upper deck.' Then, turning to Barnes, he said, 'Come on, Joe. Sod these bastards; we're gettin' out of 'ere right now!' Even while he was still pulling the sticky wheelhouse door, he was shouting to the helmsman, 'Starboard 30, Barry. Full ahead. Let's get the fuck out of 'ere.'

The motor boat crew were taken completely by surprise as *Imogen* suddenly lunged forward. They reeled with the sudden surge of her wash and the standing officer was flung savagely down into her stern sheets.

'Right, you bastards,' yelled Jackson to no one in particular. 'You want to come aboard? Well you'll 'ave to fuckin' well catch me first!'

Barnes was shouting as he followed Jackson through the wheelhouse door. 'What the hell are you doing, Skip? That bloody ship can run us down without even trying.'

'Don't you see, Joe? That sub wanted us to know who they were. They ain't being towed by choice; at least not their bloody choice. This is the best way to help 'em, Joe. She was diving, so she must have slipped 'er tow, an' if the destroyer comes after us at least it will give 'em a good chance to bugger off if they're able to.' Jackson staggered forward into his chair as *Imogen*'s bows slammed into a particularly high swell.

Imogen was making fourteen knots now, close on her limit. She wouldn't be able to hold this speed for long – not in this sea and fully loaded as she was. Barnes was also having difficulty in staying on his feet. 'Oh yeh, and what about those bloody great guns, then? You think we can outrun a shell from one of them?' He gripped the back of Jackson's chair to steady himself, but he knew that his skipper was right: under the circumstances this was about the only thing they could do.

'She won't fire on us, Joe, not in international waters.' Jackson was smiling at Barnes as if to reassure him, now talking in a lower voice, almost fatherly. He called to the helmsman, who was struggling to keep *Imogen* on course. 'Come around to 270, Barry.' Then turning back to Barnes he said, 'Go and tell Jimmy Frost to get a signal off right away. Tell 'em about the sub and the Ruskies an' don't forget to give 'em the time, date and our exact position.'

'Who's the signal for, Skip?' asked Barnes.

'I don't know. You'd best tell the fuckin' world! No, make it to the Admiralty, an' make it bloody urgent.' Barnes disappeared while Jackson made his way to the port side window of the bridge and looked aft. Already *Otvashni* was some half a mile astern of him and this gap was rapidly increasing. There was no sign of the submarine. He wiped his eyes with the back of his hand and muttered, 'Where's all that bloody mist and rain now that we really need it?'

★　★　★　★　★

Standing on the low platform in front of *Otvashni's* bridge screen, Borstoy could still hardly see over the bridge coaming, but what he could see was enough to contort his features into a blind rage. 'They are getting away, Portrova!' He hissed. 'The trawler is getting away! Do something! Stop them!'

Portrova remained calm. 'Yes, Comrad, she is getting away! But she will not get far. We will recover her as soon as we have our boat back. She may be working with the British submarine and for that reason we will interrogate her master. But we also have our main job to do. Soon we shall have our British submarine within territorial waters, and our job will be complete.' He turned to Carlov. 'Call back the boat, and resume course and speed when ready.'

On his return to *Otvashni* Bassisty had climbed miserably out of the motor boat, which was now being hauled up onto its davits. Soaking wet, with freezing water squelching from his boots, he made his way to the bridge to make his report. He feared the worst!

But Portrova had remained surprisingly calm as Bassisty blurted out his report.

'There was nothing we could do, Comrad Kapitan. They would not let us board them.'

'Nothing you could do? Pah! If—' Borstoy's voice was venomous.

Portrova cut Borstoy short. 'There was nothing any of us could do, Comrad Lieutenant. It does not matter; this trawler will soon be caught. Track her on radar.'

'But they would have seen the flag, Sir,' Bassisty blurted, still unable to believe that his report had been accepted so well by Portrova.

'Flag. What flag?' hissed Borstoy.

Portrova looked puzzled. 'Yes, what flag, Comrad Bassisty?'

'The British submarine lowered their ensign over their bridge, Kapitan. You would not have seen it from here. That is when the trawler broke away.' Bassisty felt his legs shaking, and he knew that it wasn't just the cold.

Borstoy's thin body writhed with ill-concealed rage. Portrova remained outwardly unmoved. 'So, they know our submarine is British, *da*? No matter; they will also know that we are assisting her. Soon this knowledge will be broadcast to the world.' He looked at Bassisty. 'My friend, you have done all that you could do. Now get dry clothing before you freeze.'

Bassisty saluted his captain, hardly believing that it was all over. He moved towards the bridge ladder and glanced astern towards *Spearfish*. Stopping, he blinked and looked again. The dread that now numbed his body was far worse than the cold. He looked to port and then to starboard. He even looked ahead over *Otvashni*'s bow. Surely this could not be! The British submarine was nowhere to be seen! Bassisty again turned back towards the bridge, wondering how much bad news he could give his kapitan in so short a time.

Portrova was talking to Carlov; and Borstoy was back on his platform, fuming as he watched *Imogen* disappearing into the semi-dark distance. Bassity's tongue felt like sandpaper. He opened his mouth with great difficulty. 'Comrad Kapitan! The British submarine: she is gone!'

Portrova turned. 'Gone? Gone? What are you saying, Comrad Lieutenant?' Even as he spoke, the impact of Bassisty's blurted words was dawning upon him. He bounded first across to the starboard after part of the bridge and then to the port side, gazing aft to where *Spearfish* should have been. But *Spearfish* was no longer where she should have been.

Now Borstoy was at Portrova's side, craning his neck to get a clear view aft. 'She *is* gone,' he hissed. 'You have lost the British trawler and now you have lost the British submarine, Kapitan Portrova!'

Ignoring Borstoy, Portrova lurched across to the port side of the bridge, again scanning aft. Nothing – she was gone! While they had been busy with the trawler, she had slipped her tow and quietly dived. He felt the anger rising within him. Just those few short moments was all that she had needed, and he, Portrova, had given her those moments. He reached for the sound room microphone. 'Sonar – Bridge. Report all contacts.'

'Bridge, this is Sonar. HE bearing two-seven-zero, single diesel. Speed fourteen knots.'

Portrova knew that this would be the trawler. 'Yes, yes,' he shouted impatiently into his microphone. 'Continue to report all contacts.'

'I have one other contact, Kapitan. Submarine HE moving north-west. Single propeller. She is at a depth of 150 metres and making seven knots.'

Portrova snarled. Throwing down his microphone, he swung towards the voice pipe. 'Full ahead both engines. Starboard twenty. Steer two-nine-zero.' He looked towards Carlov. 'Go to battle stations. Prepare depth charges for action.'

Otvashni's bow began to swing sharply to starboard. Then, with a shudder that could be clearly felt by those on her bridge, she came to an abrupt stop. A shrill whistle came from the engine room voice pipe. Portrova lifted the protective cover and yelled, 'Kapitan, *da*?'

'Comrad Kapitan, this is the engineer officer. I have had to stop both engines. Both propellers seem to be fouled.'

Portrova cursed loudly and slammed the voice pipe lid shut. He knew immediately what had happened. He had run over his own tow wire – a cardinal crime. Now *Otvashni* was going nowhere!

'You have lost her, Kapitan. You are an incompetent fool!' Borstoy's whining accusation shook Portrova out of his daze. 'And you will pay dearly for this day's work!'

CHAPTER NINE

Bradley leaned across *Spearfish*'s chart table, and again checked the local time clock: 08.45 exactly, and today's date was Sunday, 25th of October. He had spent most of the three days or so since his break from *Otvashni* in the sound room, listening for the destroyer's HE on what was left of his passive sonar, and which should now have been coming from somewhere astern of him, but was not! Or was that simply because of his damaged passive sonar?

This absence of HE, or of any other sign of pursuit, puzzled him, made him uneasy. Where is this bloody Ruskie? He must be out there somewhere. Surely he wouldn't just give up and let us go – not after all the trouble he's been to. He should be after us by now, so why isn't he? What is the bastard playing at?

Ravoski stood next to Bradley. He too had seldom left the control room since *Spearfish* had dived. They had spoken very little. Bradley gave the Russian a quick sidelong glance. Here was another mystery. Just what the hell was *he* thinking, this quiet Russian? What was his *real* game? Could he *really* be trusted? Ravoski had certainly played his part to the full when they had broken away from the Soviet destroyer. But why? Was he perhaps playing towards some sort of devious end game – something that he, Bradley, hadn't thought of? Or was it simply that he had seen his chance of escaping at last from the system in which he had lived and worked for all his adult life and, as he had implied to Bradley on several occasions, intensely disliked. Could it really have been *Spearfish's* good fortune that out of all the Russian officers Portrova could have placed aboard her, he'd chosen the one man who wanted to defect? He let go an involuntary sigh. Perhaps it really was just as simple as that; he wanted to believe it was. He shot another sideways glance at Ravoski. Ah well, first things first. Ravoski was not his prime concern at this moment. There were other things to worry about right now, like this complete absence of any sign of pursuit.

On diving away from the destroyer, he had closed up attack teams in readiness for the inevitable chase. He had kept these teams closed up even though as yet there was no sign of the Russian, but in a relaxed state. When *Spearfish* had broken away, she had dived at full speed on the port shaft. Then, after fifteen minutes, taking into consideration propeller noise, the depletion of her battery, and the fragile state of her port stern gland, he had reduced to half speed, slowing down at fifteen-minute intervals and turning a full circle to listen on what was left of his passive sonar for the noise of pursuit. But there was nothing. They were alone! Or were they? The sensors of his active sonar outfits had been rendered completely useless by the battering that they had taken earlier. The only sonar left in effective use was the long-range passive type 186, whose transducers were fitted in the port and starboard ballast tanks, and most of these transducers had now been reported as suspect. He would stay on this course and depth for a further hour and if by then there were still no contacts he would come to periscope depth for a quick look around. He instructed Strong accordingly, before going to his cabin and flopping gratefully onto his bunk. Even after this time his mind was still competing frantically with his pulse. The escape from the destroyer had been quick and easy – unbelievably easy. Too easy, perhaps? This thought now only added to his worries. From somewhere deep inside him that small niggling voice – the one that had been whispering to him on the morning of the missile firing – was back, and somehow he knew that his problems weren't over yet, not by a long chalk. His mind returned to the break from the destroyer. The whole event had taken less than six minutes, but even now it had seemed like an eternity. Strong and Crane had done their work well. In fact they all had. It couldn't have been easy in the short time they'd been allowed. To a man, the crew had been carefully briefed on the need to avoid arousing the suspicions of the sentries, who were now securely tied up under guard in the fore-ends. Relaxed nonchalance had been the order of the day, and it had succeeded. So easy – a complete anti-climax, in fact. Looking back now, even those brief skirmishes with the guards hadn't been too difficult, even though he dreaded to think what would have happened if they had got their fingers on the triggers of those bloody guns, which Bishop had informed him were the latest AKM, only introduced in the spring of this year, and lighter and more efficient than the AK47s they had replaced.

Now still sprawled on his bunk, Bradley was half dosing when at 09.05 the familiar voice of Willie Kinross brought him sharply back to life. 'Captain, Sir, sound room. Faint HE bearing red two-zero. The contact is moving south-west. About four miles away.' Kinross stopped his report, realising that his captain was now standing beside him, crumpled, dishevelled, but very alert. Bradley leapt the few feet from his cabin into the sound room within a split second.

The headphoned figure of Kinross, slumped in front of a pen recorder display, looked up at Bradley. Removing his headphones, he spoke in his usual sharp Scottish burr. 'Bit of a funny one, this, Sir. Picked up this noise a few minutes ago. It's off the port bow, bearing three-one-zero relative. Then I lost it again almost right away. It's intermittent. Keeps stopping and starting. There, it's just stopped again. Whatever it is, it's a single-screw diesel. Maybe it's a fishing boat or something like that.'

'What about our friendly trawler?' Bradley asked. 'She could well be somewhere in that direction.'

'Ay, the trawler. That's what ah was thinking, Sir. But if it *is* her, then she's no passed us! Ah hav'nae heard her. But then, this set is a load of shite!'

Perplexed, Bradley rubbed his fingers through his hair, 'Well, this is not the Russian destroyer and that's for sure, but it could well be that trawler. On the other hand, as you say, it could be this bloody set playing up. I'll bring us around to close in on her. If it *is* that trawler then we may have found a friend we badly need.' He picked up the microphone. 'Officer of the watch – this is the captain. Come around to two-five-zero.'

Now both men turned to study the pen recorder, with Kinross again donning his headphones. But the pens now remained stationary. They waited for a further ten minutes before Kinross removed his headset, shook his head, and looked directly at Bradley. 'Well, Sir, whatever's out there, she's no movin' the noo!'

Bradley grunted and stood up. 'OK, Kinross, keep an ear on her. I'll be in the control room.'

Now back in the control room, Bradley nodded to Strong. 'We have a contact, Oliver. I want to get a closer look at her. Close up "diving stations".'

Forty-five minutes later, with the spurious contact now barely one mile away, Bradley ordered, 'Come to fifty-eight feet, Number One.' Stood behind the attack periscope, he felt the deck beneath his feet angling upward. 'Depth now?'

'Sixty-two feet, Sir,' from Strong.

'Up attack!' Bradley crouched, ready to receive the handles as the periscope emerged from the well. Then rising with it, he watched through the eyepiece – first black, then a slightly lighter shade of black as the head broke water, momentarily clearing then obscuring again in a mass of spray and bubbles.

'Depth now?' The water finally cleared from the glass. Now there was only occasional spray, and Bradley was already starting his all-round sweep.

'Fifty-seven feet, Sir'

'Very good. Well it's still relatively flat up there, just a bit of a swell, but we're going to have to be careful with the periscope. Keep fifty-eight feet.' He completed his sweep. Just as he suspected, there was nothing up there except the one vessel. He could barely make her out, but her lights told him that she was not a big vessel. He judged that she was now under half a mile off his port bow. Kinross was right; she certainly looked like a fisherman from here. Why don't these bastards fly some sort of a flag? Not that he'd be able to see it in this light.

Now he felt the tension in his body being replaced by an indescribable sense of relief. For the first time since meeting up with the Russian destroyer he felt that he was winning again. He was calling the tune, even though he realised that he should have been approaching the North Cape by now and preparing to send his surfacing signal. Humming quietly to himself, he completed a further all-round sweep. Nothing else in sight. He turned back to study the fishing vessel. She was definitely stopped, and very low in the water. He sensed immediately that something was wrong with her. Now he had to make yet another decision. Should he disregard this vessel, and get on with the business of making good his exit from the Barents? Or should he have a closer look at her? Maybe she was in some sort of trouble and needing his help. Maybe she was British. She did look very much like the trawler that had approached them this morning – the one that had given them the chance to break away from the Russians – but he couldn't really tell from this distance, and he still didn't feel safe, not by a long chalk. Where was that bloody Russian destroyer now? If only he could really trust what was left of his sonar.

Then he knew what he must do. 'Let's have a closer look at her. Half ahead port, Oliver.' He made another all-round sweep, then lowered the periscope, feeling the deck beneath him trembling slightly as *Spearfish* increased speed.

Bradley slowed *Spearfish* when she was barely 200 yards off the stationary trawler's starboard beam and, between the deluges of spray over his periscope head, he could now make out a small ragged flag streamed from her topmast. Yes – she was British.

'She's our old friend from this morning. Come and have a look, Oliver.' Bradley stood aside to let Strong peer through the periscope.

'Yes, that's her all right.' Strong was squinting carefully. 'She's stopped and she's very low in the water. She's not got any trawl out. Perhaps she's in some sort of trouble.' He squinted again. 'I can't make out a name or any pennant number at this distance.' He continued to study her for a few moments, then pulled his head away from the eyepiece and handed the periscope back to Bradley.

Bradley said, 'Right, let's move in a bit closer, but stand by for anything!'

★　★　★　★　★

Jackson slumped dejectedly in his chair on *Imogen*'s bridge, his usually cheerful features set in a glum scowl as he gazed for'd towards her bow. A bow that should now be surging forward; carving a path through this grey heaving swell, taking them home.

But *Imogen*'s bows were doing neither of these things. Now they were simply oscillating lazily in time with the swell, and *Imogen* was going nowhere. Her stop-start engines had been giving trouble for the last hour or so, before finally bringing her to a permanent stop. Her engineer was feeling and looking concerned. 'Feed-water problems, Skip! Somehow we've got sea water in the fuel system. Fuck knows 'ow it got there. Must 'ave been all that dashin' about we've been doin', but we can't move again till we get it sorted!' He looked Jackson in the eye, and saw his skipper's ill-disguised annoyance. Then, as he left the wheelhouse to return to the engine room, the engineer, as though deliberately rubbing salt in the wounds, called over his shoulder, 'Could be quite a while.'

Bloody engineers! Bloody engines! Jackson was becoming more frustrated by the minute. His hopes for a fast run home were beginning to recede rapidly. He was not a technically minded man. He believed in the sea, and he believed in *Imogen*, but he knew nothing of engines, and cared even less. To him, engines were just a necessary evil. He paid others to look after the bloody engine. He would happily go back to sails if he had the choice.

Now he talked aloud, softly, coaxing her as a father would coax a reluctant child. 'Ee, Lass, what the 'ell's wrong with thee? Tha knows we need to be gettin' 'ome. Come on, Lass, let's get on wi' it. Don't let me down now.'

Beside him, the man at the helm smiled to himself. With no way on *Imogen*, he was superfluous as a helmsman. She would go where the sea cared to take her. He was used to hearing the skipper talking aloud to his ship. He was always doing it. Wouldn't he be surprised though, if one day the bloody ship talked back to him!

Down on the trawler's main deck, Joe Barnes pulled himself up through the engine room hatch, slamming it shut behind him. Like his skipper, Joe had no great liking for engines or engine rooms. He had only gone down there to see for himself what was going on, and to get a situation report for

Jackson. He walked for'd and stood in the shelter of the bridge structure, groping in his oilskins for a cigarette. Finally lighting up, he took a deep drag and, exhaling contentedly, surveyed the surrounding sea. Then his eyes narrowed. 'Hello!' he muttered. 'What the 'ell's that?'

He looked again, fixing his gaze to a point about 200 yards off the starboard beam. Something had caught his eye. A brief splash of white, it had stood out vividly against this undulating blanket of grey sea. Barnes wiped his watering eyes with the back of his hand, wishing that he had his binoculars with him. Yes – there it is again. It's not a wave crest, I'm sure of it, and it won't be a bird. He continued to watch. There it was again. He frowned. But I bet I know what it bloody well is though! Flicking his part-smoked cigarette over the side, he turned and hastily scrambled up the ladder to the wheelhouse.

Jackson turned as the wheelhouse door opened and Joe Barnes lurched in, again slamming the door shut behind him and again roundly cursing the swollen woodwork. 'What's the story from down there then, Joe? Not good news, I'll bet.'

Barnes was excited and it showed in his voice. He shook his head. 'You're right; it's not good, Skip. All I know is there's no change. Still no nearer to sorting the problem. But never mind what's happening down there. Dammit, where's my glasses? I think we've got a visitor.'

Jackson's scowl turned to a look of part puzzlement and part dismay. 'A visitor, you say? Where away? What the 'ell are you on about, man?'

Barnes ignored Jackson. Locating his glasses, he pulled open the wheelhouse door and moved outside to train the glasses on the starboard beam. He picked up the white splash straight away, but now it seemed even nearer. 'I thought as bloody much.' He turned to look for Jackson, who now stood by his side, and with his glasses raised, 'There you are, Skip. If that's not a periscope then I'm a bloody Dutchman! Look! Almost beam on. Can't be more than 200 yards off, if that.'

Jackson carefully studied the area indicated by Barnes, then let out a low grunt. 'Aye, 'appen you could be right, Joe. Now who the 'ell might they be? It'll be another friggin' Russian, won't it. But what might they be wantin'?' He turned to Barnes and winked. 'I bet those bastards think they're real clever! They'll be down there thinkin' they got the drop on us. Let's give 'em a surprise.' With that he dropped his glasses onto his chest, stepped outside the bridge door, and began to wave both arms wildly in the air. Joe Barnes did the same.

Spearfish was now just 150 yards off the trawler and closing fast. Bradley studied the trawler carefully through the attack periscope. Although she was half hidden in the swell he was sure now that it was the one they had seen earlier. He could make out two figures standing on the decking outside her enclosed bridge. He studied them carefully. They were waving – yes, they were waving. A medium-sized stern trawler, and by the tattered remnant of the flag she wore at her masthead, British. 'Stand by to surface, Number One.'

Bradley manoeuvred *Spearfish* until she was about fifty yards off the trawler's starboard beam before bringing her to the surface. Still on the periscope, he carefully completed another all-round look. Satisfied, he called across to Strong, 'Open the lower hatch. Get the signalman to the control room. Tim, take over the watch. Number One and I are going upstairs. We'll take over the watch from there. Better get into some warm gear, Oliver.'

Minutes later Bradley, now back in his heavy duffel coat, was on the bridge, closely followed by Strong, the signalman, and a lookout. Bradley briefly studied the trawler through his binoculars.

The two figures were still on the starboard wing of her bridge, and now others were gathering on her decks. He lowered his glasses and reached for the battery-powered megaphone that the signalman had brought with him.

'Hello, the trawler. What ship?' He lowered the megaphone and watched as the larger of the two figures on the bridge platform withdrew into the bridge and emerged almost immediately with a megaphone similar to his own.

'Hello, the submarine,' bellowed a voice with a distinct Yorkshire accent. 'This is the fisherman *Imogen*, homeward bound for Hull. 'Aven't we met before?'

'Yes, I think we have. Why are you stopped?'

'We got sea water in our fuel system!'

Bradley looked at Strong. 'Well, I guess that's a good enough reason.' He turned back to the trawler. 'This is the British submarine *Spearfish*. Do you need assistance?'

'Yeh! We could do with a hand.'

'Why are you so low in the water?'

'We got a full load, an' we're tryin' to take it easy on the bilge pump! Got to conserve power, you know? You want a fish supper?'

'Yes please! Can you send a boat across to pick up my engineers?'

'Our boat's on its way.' The big man with the megaphone stepped back inside the bridge, while the other ran down the ladder to the main deck, obviously to organise the launch of the motor boat.

Bradley called down the voice pipe, 'Captain – Control. Ask the engineer officer to speak on the voice pipe.' Then turning to Strong, he grinned, 'I don't know about you, Oliver, but I quite fancy a nice fresh piece of cod.'

'Sounds good, Sir.'

Now from the voice pipe, 'Captain, Sir. Engineer speaking.'

Bradley bent towards the voice pipe. 'Listen, Eric. This trawler up here seems to have a problem in her engine room – water in her fuel system or something. Can we spare a couple of your boys to give 'em a hand?'

'I should think so, Sir, if that's what you want. I'll detail off a couple of me "tiffies" to volunteer.'

Bradley smiled to himself. 'Good man. They'll need foul-weather clothing, with plenty of warm stuff underneath. Send 'em up here to the bridge when they're ready, and tell 'em to make it quick! Tell them there's a boat waiting. Oh, and tell Ross to get three of the casing party kitted up and ready to receive this boat.' Now he turned back to the lookout and the signalman. Keep your eyes peeled, both of you, I don't want any more nasty surprises while we're up here.'

Now a small boat had left the trawler and was heading towards *Spearfish*, riding fast and high on the long grey swell, belching out a mixture of exhaust and water spray from its overworked outboard motor. Bradley trained his glasses on the boat, seeing clearly the two-man crew – one sitting aft at the tiller with the other crouching in the bows. Already soaked by freezing spray, the bowman's gloved hands clutched a coiled heaving line. He heard someone climbing the ladder below him and turned to watch as two oilskin-clad engine room artificers scrambled awkwardly up onto the bridge, to stand blinking in the daylight – their first breath of fresh air since leaving Faslane. Although wearing thick clothing under their oilskins and lifejackets, already both were shivering violently at this sudden rude introduction to the bone piercing-cold that came with this air. The first one up now peered through slitted eyelids and mumbled half under his breath and half into his turned-up collar. 'Christ, Slinger, it ain't 'alf taters up 'ere!'

Bradley ignored this, and looked closely at the faces half hidden under the flopping hoods. 'All right, gentlemen? Now who have we got here?'

The figure nearest him spoke, his voice muffled under his hood. 'Woods and Allen, Sir.'

'Right, Woods and Allen, I want you to go over to that trawler, have a look at their problem, then let me know how long you think it will take to get her going.' He pulled the cuff of his mitten down and looked at his watch. 'Seems they've got sea water in somewhere where it shouldn't be. Let me know the situation as soon as you can, and certainly within fifteen minutes of boarding her. Is that clear?'

'Yessir!' Woods and Allen answered simultaneously.

'Good. Now it's becoming a bit crowded up here, so get yourselves down by the fin door and wait for the boat. And for Christ's sake try not to fall in, because if you do we may not be able to get you out again!'

Bradley watched as Woods and Allen disappeared down the ladder into the fin, and then turned his attention back to the approaching motor boat, which was now almost alongside. 'OK, Oliver, get your casing party out onto the casing, and let's see if we can get those two transferred without drowning the poor sods. They've had a big enough shock to their systems already!'

Strong bent over and shouted down into the fin, 'Right, lads. Onto the casing with you, and remember, Second Cox'n, I want every man properly secured with a line. Take no chances.'

Now the side of *Imogen*'s motor boat was bouncing roughly off *Spearfish*'s port ballast tanks, compressing the water trapped between into freezing fountains of spray, which drenched both her crew and the casing party. The boat's bowman threw his line, which was caught first time by one of the casing party. The helmsman cut his engine and picked up a second line, which he, too, threw over *Spearfish's* casing, again to be caught expertly by another of the men in the casing party.

Bradley knew that any sort of transfer via a submarine in this sort of sea was never an easy task. *Spearfish's* casing was surging up and down and heeling from side to side on the heavy swell, and by now it would be covered with a skin of ice. It was a miracle that they were managing to stay on their feet down there, let alone haul in the motor boat.

Now the Second Coxswain emerged from the fin door and guided the two artificers onto the heaving casing. Both had lines tied firmly around their waists and the men in the casing party now lowered the men carefully down onto the ballast tank, where they crouched, clinging to the free flood holes in the side of the casing, waiting for their chance to jump. Bradley wanted to shut his eyes. He just didn't want to watch this, but he knew he must. The first man jumped, landing on his feet safely in the tossing motor boat. He wondered which one that was: Woods or Allen? It didn't really matter. Then the second man was on his feet, tottering momentarily before half jumping, half sliding into the boat to join his companion.

Bradley breathed a sigh of relief, suddenly realising that he was stiflingly hot. Beneath those multiple layers of clothing under his duffel coat he was, in fact, sweating profusely. He watched the men on the casing below as they threw the lines back into the boat, and scrambled for the safety of the fin. The motor boat's engine once more burst into life as she sheered off and headed back towards the trawler.

'What do we do now, Sir? Dive?' Oliver Strong was watching the receding motor boat.

'No, we'll wait up here until we get a situation report from the trawler!'

'I don't much like this, Sir.' Strong was plainly uneasy. 'We're pretty vulnerable up here. And where's that blasted Russian? That's what's worrying me. The truth is I feel that we've got enough problems on our hands as it is, without hanging about here mothering some lame duck fisherman.'

Bradley nodded, apparently unperturbed. A week ago Strong would never have dared to speak to him like this. But then, a week ago Strong had been a different person. Since that first fateful meeting with the Russian destroyers he had changed completely from his former quiet, reserved self, obliging and eager to please, but not yet quite up to his job. The shared experiences over the past days had brought out the best in all his officers, but especially in Strong. Strong now really was his right-hand man and Bradley was glad that he was now voicing his own opinion, and not necessarily the opinion he thought his captain would like to hear. Now, except for that extra half-stripe on Bradley's arm, he and Strong were in many ways equal, relying upon each other, taking strength from each other, affording a mutual respect.

'I don't relish the idea much either, Oliver, but, after all, they *are* British, and they *are* in trouble. More to the point, these are the guys who gave us our chance to slip from the Russians when they could quite as easily have buggered off. God knows how they'd get on if we left them to their own resources – that's if they've got any resources.' He turned, looking to the north-east. 'Anyway, since there's no sign of our Russian friends, I'd like to believe that they've given us up as a bad job, but somehow I don't think so. They'll be out there somewhere, I'm sure of it. We'll remain at diving stations and dive off the klaxon at the first sign of trouble. So you'd better get everyone below until that boat gets back with our chaps.' He scowled to himself. 'God I wish we had some bloody radar. Just a two-minute sweep is all we'd need. But what bothers me most at the moment is that what's left of our passive sonar seems to be packing up!'

'Exactly, Sir.' Strong was talking to Bradley's back. 'If they do turn up, we'll be a sitting duck!' They both turned their glasses towards the trawler. The motor boat was back alongside her now and they could make out the dark-clad figures scrambling up her low freeboard on a rope ladder.

'Fifteen minutes, Oliver, fifteen minutes maximum. If we've not got a report back by then, I shall want our two lads off her.' Bradley stepped down on the fin ladder. 'I'm going down to the sound room. Won't be long.' Then he looked up at Strong, again with that half-smile on his face. Was it a smile of reassurance? Strong could only guess that it was. 'Don't forget though, Oliver, any trouble and it's our fastest dive ever.' He nodded in the direction of the signalman and the lookout. 'So if anything happens, you and your friends up here had better get below PDQ. That's if you don't want very wet shirts – or something a damn sight worse!'

★ ★ ★ ★ ★

Portrova was stamping his heavy fur-lined boots repeatedly on the ice-coated iron deck of *Otvashni*'s bridge, but it wasn't the intense cold of this gloomy morning that prompted him to do this. Quite the opposite. At this time he was not feeling the cold at all. He was hot, burning up in fact, and his feet stamping was not proving to be a very effective vent for the overpowering feelings of anger and frustration that he directed not only at himself, but to everyone around him. *Otvashni*'s bridge was not a good place to be at this time.

Portrova knew that the blame for the escape of the British submarine would fall squarely on his shoulders, and he had thought of little else since *Spearfish* had broken away. There would be many questions asked, and these would come from people far more important and potentially even more dangerous than that little toad Borstoy, though he had little doubt that Borstoy would fan the flames when the questions started. Portrova was finding it very difficult to accept that he had lost the British submarine, and the fact that they had escaped with such apparent ease was even more indigestible to him. Viktor Ravoski was a trusted officer with great experience of submarines. The four men with him were all fully armed and would not hesitate to use force to control any situation if ordered to by Ravoski. He had realised now that the British submarine should have been thoroughly searched before they started the tow, and any material which could be classed as "intelligence" removed and brought aboard *Otvashni*. For this omission alone, they would almost certainly castigate him back there in Moscow.

But then, no one had ordered him to search the Britisher. His orders from the admiral had been to provide a boarding party to give assistance and any help needed to ensure a safe journey under tow. Perhaps his superiors had felt that searching the Britisher, and the confiscation of any equipment or material at this stage would, from the British point of view, be taken as open aggression. Oh yes, his masters back there in Moscow would be very keen not to allow this matter to become an international incident, at least not yet – not until they chose to make it so.

'Ah well, so be it.' Portrova's voice broke the long silence on the bridge and startled the watch officer. He stamped his feet yet again, searching into his pockets for yet another cigarette. He knew now that he had badly underestimated this accursed Commander Bradley, and had also overestimated his own control over the situation. He must now locate and recapture the Britisher. Failure to do this would have dire consequences for him. But the wrath of his masters towards him was not his main spur. To him, this affair with the British submarine had become a personal vendetta – a matter of his pride and his honour, and yes, his revenge. He knew now that he would not allow rest until he had settled this matter his way. For the sake of Gregori Lenkov he would again capture this boat, together with its commander, or he would "accidentally" destroy it.

But now *Otvashni* lay stationary, crippled, useless, with at least ten fathoms of tow wire tangled vice-tight around both her shafts and propellers. Portrova had ordered his divers down to assess the problem as soon as he had realised what had happened, and their initial report was not encouraging. The shafts were jammed solid and there was a large chunk taken out of one of the blades on the starboard propeller.

His divers had worked feverishly in teams of two throughout the previous evening and through the night, labouring to remove the wire. He carried a total of eight divers and these had been split into four teams of two, but because of the intense cold the teams were never in the water for more than five to six minutes at a time. At first it had seemed an impossible task. Carlov had suggested signalling for assistance, but Portrova wouldn't hear of it. It was almost midday when these divers reported the wire clear at last. Now he was free to pursue and relocate the British submarine, and although his frustration and anger was still as sharp as it had been at the time of the break, he would not fail again. It would be *Otvashni* who escorted the Britisher into Polyarnyy

– no one else. He had been given his orders and he would carry them out, no matter what the cost.

Hardly giving his divers time to clear the water, Portrova ordered both engines to be started. Slowly at first, then gradually increasing speed, *Otvashni* at last started to move and Portrova, his gloved hands gripping the bridge rail, prayed that they hadn't damaged the shaft bearings. His prayers were answered. Both shafts appeared to turn easily, and the bearing temperatures were reported to be normal. He ordered a gradual build-up to full speed, but now, as *Otvashni* increased speed, Portrova could feel a distinct judder under his feet and knew that this was caused by a chipped propeller. He cursed bitterly under his breath, but it wasn't the increasing vibration under his feet that worried him: he knew only too well that this chipped propeller would produce a cavitation noise which would carry for miles under water, giving *Otvashni* a distinct propeller signature that would make her easily recognisable to any listening sonar operator.

Now the cadaverous figure of Borstoy again appeared on the bridge and scuttled silently across to where Portrova and Carlov were standing. Both ignored him. Portrova's thoughts were still on his damaged propeller and how it would affect *Otvashni*'s performance, and more importantly, her vulnerability if matters developed into an open confrontation with this Britisher. He was well aware that the Britisher could still bite, and bite hard if driven to it. He turned to Carlov with a look of resignation. 'It cannot be helped, Comrad. We can do nothing about it, but we *will* catch our Britisher. Steer west, remain at full speed, and make sure sonar and radar report all contacts. I am going below.'

Carlov frowned. 'The propeller, Comrad Kapitan. Do you not think we risk damage to our shaft at full speed?'

'I said full speed, Comrad.' Portrova's tone was low, almost menacing. 'Tell the engineers to keep a good watch on the shaft bearing temperatures.' He turned, making for the door at the rear of the bridge.

Borstoy stepped nearer to Carlov and prodded him in the ribs. Carlov turned and looked down into those cold reptilian eyes. 'We must find her, Comrad,' hissed Borstoy. 'She must be stopped; she must not get away.'

'So... this Britisher is that important to us?' Carlov had turned his head, watching *Otvashni*'s bows slowly swinging around as she changed course. Like most others on board, he disliked Borstoy intensely.

'She is a spy,' Borstoy spat. 'She has invaded our territory. She may have witnessed our missile firing trials and she must be recaptured. We must know what intelligence she has stolen from our country! Only as a final measure will she be destroyed. You will remember this at all times, Comrad Carlov.' Borstoy swung around with a grunt of disgust and he, too, left the bridge.

★　★　★　★　★

Bradley stood on *Spearfish*'s bridge and fidgeted. He was becoming anxious. He looked at his watch. He would give the trawler another ten minutes and that was all. Standing beside him, Strong still had his binoculars trained steadily on *Imogen*.

'What are your thoughts on our friend Viktor?' Bradley addressed Strong, as though he were thinking aloud.

Strong lowered his glasses and turned enquiringly towards his captain. If Bradley's question had surprised him, he didn't show it. 'Well, he's come up trumps so far, hasn't he, Sir? Seems a good enough sort – for a Russian that is – though I can't say I've met many of 'em before now. Knows this boat like the back of his hand already. Impresses Eric no end, I can tell you that much.'

'Yes I know.' Bradley was still thinking aloud. 'D'you know, Oliver, I sometimes think he's too good to be true. What if he *is* a plant? What if he's been put on board for a special reason?'

'Special reason?'

'Well, let's put it this way. If the Russians want to make the most of this opportunity, wouldn't it make sense to put someone like Viktor aboard rather than some gun-waving commie who would have alienated all of us from day one? What I'm saying is that Viktor now knows more about *Spearfish* and ourselves than he ever would had he adopted a more dictatorial approach. He could be playing with us. You know – softly, softly, catchee monkey?'

'I see what you mean, Sir, but after all, without his turning a blind eye we'd never have broken away from the destroyer. At least, not without a possible bloodbath.'

'Yes, but, after all, it was a blind eye staring down the barrel of my pistol.'

Strong looked uncertain. He raised his glasses again to scan the still-stationary *Imogen*. 'He certainly keeps up an interest in his four men, Sir. Checks 'em over regularly, makes sure they're properly fed, watered and comfortable. The one that took a blow from the wheel spanner has a pretty serious head wound though. Looks like he's in a bad way.' He lowered his glasses. 'What is it they say? Never look a gift horse in the mouth!' Then, turning back to face Bradley, he said, 'If you want my honest opinion, Sir, I think he wants to defect!'

'You could be right. That's the most logical answer, and it's what I was thinking as well, but I'm still not sure: it just seems too good to be true, too easy — our escape, I mean.' He sighed and shook his head. 'But at the same time it all seems so bloody surreal. Keep a good eye on him, Oliver, and warn the other officers to do the same, but be discreet.' He looked at his watch. 'Time's just about up. What the hell's going on with that bloody trawler? Either they can fix the bloody thing or they can't.'

Strong shot a further brief glance towards his captain before turning back to continue his surveillance. The anxiety was plain in his captain's voice, and he fully understood why. They *were* a sitting duck up here: no radar, no sonar to speak of, and with at least one Russian warship lurking somewhere out there whose sole aim appeared to be either to abduct them or sink them. Yes, he could understand perfectly why Bradley was anxious to be away! He lowered his glasses and again wiped his watering eyes with the back of his mitten. 'Shouldn't be long now, Sir, and at least the weather seems to be with us.' But he knew even as he spoke that his words would bring little, if any, comfort to Bradley. Now he turned and looked back towards the lookout and the signalmen, who were already intently scanning the horizon through their binoculars. 'Keep your eyes peeled, lookout. And you, Bunts. There's a big bad wolf out there somewhere.' He turned to Bradley again. 'I suppose we could go in a bit closer, Sir.' Then, looking down over the fin, he said, 'Still losing oil from three starboard main ballast tank.'

Bradley grunted and raised his glasses to again study the trawler. 'What the hell are those bloody tiffies playing at over there? Fifteen minutes, I said; and all I asked for was a situation report, not a blasted engine rebuild. I thought that I gave them clear—'

'There they are now!' Strong interrupted. 'Look, just coming on deck.' He reached down and picked up the loudhailer. 'Ahoy, *Imogen*. Situation report, please.'

Now one of the artificers had picked up a megaphone, and was calling across to *Spearfish*. He could obviously see the officers on her bridge. 'Nothing we can't sort, Sir. Take about an hour, but we need a few bits.' Strong looked enquiringly at Bradley.

'Tell 'em that I want them both back here now!' Bradley's voice was almost a growl.

Once again Strong raised his loudhailer. 'You are both to return to the boat at once.' He watched the two artificers shake hands with another overall-clad figure – obviously *Imogen*'s engineer – before climbing back down into the small boat which, again manned by two of the trawler's crew, started to make its way towards *Spearfish*.

Strong bent towards the voice pipe and called to the control room, 'Second Cox'n and two to the casing. Stand by to receive motor boat.' Then, straightening up, he said to Bradley, 'What do you think then, Sir?'

Bradley was looking at his watch again. He had made his mind up. 'We're not stopping, Oliver! We've pushed our luck far enough already and it doesn't sound like they've got too serious a problem over there. Get our chaps back on board, and give the motor boat crew the bits they need to fix the problem. They can fix it themselves and we can be on our way.'

Strong nodded and looked towards the motor boat; now well on its way across. He leaned towards the voice pipe again. 'Bridge – Control. Chop chop, the casing party.'

Bradley again studied the trawler through his glasses. There was now little movement on her upper deck – just a couple of men lounging over her rail, smoking, or the occasional figure entering or leaving the hatch that Bradley assumed led down to her engine room. Obviously their interest in *Spearfish* had diminished.

'Ahoy, *Spearfish!*'

Bradley focused his glasses on the large figure leaning on the rails outside of the trawler's bridge.

'I thank you for your'elp,' shouted Jackson.

Bradley reached for the loudhailer. 'I'm sorry we can't stop any longer, Skipper. I'm sending over the spares you need, and then we have to go.'

'Aye, 'appen we'll manage,' replied Jackson. Then he added, 'Dost tha not want tha fish, Captain? I'm gettin' some nice pieces sorted.'

'Sorry, can't stop'

'What's 'appened to thee then, Lad? Looks like tha's taken a right good thumpin!'

'It's a long story.' Bradley was fast getting the feeling that this conversation could last a long time; he'd best cut it short now. 'Once again, I'm sorry that we can't help you further, Skipper. Perhaps you'd be good enough to get a signal off to Admiralty, telling them about us. We have no means of transmission. We wish you good luck with your repairs and Godspeed back to the UK.' He lowered his loudhailer and ducked down out of sight.

Jackson shouted back, 'Already sent one, but I'll send another to make sure.'

Now *Imogen's* motor boat was again bumping alongside *Spearfish's* port ballast tanks, and the willing hands of the casing party helped the two returning artificers aboard.

'Go below and report to the engineer officer,' Bradley called from the bridge. 'Organise the spares they need, and get 'em up here as quickly as possible.'

Ten minutes later a bulky waterproof bag containing several individually wrapped parcels was passed up through the tower to the waiting second cox'n, who then passed it across to the two men in the waiting motor boat. 'Cop this lot then, gents; this should sort you out.' Then he looked up towards Bradley, who was leaning over the bridge.

Bradley shouted, 'Thank you, Second Cox'n. Get the men below', and watched with relief as the lines were cast off and the motor boat pulled away. Then he shot a quick glance across to the trawler. Only her helmsman was visible on her bridge now. 'Good luck to you, Captain Jackson,' he muttered. Then, turning to Strong, he said, 'I'm going below now, Oliver. Stand by to dive as soon as you've cleared the bridge.'

Back in the control room, Bradley trained the attack periscope on the trawler. He watched as her motor boat reached her, and saw the bundle of spares passed up to the waiting hands. Then, turning to Crane, who was leaning against the chart table, he said, 'Well, they've got their spares aboard, Eric. Are they going to manage on their own?'

'From what the lads have told me, it were a fairly simple snag, Sir,' Crane replied. 'With the stuff that we've just given them, which was mainly new filters, they should be up and running within the hour.'

'Well, I just hope they were right.' Bradley was looking through the periscope again. 'I really don't like leaving them until I know that they're properly sorted.' He looked around at the expectant faces of the control room team, and then glued his eye to the periscope once more. 'One thing is for sure though: we can't really afford to wait about up here for much longer. Helm, tell the officer of the watch, from the captain, "Chop chop with clearing the bridge".'

★   ★   ★   ★   ★

Portrova was still on his bridge when a call summoned him to the radar room, and in less than half a minute he was stood behind his operators in the darkened room. Now he peered intently through red-rimmed eyes at the dull orange orb of the screen on one of his sets, while at the same time trying to take in the garbled report from the operator.

At first the orange mottled patterns on the screen meant little, if anything, to him. Even had he been wide awake this ever-changing array would have needed a much closer examination before any sense could be made of it.

'So,' he growled, 'what do I look for?'

The operator was nervous. He knew his captain's mood swings only too well, and the past few hours aboard *Otvashni* had not been good hours for anyone. Just minutes earlier he had been plucking up the courage to waken Portrova, then thankfully Bassisty had come in and the decision had been taken out of the operator's hands.

Bassisty said, 'There is a small contact, Kapitan – see? There, to the south-west.' The operator tapped the outer edge of the screen with a pencil, and Bassisty continued, 'It is small, difficult to see. There is much interference due to the sea state. And the contact is very weak. It is right on the—'

'Range?' Portrova grunted.

'About thirty kilometres, Kapitan. We think the contact is stopped!'

Another grunt from Portrova.

Then Bassisty said, 'It is a small vessel, Comrad Kapitan. First she moves but then she is stopped.' He sounded even more nervous than the radar operator.

Portrova grunted again and leaned further forward to inspect the screen more closely, studying the fine line of the cursor as it completed each rotation of the screen.

'See there!' The operator again tapped the screen with his pencil. 'She bears 290 degrees off our left beam, Kapitan.'

Portrova again grunted, waiting until the cursor circled back to the spot the operator had indicated. Yes, sure enough, there it was! Now he could see it for himself. Just a blip, a small orange blip, momentarily highlighted then fading with hardly an after-trace as the cursor moved on. But he knew that in this area and at this time, this blip, this momentary smudge, could only be one thing: it would be the British submarine. He wondered fleetingly whether they knew he was approaching them fast, and if so, why they hadn't dived. But then, of course, they would have no radar; he had seen to that. But they could have sonar, if only passive, so they could be hearing him. Then he remembered his damaged propeller. By the gods, they *must* be hearing this singing propeller! He grabbed for the microphone to the bridge and yelled to the bridge, 'Stop right engine. Maintain a speed to give ten knots.' At ten knots he knew that he could be on his target within an hour and a half.

For the next ninety minutes Portrova moved constantly between the bridge and the radar office, smoking cigarette after cigarette, occasionally muttering under his breath but speaking to no one. He brought *Otvashni* around towards the radar contact and now he was rapidly closing the range between *Otvashni* and this small orange blip on her radar screen. Now the time was 10.45 and it was still very dark. The target was now less than nine kilometres away.

He stood on the bridge beside Carlov and the watch officer. As *Otvashni* slowed, her pitching and rolling into the head swell became even worse. They braced themselves against anything that was solid and stared through binoculars straight ahead across *Otvashni*'s seesawing bows into the still-dark forenoon.

The contact had stopped four times since they'd first detected it, each stop lasting between periods of five to ten minutes, except for the last one, and that had been for almost an hour. But now it was moving again, and it was very near. The range on radar was now less than two kilometres, and each watcher aboard *Otvashni* was straining through watering eyes, determined to be the first to turn this contact into a visual sighting.

Portrova was convinced now. This contact was *Spearfish* – it had to be. Everything pointed to it being *Spearfish*. The size of the contact was that of a submarine. The general course of the contact was that which *Spearfish* would be taking. And the stops? Well, obviously she was stopping intermittently to listen for signs of pursuit or, better still, she was having severe technical problems.

'So, my English friend, soon we will meet again, eh?' Portrova's heavy jowls creased in a humourless smile. 'But this time there will be no escape, this time you will—'

'Kapitan.' The loudspeaker at the back of the bridge interrupted him. It was Bassisty, still in the radar room. 'Kapitan, we now have two contacts, both in the same position. Both appear to be of the same size. Range now is three kilometres.'

Portrova again rushed down to the radar room, calling to Carlov over his shoulder, 'Keep a good watch there, Comrad. I will return soon.'

Now in front of the radar set once more, Portrova studied the screen. Bassisty was right. There were two distinct blips on the screen, almost on top of each other, dead ahead at a distance of three kilometres. He groped for his cigarettes, needing time to think.

Bassisty spoke over Portrova's shoulder, his tone now a mixture of apprehension and apology. 'We have two contacts, Kapitan. Both are stopped. They are almost identical. We could not see the second. Only when the range was reduced could we see him, but...' He stopped in mid-sentence, leaning forward to peer at the screen more closely, the darkness of the radar room hiding the puzzlement clouding his features. Turning to Portrova he muttered, 'Kapitan, we have lost one of the contacts. She is no longer there!'

To Bassisty's surprise and relief, Portrova answered quietly, calmly, 'No, my friend, you have seen two contacts and I have seen two contacts. There are two vessels, but they will now be so close to each other as to be indistinguishable on radar.'

Although outwardly calm, Portrova's thoughts were now racing. The Britisher meeting up with an ally was something that he had not foreseen. Again the question of Ravoski and the four armed guards aboard *Spearfish* came into mind. How had Ravoski and his men let this happen? There was only one answer: they had somehow been overpowered at the time the submarine had slipped the tow. They would now be prisoners aboard the British, and as such could be of no help to him. He grunted, then aloud but to no one in particular he muttered, 'So, Britisher, you seek to make a rendezvous, eh?' He drew hard on his cigarette and remained deep in thought. With his enemy just one kilometre away what action should he take? Darkness was still his ally, and the Britishers were obviously unaware of his presence since they hadn't attempted to move or dive. So, should he risk a stealthy approach and try to take them both unawares, or should he now simply rush them? Either approach contained a high risk of losing them: they would split up and dive independently and he would almost certainly lose one of them, if not both. No, he wanted both of them now. Important information would have been exchanged. He would rush them, and if they tried to dive he would use his radar-directed heavy guns. He *must* take both of them. At this short range he would be accurate enough to warn them not to try and escape. Then he would close in, using his active sonar for the capture. He stood up and, after grinding his cigarette into an ashtray, made for the door and climbed the ladder back to the bridge. Rejoining Carlov and the watch officer, he raised his glasses and peered into the darkness. In the direction of his enemy he muttered, 'So, Commander Bradley, you seek to speak to a friend? OK. Well now I will be your friend and I will speak to you, and how is it you say? We will catch two birds with one stone! Prepare all weapons, Comrad Carlov. We take our ship into action. Report immediately when ready.'

★ ★ ★ ★ ★

The time was 12.07. *Spearfish* was again at periscope depth, with her crew still closed up at diving stations. She was moving slowly – just enough to maintain a distance between herself and *Imogen*, who was now lying about 1000 yards off her stern. This combination of slow speed with the heavy surface swell made accurate depth-keeping difficult. Strong was kept busy holding the trim. Bradley, on the attack periscope, carefully studied *Imogen*, as he had been for the last twenty minutes or so. *Imogen* was still stopped, yawing, apparently helplessly in the heavy swell.

Bradley was becoming increasingly impatient. Why the hell were they taking so long to sort out what had been reported as a simple problem? He had given them the spares they needed but as yet there were still no signs of her getting underway. He was loath to leave her like this, and in any other circumstances would have had no hesitation in staying. But these were special circumstances, special times. He couldn't afford to wait here for much longer. Stepping back from the periscope, he muttered, 'Dip and raise', and as the periscope again slithered up from its well he immediately trained it back on the trawler. Then turning to Ravoski, who was standing by the chart table, he stepped back and motioned to the Russian, 'Here, take a look, Viktor. Nothing much happening up there, I'm afraid.'

'Thank you, Kapitan.' Ravoski watched the trawler intently for less than two minutes, and then began to swing the periscope around through a full circle, slowly, carefully. Bradley knew that the Russian was studying the horizon. What was he looking for? He nudged the Russian's shoulder and Ravoski immediately stepped away from the periscope. He was smiling.

'How is it you say, Kapitan? One all-round sweep complete; nothing to report.'

Again all those doubts and suspicions started to flourish in Bradley's mind. Nothing to report, eh! What the hell did he expect to report? Had he been looking for something? A Russian destroyer, perhaps? He again glued his left eye to the monocular eyepiece and resumed his watch on *Imogen*. 'For Christ's sake,' he muttered to no one in particular, 'what the hell are they doing over there? We've given them the spares. They've told us they could sort it. So what's the bloody hold-up?' This was a situation he hadn't expected, and certainly hadn't needed. If it continued it would, at best, delay *Spearfish*'s escape or, at worse, could prevent her escape altogether. He would give them just another ten minutes, then, whether the trawler was ready to proceed or not, he would leave the area and be on his way. He turned to Bishop, who was leaning over the chart table. 'Here, Tim, take over the stick for a while and keep a close watch for any sign of her getting underway. I'll be back in a short while.' He went towards the sound room, pausing briefly to nod at Strong. 'You're doing a grand job there, Oliver. I know it's not easy in this sea but it won't be for much longer.' Strong made no reply, continuing to concentrate on the depth gauges in front of him.

Bradley, now in the sound room, mentally cursed the situation he'd put himself in. Should he really be waiting here like this, playing nursemaid to this bloody fishing boat while putting his own vessel at extreme risk? These Russians wanted *Spearfish* and they would surely take her if she didn't stay ahead of them. And what about Ravoski? Whatever the reason, his doubts about this Russian had again been steadily growing, though he didn't know why. But these doubts would be bound to shadow his future decisions, his thinking. Or was he simply being paranoid? The only thing he was really sure of at this time was that he could take no chances. He would be watching this enigmatic Russian like a hawk from now on in. Then without warning, *Spearfish* jerked violently, almost throwing him off his feet.

In the control room Bishop, still with the attack periscope trained on *Imogen,* straightened and blinked in astonishment, while from the sound room an equally startled Kinross tore off his earphones and yelled into his intercom, 'Sonar — Control. Three loud surface explosions. Dead astern. Fifteen hundred yards.'

'Bloody hell! Flood "Q". Go to 200 feet.' Ignoring his microphone, Bishop then bawled, 'Captain to the control room at the rush!' But Bradley was already by his side.

★　★　★　★　★

Aboard *Imogen* Jackson was saying, 'Well, they buggered off a bit sharpish, didn't they? Couldn't even be bothered to 'ang around for the fish we 'ad ready fer 'em. The boys picked out some nice ones an' all.'

'Yeah, well, that's the navy for yuh — rushing here, rushing there,' replied Barnes.

Both Jackson and Barnes had been standing together on *Imogen*'s winch deck, waiting by the engine room hatch for their engineer's progress report. They had just watched *Spearfish* disappear beneath the surface some twenty minutes earlier, and were wondering why the hell she had shot off without even waiting to see that they were going to be all right.

'Well — can't say as I blame 'em,' replied Jackson. 'They obviously didn't appreciate that bloody destroyer's company a while back. Can't think why they were under tow though. They must 'ave got power, or they wouldn't 'ave been here just now to lend us an 'and!'

Barnes nodded. 'I don't know about that, but I just wish our boys down below would pull their bloody fingers out and give us some power to get movin' again. Anyone would think that… Jesus Christ! What the hell's that?'

Jackson and Barnes simultaneously turned towards *Imogen*'s port side, both looking upward, both trying to locate the source of the noise that now suddenly blotted out their conversation. There was a high-pitched whistle, or perhaps more of a low angry roar which, in reality, lasted for just fragments of a second before being eclipsed completely by the loud explosion in the water. Both watched in complete amazement at the huge spout of white water now rising to at least eighty feet above the surface of the sea, some 500 yards off their starboard beam.

'Bloody 'ell, Skip, I may be wrong but that looked like a bloody bomb to me!' Barnes was visibly shaken. 'Fer Christ's sake, wot the 'ell's goin' on 'ere?'

'You tell me, Joe.' Jackson was equally shocked. 'That were bloody shell fire! Some bastard's 'avin a go at us. I know a...' His words were now drowned out by the noise of another angry roar directly overhead. This time the noise was more of a growl, and low enough for them to feel the shock of displaced air before the shell exploded into the surface. It was closer this time – no more than about 300 yards off their port beam, and again sending a spectacular waterspout skyward. But this time the force of the explosion was close enough to send *Imogen* heeling sharply to starboard.

Both men grabbed wildly for the upper deck rail, and Jackson shouted, 'Fuckin' 'ell, Joe, we're bein' shelled! Some bastard's tryin' to do fer us. Get yerself to the wireless office. Tell Jimmy Frost to get a signal off now! An' don't forget to give 'em our exact position. I'll warn the rest of the boys below.'

Barnes rushed up the bridge ladder, calling over his shoulder, 'I'll check our position from the chart first, an' give it to—'

Those were the last words that Joe Barnes was ever to utter; he died instantly while frantically pushing open the ever-jammed bridge door. Inside the bridge, Barry, the helmsman, departed this world with the same alacrity. No time for fear, no time for pain, no time for anything. Both died instantaneously, neither knowing why.

In the radio shack, beneath and just aft of the bridge, Jimmy Frost, the "sparker", was not quite so lucky. He did feel pain – excruciating pain, though only momentarily. And he experienced the nauseating horror at the sight of the skin peeling from his blackened smoking frame, though only for the time it took the blast and searing heat to propel his melting body though the open door of the wireless office and over the guard rail, where he died before hitting the water.

This third shell from *Otvashni*'s 5.1 inch forward turret landed directly on *Imogen*'s bridge. Now there was no bridge – at least nothing recognisable as a bridge. But there was a gaping hole in her starboard side through which the icy Barents was now gushing. *Imogen* was sinking.

Jackson had been about to lift the hatch down to the engine room. Now he awoke to find himself draped around one of the twin-stern trawl posts. Opening his eyes, he stared through a red haze that wouldn't clear. Both his hands were locked around a trawl wire with a grip so fierce they now oozed blood. He never noticed this blood and he felt no pain. The trawl winch was secured and was not going to move. He blinked again, but the red haze covering his eyes still wouldn't clear, and at this moment in time he could still think of no good reason why he should be where he now was. Coughing, he spat up a mouthful of thickly clotted blood. Then he felt the pain in his legs – sharp, agonising stabs that now spread upward through his whole body like a series of electric shocks, forcing him to scream out in agony. 'Christ! What the hell's happening?' He tried to open the aching fingers of his right hand, attempting to release his grip on the wire, again screaming at the acute pain, but his fingers still wouldn't move. Now he was moaning, completely bewildered. 'What the fuck's goin' on?' he repeated, the question bubbling through another mouthful of blood. But there was no answer. There was no one there to give him an answer.

At last, as if with a will of its own, his right hand suddenly unclenched itself from the wire and his legs jerked downward. Again he screamed in agony as a fiery pain in his left leg shot through his body. Then his left hand released its hold on the wire and he fell heavily to the deck. The pain in both his legs was now excruciating – more than he could bear, blotting out all other feeling. Again he lapsed into unconsciousness, while his precious *Imogen* heeled ever more to starboard.

Jackson returned to consciousness in less than a minute. He could no longer feel his legs but now the red mist had cleared from his eyes, and for the first time since the shelling had started he began to think coherently. He called loudly, 'Where is every bastard?' There was no answer. Climbing painfully to his hands and knees, he slid across the steeply listing deck and landed heavily into the starboard scuppers. 'Oh my Christ,' he gasped as the searing pain in his legs came back. He began to crawl forward, gritting his teeth against the pain and the thick clogging blood bubbling from his mouth. Somehow he knew that *Imogen* was dying, but he still didn't know why.

Finally he reached the foot of the ladder to the starboard side of the bridge, pulling himself to his feet and ignoring the pain as he gripped the blackened and bent steel rungs. Now completely oblivious to the burning flesh on the palms of each of his hands, he hauled himself upward, rung by rung. Reaching the top, he caught his breath and leaned heavily against a steel bridge support rail that still glowed red. The left sleeve of his jacket burst into flames and with a curse he discarded it and stumbled into a wheelhouse which was no longer there.

He felt something soft under his feet, and looked down. It was an arm – still smouldering, charred, blackened, but definitely an arm, complete with Joe's big chrome watch: the one that he had always joked would take him to the bottom if he were ever washed over the side. He stared down at the arm and began to sob uncontrollably, the tears carving channels down his smoke-blackened cheeks. 'Fuck you, Joe. It shoulda been me up here, not you. What the 'ell happened anyway?' Again, his question would not be answered.

Then, exactly seven minutes after the third shell struck, *Imogen* abandoned her short struggle for life and with a final violent shudder, rolled over onto her starboard side and sank.

Instinctively swimming for his life, Jackson didn't even know that he was in the water. He should have followed *Imogen* to her grave. That would have been his wish. There were no other swimmers in that cold and empty sea.

★　★　★　★　★

Even at this short range and firing by radar, scoring a direct hit with the third shot on a target as small as *Imogen* would have been classed as very satisfactory shooting in any gunnery officer's book. Many would have called it a fluke.

Surely only fate could take the credit for this sort of accuracy. Certainly *Otvashni*'s gunnery officer would never see the success or, in this case, the absolute pointlessness of the devastation his guns had caused that morning, since the object of their fury was now lying in pieces on the seabed.

The thundering reverberation from *Otvashni*'s forward turrets had wrenched Dimitry Borstoy out of a sound sleep, his first real sleep for many days. Now, as he scrambled, still fully clothed, from his bunk, his legs got caught up in the bunk rail and he landed in a cursing heap on the deck. 'That was gunfire!' he muttered. 'That was our guns! What is that fool Portrova playing at now?' Still muttering, he hauled his skeletal frame up from the deck and struggled into his oversized heavy black leather coat. Then reaching for his ushanka, he burst from his cabin and scurried up to *Otvashni*'s bridge. 'What is happening, Comrad Kapitan?'

Hearing Borstoy's shrill squawk, Portrova swung around to face him, fully prepared for another confrontation with this man whom he detested so much. 'While you peacefully sleep, Comrad, we have again tracked down our quarry. The Britisher will not escape this time!' Portrova's voice was cold, flat. There was no attempt to conceal the contempt he felt for this KGB agent. 'We have fired warning shots to deter them from escape. Now we will proceed to capture them. Do you not think that that I have acted in accordance with my orders, Comrad Borstoy?'

Portrova's contempt was not lost on Borstoy, or to anyone else on the bridge. Borstoy's reply came in a vociferous snarl. 'You will not sink this British submarine, Kapitan! It must be taken back with us for investigation. This is the wish of the admiral. These are your orders from Moscow, and you will comply with them, Comrad Kapitan. You will not sink her! We have our—'

Borstoy's outburst was interrupted by the voice of Bassisty echoing once more through the bridge loudspeaker from the radar office.

'Kapitan! We now have no contacts on radar.'

'So, Kapitan Portrova, it seems that she has either escaped you once more or you have destroyed her.' Borstoy's voice was a slow malignant hiss. 'In either event, you have *again* failed to carry out your orders.'

Portrova was trying hard to ignore his overwhelming hatred for this man and, despite the bitter cold, he could feel his face burning with anger. He swung around to Carlov, his voice shaking with rage, 'Maintain your course, Comrad Carlov. Go to full speed on your port engine and double the lookouts. She must be here somewhere.' He raised his glasses and stared out across *Otvashni's* bow. They had to be here somewhere; surely they could not have sunk two targets with just three rounds? If there were two stationary submarines, then they must have both dived at his opening shot. So his plan had not worked. Inwardly he cursed himself for his impatience. Again he had acted impetuously. Perhaps he should have waited, given it more thought. Perhaps he should not have used his big guns. In this visibility *Otvashni* could have been on them before they realised she was there. They had been stopped and very close together, almost certainly transferring information. Now they were gone, and one of them would doubtless have a full weapons system with active sonar and radar and, more importantly, the means to transmit on her radio. It could have been so easy, but the fact that Borstoy could be right made him feel even worse.

Again Borstoy's whining voice interrupted his thoughts. 'This must be reported to Moscow, Kapitan. They will need to know at once that we have destroyed, or again lost, the British submarine. We will—'

Now again Borstoy was interrupted, this time by a voice from the loudspeaker at the front of the bridge.

'Bridge, this is Sonar. We have a contact bearing 10 right. Possibly a dived submarine.' Portrova was halfway down the ladder to the sonar room before the broadcast had finished.

Now in the darkened sonar room, Portrova crouched behind the two operators, peering over their shoulders at the visual display. The right-hand operator removed his earphones and spoke over his shoulder in a voice that was almost a whisper, 'We picked up this contact four minutes ago, Kapitan. At first it was unclear. We were not sure. Then after the guns, it became more clear. Her bearing is ten degrees to the right of our ship's head. The contact is at a depth of seventy metres. Her range is now about two kilometres. We are closing rapidly.'

The operator replaced his headset, and continued to turn the small wheel on the front of the set, fingering it lightly, delicately tuning it with just slight movement while listening carefully, concentrating. Now he again removed the headset. 'Yes, Kapitan, the contact is a submarine. She is speeding up but, like ourselves, is using only one propeller.' He pointed to a hazy pale green trace on the display. 'There are no other contacts.' Portrova studied the screen carefully, and then the contact was gone. 'See. She is changing depth, Kapitan; she is moving upward.' The operator sounded excited, and then in a lower tone he added, 'The visual is not good; the sea state gives much interference and there are many thermal layers. But she is a submarine, Kapitan, and I say that she is moving south-west.'

Portrova straightened up. So this Britisher was still there. But where was that second contact? He suddenly felt an overwhelming sense of relief, though he didn't know why. What he did know now was that the game was still on. Never mind Borstoy, or his masters back at the Kremlin, or even his own naval prospects, for that matter. Now this game was between himself and Bradley. Together they would play it to the end, no matter what that end might be. He patted both operators on their shoulders. 'You have done your work well, my friends.' Turning, he made his way back to the bridge.

★   ★   ★   ★   ★

Bradley had cautiously brought *Spearfish* back to periscope depth and was now doing an all-round sweep. Behind him Bishop was muttering, his face strained, confused. 'She's blown up, Sir. She just bloody well blew up.'

Bishop was right. *Imogen* was now heeled over to starboard by at least forty-five degrees, with flames and black smoke belching from her decks, and a bridge structure that was now barely recognisable. 'My God! She's in a bad way! What the hell's happened?' Bradley spoke through clenched teeth. 'Come around to one nine five, Oliver, and go to half ahead. We'd better get a bit closer. Maybe there's survivors, though by the look of her it'll be a bloody miracle if there are!'

Slowly and carefully, Bradley conned *Spearfish* towards the stricken trawler, his limited vision searching the white-crested swell for any sign of swimmers.

Now the voice of Kinross came across the sound room intercom. 'Captain, Sir – sound room. HE bearing zero-five-zero. Single diesel recip, approaching fast.'

Bradley swung his periscope around to zero-five-zero. 'Can't see anything, but the visibility's not up to much: dark up there.' He moved the periscope back to focus again on *Imogen*, now lying almost on her side in the water, and still belching smoke and flame. Then suddenly there was no more smoke, no more flames, and no more *Imogen*.

'Jesus! She's gone!' Bradley continued to stare almost in disbelief at the spot where the trawler had been. 'Can't see anyone in the water. Doesn't look like anyone got off. Poor bastards. What the hell went wrong? Go to 200 feet again, Oliver. I'll be in the sound room.'

Kinross was now in front of the set. He removed his earphones and turned as Bradley came through the door. 'It's me thinking we've got the Russian again, Sir. She's coming in at about sixteen knots, but she's only using one screw.'

'And it's me thinking she's on to us again,' muttered Bradley wryly.

Kinross nodded. 'Anyway, Sir, her range is now down to less than 1500 yards and she's closing fast!'

'Keep on her, and keep me up to date.' Bradley hurried back to the control room and ordered 'ultra-quiet routine'. There was nothing he could do here now, no reason for him to stay. As *Spearfish* passed 150 feet, Bradley ordered a homeward course of two-one-zero, and *Spearfish* quietly slipped away.

CHAPTER TEN

Ossie Jackson was not aware of the hands that had hauled him from the freezing waters of the Barents. *Otvashni* had come to a stop almost at the spot where *Imogen* had sunk. An alert lookout had sighted his inert body, face down on the crest of a swell, and they had lowered a boat to recover him. All the signs indicated that he was dead, but as they dragged him over the low gunwales of the motor boat he had groaned loudly in pain. They had lain him face down in the bottom of the boat, where he retched and gagged violently, bringing up mouthfuls of sea water, vomit and blood before again lapsing into unconsciousness.

On reaching *Otvashni*, the motor boat's crew had tied a line under Jackson's arms and pulled him unceremoniously up the ship's side, where he was now flopped face down on the upper deck, surrounded by a circle of curious Russians. Portrova, Carlov and Borstoy had now come down from the bridge, and the three of them pushed their way to the front of the growing circle of crewmen. Carlov and Borstoy leaned over the prone figure, and Carlov turned him over so that he lay on his back, still unconscious.

Portrova said nothing. Looking down at the body now lying at his feet, all the memories of his first meeting with the British on that cold December night in the North Sea almost fifteen years ago came flooding back to him as though it had been yesterday. He felt no pity for this man – just hate. All he could see now was the drink-sodden face of that trawler captain. Then, no longer able to control this hate, impulsively, almost instinctively, he raised his foot and kicked the man at his feet hard in the ribs. 'This, English fisherman, is for my friend Gregori,' his words barely audible to those around him.

Borstoy now stepped forward to nudge Jackson with his foot. Getting no response, he too kicked him hard in the side. Carlov reached out and clutched Borstoy's bony shoulders, pulling him away from Jackson. 'That is enough, Comrad. Can you not see that this man is badly injured?' Borstoy muttered something under his breath, and shook himself free from Carlov's grasp. Carlov now bent forward, his face close to the ear of the unconscious Jackson. He spoke slowly and clearly. 'Who are you, my friend?'

Jackson groaned loudly. His eyes flickered briefly, then opened fully to stare up at the sea of faces above him. Again groaning with the effort, he forced himself up to rest on one elbow, his face white, contorted with pain. But he had lost none of his spirit.

'The name's Jackson.' His voice was hoarse, defiant. 'Cap'n Jackson to you lot! Skipper of the British trawler *Imogen*, which I've just lost. Christ knows why – she just blew up. An' among other things, I think me fuckin' legs is busted!' He looked around him and groaned again. 'Where are the rest of my boys?' Exhausted with the effort of talking, he coughed again violently, collapsing flat on his back before breaking into a further unbroken paroxysm of vomiting which lasted for a full five minutes.

Portrova eyed him coldly. Now, at this moment, all those years of what had become a semi-dormant hatred rose up, and it was now consuming him. It was as though that fateful night of events in the North Sea had happened only yesterday, but now the roles were completely reversed. Here he was, the kapitan of his ship, standing over the half-drowned body of a British trawlerman. Surely this was more than coincidence? No, this was fate. At last the gods had answered his prayers for revenge, and he would take that revenge in full measure. It would have been far better for this Britisher if he had been left to drown.

Jackson had finally stopped coughing and Carlov ordered two watching seamen to raise him to his feet. 'Take him to the sick quarters. Tell the medical staff to make sure that he is dried and made warm.' Carlov turned to Portrova. 'As you can see, Kapitan, there is no point in further questions at this time.'

But had the light been better, and had Carlov paused long enough to look more closely at his captain's face, there would have been no missing the raw hatred still burning in Portrova's eyes.

Borstoy again stepped forward, his yellow eyes gleaming malevolently at the man now supported in front of him. 'You are a fool, Jackson, but do you think that we too are fools? A short while ago you were meeting with a British spy submarine! Do you think that we do not know this? You say that your vessel somehow exploded, but you do not know why. Well, we have an excellent gunnery officer aboard this ship. Yes, we sank your ship, Captain Jackson. You are the only survivor. We will now go on to track down your friends in the submarine, and they too will be caught, as you now are.' But by now Jackson was in no condition to either hear or understand Borstoy's tirade.

'Enough! That is enough, Comrad Borstoy.' Carlov beckoned to two seamen. 'Take him to the sick quarters now!'

Portrova's sloe-black eyes remained impassively fixed on the Englishman's back, as now, with a thick blanket draped over him and two seamen supporting him on their shoulders, Jackson was dragged across the deck towards the watertight door of the after deckhouse. Jackson cried out in agony as, without pausing, they hauled him through the open door, and his mutilated legs scraped over the low steel coaming. As Portrova watched them go, all his instincts told him that this trawler had been a spy ship and that she was the second contact. But he doubted he would ever prove it now. Again he'd acted impetuously: he should never have opened fire on her. He also knew that he may well have stirred up an international hornet's nest and his masters would not thank him for that. She had been stopped, a sitting duck, perhaps broken down. Should he not have just closed with her and boarded her? Yes, of course, that is what he should have done. But those guns: he had certainly never dreamed that he would score a direct hit in just three shots – something else they would not thank him for back in the Kremlin. He reached into his pocket for his cigarette case. Lighting up, he inhaled deeply.

Standing beside Portrova, Carlov watched Jackson being dragged through the hatch. Then he too lit a cigarette, and as though reading his kapitan's thoughts he said, 'The fisherman: she was a spy, Comrad Kapitan – you can be sure of that. She was in league with the submarine. That is the way they do their work.'

Portrova blew out a further cloud of smoke. 'I hope that you are right, Comrad Carlov, for all our sakes.'

Back on his bridge once more, Portrova settled himself in his chair and lit another cigarette. Despite having regained contact with what must surely be the British submarine, he was not at ease. The sinking of that fisherman worried him deeply. He realised now that although he had never consciously meant to sink her, if this sinking came to light his country might lose any advantage they may have had in being the victim of British aggression. To sink a British vessel without warning or indeed reason would surely put a different slant on this affair, and it would then be the Soviet navy who would be seen as the aggressor.

★　★　★　★　★

Jackson regained consciousness some thirty minutes after being laid on a cot in *Otvashni's* sick quarters, and immediately wished that he hadn't. He groaned loudly as the pain now consuming his large frame returned to torture him. He tried to move his legs, which were covered by a coarse woollen blanket, but there was no movement and the agonising stabs of pain resulting from his efforts caused him to stop and cry out in agony.

A tall, heavy-set figure clad in a white coat emerged from the gloom of the dimly lit sick bay. Leaning over Jackson, this figure placed an ice-cold cloth on his forehead.

Jackson looked up through glazed eyes at the pale, round-faced shaven head above him. 'Where am I? An' who the 'ell are you?'

Cold water from the cloth now started to run into his eyes, making it even more difficult to focus. He reached up with both hands and angrily threw the cloth aside. Both his arms were heavily bandaged and the agony brought about by his sudden movement caused him to snort with pain. His tears began to mingle with the cold water from the cloth. 'Who the fuck are you, fella?' He was now shouting in what was a fruitless effort to blot out his pain.

The Russian sick berth attendant reclaimed the cold cloth from the deck and placed it once more over Jackson's forehead. '*Vrach, nam noojen vrach.*'

'For Christ's sake, speak English!' Jackson's voice was barely a croak.

'*Savyetskee.*' The eyes in the moon face clouded with a mixture of sympathy and puzzlement. '*Savyetskee!*' He placed a hand on his chest. '*Ya, Yuri, Kapitan. Otvashni. Jdat!*' He straightened and moved towards the door while beckoning to Jackson with a reassuring palm. '*Preenaseet, Kapitan.*'

Jackson now lay silent, feverish, sweating profusely, still not knowing where he was. He gritted his teeth, fighting the pain in his arms, which now even eclipsed the pain in his legs. 'Come back, yuh little bastard; don't just leave me 'ere.' Now he began to realise that the pain wracking his body was made even worse by the movement under him. He was in a ship. Then he remembered *Imogen* and his last moments aboard her. He shot upright in his bed, staring, horrified, before collapsing back once more into the merciful arms of sleep.

Less than five minutes later he again awoke with a start to find another face leaning over him. This time it was a younger face – a dark, bearded man in his early twenties, again dressed in a white coat which, though meaningless to Jackson, bore the shoulder insignias of a Starshl Leitenant. The moon-faced sick berth attendant hovered behind him.

'So, my friend, you are a British seaman.' It was a statement rather than a question. The voice coming from the white coat was soft, moderated, and the English was good. He reached out and removed the cloth from Jackson's sweating brow, replacing it with the back of his hand. 'You are a very sick man. You are the only survivor found. I am a doktar! You are in much pain?'

Jackson tried to focus through pain-filled eyes. 'Fuckin' agony, doc,' he groaned. 'I'm in fuckin' agony, an' you can take my word for that!'

'I will do whatever I can to help you. One of your legs is badly crushed and you are very badly bruised but I think that no bones are broken. Also, you have many burns on your arms. They will be very painful, but not serious. Given time and rest, you will recover. I will see to that. Now I will give you something for this pain.' The doctor straightened and spoke quietly to his assistant standing behind him, who promptly disappeared into the background to return almost immediately with a glass of water and two white tablets.

The doctor again leaned over Jackson, pushing the tablets through his dry lips. 'These will help you, my friend.' He then placed the glass at Jackson's mouth, and Jackson gratefully gulped down the cold water.

'Thanks, Pal.' Jackson lay back and closed his eyes but he opened them again almost immediately, startled at the loud bang on the metal door of the sick bay, which swung open to reveal the diminutive figure of Borstoy.

Stepping carefully over the raised coaming at the foot of the watertight door into the sick bay, Borstoy's eyes were already fixed on the inert figure lying in the bunk. He motioned to the doctor. 'You will leave us, Doktar. I wish to interview our guest.'

'This man is very weak, Comrad Borstoy. He is also very unwell and should not talk at this time.'

But Borstoy wasn't listening. 'You will leave us, Kapitan, and you will take your assistant. I will tell you when to return.'

'But,' the doctor repeated, 'the patient is very weak, Comrad Borstoy, and he is still in much pain. I have just given him a sedative. He cannot answer your questions at this time.'

'So, he is in much pain, eh? That is good! But you *will* leave now, Comrad Doktar.'

Even in the semi-darkness of the sick bay, the doctor couldn't fail to notice the gloating look of satisfaction now in the KGB agent's eyes. He motioned towards his assistant. 'Come, Yuri.' Together they left, shutting the door behind them.

Borstoy moved towards the bunk, his yellow, snake-like eyes fixed unblinkingly on Jackson. 'So, Englishman, first you spy upon us, and then you look to us for your salvation!'

The tablets were beginning to work and Jackson's pain was now more bearable. He began to feel distinctly drowsy. 'An 'oo the 'ell might you be? Not that I give a shit!' Jackson spoke warily through clenched teeth, sensing immediately that this man was no friend.

'I am called Borstoy. I am of the Russian Intelligence Service. And you, Englishman, will listen to me. I will ask the questions, and you will answer me!'

'I ain't in no mood fer questions an' answers, Pal, so why don't you just bugger off and leave me alone.'

Borstoy leaned forward and, showing surprising strength, he grasped the prone skipper by both shoulders and roughly pulled him into a sitting position. Then he stuffed two pillows behind Jackson's back to keep him upright. 'You will listen, and you will answer.' Borstoy spat his words into Jackson's face, his voice high-pitched, squeaky, excited. 'What is your name? What was the name of your ship? And what were you doing in these waters?'

Jackson looked long and hard into the mean yellow eyes now just inches from his face. 'My name's Jackson, Captain Jackson to you. My ship *was* called *Imogen* — trawler, but you already know that! An' what the 'ell do you think we were doing? Fishin', of course! There ain't no law against that, is there? We was well in international waters an' 'ad every right to be there.'

'Why were you in the company of a British submarine?' Borstoy's voice was now even higher-pitched as he pushed his face closer towards Jackson's. Leering malevolently, he went on, 'You were in command of a spy ship, Mr Kapitan Jackson, and you were liaising with the British submarine, which we know was also spying.'

'Don't be bloody daft, man.' Jackson's tone was contemptuous. Already he was growing very tired of this conversation. 'We broke down, didn't we! Some'ow we got sea water in our friggin' fuel system and the sub stopped to 'elp us. Then somehow we got blown up. God only knows 'ow that 'appened, but I'm beginnin' to get a fair idea. We 'ad a bloody good catch an' we shoulda been 'alfway 'ome by now!'

'Lies! Lies! I do not believe you.' Borstoy's voice was a venomous hiss. Then his tone suddenly moderated and he spoke almost normally. 'Tell me, Kapitan, was there any transfer of intelligence between your ship and the submarine before you so strangely exploded?'

'Intelligence? What the 'ell would I know about bloody intelligence?' Jackson yawned widely, his tiredness now becoming almost overpowering. 'Christ, what were in them pills?'

Borstoy ignored the question, still managing to control his tone. 'You are very tired, Comrad Kapitan, I know this. Soon you shall sleep all you want, but first you must answer my questions. Did you transfer intelligence information?'

Jackson yawned again but this time it was intentional. 'The only thing that were transferred was some spare parts to sort my engine out. I were goin' to give 'em some fish, but we never got around to that. Seems they was in a bit of a hurry.'

'Pah. You still lie to me!' Now Borstoy was back in high pitch. 'But I *will* have the truth.'

Jackson stared straight back into Borstoy's face. 'I've just told you the bleedin' truth, an' you can believe it or not believe it. Now piss off; I need to sleep.'

'Oh no, my foolish friend. You have no truth for me,' hissed Borstoy, 'but I have truth for you. You think that you can outwit us, eh? Never fear, we will soon catch up with your friends in the submarine; then we shall have the truth from them as well.' Now he leaned forward and glared malevolently into Jackson's face. 'But I will make you talk, Kapitan, and I will have the truth, even if I have to force this from you. We sank your ship, Kapitan, do you hear me? It was our guns that sank your ship! You are the only survivor. All your crew have died. That is my truth! Now perhaps I will have your truth.'

Jackson stared straight ahead, his face a complete blank as Borstoy's words slowly penetrated his mind. Now the memory of those last minutes aboard *Imogen* began to return. After a full minute of silence, he spoke in a voice that was no more than a low mutter.

'So it *was* you bastards! You sank my *Imogen*? An' you killed all my boys? Fouteen of 'em dead just 'cos you thought we were bloody spies?' His voice was now a mixture of incredulity, misery and anger. Turning again to stare into the face of his tormentor, the tears again ran freely down his cheeks, but this time they were tears of savage anger. Now he was again shouting, 'You sank my ship an' killed all my boys because you thought we was bloody spies?'

'We did only what was necessary.' There was no remorse in Borstoy's response, no pity for this man on the cot – just a gloating satisfaction.

'You're a shower of bloody 'eathens, 'an you'll pay in full for what you've done today.' With no change of expression on his face Jackson's right arm shot out from beneath the blanket and grasped the Russian tightly around the neck.

Borstoy squeaked in shocked surprise. That was all he was able to do as Jackson's grip tightened relentlessly around a neck so scrawny that his fingers almost met his thumb at the nape.

'So yuh did what yuh 'ad to do, eh? Well now I'm goin' to do what I 'ave to.' Ignoring the vicious pain in his arms, Jackson now reached out with his left hand and, locking both thumbs over Borstoy's bulging Adam's apple, he began increasing the pressure. Nothing would break his grip now; he must kill this Russian. Borstoy twisted and squirmed, trying to speak but making no real sound. Now his mouth sagged open and he began to drool over Jackson's bandaged arms. Jackson dragged Borstoy onto the cot almost on top of himself. The Russian's legs began to kick violently and his fear-filled eyes began to protrude from their sockets like pale yellow egg yolks as, slowly but surely, Jackson's huge hands squeezed the life from him. Then came the dull crack, the sound of breaking bone. Borstoy's neck had snapped and his body stopped squirming. Thrashing legs now lifeless, he lay motionless, like a rag doll, across Jackson's legs.

He had not heard Borstoy's neck snap and it was a full three minutes before he relaxed his grip on the Russian's throat. Then he had simply sat there, bolt upright in the cot, with Borstoy's frail corpse lying face downward across him, but through his tear-misted eyes he saw or felt nothing. Then, suddenly returning to reality, he shifted his gaze down to the face of the man he had just killed. Still feeling no regret, no remorse, he looked down almost vacantly at Borstoy's bulging eyes and his drool-stained open mouth. Then, as though filled with a sudden revulsion, he threw the body off the cot and fell back on his pillows, sobbing uncontrollably.

Some five minutes later the door of the sick berth opened and the white-coated doctor appeared, together with his assistant Yuri. Both men stood looking down at the crumpled body of Borstoy. The doctor leaned over Borstoy, feeling his neck for a pulse. Straightening, he turned to his assistant.

'Yuri, get the kapitan down here right away and say nothing to anyone but the kapitan.' He spoke in a rapid Russian staccato. Then turning to the still sobbing Jackson on the bunk, he shook his head and muttered, 'Oh, my friend, what have you done? Where will this lead?'

★ ★ ★ ★ ★

Portrova was once again back in *Otvashni*'s sound room. Standing behind his senior sonar operator, he carefully watched the visual display in front of them and listened to the constant ping that now echoed from *Otvashni*'s active sonar to the target on the screen and back to the headset of the operator. He had wiped all other matters from his mind. To him all that mattered now was this small contact on the sonar screen in front of him.

'It is the submarine, Kapitan, the same submarine. She is at a depth of forty metres and is moving on a course of two–one–zero, and has again increased her speed to eight knots. Her range is now just less than three kilometres.' The senior of the two operators spoke nervously, trying to judge Portrova's mood.

Portrova grunted with undisguised satisfaction. He leaned forward and patted the man's shoulder. 'Again you have done well, my friend. This time I think we have her. Do not lose contact. Switch your speakers through to the bridge, and call me if anything changes.'

Once back on the bridge, Portrova ordered half ahead on the port engine and set a course to intercept his contact. This time he would not rush things; he knew that again he was hunting Bradley and *Spearfish*, and that *Spearfish* was badly wounded. Then he lit yet another cigarette and gave the order to prepare depth charges, before climbing back into his chair to await events. Within seconds his thoughts were disturbed by a fierce tug at his right sleeve. He looked around, annoyance immediately turning to surprise as he recognised the pale, anxious face of Yuri, the sick berth attendant. 'Kapitan, you must come right away to the sick berth. Comrad Borstoy is dead!'

'Dead? How is he dead?'

'The Britisher has killed him, Kapitan. You must come now, please. 'Yuri turned to scuttle back down to the sick berth, and Portrova slid off his chair to follow him, shouting over his shoulder to Carlov, 'Take charge, Comrad Carlov, and be sure to call me when we reach the target.'

Portrova entered the sick berth on the heels of the flustered Yuri, and looked down at the dead KGB agent. Then he turned to the doctor, his dark features impassive. 'He is dead, Kapitan?'

'*Da*, Kapitan, he is dead. His neck is broken,' the doctor nodded.

'How has this happened?' Portrova's question sounded academic, showing no hint of concern for the crumpled corpse at his feet.

The doctor cast a fleeting but clearly uncomfortable glance towards Yuri. 'Comrad Borstoy was interviewing the Britisher. They were alone. We were dismissed and we returned to find this.' He gestured to the body of Borstoy and the silent Jackson.

Portrova shifted his gaze towards Jackson. 'So, Englander, now you have committed murder, eh? Is this how you repay us?' Then in a vague tone, almost as an afterthought, he added, 'I am Kapitan Alexci Portrova, commander of this ship.'

Jackson lifted himself painfully to one elbow and turned his tear-soaked face towards Portrova. 'So you're the fuckin' captain eh? Well, Mr fuckin' Captain, come a bit closer if you will, an' I'll do fer you as well! As God is my witness I'll do fer the fuckin' lot of you. You're a bastard murderer, Mr Captain whatever your name is, 'an I'll see that you pay fer what you've done to me an' mine.' Exhausted, he again fell back on his pillows.

'You are the one that will pay, my friend.' Portrova's voice was still, level, moderated and completely devoid of emotion. In his mind he was still looking into the whisky-sodden face of another trawler captain some fifteen years ago. Then he said, 'You will be taken back to our country, where you will be tried for the murder of a Soviet citizen.' Now there was clear emotion in his voice. 'Believe me, Englishman, this will not go well for you.'

Jackson looked straight ahead. Now the tablets were really beginning to tell – he was almost asleep. In one final gesture of defiance he looked up at Portrova and mumbled, 'Bollocks! Yuh really think I give a shit?' Then he was asleep.

Portrova turned to the doctor and, indicating the body of Borstoy, he said, 'Get Comrad Carlov to arrange a burial service. We will dispose of Comrad Borstoy right away, while we are stopped. And you, Comrad Doktar, will arrange for an armed guard to be here with the prisoner at all times. Now I have things of greater importance to do.' Turning abruptly, he left the sick berth and quickly made his way back to the bridge.

Some twenty minutes later a short service was held by Carlov and watched by a small party of officers and ratings on *Otvashni*'s icy upper deck. On completion, Borstoy's blanket-covered body was slid overboard. Portrova was conspicuous by his absence.

★ ★ ★ ★ ★

It was now snowing heavily. Thick, heavy flakes were settling on *Otvashni*'s decks and superstructure as well as on the shoulders of her bridge team. From his bridge chair, Portrova grunted with displeasure, all thoughts of Borstoy's death gone from his mind as he listened intently to the metallic pings from the sound room now coming over the bridge speaker in front of him. The time period between the transmitted signal from the active sonar and the return echoes was rapidly becoming shorter. He listened impassively, drawing heavily on his cigarette. Now, at last, the two echoes were almost simultaneous, virtually indistinguishable.

'Kapitan.' The sonar operator's voice was plainly excited, urgent. 'Kapitan, we are almost over the target.'

★ ★ ★ ★ ★

Aboard *Spearfish*, what was left of her passive sonar had picked up the rapidly approaching *Otvashni*. Bradley had no doubt that this was *Otvashni*, even though her propeller noise had changed significantly since their last meeting. This time she was using just one propeller and he wondered why. But he knew what to expect, and he knew that if *Spearfish* was to survive any further charges she would have to come shallow – he couldn't trust that stern gland. So he had now come to ninety feet and reduced speed to slow ahead on his one good propeller, and ordered a blanket silence throughout the boat.

Still the Russian came directly towards them. Now Bradley didn't need his sonar: the thrashing propeller of the approaching destroyer was plainly audible to all in *Spearfish*. He leaned against the chart table, head tilted back, eyes gazing upward as though willing himself to see through the pressure hull and the rapidly narrowing expanse of water between *Spearfish* and her hunter. Despite the cold outside, he constantly wiped beads of sweat from his forehead with the back of his hand.

Ravoski stood beside Bradley, his face impassive, expressionless. If he felt the discomfort that Bradley and the rest of the control room now shared, he certainly didn't show it. His eyes were everywhere, missing nothing as they darted around the dimly lit control room, but mainly they concentrated upon Bradley and on Strong, who, stationed behind the two planesmen, was desperately trying to maintain the depth and trim on his slow-moving boat while making an absolute minimum use of the ballast pump or trim system.

The destroyer continued to close. Throughout the boat many more eyes now looked upward. They also looked towards each other, questioningly but silent. There was no need for words; there was nothing to say. Were they in for another pasting? Yes, that seemed inevitable. The last time it had been bad enough, but at least then it had been completely unexpected and soon over. This time it was worse. The waiting made it that way. But were these Russians out for a kill this time? Were they really out to deliver the *coup de grace*? Surely not with five of their own men still aboard.

The thrashing propeller was now almost directly above them, and then suddenly it slowed and stopped. The resultant silence was in many ways worse. Bradley now knew for sure that *Spearfish* was trapped. He now had two options, both of which he had considered deeply during the past thirty minutes. He could either go deep and try his luck at a game of hide-and-seek in an attempt to lose the Russian, but this, he reasoned, was a pretty forlorn hope under the circumstances. Secondly, he could again surface, but to surface with no active sonar, no radar and no effective W/T transmission would be tantamount to surrender. He could let them make the first move – see how far they were really prepared to go. If the Russian did choose to attack, then Bradley knew that *Spearfish* in her present condition might well never survive another pounding like the last time. So should he now risk his boat and his crew merely in order to avoid what at worst could only be a very embarrassing international incident?

No, he knew what he had to do; he had made his decision and there would be no going back on it. The crew were reliant on him, and him alone, to keep both them and *Spearfish* alive, and that is what he must do. He suspected that this Russian would happily sink him for little or no reason. They would be lost without trace and who back home would not come to the conclusion that this loss was just another of those tragic peacetime submarine accidents – part of a submariner's lot?

Now that his mind was made up he felt at least a partial sense of relief. Unless the present situation changed dramatically, at least he knew what he must do. Crossing to the helmsman's position he used the sound–powered telephone to pass an order to load the forward and after submerged signal ejectors with red grenades. Then he asked for the torpedo officer to report to him in the control room.

At the mention of the red grenades Strong turned from his depth gauges to shoot a questioning glance at Bradley, even though he knew now what his captain was planning.

'I'm sorry, Oliver,' Bradley answered his first lieutenant's unspoken question. 'Can't risk any more games, any more lives. We've given it our best shot. I can do no more.' Suddenly he felt physically sick. All those weeks on patrol, all that intelligence and information so arduously and carefully gathered, and now here he was with nothing.

One of the hydraulic pumps in the auxiliary machinery space beneath the control room abruptly cut in, its harsh roar finally breaking the silence in the control room and doing nothing to improve the nervous tension, which remained as sharp as ever.

Now the propeller of the destroyer above them started to turn again. She was moving slowly ahead.

Murray appeared in the control room. He had heard the order to load the SSEs with red grenades, which, conventionally, were only used prior to emergency surfacing. For once even Murray looked nervous, unsure of himself. 'Things are as bad as that, Sir?'

'Yes, Ross, I'm afraid they are.'

'Well, Sir, but—'

'But what?' Bradley's tone was sharp, angry, and he immediately regretted using it.

'Well, Sir.' Murray seemed unaware of any rebuff. 'We could use bubble decoys. You know, try to fox the bastards. Or...' and now he looked at Bradley apprehensively, '...they've been giving us a bloody hard time. Why not return the compliment? All tubes except number five are loaded with warheads!'

'Sorry, Ross. I hear what you're saying, but I don't want to compound my crimes by starting World War Three. Go forward and wait for my word.'

Bradley moved back to the chart table. Now from the sound room, 'Contact has stopped, Sir, 400 yards directly ahead and—'

Before Kinross had finished speaking *Spearfish* bucked and trembled violently as a charge exploded over her bows, thankfully too far away to do her real damage. Then again from Kinross, 'Contact has turned, Sir, and is now approaching down our port side.'

Bradley gripped the attack periscope supports tightly, more as an impulse than a need. What's this bastard playing at? Maybe his sonar operators aren't so hot after all.

Then the second explosion. This time about 300 yards off *Spearfish*'s port beam, again too far away and too deep to do any damage.

'Surface contact still moving aft, Sir,' from Kinross in the sound room.

The third charge exploded directly astern of them, closer this time, but still too far away and too deep to pose any danger to *Spearfish*.

Again from Kinross, 'Surface contact turning towards us. Contact will pass to starboard.'

Now suddenly it dawned upon Bradley. They weren't *looking* for him – of course they bloody weren't. They were telling him that they'd already found him. They knew exactly where he was – his location and his depth. They were sending him the message through these charges, almost as though they were using them as precision surgery.

'Stand by for a charge off the starboard side.' It was all the warning that Bradley could utter. But this time the charge was much closer and set almost at the same depth as *Spearfish*. This would be the final warning. The shock wave lurched *Spearfish* violently to port, and it was only his firm grip on the periscope standard that stopped Bradley from being thrown across the control room. The lighting went out but almost immediately flickered back on, and the sound of smashing glass and loose messware came from forward. Once again the gyrocompass in the machinery space beneath them toppled, its warning bell adding to the noise and confusion in the control room.

Strong pulled himself back from the shoulders of the two planesmen on which he'd been thrown, his normally pallid features now ashen. He turned towards Bradley. 'That was close, Sir. Surely a couple of anti-personnel charges would have done the same job?'

'Close, yes, but only as close as it was meant to be,' breathed Bradley. 'They're not warning us off; they want us up there and at the end of their bloody towline again.'

'Bloody 'ell, Sir! It was close enough for me an' that's fer sure,' muttered Able Seaman Charlie Collam from the helm. Then in a louder voice he continued, 'Why don't we just go up there and stuff a couple of fish up their arse? That would take the wind and piss out of 'em!' The usually quiet and reserved Collam's broad west midlands accent was filled with a mixture of anger and fear. Under any other circumstances Collam would never have spoken out like this but Bradley knew that Collam's feelings would be reflected in the whole of the control room team and indeed throughout the whole boat. He suddenly became conscious of the continuous harsh jangle of the gyro alarm bell. 'Helm, switch off that bloody alarm! And someone get the EA to sort out the compass.' Bradley moved back to the attack periscope. 'Switch to red lighting in the control room.'

'EA's already down there, Sir,' called Collam from the wheel. As if in confirmation of his reply, the gyro alarm bell suddenly went silent.

'Come to sixty-five feet, Oliver. Hold your present course, but no more forward movement than necessary: we don't want to inconvenience Ivan by moving outside of our designated position.' He reached for the main broadcast microphone above his head.

'D'you hear there, all compartments? This is the captain speaking. We shall be surfacing shortly, at which time we can expect to be boarded once again by the Russian navy. The situation is extremely regretful, but cannot be avoided, certainly not without severe risk to all of you and to the boat. My main aim now is to get you all home in one piece, and that I will do, though it may now take a little longer than anticipated. In the meanwhile, I would ask you to do only what you are told by either myself or your officers. Please do nothing to make the situation worse than it already is. That is all.'

From Oliver Strong, 'Captain, Sir, depth now ninety feet.'

'Very good.' Bradley lifted his microphone. 'Fire the forward and after SSEs.'

Almost immediately there came two dull thuds – one from forward, the other from aft – as the submerged signal ejectors sent their canisters fitted with red grenades rocketing towards the surface.

'Captain – Torpedo Officer. For'd SSE fired, drained down, bore sighted clear.' Then, from the after ends, came a similar report on the after SSE.

Bradley called across to Strong. 'Stand by to surface, Number One.'

'Stand by to surface, Sir.' Strong reached for his main broadcast microphone. 'All compartments stand by to surface. Report main vents.'

Bradley went to his cabin, where he pulled on a submarine sweater and his heavy camel-coloured duffel coat. He then struggled into a full set of oilskins, while all the time listening to the pre-surfacing reports coming to the control room over the main broadcast system. Returning to the control room, he took up station by the attack periscope, noting that Bishop, the signalman and the lookout were also dressed for the bridge. There was no sign of Viktor Ravoski.

Strong turned to look at Bradley. 'Ready to surface, Sir. '

Bradley took a deep breath, hesitating. This wasn't coming easily. 'Thank you, Number One. Surface the submarine.'

★ ★ ★ ★ ★

Alexci Portrova sat in his chair on the bridge of *Otvashni*, waiting, seemingly impervious to the bitterly cold wind and the driving snow which now covered his heavy black watch-coat and his black fur ushanka. He was now waiting for his moment of triumph; which was very close now.

Then, from the port lookout and almost simultaneously from the starboard wing lookout, 'Kapitan, look!' The snow-covered figure of Carlov turned to face his captain. 'Kapitan, look,' he repeated, pointing upward and off to the port beam, where two red flares soared skyward, exploding at about seventy feet into myriads of bright red showers.

Now came an excited call from the sonar operator. 'Kapitan, the submarine is coming to the surface.'

Portrova smiled to himself. 'So, my friend,' he muttered, 'you wish again to surrender. You think that maybe you can save yourself, eh? But you have caused me much trouble. You have a lot to be accountable for. Things will not be easy for you now.' He watched intently through the falling snow as the bright red glow of the grenades continued to light up the sombre grey of the sky, until the very last falling glow was extinguished by the heaving dark surface.

Carlov was again pointing towards the port beam. 'Kapitan, the submarine has surfaced. She is 300 metres to our left.'

'Thank you, Comrad Sergei.' Portrova hauled himself off his chair, brushing the thick covering of snow from his coat. Clutching his binoculars, he made his way across the bridge to stand beside Carlov, levelling the binoculars on the black shape of *Spearfish*, which was now settled low in the water. Then he turned to Carlov. 'Yes, Sergei, she is our British friend. See her damaged bridge? Come, let us take a closer look, and prepare a boat. We must again welcome her commander as our special guest.'

★ ★ ★ ★ ★

Standing on *Spearfish*'s bridge, with Bishop beside him, together with the lookout and the signalman closed up behind, Bradley eyed the Russian destroyer through his binoculars, trying to ignore the choking cold that froze each intake of breath to a painful gasp and then went on to sear the lungs. It was a cold that didn't encourage conversation.

'Strains of déjà vu, Sir?' Bishop spoke in a low voice.

'Yep, I'm afraid so, Tim. This one's not a stranger to us.'

'She's altering course towards us, Sir.' Bishop, too, was looking through binoculars, which he now lowered to wipe snow off the already freezing lenses.

'And no doubt we'll be receiving another cordial invitation to go aboard her,' muttered Bradley.

Both men watched in silence as the dark-grey shape of the Russian destroyer plunged towards them out of the gloom, white spume flying back from her knifelike bows as she closed. Now she was again broadside off *Spearfish*'s starboard beam, her white pendant numbers clearly visible. When she stopped, the gap between *Otvashni* and *Spearfish* was barely 100 yards.

'They're lowering a boat, Sir,' said Bishop.

'Yes, I figured they would.' Bradley's response was emotionless as he lowered his glasses and abstractedly brushed snow from the front of his coat.

Bishop turned to glance quickly at his captain, knowing that Bradley had resigned himself to whatever action the Russian might choose to take, and at that moment he didn't know whether to feel relieved or disappointed. But the look of pure agony on his captain's face sparked a feeling of pity inside him which now completely eclipsed the piercing cold he felt.

They watched in silence as the motor boat approached. Bishop turned to the signalman, 'You OK, Bunts? Be ready for anything!'

The motor boat was now turning alongside *Spearfish*'s starboard side. An oilskinned figure standing in the stern sheets raised a megaphone and called, 'British submarine, you are under our guns. Your kapitan is ordered to accompany me to our ship. He must come now!' This was no polite invitation!

'Ah well, here we go again.' Bradley turned to Bishop. 'Acknowledge their message, Tim. I'll just go below and have a quick word with Oliver. Meanwhile you'd better get the second cox'n and his gang up to the casing.' He grinned bitterly to himself. 'And make sure that bloody boat doesn't damage our paintwork! I'll see you later.' He disappeared down through the conning tower for a hurried conversation with Strong.

Some five minutes later, after leaving Strong in charge of *Spearfish*, and now wearing his cap and an inflated lifejacket over his oilskin top, Bradley made his way up to the casing. Climbing through the fin door, he was surprised to find not only the second cox'n and three members of his casing party, but also the tall figure of Carlov, backed by six Russian seamen all armed with submachine-guns and now menacing the casing party with these guns. Carlov stepped forward. Again he wore the long leather coat, complete with belted holster containing his side arm. Under the black ushanka his thinly chiselled features were, as always, unreadable. Bradley dropped on the casing to stand facing the Russian officer.

Carlov said, 'You will board our motor boat now, Commander. I will remain here in your absence, but first I will speak with Lieutenant Ravoski.' He turned to one of his men, who was dressed as a petty officer, and muttered something in Russian. Obeying what was obviously an order, the petty officer turned and motioned two of his men to escort Bradley forward towards the still turned-out fore planes. With the help of the casing party the Russian motor boat had been secured just below *Spearfish*'s starboard for'd hydroplane. This at least provided Bradley with a platform for embarkation – much safer and more dignified than on his last visit to the Russian destroyer.

Carlov watched as Bradley was bundled unceremoniously into the motor boat, then, together with the four Russian seamen behind him, turned and climbed through *Spearfish*'s fin door to make his way below to *Spearfish*'s control room.

Strong had been forewarned of the Russian officer's imminent arrival by Bishop, who was still on the bridge, and now stood waiting in the control room as Carlov climbed down the ladder, closely followed by four of the guards.

Now Carlov turned to face Strong. 'I am Kapitan Lieutenant Carlov. In the absence of your commander I would speak with your first officer.' He spoke stiffly, but his eyes were everywhere except on the man he was speaking to.

Strong, somewhat taken aback by this direct approach, quickly gathered his senses and replied equally stiffly, 'I am Lieutenant Oliver Strong, Royal Navy. And I am in command of this vessel in the absence of Lieutenant Commander Bradley.'

'Very well, Lieutenant Strong, I will now speak with Kapitan Lieutenant Ravoski. You and your men will remain as you are.' As if to emphasise his point he reached down to his right side and unclipped the top of his holster.

Then Ravoski stepped forward from the shadows at the after end of the control room. 'I welcome you aboard, Comrad Carlov. By the stars, it is good to see you.'

Ignoring Ravoski's genial welcome, Carlov turned, and together they talked in Russian, in tones low enough to be inaudible to anyone but themselves. After some three minutes Carlov stepped back to allow Ravoski to make his way across to the waiting Strong.

'What's going on, Viktor? Tell me what the hell's happening.' Strong spoke in a low voice, almost a whisper, looking as he felt – anxious, completely puzzled.

But now there was no geniality in Ravoski's voice, no twinkle in his eyes. He spoke loudly. 'You will do as you are told, Lieutenant Strong.' Pausing, he cast a swift glance towards Carlov before continuing, 'Firstly, you will release my men, and the two that are wounded will be prepared to return to my ship. I, too, am returning to my ship. My kapitan needs to be informed first hand of recent events, but I shall return to supervise your safe passage to Russia. While I am away my comrad, Kapitan Lieutenant Carlov, will remain here, together with our guards. You will obey his instructions. Make no mistake, Lieutenant Strong, Comrad Carlov has no liking for the British. It will be far better for you and your crew if you accept our offer of help and let us take your submarine to a place of safety, as we tried to do before.' Again he shot a swift glance towards Carlov, who was listening intently. 'Now, you will please arrange for my two injured men to be brought to the control room, and for the other two men to be released. You will do this immediately! My kapitan will be losing patience.'

Strong looked hard at Ravoski. This was a new and completely different Ravoski, and a completely different scenario than the one he'd anticipated. 'But I—'

Ravoski walked towards to the wardroom, calling over his shoulder, 'Say nothing, Lieutenant Strong. Just do as you are ordered.'

Strong shrugged his shoulders. Still trying to grapple with the situation, he reached up for the main broadcast microphone. 'All compartments, d'you hear there?' His tone was bitter, edging on sarcastic. 'We are again hosting a reinforcement of our Soviet friends. The captain is at this time preparing to liaise with the captain of the Russian destroyer. In the meanwhile no one will do or say anything that may lead to further aggravation between ourselves and our guests. I have now assumed command. Cox'n Greene, report to the control room at the rush. That is all!'

Replacing the microphone, Strong turned back to Carlov, who acknowledged him with the briefest of nods before beckoning the petty officer guard forward and giving a brief series of orders in Russian. The guard listened intently, then, bringing his weapon sharply to his side, he came to attention. 'Da, Comrad Kapitan Lieutenant.' Turning to the other guards, he issued his own short stream of orders. Strong and his control room team looked on as two of the guards placed themselves at the forward end of the control room, blocking passage forward, while the other four moved aft towards the diving panel, prohibiting any passage aft.

Then Greene was standing beside Strong. 'You called, Sir?'

'Ah, Cox'n, get the two Russian headcases to the control room. Make sure they're dressed properly. They'll be leaving us shortly, together with Viktor and the captain. Oh, and you'd better untie the other two guards and send them back here as well.'

'Aye Aye, Sir.' Greene disappeared and returned within minutes with the four original guards – two with bandaged heads and now dressed in their heavy clothing, and the two uninjured guards carrying their reclaimed submachine-guns. Ravoski appeared from the wardroom, now dressed in his long leather coat and black ushanka, and a Makarov pistol strapped to his waist. Speaking a few more brief words to Carlov, he turned and made his way up the conning tower ladder, followed by the two injured guards.

Carlov turned to Strong. 'You will dismiss all your men from this area, Lieutenant, but you will remain here and keep in contact with your officer on the bridge. My guards will be deployed within your vessel, and any of your men attempting to operate machinery without my knowledge will be shot! Now, I will wait in your kapitan's cabin, *da*?'

Strong nodded dumbly, unable to a find a suitable reply. So this is it, he thought. Finally the game was over. Carlov was certainly no diplomat. His attitude was not that of a man wishing to provide assistance or indeed safety to *Spearfish* and her crew. Threatening to shoot his men? My God, they must really want *Spearfish*. Now she was indeed a prisoner; they all were. But what about Ravoski? There was a man who was now once more a complete enigma, or was he was just simply another bloody Red?

*   *   *   *   *

Ravoski and the two wounded guards had boarded the waiting motor boat. Ravoski had not even spared a fleeting glance towards the shivering snow-covered Bradley, now hunkered down on the lee side of the engine housing next to the two bandaged-headed Russian guards. The second cox'n and his two seamen threw the head and stern ropes back into the motor boat then, nudged by the two guards, made their way aft to the fin door, while the boat sheered off and headed towards *Otvashni*, leaving a total of eight Russian guards, together with their leader Carlov, aboard *Spearfish*.

Bradley eyed the oilskinned Russian officer in charge of the boat. Again he couldn't decide upon his rank, since there was no visible indication of this either on the oilskin jacket or his hood, and just as before, this officer had paid no formal deference and respect to Bradley's rank. This was a young man

– probably another sublieutenant or maybe a midshipman, if they had those in the Russian navy. What the hell did it matter anyway? He had far more important things to think about now. And whatever his rank, this young officer was obviously not interested in him.

The motor boat rapidly approached its mother ship, its cox'n guiding it expertly alongside the lowered ladder at *Otvashni*'s side, while a seaman stationed in the bows dextrously hooked the ladder with a boathook. Ravoski was the first to climb this ladder, followed by the two guards wearing the head bandages. Now the young Russian officer gestured to Bradley to go next. In spite of the heavy swell Bradley had no difficulty in making his way up to the destroyer's snow-covered upper deck, where two armed guards grabbed him by either shoulder and practically frogmarched him to the cabin that he and Bishop had been held in on his last visit to *Otvashni*. He made no effort to resist the roughness of his guards as they practically threw him into the cabin and shut the door. Hearing the door clips being pulled into place, he moved across to slump tiredly into a chair. 'Oh well,' he muttered to himself, 'here we go again!'

★ ★ ★ ★ ★

Portrova had prepared himself to welcome his guest. Having discarded his normal seagoing clothing in favour of his best uniform, he was now waiting in the cabin that he and Bradley had first met in. This time he sat at a smaller table, upon which sat a pile of papers and notes he had hurriedly dictated to his ship's secretary shortly before closing in on *Spearfish*. These were there more to impress Bradley than for any other reason. He picked a Sobranie from the open case in front of him, lit it, and inhaled heavily. He was satisfied now that this matter could finally be brought to an end. This arrogant submarine commander would be taken back to Russia, where the Kremlin would then expose the British government and their American allies for the warmongers that they really were. Bradley would face trial for espionage, after which he would either suffer execution or, much more likely, an indefinite detention in a Russian prison, which for him would be little more than a living death. Also the whole British nation would be made to look foolish, being accused in the world press of antagonising an already delicate situation between Russia and the West. And he, Kapitan 1 Ranga Alexci Portrova, would be the man who had brought all this about. But in the meantime he held Bradley responsible for all the trouble and expense caused to him since their first meeting, and he would do all within his power to make this arrogant pig suffer while he was aboard *Otvashni*.

Again he raised himself from his chair to walk across the cabin and look into a small, round unframed mirror fixed to the bulkhead. Staring intently at his reflection, he carefully smoothed down his jet-black hair with both hands and then checked his moustache: he had to look his best in front of this Englishman. But first he would meet with Ravoski and find out how the British submarine had managed to slip her tow and escape. Returning to his chair, he again started to shuffle the pile of paper in front of him, waiting expectantly.

Two loud bangs on the steel door of the cabin signalled the arrival of Ravoski. Portrova grunted to himself and lit yet another cigarette. Straightening himself in his chair, he called, 'Come.' The heavy door swung open and the stooped figure of Ravoski entered the cabin, freezing sea water still running freely from his coat. Ravoski straightened briefly and brought his heels together in a vague motion of deference to his kapitan and, then relaxing, he removed his sodden ushanka and slumped into the straight-backed chair, facing Portrova across the desk.

Portrova eyed Ravoski closely but said nothing. Then carefully stubbing his cigarette into the already overflowing ashtray in front of him, he stood up and walked across the cabin to gaze through the ice-covered glass of the porthole, his back to Ravoski. Finally he spoke. 'These have not been happy days, Comrad Viktor. This Britisher has caused us much trouble and much delay, *da*?' Now he turned to fix his gaze directly on Ravoski. 'Trouble and delays that should never have happened, eh?'

Ravoski, appearing completely unruffled, rose to his feet. 'These events are regrettable, Comrad Kapitan, but under the circumstances they were unavoidable. I too have many regrets. I would—'

Portrova cut him short. 'Regrets? You have regrets! Regrets are not what our friends in Moscow will want to hear.' Portrova sat back in his chair and motioned Ravoski to do the same. He reached for another cigarette and lit it, his eyes still fixed on Ravoski. Now his tone mellowed slightly. 'They will see it only as incompetence and failure — failure to carry out the task they entrusted us with.' He drew deeply on his cigarette and continued to study Ravoski's face, waiting for a reaction that did not materialise, so he continued, 'We were a designated guard ship for the missile firing — a firing that was to be in every respect top secret, but which I believe is no longer a secret! Our task was to deter intruders, spies. And you, Comrad Ravoski, together with Dimitry Borstoy, were placed aboard this ship to deal with the very events we have recently experienced. You have both been trained for this task and so far you have both failed. I never liked or trusted Borstoy, but I would have expected more from you, Viktor.' He paused, again drawing deeply on his cigarette. 'You, Viktor,' he continued, 'have been with me for much longer than Borstoy, and I trust your judgement more than his.'

Now Ravoski answered with a voice as hard as his eyes. 'Borstoy is a fanatical fool, Kapitan — we both know that — but he has many friends in high places. And yes, Comrad Kapitan, we were placed here on your vessel for the reasons you describe.' Now, looking fully into Portrova's face, he continued, 'But I should remind you that we are not under your direct command; we answer only to our masters in Moscow!'

'And so you will, my friend, have no doubt about that.' Portrova's tone remained moderate, deliberate. 'Borstoy is dead!'

Now Ravoski jerked upright in his seat. 'Dead?'

'Yes, dead — murdered just hours ago by the kapitan of the British trawler we sank. He was the only survivor, but that is of no consequence. He will pay for his crime!'

Ravoski's shoulders slumped and he let go a heavy sigh. Now things were falling into place. 'Ah, so you did sink the trawler?'

'More by accident than intent,' replied Portrova. 'We suspected that she had met up with your British submarine to exchange intelligence. Our intention was only to board and search her but our gunnery was too accurate.'

'And only her kapitan survived?' Ravoski sighed again. 'You are right, Comrad Kapitan, we did meet up with this trawler, and she had troubles with her engines. Commander Bradley stopped to give her assistance. Some mechanical equipment was passed across to her, but certainly no intelligence, of this I am sure!'

Portrova looked puzzled. 'And you found no evidence of her surveillance operations?'

'Nothing,' replied Ravoski. 'It would seem that you sank the trawler for no valid reason, Kapitan.'

Portrova ignored this. 'And how did you allow the submarine to slip her tow?'

'Commander Bradley is a very determined man, Comrad Kapitan, and I had insufficient men. We were caught off guard during your first meeting with that trawler.' He reached down and withdrew his pistol from its holster. 'Even now I have no ammunition for my weapon.'

'And the submarine: is she still badly damaged?'

'She has no usable communications, Kapitan, or reliable sensors, and you have seen the damage to her bridge. She has only one usable periscope and can propel on one shaft only. She also has much interior minor damage, but both her engines and motors are working.'

'And her crew: their morale?'

'Until this time they are in good spirits. Commander Bradley is an excellent leader. But with their food, and, as always, their fresh water, there is rationing. They will soon be reaching a state where they will need to impose very strict rationing. We have detained them from their return to their base and they will need more food and water, especially with our extra men on board.'

Portrova rose from his chair and again walked over to the frosted porthole, keeping his back to Ravoski, hiding the deep scowl that now crossed his dark features. 'This will be arranged. And you, Comrad, what were your plans?'

Ravoski's grey eyes were completely expressionless. 'I was waiting for the opportunity to retake her. It could have been done. I have gained the full trust of her commander and her officers. I would have succeeded.' Then he added, perhaps for reasons of diplomacy, 'Though, under the circumstances, your arrival here this morning was most fortuitous.'

Without turning from the porthole Portrova said, 'You will return to her. That is my wish. Your knowledge of that vessel is equal to that of her commander. At this time we are again preparing her for tow. You will have more men with you this time, together with one of our junior officers. This time there will be no mistakes. Commander Bradley will remain aboard this ship. Go now, Comrad, and prepare yourself. We will speak again before you leave. You will arrange for Bradley to be brought to me now.'

Now came two more loud bangs on the door of Portrova's cabin. Again the door swung open and an armed petty officer stepped inside, followed by Bradley together with two armed seamen. These guards now nudged Bradley forward with the muzzles of their submachine-guns until he was standing some three feet directly in front of Portrova's table.

The petty officer snapped to attention. Speaking in Russian, he said, 'The British officer, Comrad Kapitan.' Then he relaxed and moved behind Bradley to stand next to the two seamen.

Now, almost wearily, Portrova raised his bear-like frame from the chair. 'Ah, Commander Bradley, how good it is to see you again,' he said in his deep guttural tone, with a mixture of sarcasm and triumph. Then he slumped heavily back into his chair.

'I'm sorry that I can't say the same thing, Captain Portrova.'

Bradley was already fighting back his anger. Just the sight and the sound of this Russian sickened him to the core, but he decided to go in hard. Struggling to maintain a moderate tone while at the same time knowing that he could never conceal the contempt and anger that he felt for this man, he looked down at the seated Russian. 'You, Sir, have committed yet another act of extreme piracy. You have attacked one of Her Majesty's submarines whilst it was in pursuance of its lawful operations within international waters. Using blatant aggression, you have endangered the lives of my crew and the safety of my vessel; in addition to which I have reason to believe that you have attacked a British trawler, causing her loss and the loss of all those aboard her.' He paused, drawing a deep breath. Now he was no longer attempting to control his anger. 'You may rest assured, Captain, that as the commander of this ship these violations, together with any backing you may have had from your government in this affair will not be taken lightly. I will be making a full report as soon as I have the opportunity to do so. In the meantime I insist that you allow me to return to my ship and permit me to proceed to the United Kingdom before any further action on your part compounds the breaches in international relationships already made.'

Bradley drew another deep breath, already knowing that his outburst had not had the slightest effect on Portrova, and he wondered briefly whether his words had been properly understood by this peasant-like figure seated in front of him.

Portrova stubbed out a half-smoked cigarette and immediately lit another. Inhaling deeply, he gazed up at Bradley and deliberately blew a cloud of dark smoke directly into his face. He sensed the frustration now within this Britisher and knew now that he had the upper hand.

'So, Commander, I have listened to what you say. Now perhaps you will permit me to speak?'

Portrova's voice was even lower now and even more controlled, but still the sarcasm was plainly obvious. 'I took the action necessary to protect the interests of our country. You, Commander, were spying. You had no right to be where you were, and your vessel was accidentally damaged during our efforts to trace you. We took you in hand and offered you safe passage to a place where your vessel could properly be repaired. This you declined, causing much damage to my vessel in the process. Why was this, Commander? Did you have something to hide? Yes, we did pursue you, but only in the interests of your own safety. There are many miles between the Barents and the United Kingdom. Who could say that your vessel would make this journey with safety?' Portrova paused, studying the glowing tip of his cigarette before continuing. 'And yes, we did open fire on the fishing boat, but it was not intended to sink her. That was most unfortunate, even though we believe that she, like yourselves, was spying on the activities of our Northern Fleet.'

'Were there any survivors?'

'Yes, we sank this trawler, and yes, I do regard this as unfortunate. Our gunnery officer is very good, but to sink her was luck! In this case bad luck. I had wished only to board and search her. Our gunfire was intended only as a warning. But we know that she was working with you, Commander, and we know that this trawler made a rendezvous with your vessel shortly before we sank her.' Portrova again feigned a temporary puzzlement. Now he was really enjoying himself. He looked up at Bradley, the lazy, mocking indolence in his face now fading. He was studying Bradley very carefully, watching the Englishman's reactions.

Bradley remained silent. This bastard's got us thoroughly stitched up. But why would he admit to me that he sank the trawler? He glanced quickly around the cabin. Wonder where that little KBG bastard's got to.

'And so, Commander Bradley, I will once again offer you the courtesy of escorting your vessel to one of our bases, where it can be properly inspected and repaired before we let you continue on your way.'

Bradley knew now that he had already lost; nothing was going to stop this Russian. But he also knew that he must not give up trying. He spoke through a dry mouth, 'So you are again proposing to detain both myself and my ship? You say that we were spying. Where is your evidence? I give you my permission to board my vessel and carry out a full search. You will find nothing!'

'Of course we will find nothing; you will have already seen to that,' Portrova sneered. 'You British, along with your American allies seem to think that we Russians are stupid. We fought a long and bitter war, Commander, and we paid a high price for victory. Oh yes, you helped achieve that victory, you and your capitalist friends, but only because it suited you to do so. We know that you now seek to destroy us when you feel the time is right. Your politicians will see to that!'

Now Portrova was on his feet again, leaning forward across the table towards Bradley, his dark sloe-like eyes filled with hatred and a voice that was now a snarl. 'No, Commander, we are not fools, and we will not be dragged into your capitalistic system. Despite what your masters would have you believe, we are a great nation, growing in strength, and we will grow stronger yet. Soon our defences will again match those of the West and we will combat any aggression blow for blow.'

Surprised by Portrova's sudden outburst, Bradley took a step back and one of the guards at his back immediately prodded him forward with the muzzle of his submachine-gun. Portrova sat back down in his chair and stubbed out yet another half-smoked cigarette. Then he looked up at Bradley. 'But have no fear, my friend. My men will board your vessel, and they will make another search. No matter if we find nothing. We know what you have been doing and if you have now been forced to dispose of this – what was it you called it – evidence? then we of course have still succeeded in our task, while you, Commander, will remain here, not as my guest, but this time as my prisoner!'

Bradley tried hard to conceal his feelings at the Russian's gloating tones, knowing now that there was nothing he could do. But he did know that he needed to prolong this conversation, to find out everything that he could, in order to assess his situation.

'Tell me, Captain, how is the injured officer that I sent aboard you for medical care?'

Portrova nodded his head in the affirmative while adopting a deliberately puzzled expression, which did not fool Bradley. 'Injured officer? Ah yes, your officer – the one with the head wound, *da*?' His deep sigh was so obviously bogus. 'It was a very bad wound, Commander. Unfortunately, your brother officer did not survive his injuries, and his body was – how is it you say? – committed to the deep. This was done shortly after you slipped our tow.' There was no sympathy, no regret in Portrova's voice.

Again Bradley felt the bitter bile rising up from his stomach to his lungs. So Toby was dead. He had feared that this would be the case but even so he felt himself trembling at the shock of this news.

'Yes, yes, Commander, but as for the trawler, was not this trawler present at the time you slipped our tow? And her subsequent meeting with you again: was this not a deliberate liaison? Or perhaps that meeting, too, was purely coincidental, *da*? We did all we could to save her crew, and we did manage to rescue her kapitan, but he was the only one, the only survivor. Jackson, I think is his name. But this man Jackson then repaid us by murdering one of our people – Comrad Borstoy of the KGB. You will remember him, *da*? You will understand that Jackson will of course pay for this crime with his life.'

'So that's why the little bastard's not here now,' Bradley said to himself. 'Well done, Captain Jackson!'

'So, is Jackson aboard here now?' he asked.

'*Da*, he is still with us. We intend to keep him alive. Kapitan Jackson will accompany you and your crew back to Russia with us, where he will stand trial for the brutal killing of one of our comrads. He is presently under escort in our sick berth. He has suffered much serious injury and is in much pain, you will understand.' Portrova's tone was again patronising, mocking.

'You bet I bloody understand!' Now Bradley could no longer contain his anger. The strain and tension of the past two weeks had finally manifested in a rage he could no longer control – a rage that he now had no wish to control. He lunged forward towards the figure seated in front of him, arms outstretched, grabbing for the shoulders of this man for whom he now felt so much hate and loathing. 'And you won't get away with this either, you bastard. I'll see you in hell before—'

But as quick as his move had been, his guards were quicker. Before Bradley had gained one step towards Portrova, the guard on his right-hand side had rammed the butt of his weapon hard between his shoulder blades with force that brought him to his knees. He looked up towards Portrova, desperately trying to regain his feet, a grey mist slowly descending over his eyes. Then the second guard stepped forward, swinging the butt of his submachine-gun hard against Bradley's left temple, and Bradley watched the deck come up to meet him before finally losing consciousness.

The petty officer motioned to the two guards to remove Bradley's inert body from the cabin, while Portrova settled back in his chair and selected yet another cigarette, watching the guards as they dragged Bradley's unconscious body roughly over the door sill. He felt content; he had stood against this arrogant Britisher and he had held his ground. What did he care for politics? He disliked his own masters but on a personal basis he disliked this so-called enemy much more. He had been playing a game, and he had won. He closed his eyes in deep thought, his mind travelling back in time, as it had done so many times before, to again relive that fateful night aboard *Ocean Harvester* in the North Sea – the night that had changed his life so completely, the night he had watched his best friend die. Now we have them, Gregori. Soon the circle will be complete and this business will be over. Justice will be done. I, Alexci Portrova, will make it so. The British fisherman will die, but the British submarine commander may suffer a far worse fate. He looked towards the back of the disappearing petty officer, and called, 'So the Britisher has still some spirit, eh? No matter: we will soon change that. See that he gets to the sick berth and be sure to tell the doktar that I want him kept alive.'

Bradley awoke some fifteen minutes later in *Otvashni's* sick berth. He lay in a metal-framed white-painted cot. A blinding headache forced a groan from his dry mouth as he instinctively shielded his eyes against the white overhead lighting. He raised a hand gingerly to his face. Gently exploring, he could feel the stickiness on his fingers. Looking at his fingertips, he could see that they were covered in dark, partly congealed blood. He tried to raise himself to a sitting position, but an excruciating jolt of pain between his shoulder blades forced him to collapse limply back on the mattress. 'Where the hell am I?' he muttered weakly to no one in particular.

'You're in the sick berth of a Russian bloody warship, Laddie, that's where you are!'

The gruff Yorkshire tones that came from the cot positioned at right angles to the foot of the cot upon which he lay surprised Bradley, but almost immediately he knew that he had heard that voice before. 'Aye,' the voice from the other cot continued, 'they brought you in about fifteen minutes since. The doc's 'ad a look at you. He reckons you'll live.'

Then Bradley remembered. 'You're the trawler skipper! Jackson, wasn't it?'

'It still bloody well is, as far as I know,' the voice grunted in reply. 'Ozzie or Skipper to my friends. An' who might you be, then?'

'The name's Bradley. I command a British submarine which is, or rather was, carrying out independent exercises in this area. Looks like we've both fallen foul of Ivan.'

'Commander Bradley, eh!' The voice had lost some of its aggression. 'It was your guys who tried to help me with my *Imogen's* feed-water problems.

Pity you didn't 'ang on for those fish I promised you. But then you'd have probably copped a packet as well! Those Russian bastards blew us clear out of the water soon after you left. Seems I'm the only one of us left alive, an' that's down to a friggin' fluke if ever there was one. All the rest of 'em are gone to the bottom, together with my *Imogen* and a full load of fish.' No one could fail to miss the anguish in Jackson's voice, and it wasn't over the loss of his fish.

Bradley remained silent, his head still throbbing. This all seemed so surreal. Just what the hell was going on here? What was happening? How come this man Jackson was involved? Then it was as though his mind and memory had suddenly become unlocked. It was all starting to come back to him: the depth charges, the surfacing of *Spearfish* off the beam of the Russian, and his subsequent meeting with Portrova. He groaned to himself as the memories began to unfold. Then, without warning, he succumbed to sheer unreasoning panic. Oblivious to his pain, he shot bolt upright in the cot, heavy sweat breaking from his forehead and running down his face in thick liquid beads. He was now staring straight ahead but seeing nothing, feeling nothing but total fear. Had he been able to reason at this time, he would have known that this was the perhaps inevitable result of his experiences during the past week, or even the past hours, but he was not reasoning. 'I've got to get out of here. I must get back to the boat. Where is everyone? Where's Oliver? Oh for Christ's sake, someone help me!'

''Ee, Lad, I'd give you a hand if only I could, but the bastards 'ave got me in a straitjacket, an' I'm roped down to this friggin' bunk like an upper deck tarp! Keep on shoutin' though, an' you'll get the doc back in here. I was 'oping that you an' me could have a bit more of a chat before that 'appens.' Jackson's tone was quiet, soothing, paternal almost, and it had the desired effect.

Now flopping back into the cot, Bradley lay silent, gathering his thoughts while Jackson waited patiently.

It was a full five minutes before Bradley spoke again. Now he was calm. The panic attack had left him as abruptly as it had started. Now he was thinking again. 'What are you doing here?'

'Oh, I'm a prisoner – the same as you are, Commander. We're both in the same boat.' Jackson chuckled to himself, but there was no humour in his chuckle. 'We're both on our way back to Russia, or we will be as soon as those bastards in charge of this ship get themselves sorted out. Only difference is, you're going to get a bollicking, an' I'm going to get a bullet!'

'A bullet?'

'Well, yeah, probably more than one. They'll want to do the job properly. Nothing less than a firing squad – that's what I've been promised. Or then, come to think of it, I suppose it could be the rope!'

'Why?' Bradley asked, though he already knew the answer.

'Well, I lost me temper, didn't I? Killed one of the bastards. Scrawny little sod. Seems I broke 'is bloody neck.' Jackson coughed up yet another mouthful of blood. 'But 'e deserved it fer what he did to my mates and to my *Imogen*, an' I ain't sorry about that; I just wish that I could get at the rest of the bastards. Jesus, I'd show 'em a thing or two!'

'Who was it? An officer or what?' Bradley continued to ask questions, the answers to which he already knew, but he wanted to gain the confidence and friendship of this trawler captain.

'Well, according to the doc, this little bastard was a KGB man. Ugly little sod. Can't remember what 'e called 'imself, but the bastard was well pleased with what he'd done, God curse 'is soul. Would you believe it, the little bastard shit himself before he went, and I can still smell 'im.' Jackson suddenly broke into a peal of uncontrollable laughter, which quickly subsided into a further bout of sobbing. 'Is there a place in 'eaven for people like that? You tell me, Commander.'

Bradley lay there. Now at least he had one ally aboard this ship. Already he knew that he could trust Jackson.

A further five minutes elapsed before either man spoke. It was Bradley who broke the silence.

'Skipper?'

'Yeah?'

'Are you badly hurt?'

'Well, let's put it this way, Commander, I've felt better! I did get a bit of a kicking, just to add to the problems I already 'ad, and I weren't in too good a shape before that.'

'But could you move if you had to?'

'Ow the 'ell do I know? I already told you, I'm tied up. I know that the legs are a bit dodgy – I thought they was busted, but the doc says they ain't – and me arms are a bit burnt.' He paused for a moment, as if in thought, then he said, 'But I suppose it's nowt that would keep me out of the pub on a Sunday lunchtime. 'Ow about you?'

'I've got a blinding headache, and they seem to have had a good go at wrecking my spine, but I think I'm OK. We're going to have to work something out, yes? With a bit of careful planning we can save me from a bollocking and you from a bullet.'

'Amen, I'll drink to that,' muttered Jackson.

★ ★ ★ ★ ★

Ravoski, having enjoyed a long hot shower and a hot meal, was now back in his cabin, hurriedly stuffing a grey canvas bag with the last of the few items that he would need for his forthcoming passage aboard *Spearfish*. He was fully dressed and ready for the boat transit. Leaving his bag just inside his cabin door, he went to have another short talk with Portrova, just to make sure that their previous plans hadn't changed. They had not. He made his way back to his cabin to pick up his bag before making his way to the wireless office, where he stood behind the operator for a few moments, listening to the wireless traffic. Then, leaning forward, he nudged the wireless operator on the shoulder. 'Is there anything of interest in the air tonight, Alexsander?'

Since his time aboard *Otvashni*, Ravoski had got to know the names of most of her crew, at least their first names. Now the young blond-haired and barely nineteen-year-old wireless operator Alexsander Mornov turned in his chair to look up at Ravoski. He, like many others aboard *Otvashni*, had developed a liking for this fatherly old man.

'There is much wireless traffic, Comrad Kapitan Lieutenant. It has been busy, but it is all routine traffic and is of no concern to us.'

Ravoski rested his hand on the operator's shoulder and said, 'That is good, eh, Alexsander? But I have been ordered to transfer myself back to the British submarine in order that we may tow her to harbour. It is work that I would rather not do, but it is the kapitan's order, and I will always do my duty.'

'*Da*, Lieutenant, this I know.'

'I do not look forward to my stay aboard the Britisher, my friend. Maybe you would go and get me two bottles of vodka from the steward. Make my duty easier, *da*? I will maintain your watch until you return.'

'*Da*, Comrad Lieutenant, this I will do.' Mornov grinned knowingly. He trusted this officer completely and he knew that Ravoski was perfectly capable of looking after his office. In any case, he would be grateful for a relief, if only for a brief period. He rose from his chair and left the office.

Ravoski shut the door behind him and, seating himself in the operator's vacated chair, he leaned towards the transmitting panel.

CHAPTER ELEVEN

Ravoski again crouched under the lee side of the motor boat's engine cover as it approached *Spearfish*. Behind him, standing errect in the boat's stern sheets, the young Starshl Lieutenant Nikita Gorski, who was to accompany Ravoski aboard *Spearfish*, appeared impervious to freezing spray. His only concession to the weather was to occasionally grab for the support of the varnished wooden engine cover as the boat encountered a particularly heavy swell. Behind him the helmsman deftly guided his small craft alongside *Spearfish*, while forward of the engine cab eight heavily armed seamen huddled together in a vain attempt to find some sort of protection from the weather. Ravoski looked up at Gorski. Gorski was young, inexperienced and impetuous. He was also keen, energetic and intelligent. He would doubtless go far in the Soviet navy

Spearfish was still lying very low in the water, and Ravoski could make out at least five men on her casing, while at least another four heads appeared above what remained of her battered bridge. Gorski now raised a battery-powered megaphone and called, 'Hello, the submarine. You will take my line.'

Aboard *Spearfish*, Bishop had been officer of the watch, and he had summoned Strong to the bridge as soon as the approaching motor boat had been sighted. Now Strong replied, again through a megaphone, 'How can we help you?' His voice held no hint of warmth or welcome.

'I am Starshl Lieutenant Gorski. I am returning with Kapitan Lieutenant Ravoski, and more guards. You will take my line.'

'Where is our captain?'

Ravoski, now standing, took the megaphone from Gorski and called back, 'Unfortunately, Commander Bradley has suffered a slight accident. Our doktar is looking after him. He is in good hands. You will give me assistance to board you!'

Strong turned to Bishop. 'They've got us by the short and curlies, Tim. Look at the firepower he's got with him. Just a few bursts into our main ballast tanks from those machine guns could finish us, not to mention that big grey bastard parked over there! Apart from blowing her out of the water with a torpedo, what can we do?'

'And they *have* got our captain aboard them.' Bishop was thinking aloud. 'If anything, he'll be trying to stop this from escalating to a major international incident. But in any case, if we have to have Russians aboard I'd rather have Viktor than that pompous bastard sitting below in the captain's cabin. I'll be glad to see the back of him.'

'Looks like we'd better let 'em on board, then.' Strong's voice was flat, emotionless. He felt completely out of his depth. 'Better get them aboard over the starboard fore plane. Get the second coxswain to rig some sort of a lifeline back to the fin. We don't want any nasty accidents, do we?'

'Well, we could always knock the bastards off one by one as they come down the tower.'

Strong allowed himself a wry grin. 'Believe me, Tim, there's nothing I'd enjoy more. Well, I'd better go down and make them welcome.'

Ravoski had been first off the motor boat, leaping with surprising agility onto *Spearfish's* starboard fore plane, and the second soxswain stepped forward to help him up to the casing. ''Ere, I'll take yer bag, Chum.' He grabbed Ravoski's grey canvas bag. Surprised at its weight, he muttered, 'Christ! What the 'ell 'ave you got in 'ere: another of yer oppos?' He called to his leading hand, 'Get the rest of 'em off, Nobby. Try not to drown any of 'em yet! I'll go down first. You lot can follow.'

Strong, Bishop and Cox'n Greene were waiting in *Spearfish's* control room. Carlov stood with them. Ravoski emerged from the conning tower, with Gorski and the extra guards close behind. Strong stepped forward. He had been wondering what he would say to Ravoski, but the heavy bag dropped on the deck from the conning tower hatch, followed by the second coxswain, confirmed his prediction that this would not be a short visit.

'I could say welcome aboard, Viktor, but under the circumstances you know I would be lying! Now, where exactly is Commander Bradley?'

Ravoski, his face still flushed from the cold, looked directly at Strong. He removed his snow-covered ushanka and unbuttoned his greatcoat before replying in his usual impeccable English, 'My friend, your kapitan was unfortunate to suffer an accident while aboard my ship. Luckily this was not too serious, but he is receiving medical attention from our doctor and will continue to do so for as long as necessary.' Then he indicated towards the waiting Gorski, 'This is Starshl Lieutenant Gorski. He will be riding with us, as will the extra guards. Now I will speak with Kapitan Lieutenant Carlov.'

A further deluge of freezing humanity dropped, one by one, through the conning tower lower hatch. This was the remainder of the casing party, all glad to be back in the comparative warmth of the control room.

Carlov now moved away from Strong and beckoned to Ravoski, 'Come, Comrad, we will speak alone.' He motioned Ravoski towards Bradley's cabin and when they were both inside he spoke rapidly and in low tones, 'I will now return to *Otvashni*. A towline will be arranged. You will remain on this vessel. Our kapitan will not want these Britishers to escape again! You have more men now, and you will be very vigilant, *da?*'

There was no missing the veiled threat in Carlov's words, but Ravoski's features remained completely impassive. He simply said, 'I have spoken to our kapitan, and this I already know, Comrad.'

Carlov returned to the control room and said to Strong, 'You are the first officer aboard this vessel, Lieutenant. Kapitan Lieutenant Ravoski will be your kapitan until we reach our journey's end. As you will be aware, he is a submariner and he knows this vessel well. From this time you will take orders from him alone. Do you understand?'

Strong's cheeks flushed with anger. 'This is wrong, completely wrong! It's bloody piracy! You just can't do this.'

'Oh, but I can, Comrad Lieutenant. We now have eight fully armed men and two of our officers aboard you and they will use force if necessary. I strongly advise against any further attempts at escape. How is it that you say in England? We are paying the piper, so we shall call the tune. That is how you British say it? *Da*, I think so.'

* * * * *

Portrova lay on his bunk and stared at the smoke-stained deck-head above him. Yellow smoke from the eternal Sobranie held loosely in his right hand curled lazily upward to compound this stain. He looked across at the clock: 17.40. Carlov should be reporting back to him shortly. Then, as if Carlov had been reading his captain's mind, there came a loud knock on the door of his cabin.

'Come.' Portrova stubbed out his cigarette and slid to the deck. He was back in his seagoing clothes now: dark serge trousers, sea boots and a heavy knitted black sweater. The door opened and Bassisty stepped inside the cabin.

'Comrad Kapitan, we have word from Comrad Carlov aboard the British submarine.'

'So, and what does he say?'

'He uses the signal lantern only, Kapitan. The watch officer would like you to come to the bridge.'

'So, at last!' Portrova hurriedly pulled on his watch-coat and ushanka, while Bassisty stepped quickly aside to avoid his captain's burly frame as it lumbered towards *Otvashni*'s bridge.

Portrova reached the bridge and, striding across to the port wing, he levelled his glasses towards *Spearfish*'s bridge, screwing his eyes against the non-stop staccato of bright white light from her signal lantern. It was impossible for Portrova to make out who exactly was on the submarine's bridge, but assumed that it would be Carlov on the signal lantern. He turned to the signalman standing behind him and made an impatient gesture for the loudhailer. Grasping it firmly in his left hand, he bellowed into the mouthpiece, 'Hello, the submarine. Do you hear me? I will speak with Kapitan Leitenant Carlov.'

The signal lamp on *Spearfish*'s bridge stopped blinking, and there was a full minute's silence before she made a reply, this time through a megaphone, 'To Kapitan Portrova from Kapitan Lieutenant Carlov. I wish to report that the British submarine is fully under our control. Her officers and men are co-operating with us at this time. A full search of the vessel has been carried out, but reveals nothing. Kapitan Lieutenant Ravoski and his men are now aboard.'

Portrova grunted. Lowering his megaphone to wipe the gathering snow from his mouth, and then raising it again, he bawled. 'You will now pass command of the submarine to Kapitan Lieutenant Ravoski, then you will return to *Otvashni*.'

Portrova turned to the watch officer. 'See that Kapitan Lieutenant Carlov comes to my cabin as soon as he returns.'

★　★　★　★　★

Some twenty minutes later, Carlov was back aboard *Otvashni* and knocking hard on the door of Portrova's sea cabin.

'Come.' The usual bellow from Portrova.

Carlov pushed the door open and stepped inside. Portrova was again lying fully clothed on his bunk, but slid to the deck as Carlov entered.

'So, Comrad, you have news for me?' Portrova now settled himself into one of the two chairs, beckoning Carlov to use the other.

Carlov was still dressed in oilskins and heavy leather watch-coat, topped with a black fur ushanka. Now dripping water and ice particles over the deck of the cabin, and his thin features tinged blue with cold, he was plainly uncomfortable. Portrova could clearly see this discomfort but chose to ignore it. Civilities like hot coffee or vodka were of secondary importance to him now. 'Come, Comrad, make your report.'

'The British were not happy, Comrad Kapitan, but we were allowed to board with no resistance. Comrad Ravoski has done well; he has their trust. But he tells me that he could not, however, prevent their previous escape without risking the total loss of the submarine. He confirms that all intelligence material has been disposed of, and our search of the vessel bears this out. The British first officer has agreed to comply with our instructions, but he wants an assurance on the welfare of his kapitan.'

Portrova raised a hand dismissively. 'Assurance? Does he not yet know that he is in no position to ask for assurances of any kind? But no matter, Sergei, continue.'

'Their food stock is low. They have no bread, and adequate fresh water is becoming a problem, though they are able to produce their own in limited quantities. With our men now aboard we will have to provide them with extra provisions.'

'Yes, yes, that will be done! Comrad Ravoski has told me of this.' Portrova leaned back in his chair. 'We will show them that we know how to feed our men. We will send over one week of supplies. That should be sufficient. You will arrange that.'

'They are ready to accept our tow, Kapitan.'

'This is good. You will see that our line is passed to them.' Portrova paused and looked directly at Carlov. There was no mistaking the thinly veiled threat. 'This time, Comrad, there will be no escape for them.'

★　★　★　★　★

Portrova had remained on *Otvashni*'s bridge for a full hour after the towline had been secured to *Spearfish*, and had watched as the bulky boxes of food supplies were transferred via the submarine's turned-out fore planes. Then, together, the two vessels had restarted their long journey southward. Within the hour they were battling head-on into a force ten gale.

Portrova had now slumped in his bridge chair, eyes closed, motionless, seemingly oblivious to the biting cold and the fiercely pitching motion of the ship beneath him. *Otvashni*'s bows were now taking the brunt of the increasingly heavy seas. Then, suddenly stirring, he shuddered violently, as though awakening from a bad dream. Grunting with the effort of raising his bulk from the chair, he stamped his frozen feet on the steel deck. Groping into his pockets with gloved hands, he produced his cigarette case. Removing a glove, he selected a Sobranie and placed it between his lips before carrying out a further search for his lighter. Finally the cigarette was lit, and he inhaled deeply before striding over to stand beside Bassisty, who was his watch officer.

Together they turned to look aft towards *Spearfish*, and Portrova gave another satisfied grunt as he watched *Spearfish* wallowing at the end of the bar-taut tow wire, now thickened with ice along its entire length. *Otvashni* was not making the progress that he would have liked. Her stern was digging deep in the water under the weight of her tow, and although she was now using both engines, she was not helped by this south-westerly sea. Her speed was barely three knots.

Turning back to Bassisty, Portrova said, 'Keep a good watch, Comrad Lieutenant. I do not trust this Britisher. Maybe she has yet more tricks up her sleeve, eh? But we will give her no more chances, *da?*' He again stamped his numbed feet on the steel deck. 'Maintain your course and speed. I go now to my cabin. Do not fail to call me if anything changes.'

Back in his sea cabin, Portrova paused only long enough to pull off his wet coat and throw it into a nearby chair before, still booted and fully clothed, throwing himself onto his bunk, where he lay motionless, one arm hanging over the bunk rail with the eternal Sobranie clutched between fingertips, the other arm covering his eyes. Physically inert but mentally in a state of turmoil, he knew that he had not handled this situation well from the outset. He had made hasty decisions and misread situations. He had become a changed man since his meeting with this British submarine. His hatred of the British, which had lain mainly dormant inside him for the past fifteen years, had now rekindled and had redeveloped to a point of fanaticism, which now burned inside him like a searing flame. When he turned Bradley over to his masters in the Kremlin, the Britisher would be made to pay dearly for all the trouble he had caused; and as for the other one, the trawler captain, he would pay with his life. He, Portrova, would see to that, not for the sake of his masters, or for the sake of that toad Borstoy – may his soul burn in hell. He was doing this for himself, and for the man who had died saving his life all those long years ago. Then, and only then, perhaps he could find some peace.

He knew that back there in Moscow they would blame him for the death of Borstoy. They would also blame him for the escape of the British submarine, days earlier, and for the subsequent injuries to two of his crew members, who were now being cared for by the doctor in a compartment away from the sick berth where the two Britishers were being held. But he did not care about any of this. He had long been regarded by his masters as a renegade, and had long since lost any feelings of respect or proper allegiance either to his masters or to his job. Much against his will, they had removed him from service in submarines shortly after the *Shtshuka* incident, declaring him to be unfit for that branch of the service. His subsequent advancement through the ranks had been long and hard fought, but by now the command of *Otvashni* had to him become more of an occupation than a calling. His second command, she had been his for just over two years now, and had afforded him the relative independence which he had always sought, as well as a large degree of personal privacy which, as time went by, had become increasingly more important to him.

So what could they do to him – these puppets that nestled beneath the protection of Khrushchev's wing back there in Moscow? At worst they could take away his command and give him a shore job, or perhaps they would retire him from the service. Either way it did not matter, since either way would enable him to drink more and thereby hasten his reunion with Anna. But whatever happened in the longer term, his job now was to take this British submarine back to Russia, and to hand her officers and crew over to the authorities, and this he would do. After this he cared not what might happen. A sharp knock on the door of his cabin shook him from his kaleidoscopic thought pattern.

'Come.'

The door opened to reveal the slim white-coated figure of the ship's doctor. '*Da*, Doktar, what is it?'

'I am sorry to disturb you, Comrad Kapitan, but I need to report that one of our two seamen injured while aboard the British submarine is in a serious condition; his head injury is very severe. I have put him in a cabin separate from the two British prisoners.'

'And the other man?'

'His wounds are not so serious: just some bruising.'

Portrova lit another cigarette and turned away to stare at the deck-head, while the doctor awaited a further response. But there was none.

CHAPTER TWELVE

00.05 Thursday, 29ᵗʰ October 1959

The overnight train from London Euston had arrived in Glasgow Central station at 06.52: precisely two minutes early. Hissing and clanking down the length of the platform, it coasted to a stop some ten feet short of the buffers that marked its journey's end. Then, as in an overt display of self-indulgence, perhaps rewarding itself for a journey successfully completed, the weary smoke-stained engine proceeded to noisily disgorge voluminous gouts of steam from the dark oily voids of its dripping undersides. Surging wetly upward from beneath the level of the platform, this cumulus wet cloud ballooned outward to envelop the engine in a giant snowy candyfloss, providing, as if by design, a perfect isolation from the bustle of activity now taking place on the platform behind it.

Some seven hours earlier, at London's Euston Station, a shrill blast from the guard's whistle had jolted the dozing engine into life. Responding with a long hoarse screech of protest, it had shuddered into a reluctant motion. Barking huge gouts of grey-black smoke high into the gloomy reaches of the station canopy, the drab blue steel-plated mammoth began to take up the strain. Snorting and wheezing, with its huge wheels spinning sporadically on the cold steel of the rails, it struggled to haul its thirteen equally drab blue carriages away from the sanctuary of the station, out into the rain of the waiting night.

The three first-class carriages at the front of the train were far less crowded than the rear ones. So much so that one man in the carriage nearest the engine presently had a compartment to himself. This man, at first appraisal, would convey to a stranger all the hallmarks of the archetypal middle-aged academic. But in this case any such appraisal based on outward appearance would be completely wrong. The lean figure in the dishevelled brown tweed suit now slumped in the window seat facing the engine, and looking distinctly uncomfortable in spite of the relative opulence of first class, was no woolly-minded university don – nothing could be further from the truth. A closer look at those keen piercing eyes and firm jawline would most certainly call for a rethink.

Lieutenant Commander James Cunningham DSC RN, commanding officer of Her Majesty's Submarine *Sturgeon*, had been one of the first to board the train that evening. Unable to book a sleeper, he had arrived at Euston just after 23.00 – early enough to take advantage of any last minute cancellations, but there were none. So now settling himself in the seat of his choice, with his long legs splayed across the floor of the dimly lit compartment, he contemplated the long boring journey that lay ahead.

A tall man, just short of six feet four inches, Cunningham's features gave the impression of an age well beyond his thirty-seven years. His penetrating grey eyes were set deep beneath sand-coloured brows topped by a pale expanse of sloping forehead, which carried a rash of faded freckles deep into his receding, sandy hairline. This, together with the long and slightly hooked nose dominating his chisel sharp jawline, presented a remarkable similarity to the features of Mr Punch. It was by any standards a striking face, conveying an unmistakable strength of character together with an assertiveness and wisdom accrued from a very detailed experience of life. But beneath this, again, there was something else: a sensitivity, perhaps? Even at this late hour those grey eyes revealed a distinct sparkle, a zest for life.

It was still cold in the compartment; the steam heating not yet having time to permeate through the train. Cunningham had never found it easy to sleep on trains and on this journey he doubted he would sleep at all. There was far too much on his mind for sleep. Even now he was deep in thought, completely oblivious to his surroundings and to the noisy pushing crowd on the platform outside.

The compartment door slid noisily open and two men entered, both of them dressed in dark overcoats, wearing trilby hats, and carrying suitcases. They pushed their cases and hats into the overhead racks, but kept their coats on. Nodding briefly towards Cunningham, they sat opposite each other in the corner seats next to the corridor. One mumbled to the other something about being just in time. Cunningham had hardly noticed their arrival.

Finally, with all doors now slammed shut, and with a fierce jerk, the train started to move. This sudden movement jolted Cunningham out of his thoughts. Looking out of the misted window, he cleared a patch in the glass with the back of his hand and watched as the station buildings and the small groups of people still on the platform slipped silently by before disappearing from his view.

Clearing the station, the scene through the window changed to a seemingly endless procession of shadowy buildings. Cunningham watched without really seeing, as dark terraces of houses, relieved only by the occasional lighted window or by dull yellow splashes from street lighting, passed across his vision. Now, with the train gathering speed and the engine seemingly resigned to its long haul northward, he settled back into his seat and closed his eyes, once more deep in thought.

Whoosh! The gentle swaying motion of the train and the rhythmic drumming of its wheels were rudely interrupted by the thud of air impacting against the window at Cunningham's side. The compartment rocked violently as a train passing in the opposite direction thundered by with a dull roar and a stream of flashing lights, disappearing into the darkness as quickly as it had appeared.

Cunningham stirred. Already his legs were beginning to ache. He looked at his watch: 00.40 – just thirty-five minutes into the journey. His two travelling companions appeared to be asleep. He felt the need to stand, so he did, gratefully stretching to his full height. Even though he had spent so many of his years within the confines of a submarine, his height had never been a problem to him. A few cuts and bruises to his head during the early days had taught him well, and as a countermeasure he had developed a distinct stoop over the years; a stoop that had now grown on him, and was now a part of him, whether afloat or ashore; a stoop which added further to the impression of age. When they knew that he was well out of earshot, his crew often referred to him as the "old man", but this was a term of endearment rather than a reflection on his looks.

He reached up into the luggage rack and pulled down a scuffed brown canvas holdall with a broken zip, from which he extracted last evening's London paper. Flopping back down in his seat, he scanned the front-page headlines. He grunted, realising that he wasn't really in the mood for reading. Refolding the paper, he groped in the side pocket of his jacket for his cigarette case. One of the two newcomers looked across at him and asked, 'Do you mind if we turn off the lights?'

Cunningham nodded. 'No, of course not; please do.' Inhaling deeply on his cigarette, he studied the dark of the night and the now almost horizontal "snail trails" of raindrops ceaselessly scurrying across the window at his side. He could see more clearly through the window with the main lights off. The only light left in the compartment was a dim yellow glow from the reading light directly above his left shoulder.

His thoughts turned to Sarah and his two boys back there in the house at Harrow. They would be long asleep by now. It had been such a short visit, but even though short, the unexpected opportunity to visit them had been a bonus, and he was grateful.

Sarah had understood though – she always did. Even though sensing an even greater than usual preoccupation within him during this visit, she had known that though he had been with her in body, his mind had been up there in Faslane with *Sturgeon*, his second wife. And like the good navy wife that she was, she had understood and accepted this.

A shrill screech from the engine's whistle again jerked Cunningham back to the present. The steady beat of the wheels beneath him now became a harsh clatter as the train careered over a jumble of points and then, just as suddenly, resumed their original rhythm. Now they were hurtling through an anonymous station. Bright platform lighting blurred past his window in a single long streak before giving way to the slower-moving, more distant lights of the passing town. He yawned widely, fumbling for the ashtray. Then easing himself into a more comfortable position, he closed his eyes, and let his thoughts drift back to the previous Monday morning.

Sturgeon was in the final week of a self-maintainance programme and was now lying alongside the depot ship HMS *Adamant*, based at Faslane in the Gareloch. He had been in his cabin aboard *Sturgeon*, making a determined attempt to reduce a seemingly never-ending pile of paperwork, when at about 09.30 he had been interrupted by a phone call from Commander Henry Mearsom, Cdr SM3. Mearsom had requested Cunningham's immediate presence in his office. Minutes later, and somewhat puzzled by the apparent urgency of the message, he had arrived at the door of Mearsom's office. The door was slightly ajar and he could hear voices. There were others already in there. Were they waiting for him? He had knocked twice and, without waiting for an invitation, pushed the door open and walked in.

He'd been faintly surprised to find not only Mearsom and his secretary, Lieutenant Chris Long, in the office, but, seated next to Mearsom and clutching a very large tortoiseshell fountain pen, with which he was now scribbling intently in a notebook, was the bulky figure of Captain Richard Sterne DSO, DSC, Captain SM3. Also, sitting to Mearsom's right, was the squadron operations officer, Lieutenant Commander Dickie Bird.

Christ, a reception committee! Cunningham had felt vaguely uncomfortable though he didn't know why. He and Mearsom went back a long time and Bird was also a good friend. Mearsom and Bird had been talking quietly and had looked up as he entered the office. Sterne continued his writing without looking up.

'Ah, there you are, James. Come and sit down.' Mearsom indicated to the empty chair in front of his desk.

'Coffee?'

Then, turning to Long, he said, 'Thanks, Chris, that'll be all for now.' Long nodded and left the office. Cunningham noted that the others were not taking coffee, so he raised his hand in refusal before sitting down. Sterne continued to concentrate on his notebook.

Cunningham waited expectantly. Despite Mearsom's cordial welcome, he could sense tension. Mearsom was obviously not at ease, and certainly not his usual affable self. But then it was no secret that Mearsom's relationship with Sterne had been strained almost since the day he had taken up his appointment. Richard Sterne was not an easy man to work with, or for. Large and thickset with florid heavily jowelled features bearing a permanent look of agitation and impatience, he was so aptly named. It was a well-known fact among the rank and file that you didn't deliberately upset Captain Richard Sterne.

Mearsom glanced towards Sterne, but it became clear that Sterne expected him to start the conversation. He coughed quietly, clearing his throat. 'Right, this won't take long, James; at least not at this time. We've got a potentially nasty situation brewing, which we hope won't escalate, but at this stage we're not quite sure what—'

'When can *Sturgeon* be ready for sea?' Sterne had looked up and interrupted Mearsom with his customary blunt bark.

Cunningham had been caught completely off guard, for this was not a question he'd been expecting. According to her programme, *Sturgeon* was officially out of action for at least another seven days.

'Well, as you know, Sir, officially we've got until Sunday to complete our maintenance period. As you also know, we've had serious problems with our main generators. These problems have taken precedence over a lot of our other jobs, and have put some of the other work slightly behind. However, as you also probably know, both our own engineers, as well as those from *Adamant* and those sent up by the makers, appear to have cracked the problem. We've run extensive trials over the past two days and, thankfully, it's all looking good. But there is a smallish amount of maintenance work to do, as well as a few more outstanding minor defects to clear by the weekend. Why? Is there a—'

Sterne interrupted him, again with his customary blunt bark. Closing his notebook with a snap and pocketing his pen, he glared at Cunningham, dark eyes piercing beneath heavy iron-grey brows. 'Yes there *is* a problem! At least it's growing more likely by the hour that there may be a problem, and it could be a serious one. It's imperative that *Sturgeon* will be fully ready for sea by next Thursday morning, the 29th. If push comes to shove, your men and some of our men will work night and day to clear these outstanding defects, but you must be ready to sail by Thursday forenoon!'

Again Mearsom coughed, this time almost apologetically. He was a small man, slim in stature, with finely chiselled, pale, almost delicate features, and always immaculately turned out – an exact opposite of Sterne in just about every way.

'We may have a problem, James. *Spearfish's* surfacing signal is overdue, well overdue. In fact, it expired at 12.00 on Thursday the 22nd. Now I know that's only a few days ago and could well be nothing more than a communications problem, but on that same day we received a rather garbled signal from the trawler *Imogen*, telling us that she sighted a British submarine being towed in a southerly direction by a Russian destroyer of whom we know nothing, but the trawler's position does make her signal credible. We've run a check on her: she's definitely British, apparently out of Hull. Haven't heard a thing from her since, though. Then last Friday, through sheer chance, we happened to pick up an even more confusing signal, unencrypted, and in English! This seems to have originated from somewhere in the Barents, telling no one in particular that she was heading south towards the Russian mainland. We've tried to do some follow-up on it, but without success. Could be from anyone about anything, really. It's just the fact that the word "tow" is used.'

He handed Cunningham a signal sheet lying on his desk top. Cunningham studied it briefly. It read: 76N 47E To... again we... in... tow... Weather poor... Estimate time... to be 5... Cunningham read it twice before handing the signal back to Mearsom, who raised his hand. 'No, you keep it, James. We've got a copy in our log. I doubt whether it'll be of much use to you though. Could be about anything. Strange it was uncoded though.' Cunningham stuffed the signal sheet into his trouser pocket.

Mearsom coughed again, nervously now, plainly aware of Sterne's baleful glare. 'So, as I was saying, this could be a tricky one. Because of what she's doing and her likely location, the powers-that-be were, and still are, anxious to initiate sub-miss procedures, not at this stage anyway. We've been hanging on in the hope that it's just a communications problem, but that's beginning to wear a bit thin now. From that trawler's report, *Spearfish* may have suffered a complete power failure: generators, perhaps? Understandably, the boys down in London have been getting more concerned as each day passes. They've already carried out five Shackleton air searches. There are trawlers up there. Of course, many of these will be foreign, but as for a Russian towing a British submarine, well, there's been no joy as yet. Now the politicians want to discuss further action. In other words, they probably want us to go up there and look for her!' Mearsom had cast a sideways glance at Sterne, who was still glaring fixedly at Cunningham. 'I don't have to tell you, James, that if there *is* a problem, then because of where she is and what she was doing, at best things could get embarrassing, and at worst, bloody serious or possibly even dangerous!' He paused again, shooting another glance towards Sterne, who remained silent, still watching Cunningham.

Then Bird spoke for the first time. 'Someone has to make a decision, and under the circumstances – time is marching on – we need to know what's happening up there—'

Again Sterne interrupted. 'I'll be in London on Wednesday, James, and so will you. There's a meeting at the MoD at 10.00. The objective is to go through all the facts we have, get 'em clear and sorted, then decide what to do. Those buggers down there will be frightened of muddying the water – they always are. Decisions don't come easy to them. I already know what the outcome of this meeting will be, or at least, what it should be, and that's to get someone up there to try to locate *Spearfish*, and if possible get her back here without causing too many waves for the politicians.'

Bird said, 'Of course, we don't want to exacerbate any problems we may already have, and at this time we're still dealing with speculation, but if we must send someone up there, then we'll use the best tool available.' He had looked directly at Cunningham. 'Since *Shark* is presently working down in the eastern end of the Med, and *Sealion* is high and dry in the floating dock up here with worse generator problems than your boat, I'm afraid it looks like you've drawn the short straw. Unless we get some definitely positive news between now and Thursday, you and *Sturgeon* will be on your way…'

Bird paused, his tone now almost apologetic, looking towards Mearsom and Sterne, who both remained silent. He continued, 'As you know, James,

Sturgeon's immediate programme was for five days of exercising with the Home Fleet, commencing a week from tomorrow, followed by a four-day jolly in Rotterdam. As things currently stand you could, of course, say goodbye to those – they're not important. Anyway, we can only hope that this situation will be much clearer by Thursday.'

There had been no expression on Cunningham's face, but his mind was working overtime. What would all this mean? And in any case, could *Sturgeon* be ready in all respects for sea by Thursday morning? He was trying desperately to remember the items of outstanding work. Now he spoke slowly, deliberately – this was not the time for hasty decisions or rash promises. 'Thanks, Dickie, I get your drift. So at the moment it's a case of waiting for something—'

'Do you? Do you get the drift?' Sterne too, had spoken slowly, but still with his usual bellow. 'Because I'm damned if I do! One of our boats is missing, and I want it back! All this bloody waiting about while a pack of blasted politicians try to make up their minds what to do. I know what I'd do if I had my way. I'd have a boat away this afternoon, and maybe a couple more besides!' He stopped, as though suddenly becoming conscious of his outburst; then clearing his throat with a low cough which for anyone else could have been attributed to embarrassment, he again groped for his tortoiseshell fountain pen, rolling it between his fingers before continuing in a slightly modified tone, 'We will, of course, provide you with all the extra manpower and equipment that may be needed to bring you back to your full capability, but *Sturgeon* must be ready in all respects by Thursday morning!' He shot a quick glance towards Mearsom.

Mearsom, pointedly ignoring Sterne's outburst, said, 'You'll be storing for war. Torpedo loading has been arranged for tomorrow and you'll start embarking stores on Wednesday. I've got everything organised with the inboard departments but you'll need to get your people sorted pretty quickly for some liaison work. Oh, and we'll need to get your fin beefed up a bit: there'll be a lot of ice up there by now, but we'll do that.'

Mearsom had paused, briefly drawing breath before going on. 'Give as much night leave as you can before Thursday, though under the circumstances I don't suppose you'll be able to spare many. To all intents and purposes you may consider *Sturgeon* to be under sailing orders! Do you have any other questions?'

'Not immediately,' Cunningham replied, 'but no doubt there'll be plenty once all this has properly sunk in.'

Then Sterne rose to his feet. Suddenly he looked very tired. Gone was the blunt arrogance. Now his tone was almost docile. 'I'll leave you to arrange the detail, Henry. I'll be in my office if you need me. Things to do, you know!' He looked towards Cunningham and now there was the mere hint of sympathy in his voice. 'I'm really sorry about all this, James. I'll see you in the MoD at 10.00 on Wednesday. Damned nuisance! We could all do without this.' Pushing his chair back, he moved towards the door, then stopped and turned back to look at the others, his voice now no more than a mumble. 'Something seems to have gone badly wrong. Not like young Bradley to upset the applecart.' Then he seemed to relax. The aggression in his tone had faded and the scowl on his florid face had suddenly turned into what Cunningham vaguely supposed could have been the hint of a grin. 'Well, good luck! Make your own way down south tomorrow. Spend the evening with your family. Keep me in touch, Henry. Thank you, gentlemen.' Then he was gone, slamming the door shut behind him.

'Well, there you have it, James.' Mearsom looked distinctly relieved, obviously glad that this meeting was over. He'd done his job for the time being and there wasn't much else to be said at this time. 'But whatever,' he added, 'we'll meet again tomorrow at 09.00 for a progress report, but if there's no change in the current circumstances, then *Sturgeon* will almost certainly be sailing on Thursday.'

Then Bird said, 'Of course, all this is classified. Obviously you'll have to tell your officers what's going on. Do that as soon as you can after you leave here, but keep it strictly on a need-to-know basis, and don't say anything to the troops about *Spearfish* yet. We know they're probably going to go to sea a few days early, but there's no need for them to know why – not yet, anyway – and we can certainly do without wild rumours at this stage.'

After Sterne had left the office nothing in the continued conversation between the three remaining men threw any further light on the subject, and by the time Cunningham departed he was fully convinced that *Sturgeon* would be sailing, as discussed.

★ ★ ★ ★ ★

Cunningham stirred and opened his eyes. He had actually slept. He looked at his watch: ten past six. Not long now. His mouth was dry. He lit a cigarette and wondered what was going to happen this morning. Probably get back there and find that everything's changed. *Spearfish* had been located. Stand *Sturgeon* down and revert to her original programme. He knew Bradley very well, and had a lot of respect for him. A bit brash perhaps, and sometimes sailed "close to the wind", but he knew his job and was, in Cunningham's opinion, a good submarine CO. In spite of his worries, he smiled wryly to himself, thinking, What's the young bugger been up to now?

He rubbed his eyes, really feeling the need for some sleep now, but he knew that sleep wasn't going to happen, not with so much else to think about. Settling back in his seat, he drew deeply on his cigarette. Somehow he knew that he would be at sea before this day was out.

Yesterday evening, travel weary after his long train journey south, he had walked into his house at Harrow. Sarah had been completely surprised at seeing him, but nevertheless delighted. She called the two boys, who had gone to their beds some thirty minutes ago, and for the next hour they all talked. He put the reason for his unexpected visit to a last-minute change in *Sturgeon's* programme, and left it at that. He also told them he was due to go to a meeting at the MoD at 10.00 the following morning. Then the boys returned to bed, and he and Sarah had made the most of the rest of the evening.

The MoD meeting added little or nothing to what he already knew. Although there was a lot of discussion and airing of personal opinions, particularly in the case of Sterne, who, with a barely-hidden disdain for the ministers, and in spite of being subordinate in rank to most of the other naval officers present, had made a very firm case for sending *Sturgeon* north in search of *Spearfish*. The meeting was over by 12.00, with the defence ministers wanting more time to discuss the situation within their departments, saying that they would signal their final decision to SM3 before midnight that day. Declining an invitation to lunch at the MoD, Cunningham left immediately to make his way back to Sarah, where he had stayed until 22.50, before taking a taxi back to Euston.

The sudden change in the rhythm of the wheels beneath him once more brought him back to the present. He rubbed his hand over the misted window and saw that it was still raining hard. There was some daylight now, but the dawn sky was an unbroken grey. The train slowed as it rolled over a long viaduct and, looking down, he could clearly see fast-moving traffic on the road below, headlights reflecting wide yellow blobs on the wet road in front of each vehicle, turning road spray into thick mantles of dirty yellow.

The other three men in the compartment were beginning to stir. The fourth – a man who had joined the train at Crewe and was now seated opposite Cunningham – had also lighted a cigarette and was now vigorously rubbing his portion of the window while gazing at the streaks of light in the dawn sky. The other two were now conversing in low tones.

Cunningham glanced at his watch. In the yellow light of the reading lamp above him he could see that the time was coming up to a quarter to seven. Glasgow should be just a few minutes away if the train was on time. He hoped that the staff car he had organised before leaving the depot ship wouldn't let him down. Now he stood up, feeling the relief flooding through his limbs as he stretched. Suppressing a yawn, he pulled on the thick tweed overcoat that had acted as an overnight blanket, and reached into the overhead luggage rack to pull down his tan-coloured canvas holdall with the broken zip, together with his well-worn brown trilby, which he placed squarely on his head. Now sitting back down, with his baggage between his long legs, he awaited Glasgow.

The staff car had not let him down; the driver was waiting for him in the main foyer of the station. Cunningham's dry mouth and throat told him that he really needed a large cup of strong coffee, but because his driver was already here, he would have to reserve that pleasure until he arrived back aboard *Adamant* in about forty-five minutes from now. Together he and the driver made their way to the car and Cunningham threw his hat, coat and bag into the back seat and then sat in front with the driver. The staff car was a Rover, very big and very comfortable. They travelled for less than half a mile before he was soundly asleep.

★　★　★　★　★

At about the same time that the night train from Euston was approaching Glasgow Central station, Lieutenant Andrew Watson, *Sturgeon*'s weapons electrical officer, and at this time her duty officer, was awakened with a start as the curtains in his wardroom bunk were roughly pulled open, leaving him blinking owlishly in the flickering overhead fluorescent lighting that had just been switched on to now send out a steady glare of white, providing a backdrop to the grinning black-bearded features of Gus Ramsay, the duty petty officer.

Watson instinctively raised a protective hand to shield his eyes from this light. 'Morning, Ramsay,' he mumbled, lowering his hand but keeping his eyes half shut. Then, propping himself up on one elbow, he asked. 'What's the time?'

'Mornin', Sir, it's twenty to seven an' it's Thursday. Nice cuppa coffee?' He thrust a large white mug of steaming coffee towards the bunk, and Watson reached out to take it.

Gripping the body of the mug, Watson winced in agony, 'Christ, that's bloody hot!' Grabbing the handle with his other hand, he thrust it back at the still-grinning face. 'Here, put it on the table for a minute. What's the weather like?'

'Bin pissin' down fer most of the night, Sir. Not so bad now but the wind's pickin' up a bit from the south-west. Well, more than a bit, really. Seems there's a bloody 'ooligan blowin' up further north. Right then, I'll be off to call the 'ands.'

Watson lay there for a few minutes, propped on his elbow and massaging fingers that still tingled from the heat of the coffee mug. He had been "duty officer" since 08.00 yesterday, though, as he admitted to himself, the one advantage of being duty officer was that it gave him the chance to catch up with the pile of paperwork during the previous evening. He was grateful that yesterday had been a relatively quiet day, spent mainly checking on the state of play within his department, making sure that any work which could possibly compromise *Sturgeon*'s readiness for sea was completed. At least it had been a peaceful day, and that was something that the last two weeks had definitely not been.

Both of *Sturgeon*'s main generators had been giving trouble almost continuously since leaving the builders yard. These generators were essential to the working of the submarine. They were, in effect, her heart since, together with their associated diesel engines, they provided the sole means of charging her main batteries – the main source of her electrical power. By design, these new "S" class boats had no direct drive between diesel engines and propellers, and since the two main propulsion motors took their power from the batteries, without main generators to keep these batteries charged *Sturgeon* was effectively dead, incapable of sustained movement.

During the maker's sea trials, much to the annoyance of Cunningham they had been forced to make an unscheduled return to the builders because of these generators, and still the bloody things were playing up. Although it was of little consolation to him, Watson knew that at least three of the other newly built boats of this class were having similar troubles, which must put the root of the problem down to design. But the whole business of these unreliable generators had weighed heavily upon his shoulders. He *was* the weapons electrical officer, and so, responsible or not, the buck stopped with him. He certainly hadn't missed the look on Cunningham's face when *Sturgeon*'s work-up programme had been interrupted by the failure of these generators.

He reached down to the table for the mug and took a large gulp. The coffee was still very hot, but he swilled it around his mouth and felt it eating into the musty layer that lined his tongue. Then, swallowing, he lay back, shutting his eyes, listening to the faint drone of machinery coming from the control room, together with the subdued rustle of air from the ventilation louvre above him, and he waited for the fuzziness in his head to clear.

It felt like a hangover, but it most certainly wasn't. Because of those bloody generators *he* hadn't been allowed the luxury of a hangover, or indeed any other kind of luxury during the past two weeks. Cunningham was not happy, and had made this very plain. 'Get it sorted, Andrew.' His tone had been unusually terse. 'Get it sorted.'

And so, with these faulty generators hanging over his head like the sword of Damocles, Andrew Watson had vowed that apart from meals and sleep, he would not set foot off the boat until they were right once and for all.

This was hard for him. An active social life with all the trimmings was to Watson a fundamental need – one which he liked to enjoy to the full. Almost six feet tall, with a slim build, dark wavy hair and classically handsome features, Watson, though not a womaniser, had enjoyed his moments. As yet unmarried, he had no plans to change that situation. A born-and-bred Bristolian, with a voice that still carried more than a broad hint of that Bristolian burr; his grammar school education had taken him on to university, where in spite of his fondness for the social life, he gained a BA with Honours in Electrical Engineering. He joined the Navy on a short-service commission at the age of twenty-three and, as a sublieutenant, was appointed to *Ark Royal*, essentially still in a training billet. While in the "Ark" he volunteered for submarine service, though even now he didn't quite know why. On completion of his submarine training he was appointed to *Sturgeon*, where he stood by her build at Birkenhead for almost a year, before commencing sea trials.

Now yawning widely, he took yet another gulp of coffee, and with his head now beginning to clear, he rolled out of his bunk and reached for his clothes. As he pulled on his trousers he reflected that he wouldn't be at all anxious for a repeat performance of the four months since *Sturgeon* had left Birkenhead. Fitters from Cammel Lairds, together with his own chief electrical artificer and a team from the electrical workshops of the depot ship *Adamant*, had been working practically non-stop on the main generators since *Sturgeon* had come alongside seventeen days ago for a three-week self-maintenance period, since when they had virtually rebuilt both machines. They had finished just over a week ago, and over the weekend had carried out exhaustive trials on both generators, which, thankfully, had proved completely successful.

Cunningham's announcement last Tuesday morning had come as a complete surprise and more than a bit of a disappointment to him. He had been looking forward to some social enjoyment in Rotterdam. But at least his department was completely ready for sea this morning, ready to meet today's advanced sailing date if required, and that meant more to him than a couple of runs ashore.

His thoughts were interrupted by the bawling voice of Gus Ramsay coaxing the duty watch from their bunks in the accommodation space forward. 'Come along then, you lazy sods. Feet on the deck – now! You've 'ad your time. It could be 'arbour stations at any minute. I'll be back in five an' I'll troop anyone still turned in.'

Ramsay was *Sturgeon*'s TI, these initials standing for torpedo instructor, which was the equivalent to the general service torpedo and anti-submarine instructor, or TASI. The omission of the A and the S were very apt in Ramsay's case. No one could be less anti-submarine than him. He was a big man, with a build still very powerful but now running to seed. A thick black beard mottled with grey covered the lower half of his heavily jowelled face. No one could ever remember seeing him without it, together with a seemingly perpetual grin on his face. As he was now in his thirty-ninth year, *Sturgeon* would be Ramsay's last boat. Today would probably be the start of his last trip to sea in a submarine. He had been in submarines since he was eighteen. He was one of the few on board who had served throughout the whole of the second war in submarines, and he proudly displayed the dark-blue and white of the DSM among the three rows of discoloured ribbons on the chest of his well-worn jacket. But he had been a natural-born hellraiser in his younger days, and after the war it had taken him longer than most to settle down. His career had been more than a little blighted by drink. At one stage – having completed the long and arduous climb from able seaman to leading hand, to petty officer and then to chief petty officer – he was, after a particularly boisterous and eventful run ashore, plummeted back down to AB. Had it not been for the fact that he was excellent at his job, and that his successive 'skippers' had appreciated this fact, he would never have been tolerated in the submarine service. But he was a survivor; he was lucky. And then, he had finally realised this. For the last five years or so of his service he had diligently toed the line. A reformed character, he never drank while on board, not even his daily tot, and he never went ashore unless going home. For Ramsay, maturity had arrived at a somewhat late age – perhaps a little too late, but now here he was on his last boat, a TI once again, having made a solemn promise to his long-suffering wife that he would never again put his navy pension – their pension – at risk.

'Everything all right, TI?'

'No problems,' answered Ramsay. 'Everything's under control, Sir.'

'No messages from inboard, I suppose?'

'Nothing, Sir.'

Watson shrugged his shoulders, feeling a distinct sense of disappointment. 'OK then, I'm off inboard for a shower and a spot of breakfast.' Moving forward towards the main access hatch, he noted that there was still little, if any, sign of activity in the seamen's mess. Climbing up the ladder through the main access hatch, he stepped onto the casing and surveyed the new day. It was still dark and it was drizzling. And yes, it was a bloody awful morning.

★ ★ ★ ★ ★

The large clock on the bulkhead of the junior rates' dining room in the submarine depot ship read exactly 07.55 as Leading Seaman Tom Donovan and Leading Telegraphist "Dixie" Deane arrived for breakfast. They were hungry, and made their way eagerly across to the servery, sniffing, savouring the smells. The dining area was almost empty now; as were the shallow steel trays lined up on the stainless steel hot counter. The two friends were, as usual, almost the last to come for breakfast. The cooks were now out of sight, but soon they would be back to clear the trays away, and breakfast would be over.

Breakfast always smelled better than it looked. Donovan gazed down into the first tray, where a dozen or so small off-white circular slabs with a rubbery yellowish green eye malevolently glared up at him from a pool of pale yellow cooking oil. He almost lost his appetite, but scooped up two of these and slid them onto his plate. Moving on to the next trays, they each pulled out half a dozen small rashers of even greasier bacon, together with a large scoop of baked beans. Then, after pouring themselves mugs of strong black coffee, which thankfully was still hot, each balanced four thick slices of bread on the top of his plate and, picking up knives and forks, made their way over to a table in the far corner of the mess, where Leading Seaman "Knocker" White was busily finishing a similar meal.

Laying their plates on the table, they sat down beside White, both nodding a greeting as they stabbed the hard yolks of their eggs with knives. 'Jesus!' breathed Donovan, poking his eggs with a knife. 'The great pusser's fried egg. How do they do it? Look at this bloody lot. I ask you, no matter whatever else changes in this world, here's something that will never change.' He flipped one of the eggs over. 'A pusser's fried egg! It's unbelievable.'

'Well, they send these cookies on special courses, don't they?' offered Deane. 'You know the ones. "Fifty Ways to Cock Up Good Food", an' it looks like the bastards who cooked this 'ave qualified wiv honours!'

White had almost cleared his plate, and was now swallowing hard on a grease-soaked crust, which he washed down with the remnants of his coffee. Then, wiping his mouth with the back of his hand, he rubbed his greasy fingers over the front of his shirt and said, 'Ah well, roll on dinner-time. We got "pot mess" fer dinner.' Deane busied himself by scooping the whole contents of his plate between his four slices of bread to produce two ungainly grease-dripping sandwiches, while Donovan looked across the table at the burly figure still seated opposite. Dressed in worn, faded and patched number-eight working dress, White's shirt was, as usual, unbuttoned almost to his waist, exposing the mat of black hair covering his expansive chest. His shirtsleeves were rolled up tightly, high above the elbow, pulling over muscular arms that proudly displayed a variety of tattoos. His thick bull neck supported a massive head covered with tight jet-black curls crowning swarthy features, with olive black eyes set deep above a large hooked nose – a nose that had twice been broken during drink-fuelled disagreements during some long-forgotten runs ashore. With his wide full-lipped mouth and equally wide smile, he had the appearance of a Spanish gypsy, but despite these Hispanic features, and although Irish on his father's side, he was a born-and-bred Liverpudlian.

Donovan knew that White had been the duty leading hand last night. He and White had been close friends since they had together joined their first boat just over eight years ago, and although he knew that Knocker was not a person that you went out of your way to upset, he also knew that behind his tough-looking exterior, White was in many ways a big softie – a gentle giant. Full of rough scouse humour and razor-sharp wit, White laughed a lot, as often as not at himself. Although a married man with his wife and family living ashore just some three miles away in Helensburgh, the real love in White's life was his motorbike: a Norton Dominator – an immaculate machine dressed in a combination of glossy black paintwork and sparkling chrome, and very powerful. Having lovingly cleaned and polished the Norton last Tuesday evening, he'd covered it with a blanket and parked it in his shed to await his return. This morning he had given his wife her customary peck on the cheek, and patted the heads of his four children, before hitching a lift into the Faslane base, where he would be duty leading hand for Wednesday.

White had in fact recently passed professionally for petty officer, and for this trip would be *Sturgeon*'s most senior sound room operator. Soon he would be rated petty officer and placed in charge of the day-to-day operation of all sonar sets on board – a job that he was in fact already doing as a leading hand.

Finishing his beans, Donovan next applied himself to making up sandwiches from the rest of what was on his plate – two rounds of one egg and three rashers, topped off with a liberal dollop of tomato ketchup. 'So I guess that we'll be going according to schedule this morning.' Donovan took a large bite from his first sandwich and tried to conceal his niggling disappointment.

'Oh, we'll go, all right…' Deane finished off his second sandwich and reached into his trouser pocket to withdraw a crumpled grey handkerchief, surveying it carefully before blowing his nose, '…even though I don't 'ave a bleedin' clue where.'

White said, 'Seems that way, old son. Special sea duty men could be at half past ten, and harbour stations at eleven. But nothing's for sure yet.' Then, seeing Donovan's face drop, he gave him a long quizzical look. 'Why? What's the matter, Donno? Don't you want to go then? Christ, I can remember the times when you couldn't get to sea quick enough. What you want to do is to get yer missus up 'ere like I did, then after about six weeks, goin' to sea will be like a bloody 'oliday cruise. Still,' he added with a loud sniff, 'you aint got no kids yet, 'ave you? I suppose that can make a difference, an' o'course,' he added, 'you ain't been tied up fer a dogwatch yet, 'ave yuh!'

Donovan frowned, remaining silent, outwardly concentrating on his breakfast, inwardly lost in thoughts of June and the baby that was on the way. He hadn't mentioned the baby to anyone on board yet, not even to White or Deane, though he'd known that June had been pregnant for almost seven months now. 'Course I'm ready to go, yuh scouse prat. Wouldn't miss this for the world, would I? An' I'm really lookin' forward to our run ashore in 'Olland.' He took a large gulp of coffee, and then, if for no other reason than to change the subject, he said, 'By the way, is Dinger Bell back aboard yet?'

'Yeh,' frowned White. 'He came aboard at about midnight and slept down the boat. Pissed as a friggin' handcart again.' White scowled in mock disgust. 'Well, 'e's goin' to regret 'is pissy-arsed run later. From what I've 'eard, there's goin' to be some real roughers out there today. Anyway, serves the bastard right; 'e won't be gettin' no sympathy from me, an' that's for sure.'

'Jealousy will get you nowhere, me old mate,' grinned Donovan. 'You got all your gear down the boat yet?'

'Yep, I'm all ready to go. Only popped up fer a spot of brekkers; I was friggin' starving! You got all your stuff down?' Using the crust from his last sandwich, Donovan wiped the remains of the grease and ketchup from his plate. Swallowing it in two mouthfuls, he wiped his mouth with the back of his hand and said, 'Only me steaming bag to go down now. See you down the boat, then. You ready yet, Dixie?' He stood up, and together he and Deane made their way down to *Sturgeon*.

* * * * *

Now aboard *Sturgeon*, Donovan threw the remainder of the gear he would need for sea into his bunk just as the loudspeaker above him clicked on. A harsh background crackle gave way almost immediately to the clipped, crisp voice of the first lieutenant, Lieutenant Hugh Morton.

'D'you hear there, all compartments? This is the first lieutenant speaking. The submarine will go to harbour stations at 10.45 and will slip at 11.00. Special sea duty men will be required at 10.30. The weather forecast is not good, so see that the boat is properly secured for sea. That's all.' Another brief crackle, and the microphone clicked off.

In *Sturgeon*'s control room Morton replaced the microphone in its holder. Slightly overweight and with blond curly hair and soft pink features that could well be described as cherubic, Morton had joined *Sturgeon* half way through her build, and she was his first boat as first lieutenant. Very popular with *Sturgeon*'s crew, and always ready with a word of encouragement or a friendly joke, perhaps Morton's biggest attribute was that he appeared to be absolutely unflappable no matter what the situation – a quality which he had demonstrated on more than one occasion during the past four months, especially during the initial phase of the work-up.

Now he turned and grinned towards the coxswain, Chief Petty Officer "Sandy" Sanford, who had been waiting patiently at his side gripping a clipboard bulging with paper. 'Bloody paperwork, eh, Cox'n. Right then, we'll have a look at the inboard mess at about half nine, and in the meantime a clean through the boat wouldn't come amiss. Get rid of the gash and see that everything's properly secured. There's going to be a bit of a blow out there today, according to the forecast.' He paused and looked at his watch. 'Any absentees?'

'No, Sir. All present, correct an' rarin' to go, even if we are a few days early.' Chief Petty Officer Coxswain "Sandy" Sanford DSM – short, tubby and balding – had the look of one who had seen it all and heard it all before, and for the most part he had. He too had served in submarines throughout the Second World War. He shot a sly wink at Jim Beresford, the chief stoker, who had now joined them.

Morton grinned and turned to Beresford. 'Morning, Chief Stoker. How's the black gang this morning? Any problems?'

Joe Beresford, a small, morose man, lifted his thin shoulders in a shrug, pointedly ignoring Morton's friendly approach. 'No, Sir, not as I know of, anyway.' Beresford's sallow features were seldom seen to smile, and even more seldom seen without the cigarette dangling from his lips. Like Ramsay, at just short of forty years old, he was due for retirement. This would be his last seagoing trip in *Sturgeon* but, unlike Ramsay, he was glad to be leaving. Also, unlike Ramsay, Beresford was not liked by his stokers. Secretly they called him "Vinegar Joe", or "VJ", but only when they knew he was well out of earshot. The grease-stained navy blue jacket Beresford wore over his blue overalls carried a variety of ribbons. He had served in submarines for the last four years of World War II. Without further word, Beresford turned abruptly and walked forward.

Whatever else he thought of Beresford, Morton couldn't fault him at his job. He knew that, along with the rest of the engineering department, the chief stoker had been very busy, and that many of his normal pre-sea tasks had of necessity been left to the very last minute because of the generator work. Among other jobs, Beresford had supervised the taking on of fuel and fresh water on Tuesday, and then he had spent most of yesterday putting on *Sturgeon's* trim.

Morton shook his head. 'What a bundle of laughs that man is!'

'Oh, our Joe's all right, Sir,' said Sanford. 'Just getting too old for this – bit like me, I guess. Right then, I'll pick you up at half past nine, Sir?' He reached out for the microphone. 'Leading Seaman Donovan, report to the coxswain in the control room.' Again the harsh crackle over the broadcast system.

Morton called loudly over his shoulder as he walked from the control room, 'And for Christ's sake, get the EA to fix that bloody microphone!'

★　★　★　★　★

Cunningham arrived back aboard *Adamant* just before 08.00, having slept for most of his journey from Glasgow. He then treated himself to a large mug of strong coffee and a long hot shower before changing into uniform and, by chance, meeting up with Watson in the wardroom, where he used the opportunity to catch up with *Sturgeon's* current state, and her readiness for sea. After breakfast, while relaxing in an armchair in the wardroom with a second cup of coffee and the *Daily Telegraph*, he was startled by a steward nudging his arm. 'Commander Mearsom wants to see you in his office as soon as possible, Sir.'

Cunningham was surprised. His meeting with Mearsom was not scheduled until 09.00. Could this be good news about *Spearfish*? No, probably not. Nothing that would prevent sailing, anyway. He dropped his paper and gulped down the remains of his coffee, then hurried aft towards Mearsom's office.

'I'm sorry, James, still no news. Nothing from the last air search, I'm afraid.'

'Communications failure?' Cunningham volunteered, mainly for something to say.

'Possibly,' replied Mearsom, 'but what the hell was she doing hooked up to a bloody Ruskie? Was she detected and forced to surface? If so, that could be very embarrassing. Or had she suffered some sort of major mechanical problem, which she's now fixed? In accordance with her orders she would, of course, be keeping radio silence until she clears the North Cape.' Mearsom paused, frowning. 'But, whatever the case, I don't like the sound of this Russian involvement! Whitehall have made some discreet enquiries but, of course, surprise, surprise, the Soviets deny all knowledge of the matter. We received a signal from the MoD late last evening. You will be going to sea at 11.00 this morning! I'm sure you're not surprised to hear that.'

Cunningham nodded and asked, 'How did the trawler know for sure that this boat was one of ours? She certainly wouldn't have been flying an ensign and she would have scrubbed her pennant numbers.'

'Blowed if I know.' Mearsom shook his head. 'But that's all the signal said and, I agree, it provokes all sorts of questions. But if it was pukka, and I believe it is, then at least *Spearfish* isn't down, and that's the main thing.' He looked directly at Cunningham, knowing that they were both thinking the same thing. 'This whole business has a bit of a nasty smell about it, James.' He passed a large buff-coloured envelope to Cunningham. 'Your orders are here. Everything is more or less as we discussed last Monday. You'll make all haste to get up there, while we'll just sit here and hope that you meet her on the way up.'

Cunningham managed a smile. 'Well, I suppose you could always come up with us, Henry.'

Mearsom didn't smile. 'Believe me, James, there have been times over the past week or so that I wish I was going with you.' He glanced at his watch. 'Sterne will be back aboard by now, though I haven't seen him yet this morning.' He paused while a steward quietly entered the office and placed coffee on his desk. Nodding to the steward, he waited until he left the office before continuing, 'By the way, you'll be taking three extra people up north with you: a major from the Army Intelligence Corps – some sort of Soviet expert, I believe – and two Royal Marine NCOs – diving specialists. You'll collect them from an MFV off Campbeltown. It's all in your orders, They'll be with you for the duration! We'll maintain radio contact until you reach the North Cape, and of course you'll be recalled if things sort themselves by then. If not, you'll carry on, but you'll be on your own, just like *Spearfish*! And you'll need to be ready for anything! Now I won't keep you. No doubt you'll have things to do.'

A fleeting scowl shadowed Cunningham's face. 'Why can't we use our own people? And why couldn't these "passengers" have come aboard this morning before we leave? From what I hear on the forecast, it's blowing up quite rough further up. Picking them up will just be another buggerance factor.'

Mearsom shrugged his shoulders, but made no reply.

Cunningham left Mearsom's office. No surprises there, he thought. In fact things had turned out in much the way he'd expected, and already he was planning the next few days in his head. Strangely, he now felt a sense of relief. At least he now knew for sure what was happening. More importantly, it now looked a lot more possible that *Spearfish* was not lost, as he and many others had begun to fear. But then again, how much credibility could he placed on those signals? Ah well, he thought, time will tell. Returning to his cabin, he packed his seagoing necessities into the large tan-coloured holdall with the broken zip, and made arrangements for this to be transported down to his cabin aboard *Sturgeon*.

He had already briefed Morton on the main points of his earlier meeting with Mearsom, and now, seated in his cramped cabin aboard *Sturgeon*,

Cunningham settled down to pen a short letter home – possibly his last letter for quite some time. He wrote quickly, his long legs tucked uncomfortably under the drop-down flap fitted to the front of the small wooden drawer unit which also served as a desk. Occasionally he glanced towards the framed photograph screwed to the bulkhead in front of him, to the smiling fair-haired woman with the two young boys. As always, after seeing her, there were so many things that he wanted to tell her, but hadn't. In this instant he would say that his visit had been too short, but he knew that he could, and should, have made more of it.

He paused. Laying down his pen, he leaned back in his chair and yawned deeply, knowing that his virtually sleepless night on the train, combined with the pressures and stresses of the past few days, were catching up with him. No matter; hopefully he would get some sleep this afternoon. Pushing himself to his feet, he reached over to the jacket draped on his bunk and extracted a pack of Players from the pocket before throwing the jacket back in a crumpled heap on his bunk. The gold braid of the two-and-a-half stripes on each cuff had long since lost its lustre, and was now fading and lifting away from the dark navy of the sleeves. Like its owner, this seagoing jacket had seen many years of service. Leaving the Royal Naval College, Dartmouth in the autumn of 1940 as a cadet, he had served on two destroyers, as a cadet and midshipman. Then, as a midshipman, he'd been appointed to the cruiser *Birmingham* in the Mediterranean. *Birmingham* had been torpedoed soon after he'd joined her, and he'd grudgingly spent the next twelve months with her in the dockyard while she was being patched up. Then, as he afterwards came to consider, in a move born of desperation and boredom, he had volunteered for submarine service. As a sublieutenant he'd been appointed to his first boat just five months before the war in Europe had ended. But those five months had been action packed. He had spent them in a "T" class boat operating in the North Sea, and had enjoyed the distinct honour of being the youngest sublieutenant in the submarine service to be awarded a DSC, for his actions as the officer of the watch during one of the last home waters submarine actions of World War II. All in all, he was a satisfied man. Never spectacular – spectacular was not his style. Solid, dependable and safe, but never spectacular

– that was Cunningham. One of the Navy's workhorses, he had spent more time at sea than most, and had commanded four other boats before *Sturgeon*. Now well towards the top of the promotion list, he knew that, all being well, he should be made commander early next year, and then it would almost certainly be a desk job. He didn't really fancy the thought of that, but at least it would ease him gently into his retirement. Or would he perhaps be sucked into the nuclear programme he was hearing so much about from his peers these days? This, according to the pundits, was the way ahead in the submarine service, and he had no doubt that they were right. Frowning, he pulled a cigarette from the packet and lit it, drawing deeply before removing it from his mouth to study the glowing tip. No, I'm well past the age for consideration for nuclear submarine training. In any case, they're going to be too bloody big by far!

Picking up his pen, he again began to write, half listening through the thick dark-blue velour curtain that separated his tiny cabin from the control room to the snatches of passing conversation, the variety of accents, the light-hearted profanity, the occasional sharp burst of raucous laughter, together with the clink of tools as his people went about their work preparing *Sturgeon* for sea. They were a good team and he was well satisfied with them. Apart from the problems with the generators, *Sturgeon's* sea trials and work-up had been very successful. In the eight months that had followed, she had earned her place in the squadron. She had proven her mettle.

A sharp rap on the panel outside startled him from his thoughts, and the curtain was drawn back just enough to allow Hugh Morton's pink face to peer in.

'Come in, Hugh.'

Morton stepped inside. 'Thank you, Sir. Just to report that the boat is ready for sea, in all respects.'

Cunningham leaned over to a large glass ashtray and, stubbing out his cigarette, he looked up at Morton questioningly. 'Thank you, Hugh. Nothing else that I should know about?'

'No, Sir. All departments are on top line, with no serious defects. We'll be ready to slip at 11.00.' Morton hesitated, waiting for Cunningham to speak again. Then he said, 'Well, if that's all, Sir, I'll be off to check the inboard mess with the cox'n.'

Cunningham nodded and returned to his letter.

Hearing the call for him over the main broadcast, Donovan reported to Coxswain Sanford in the control room, and then sent three ABs to square off the inboard mess. Next, he organised the spare hands for'd to start cleaning through the boat, ditching gash, and securing for sea. At 10.00, with the boat cleaned through and all chores completed, he detailed Able Seaman "Pony" Moore to wet the tea, and at 10.15 they went to "stand easy" in the for'd mess.

The internal design of the for'd mess in these new "S" class boats differed markedly from that of all other classes currently in commission. Here, in the crew's accommodation space, there was a total absence of the usual tangle of pipes, valves and electrical wiring. All this was hidden behind gleaming white Formica panelling, with access to valves and gauges being provided through small hinged flaps and removable panels.

Now, with everything stowed and ready for sea, the for'd mess presented a neat, clean, appearance.

But, as in all submarines, living space in *Sturgeon* was at a premium. This was a living space for up to thirty-five men, and if it wasn't for the fact that about a third of these men were on watch all the while she was at sea, then even the most meagre comforts would be impossible.

To add to the general discomfort in his area, the main access into *Sturgeon* was via a hatch and a vertical ladder situated directly in the centre of the for'd mess. This hatch was required to be left open at all times while in harbour – an arrangement which presented obvious drawbacks to the inhabitants, especially during cold or wet weather, since the constant down-draught created by the boat's ventilation system meant that the area immediately below the hatch was, in all but the kindest of weather, extremely wet, cold and draughty. This discomfort was multiplied by at least ten when the main engines were running for a battery charge. Internal access to the torpedo stowage compartment was via a round watertight door at the forward end of the mess, while access aft was via a bunk-lined passageway on the port side, passing the senior rates' mess, through a further watertight door passing the

ERA's mess and the wardroom, before reaching the control room. Most of the stokers, together with a couple of electrical ratings and specialist seamen, lived back aft in the after ends mess, where conditions were every bit as cramped as those for'd. Now they sat on the bottom bunks – nineteen of them – crushed together on either side and end of the mess table, with the bright fluorescent lighting showing up the grubby stains that decorated most of the off-white sweaters worn by those who would shortly be going up onto the casing.

Using both hands, Able Seaman Moore deftly poured steaming tea non-stop into a line of mugs set out on the table. Donovan reached for the nearest mug, pouring fresh milk from an aluminium jug before shovelling in three teaspoonfuls of sugar and stirring vigorously. 'Cheers, "Pony".'

They were unusually quiet this morning. It was always like this just before going to sea, but today the atmosphere seemed even more strained, almost tense. Firstly, they were sailing earlier than planned and this never went down well. Neither did going to sea on a Saturday. The general assumption in the mess was just that *Sturgeon*'s planned programme had been brought forward by a few days, but nobody had told them this officially, and Donovan, together with the rest of them, wondered why. This was a period of limbo: they were not yet at sea, but now they couldn't go ashore. Donovan knew this feeling so well and yet had never become used to it. As always, there were plenty of buzzes floating about, but no one really knew what was happening – certainly no one in the for'd mess anyway. But now in the knowledge that their going seemed inevitable, they just wanted to be off.

White broke the silence. Holding his head on one side, he turned his gaze towards Bell, who was sitting head in hands at the far end of the table. White spoke in a loud, lisping, posh and much exaggerated falsetto.

'Oh, there you are, "Dinger", my dahling. Nice of you to join us. 'Ow's yer 'ead this morning, my son?'

Bell slouched, unshaven, his lank black hair uncombed. He glowered across at White, but said nothing.

Undaunted, White chirped on, 'Well really, my dear, the sights you do see when you hain't got a loaded gun.'

229

Bell gingerly took a sip from his cup. 'Piss off!' he growled.

But now White was hot on the trail. 'Oh, so it's piss off this morning, is it?' he lisped, rolling his eyes upward in an expression of exaggerated hurt. 'You gotta short memory, my old son. Who was it wot turned you in last night when you was all pissed and could 'ardly friggin well stand up? Well I just 'ope that you remember promisin' me yer tot today. Tell you what,' he continued, 'why not give us another renderin' of that friggin' song you was tryin' to keep us all awake with last night? Then we can *all* 'ate you as much as I do this morning!'

Now Bell's head was in his hands again, his eyes tightly shut. Rum was the last thing he needed to be reminded about at this moment. 'The way I feel at the moment, you can have the flaming lot,' he grated.

A contrived look of sheer delight spread over White's swarthy features. 'There you are, you lot,' he crowed, now back in his broad scouse accent, 'you all 'eard that. I got 'is tot today!'

Then the loudspeaker above them crackled harshly, 'Leading Seaman White report to the control room.'

'Aw, what the friggin 'ell's up now?' White gulped the last of his tea.

'Like I was just saying,' muttered Bell under his breath, 'piss off!'

Deane wandered up the passage and pushed himself into the seat that White had vacated. 'All right then, Donno?' He reached out for the teapot, holding it in both hands. It felt light so he shook it and then he pulled off the lid to peer inside. 'Suppose you bastards 'ave seen off all the bloody tea already.' Deane used the word "bastard"' very frequently, especially when addressing his messmates. He pulled a cup towards him and started to pour the remnants of the pot, watching the slow, almost black trickle emerging from the spout. Finally satisfied, he added milk and sugar and then turned to his waiting audience.

'Right then, you bastards; who's got all the good buzzes then?'

'We was going to ask you that, Dixie,' from Fred Coulson, a large thickset electrical mechanic whose pride and joy was the flowing red beard completely covering the lower half of his face.

'Yeah, that's right,' echoed a chorus of voices. 'You're the killick sparker, an' you got all the buzzes. At least you bloody well should 'ave.'

'Sure he has,' muttered Moore sarcastically. 'Ain't you supposed to tell the old man what's 'appening, Dixie?'

'All I know,' said Deane, 'an' I'm being perfectly straight with you on this one, is that we're goin' north, an' that's only because the navigator's got the charts out in the control room. Probably goin' up there to play with some "skimmers", I should think. After that, as you already know, we'll be goin' across to Rotterdam for a piss up. There, that do you? Cos I can't tell you anything else!'

'Well, that ain't much to look forward to then, is it? I 'ates them Dutch anyway! Flamin' foreigners,' muttered "Spotty" Samuels.

'Well, maybe they ain't so keen on you either, yuh little shit,' scowled Moore. 'Anyway, Spotty, part threes should be seen an' not 'eard, so keep yer gob shut!'

Able seaman Samuels was a "part three" – a trainee, on board to complete the third and final part of his submarine training. He was just eighteen years old, ever eager and ever his own worst enemy, already the butt for most of the banter in the mess. This was Samuels' lot – the youngest in the mess, awkward, gangling, with a face full of adolescent spots and as yet, virtually clueless. He never stood a chance. He would be the mess whipping boy, the butt of all the jokes and take all the flak that his mess mates cared to throw at him until some more junior and equally vulnerable trainee came along. That was the order of things. But woe betide anyone outside of *Sturgeon* who picked on Spotty – that would be a completely different matter.

Now they were talking more, private tensions were subsiding, and the banter was starting. They were becoming acclimatised.

Moore spoke again, fixing his gaze on Deane. 'I reckon you're full of shit, Dixie! 'Ow come we've all bin issued with long johns an' woolly vests? You don't get them for a five-day cruise off the Shetlands, 'aving a few games wiv the grey funnel line.'

'Yeh,' added George Dagwood, 'an' what about all that welding they bin doing in the fin, an' all them wooden beams they've wedged up there. What's all that for, then?'

'Yeh, well,' Deane frowned, 'like I said, no bastard ever tells me anything.'

And so the conversation continued, most of it now just a blurred background noise to Donovan, whose thoughts were once more elsewhere. At one time he would have led this chatter and loved every minute of it, but lately he'd begun to find it irksome. Again he was thinking of June and the baby that was on the way. His baby – their baby! His thoughts were interrupted as the overhead loudspeaker crackled again. It was the cox'n. 'D'you hear there? Special sea duty men close up. Dress for the casing party will be foul weather gear.'

Donovan looked up at the clock on the for'd bulkhead: 10.30 – bang on time. He stood up and reached into his bunk for his life jacket and cap. 'Come on then, casing party, let's get to it. Collect your foul weather gear from the fore-ends.'

★   ★   ★   ★   ★

Sanford poked his head through the open doorway of the wardroom, and located the first lieutenant. '10.45, Sir. Special sea duty men have been closed up for fifteen minutes. We're ready to go to harbour stations.'

Morton said, 'Thank you, Cox'n. Make the pipe.'

Sanford walked into the control room and stood by the helm. He hooked the clipboard carrying his harbour stations checklist to a pipe over the telegraphs, and reached for the microphone. There was no crackle now: the EA had been busy. 'D'you hear there? Harbour Stations! Harbour Stations! Shut clip and report all hatches. All departments make your reports.' Then, still gripping the microphone, he slumped down into the helmsman's seat to await the deluge of incoming reports.

CHAPTER THIRTEEN

11.30 Thursday, 29ᵗʰ October 1959

*S*turgeon was now stopped midway in the Gareloch, having given way to two small yachts now scudding easterly across her path, not twenty yards off her bow. She was facing south, with a sharp southerly rain squall now beating into the faces of the men on her bridge. Morton, his normally pink features now a glowing red, stood beside Cunningham, who was busily wiping rain from his binoculars. Both were clad in full oilskins, but even so they were still uncomfortably aware of the combination of stinging rain and cold wind. Now their path was clear, and Morton called down the voice pipe. 'Helm – Bridge, half ahead together.' Sterne, Mearsom, and several other SM3 officers had gathered on the upper deck of *Adamant* to see them off, but *Sturgeon's* leaving this morning was by design a low-key affair.

Now they were approaching the Rhu narrows, gateway from the Gareloch into the Clyde estuary. Lieutenant Chris Heywood, the navigating officer, was carefully checking bearings on the compass repeater, and Morton was leaning over the bridge voice pipe and calling down steering orders to the Cox'n Sanford, who was on the helm below in the control room.

Off to the port bow Cunningham could see groups of people standing about on the stony foreshore at the narrows. 'Better slow down a touch, Hugh. Don't want to give 'em wet feet.'

Morton nodded and again leaned towards the voice pipe. 'Helm – Bridge. Slow ahead together.'

'Bridge – Helm. Both telegraphs set to slow ahead together.'

The groups of people on the narrow stony beach were now waving at them. Cunningham knew that most, if not all, of this rainswept little group would be the wives and families of *Sturgeon*'s crew. They always gathered here at the narrows, complete with cameras and binoculars, to wave farewell when *Sturgeon* was going to sea. With many of them this had become almost a ritual over the past months, and he knew that many of those standing on that small beach now would be there again on *Sturgeon*'s return, though he had never discovered from where they got the news of impending returns. He always kept the casing party closed up until they had passed well through the narrows, standing them easy and allowing them to acknowledge this "families farewell".

But now, as the casing party cleared away below him, he was more concerned with what was happening off to their starboard side. There would be other people up among those craggy gorse-covered hills who were neither family nor friends. They too would be marking *Sturgeon*'s departure with cameras and binoculars, but for far more cynical reasons. But then, this was the norm these days and there was little, if anything, that could be done about them. He knew that they would be reporting back to their Soviet masters before the hour was out.

Now *Sturgeon* was clear of the narrows and, with Helensburgh seafront on her port bow, she began altering course to starboard until Greenock was on her port beam. She then turned south into the Firth of Clyde and again directly into the wind. The rain had stopped now, but a strong south-westerly head sea was building up over her bow.

Sanford's voice came through the voice pipe. 'Helm – Bridge. Permission for messenger to the bridge with a signal for the captain.'

'Bridge – Helm. Yes, please.'

The messenger's head appeared at the top of the fin ladder, and passed a sheet of signal paper up to Cunningham. 'Just came in, Sir.' Then he disappeared below.

Cunningham read the signal: 'Regret weather off Campbeltown not suitable for safe transfer of your passengers. Rendezvous with MFV cancelled.

Proceed independently.' He grunted to himself. He really wasn't bothered either way. Turning to Morton, he said, 'Well, it looks like we've lost our passengers already, Hugh. It seems the weather's a bit too loppy for 'em. I don't think we'll miss 'em too much though, and at least we'll save on a bit of food and water. But it does make me wonder just how much importance is being placed on this job by those who organised it. Still, at least it will save us a lot of time.'

Morton recognised the sarcastic tone of his captain's remark and said, 'And at least it looks like they trust us to do the job on our own, Sir.'

Cunningham had remained on the bridge for a further fifteen minutes before he went below. Morton watched him go, then turned and called down the voice pipe,

'Helm – Bridge. The captain is coming below. Go to passage routine. Stand fast, special sea duty men.' He listened to the roar of air through the tower as Cunningham made his way down, and he heard Sanford's voice over the tannoy calling for blue watch to close up in 'passage routine'.

★　★　★　★　★

Donovan had been sleeping fully clothed on the top of his sleeping bag. Now he stirred in the quiet darkness of his bunk as his senses slowly flooded back and he realised where he was. He was uncomfortable, hot, sticky, and sweating. Again he'd been dreaming he'd been with June, and again he felt an acute disappointment that the dream was over and he was back in the world of *Sturgeon*. Reaching up, he switched on his bunk light and looked at his watch: 13.30. He'd only been asleep for half an hour. He lay there, feeling the rise and fall of the boat under his back and listening to the faint drone of the diesel engines filtering through from aft, and to the sound of the sea breaking over the casing above him. He turned his head to look at the photograph stuck with strips of clear Selotape on the Formica bulkhead beside him. June was smiling, dressed in a white summer frock, sitting on a bench in a park at Southend. She had gorgeous legs. He had taken this photo early last summer. It was one of his favourites and one of the only coloured photos he'd got of her. That had been such a marvellous day, a day that he would always remember. Again he closed his eyes, feeling sharp pangs of frustration and loneliness wash over him. His thoughts went back to last Sunday evening and the weekend that he had spent with her. He had left her at 22.30, having resisted the strong urge to wake her. Quietly pulling on his uniform and carrying his shoes and his holdall, he had left her sleeping on the settee in their tiny one-bedroomed flat over the butcher's shop on the High Road in Willesden. They had said their goodbyes many times during that evening, and he was happy in the knowledge that he would be with her again at the following weekend. Silently closing the door behind him, he had made his way down the darkened stairway to the street door, where he put on his shoes and headed towards the underground station and the last train of the day to Euston. Already it seemed to him a lifetime since he had seen her last. He had written to her last evening to tell her that it was unlikely he would be home for the coming weekend after all.

It was quiet in the mess now. Outside his curtained bunk all those off watch had turned in. The daily tot had come up as soon as they had fallen out from special sea duty men. White and a few of the others had, as usual, held court until the rum fanny was empty, and then they had got the dinner up. It had been a simple, quick and easy meal for the first day out – "pot mess", the navy's version of stew. *Sturgeon* boasted two cooks for this trip, not usual, but the second cook was on board for sea training. It had been a noisy meal, everyone seeming excited and all wanting to talk at the same time.

Now *Sturgeon* progressed steadily southward down the Firth of Clyde with a still-strengthening southerly sea breaking over her bows. Soon they would get their sea legs again, but for now the motion of the deck underfoot, together with the dark claustrophobic surroundings, had started stomachs churning, and their chatter became subdued as they quickly washed up and stowed the mess crockery before seeking the refuge of their bunks.

Donovan had been glad to climb into his bunk as well, not that he was particularly tired, or that he was affected in any way by *Sturgeon's* motion. More and more these days he was using his bunk as a retreat, a refuge, somewhere to escape the constant meaningless chatter, the tall stories and the petty arguments that were an everyday part of mess deck life.

From somewhere out in the passageway, a loud metallic crash was followed by a muffled curse. One of the mess kettles had broken loose and was sliding around the deck. Donovan opened his eyes and looked at his watch. It was 15.10. He had the first dogwatch. He would get out in twenty minutes, giving himself time for a quick cup of tea and whatever else might be going before taking over the watch. He closed his eyes again.

★ ★ ★ ★ ★

At 15.30 precisely, Cunningham, now in his shirtsleeves, knocked on the wardroom door and pulled back the curtain. Morton had been waiting for him and now stood up, indicating a vacant seat just inside the door. 'Come in, Sir.'

Cunningham eased his frame between the table and the seat lockers and sat down. Apart from Morton there were four others seated around the small table: Heywood the navigating officer, Lieutenant Don May the engineer officer, Watson the weapons electrical officer, and Sublieutenant Tony Holmes, who had joined *Sturgeon* some six weeks previously as additional, under training. The torpedo officer, Lieutenant Guy Bramwell, was officer of the watch on the bridge.

Morton waited until Cunningham was seated. 'Coffee, Sir?' Cunningham shook his head in refusal, and Morton looked enquiringly towards the others. 'Anyone else?' They all declined, so Morton sat down.

The wardroom was small, sleeping six in two tiers of three bunks fitted to two adjacent bulkheads, the centre bunk in each tier being folded up when not in use, enabling the lower bunks to seat up to six on two sides of the small table, which was now covered with a dark-blue baize cloth and topped by a centrally placed heavyweight glass ashtray. A padded-topped locker provided seating for a further three on the third side of the table, while the blue velour-curtained doorway angled into the inboard corner decreased the usable space even more. The remainder of the off-white Formica bulkheads accommodated the obligatory picture of the Queen, a large black framed aerial photograph of *Sturgeon* on her sea trials, and a small glass-fronted display cabinet housing a trophy gained at last year's builders' golf tournament. But with even just the six men now seated, this tiny wardroom seemed cramped to the point of discomfort.

Cunningham motioned towards the curtain and Morton reached out to pull it across the open doorway. The five officers looked expectantly at their captain, who now glanced quickly around the table, piercing grey eyes dwelling fleetingly on each face in turn.

'Well, gentlemen, here we are on our way at last, so let's get the basics sorted out first. We've received a further signal concerning some passengers. As you know, we were going to pick 'em up from an MFV off Campbeltown. But now it looks like we're not going to get the pleasure of their company after all, but then, that could be just as well anyway.' He rubbed his chin thoughtfully and looked towards Morton. 'We'll do a trim dive once we clear the Minches, Hugh, and perhaps a few shakedown evolutions wouldn't come amiss, but nothing that will hold us up.' He paused, again rubbing his chin – a habit that had grown on him over the years in the same way as his permanent stoop. It was a habit that his officers had grown to know so well, but by now barely noticed. 'With regard to our end objective,' he continued, 'unfortunately there's very little more I can add to what I told you last Tuesday morning. Even now, the reasons for this trip still appear somewhat tenuous, and the possible outcome even more so. But since we're now on our way, it goes without saying that I've heard of no major change in the situation since our last chat.'

He paused, and Morton again spoke for the rest of them. 'Assuming the worst, Sir, if *Spearfish* can't be located, then we've got to assume a "sub-miss" or a "sub-sunk" situation?'

Cunningham nodded. 'That's right, Hugh. That would be the normal procedure, and if there were anything normal about this, then the procedures would have been initiated several days ago, but under the current circumstances, our lot are not likely to be initiating a sub-sunk up there in the Barents, it's too early in this case, and we have to place some credence on the information in that signal from the trawler, which, incidentally, I see no reason to disbelieve.' He paused, again looking closely at his officers. 'No, rather I think in the first instance that our people back home will be hanging their hats on us meeting up with *Spearfish* and perhaps her Russian escort somewhere along the way – certainly well before they make landfall. *Spearfish* could well be suffering a total breakdown – no drive, complete loss of power, unable to transmit, you name it! There are all sorts of valid reasons why she hasn't sent off a surfacing signal, and all sorts of reasons why she is taking a tow from the Russians, none of which can be discounted at this time. But a breakdown, a complete loss of power would be the most likely scenario now.' He looked pointedly across at Watson. 'What say you, Andrew?'

Watson nodded and nervously cleared his throat. 'Very possibly, Sir.'

Sensing Watson's discomfort, Cunningham allowed a fleeting smile to cross his eyes. 'Possibly, but yes, I know – just another reason, eh!' Watson relaxed visibly. 'But,' continued Cunningham, the twinkle now gone from his eyes, 'even now these bloody generators don't exactly fill me with confidence! I certainly wouldn't be in a rush to stake my life on 'em, and it may well be that those poor buggers up there are doing just that at this very moment. No generators – no power, and that could well be their problem.'

Coming from anyone else, Watson could easily have interpreted his captain's last remarks as badly concealed innuendo, but he knew that this was not Cunningham's way, and that what his captain was saying was a statement of fact.

Cunningham paused, again studying the faces of his listeners before continuing, 'Of course, the other thing to bear in mind is that if we do find her and she *is* in the company of the Russians, they might not be too happy about handing her back, especially in the light of what she was doing up there.'

Heywood said, 'The weather's not good in the Barents, Sir: very strong south by south-westerly gales, unusual for this time of the year – the same wind we've got down here now. Our wind force is building, and so will theirs be. That, of course, won't be good for them, but it will almost certainly be in our favour. Towing *Spearfish* into a heavy southerly gale will be a slow and tedious job for the Russian. According to her position from that trawler's signal, it's my guess she's heading south, probably making for the White Sea.' He looked pointedly at Cunningham. 'If that *is* the case, then we haven't got much time to waste if we're to stand any chance of bumping into them.'

Cunningham nodded. 'Exactly! And therein lies our problem. It's essential that we time any meeting with *Spearfish* for while she's still in international waters. We'll have to average at least ten knots, which would get us up off the Kola in just about nine days. From that trawler's signal, the Russian would have to cover about 950 miles to reach the White Sea. Under normal circumstances she could easily make that journey in three days, and bear in mind that the trawler's signal was sent several days ago!' He stopped and again scratched his chin. 'However, I'm banking on the weather. If she has to head into heavy gales her progress will be slowed significantly. That, coupled with the fact that she could be towing *Spearfish*, could slow her passage even more, possibly down to eight days even. Whereas a stern sea will help us no end, it's going to be a close-run thing, perhaps too close, and, gentlemen, I really don't want to follow them into the White Sea!'

'Do you mean you'd really consider doing that, Sir?' Morton had raised his eyebrows but tried to make his question sound casual.

'Doing what?'

'Going into the White Sea!'

'I really don't know. Our orders give us carte blanche, so let's just hope we don't have to make that decision,' replied Cunningham. 'As things stand at present, whatever happens, it's going to be a race against time, so all we can do is get up there as fast as we can and hope, as I've already said, if the weather up there really detioriates she may be slowed considerably. That would then give us a fighting chance of intercepting her in safe waters.'

'So what 'appens if we do find 'em but the Ruskies don't want to give her back, Sir?' asked Don May, a small sallow-featured man, prematurely grey and the eldest member of the wardroom. A commissioned engine room artificer, May was still proud of his strong cockney accent, and had a tendency to be rudely outspoken at times. 'Are they likely to give us bovver, then?'

'It's hard to know.' Cunningham shook his head. 'Your guess is as good as mine. Again, as I've already said, anything could happen and so we've got to be ready for anything! This situation could either be resolved completely amicably, or it may well develop into the biggest row since the last war. But my gut instinct tells me that they're not going to be happy to see us and, from what we hear, Nikita Khrushchev has been playing up again, so something like this could provide him with just the excuse to stir things up even more. I'd be very surprised if they handed *Spearfish* back without making one hell of a stink about it. No, for my money, I think they'll want to turn this into a major political issue, an international incident even, and they'll make damn sure the resultant crap really hits the fan!' He paused briefly, and then continued, 'Our sole aim is to get *Spearfish* home safely and with as little fuss as possible. The RAF has completed several Shackleton searches already, obviously with no success. They'll probably try at least one more, but no one is anxious to put on too much of a show at the moment. We'll be doing dived searches and using only passive sonar once we've rounded the Cape: less chance of attracting any premature attention from the Reds.'

'Sounds like we'll be lookin' for a needle in a bleedin' 'aystack, if you arsk me,' May muttered. No one took up his point.

'Is there a chop date on the search, Sir?' Morton enquired. 'Obviously we've stored for a lengthy capability.'

'Not really – at least we haven't been given one – but I'm banking on the fact that if we do locate her, it will be within the first week of our arrival off the White Sea. Anything after that, then I reckon we'll have missed her. If the Russians do get past us and take her in, then that'll be a different story, and one that I don't want to think about at this time. But if that does happen then the probability is that that we'll get recalled and this whole mess will be left to the politicians to sort out.' Cunningham looked around at the now-serious expressions of his officers, and again scratched his jaw.

'Well, gentlemen, I don't think there's much more to be said at the moment. In the meantime, keep hoping for some good news. Another thing I would add is that from now on it should go without saying that we go very carefully with the fresh water and food.'

He turned to Morton. 'As I said, Hugh, we'll dive and catch a trim once we're clear of the Minches, but, on second thoughts, scrub the evolutions: can't spare the time.'

Then he turned to Watson. 'Keep the battery on top line from now on in, Andrew, and keep a bloody good eye on those generators as well! Let me know immediately if you have any concerns. Are there any more questions?'

There were no more questions so Cunningham stood up. 'Very well, thanks for your time. Our time starts now! This is no exercise. Stay on the ball, and make sure you keep the lads on their toes as well.' He turned and stepped through the curtained doorway. Morton followed him out.

'Thanks, Hugh.' Cunningham looked at his watch. 'I'll make a main broadcast to the troops during the first dogs. You know Bradley very well?'

'Only socially, Sir. Seemed like a good bloke. I liked him.'

Cunningham grunted. He hadn't missed the past tense in Morton's reply. 'He *is* a good bloke – one of the best. He was my number one in *Trojan*. A good bloke, but perhaps a trifle too keen at times, and that's what's worrying me a bit now.'

Then, not knowing what else to say, Morton said, 'I have the first dog on the bridge, but I'll make sure that the PO of the watch is in the picture before I go up.'

★   ★   ★   ★   ★

In the dark warmth of his bunk Donovan again checked his watch: three thirty. He yawned. He had been lying there awake, wishing for sleep. But now that he felt he could sleep, it was time to turn out. With a deep sigh of resignation, which then turned into another yawn, he slid back the curtain of his bunk. Easing his stockinged feet over the edge while gripping the overhead handrail, he lowered himself down into the passageway.

'Sod it!' he muttered, as his feet landed in the cold water now sloshing continuously across the deck, probably from the mess kettle that had been sliding about earlier. Still muttering to himself, he located his shoes and pulled them onto his now-cold and soggy socks. 'Here we go again. Situation bloody normal!' Half of the lighting in the mess was now on and he could see young Samuels manfully struggling to pour steaming tea from the large tin mess kettle into a cup, his slight frame wedged firmly between the table and the seat lockers. Donovan could see the look of determination on Samuels's puce green features as he tried to counter the now vicious motion of the deck beneath his feet. About seventy per cent of the tea was actually hitting the target area of the cup.

'You're doing a grand job, Spots. You called the watch yet?'

'Yeah, well...' Samuels frowned and pushed out his thin chest, a temporary feeling of importance overcoming the heavy queasiness in his stomach. '... they all bin shook twice but they ain't takin' no friggin notice, lazy bastards.'

A set of curtains scraped back and the tousled head of Able Seaman Darby Allan looked out. 'Aw shite! I 'ate this friggin trip already.'

'Never mind about that,' retorted Donovan, 'the good news is you're first look out up top, and it's startin' to blow a bloody hooligan. Jimmy's got the watch, so don't be adrift.' He turned back to Samuels. 'Right, Spots, I'm off fer a quick gypsies, an' you're in charge, so make sure the rest of the first dogwatchmen are out before I get back.' He paused and glanced at the tea kettle still in Samuels's hands. 'Mine's white with three sugars, an' I'll be back in two minutes.' Turning, he made his way aft to the heads.

★ ★ ★ ★ ★

Morton crouched behind the raised glass bridge screen, which was again proving completely useless against the bitterly cold sea spray constantly breaking over the back of *Sturgeon* from her port quarter, and more often than not, breaking over her bridge. The larger waves were now breaking at twenty to thirty feet. Having rounded the Mull of Kintyre, *Sturgeon* was steering north by north-west, headed towards the Inner Hebrides. It was dark now. Up here at this time of the year you were lucky to get as much as five hours of full daylight each day, and this would get less the further north they went. The grey coastline off the starboard side had long since disappeared. There was nothing but sea out there now, a sea that was increasing by the hour, with the wind now pushing towards force eight and with no signs of easement. A sea that gave *Sturgeon* a constant corkscrew motion, with her stern buried deep and her bows surging upward. Shuddering eagerly, like a dog straining at the leash, she would shrug off this sea in cascading torrents from her fore casing, before sliding her nose deeply downward into the next trough. *Sturgeon*'s bridge was not a good place to be at this time and Morton had long since given up attempting to dodge the stinging wind and the relentless deluges of near-freezing water. He stamped his feet on the deck plates beneath him, at the same time realising that this was a futile move since the water had already found its way down inside his boots and he was already standing on what felt like twin blocks of ice.

Leaning forward towards the voice pipe, he called, 'Helm – Bridge. Time, please.' This was the third time that he had called down for a time check since coming on watch, but it saved him from removing his glove and pulling back the wrist seal of his oilskin jacket to see his own watch. In any case, he told himself, it kept the bloody helmsman on the ball!

'Bridge – Helm. 16.45, Sir.'

God, the time was dragging. An icy-cold trickle of water ran down his neck. He pressed the sodden green terry-towelling scarf more firmly into the neck of his oilskin, then pulled the collar further up around his neck, and the peak of his hood further down over his eyes. Christ, if this is what it's like here, what's it going to be like further up? Now he wished that he had put on the long johns he'd been issued with last Tuesday.

Unlike most aboard *Sturgeon*, Morton had no regrets about their shortened maintenance period. Going to sea five days before planned didn't bother him one bit. Sea time was the all-important thing to him now; he wanted and needed the experience it would give him. He wanted to show them all, especially Cunningham, what he could do. Sea time was experience, and experience was not gained alongside the jetty. Experience at sea would be a major factor in determining his assessment for fitness for a future command, and the subsequent recommendation for the Commanding Officers Qualifying

Course. This COQC was more often known as the 'perisher', since success on this course would pave the way for the command of a submarine, whereas failure would mean the immediate return to general service. There were no second chances on the perisher course. He was not married, not even attached, though, once satisfied that *Sturgeon* was completely ready for sea, he had taken the opportunity, last evening, to drive out to the Loch Lomond Hotel for dinner with Julie Carter, a second officer Wren on captain SM3's staff, with whom he had maintained an off-on relationship for the past twelve months. He was genuinely fond of her. She was fun, great company, but that was all she was. At this moment she would probably be preparing to dine out with some other young naval officer, but Morton didn't mind; he was more than happy to be where he was tonight. He was doing well in *Sturgeon*. Cunningham had taken to him, and the feeling was mutual. Morton knew that he could never have a better CO and had grown to like Cunningham a lot. It was a liking born of respect and trust. As first lieutenant, he was also fully content with the rest of the officers aboard *Sturgeon*. With the exception of young Holmes they had all been with *Sturgeon* since her building days, and since leaving the builders yard had moulded into a close and very effective team. The same applied to the rest of her crew, and Morton sensed the added satisfaction of knowing that this was mainly down to *his* efforts.

When he had first joined the boat at her builders in Barrow, his pink cherubic features and ready smile had fooled many of the crew. Here was a "Jimmy" who was going to be a soft touch, or so they thought. After his first week they saw him in a different light: it was becoming increasingly obvious to them that this Jimmy was no walkover. Submarine work-ups are never easy, especially in a brand new class of boat and, when the occasion had demanded, Morton had driven them and himself to the limit. He had ceaselessly and tirelessly coaxed, cajoled, demonstrated, remonstrated, preached and practised every evolution in the book until the crew became sick and tired of them. Then he would start all over again. The result of this was a first-class pass for *Sturgeon* when they completed SM3's sea and harbour inspections. Both captain, SM3 and, of course, Cunningham were happy in the knowledge that Her Majesty's Submarine *Sturgeon* was ready for anything that would be asked of her; and Captain Sterne, or for that matter Cunningham, were not easy men to please.

Morton had won the crew's respect and, to a man, his men liked him. He was, in their eyes, a "good hand". Defaulters were rare aboard *Sturgeon* – just the odd instance of someone being put on first lieutenant's report for either an over-zealous run ashore, the occasional slack hammock, or someone returning adrift after leave. He had been able to deal with these crimes more or less on the spot, and he prided himself that he had not yet had to refer any misdemeanour to his captain's defaulters' table. In general service terms, *Sturgeon* would be described as a "happy ship", and Morton was a very satisfied man.

He stamped his feet again. Were these bloody sea boots leaking? Or was it the water going down inside them from their tops? On several occasions during the past hour, water breaking over the bridge had risen well over the level of his knees, so his oilskin trousers were virtually useless. He turned and looked upward at the silently rotating dish on the top of the radar mast – the mast that was now providing *Sturgeon's* eyes. Further aft the tall slim spire of the wireless mast also described an erratic arc against the dark of the clouds. This mast was now giving *Sturgeon* her hearing and her voice. Thank God for the marvels of modern technology. He turned to where the shadowy figure of the lookout, Able Seaman Allen, stood braced against the port side at the back end of the bridge, elbows wedged into the side coaming supporting the heavy binoculars to his eyes, hooded head turning slowly as he scanned the murky horizon.

Shouting into the wind, Morton asked, 'You awake, Allen?' He knew that he would be: how could anyone even catnap in this weather? His question was just a way of opening some sort of conversation, and he felt like talking.

'Say again, Sir,' called Allen. Even though he had heard Morton clearly, Allen never passed up a chance to be awkward, especially where an officer was concerned.

'Never mind,' returned Morton. 'Glad to be back at sea, Allen?'

'Oh yes, Sir! Absolutely bloody ecstatic, Sir.' What a stupid frigging question! Allen had pulled the scarf from over his mouth and was grinning lopsidedly. 'Feel better about it if I knew where we was goin' to though, Sir. Any clues?'

'You'll find out soon enough,' Morton shouted back. 'All will be revealed very shortly.' He turned and faced forward again, knowing that this attempt at conversation would lead nowhere. Allen was one of *Sturgeon's* resident self-styled comedians and never lost an opportunity to put one over on the officers.

Morton raised his binoculars and again scanned forward, his thoughts now interrupted by a bellow from the voice pipe.

'Bridge – Helm. Permission to relieve the lookout, Sir.'

Now Morton pulled back his cuff to check his watch. This was not an easy thing to do. Shining the red lens of his torch on the dial, he could see that it was coming up to 16.55. 'Yes please, and make sure he's dressed for the occasion! It's bloody awful up here.'

Below him, the sudden rush of air through the conning told him that the relief lookout was on the way up. Then a hooded shape of the relief lookout emerged through the hole at Morton's feet and straightened up beside him

'Relieve the lookout, Sir?' Donovan was still breathless from his climb up to the bridge.

★ ★ ★ ★ ★

Cunningham lay on his bunk, fully clothed and fully awake. He'd been waiting for the sharp rap on the panel outside his door, but when it came it still startled him. The door curtain was pulled back and Sanford poked his head into the dimly lit cabin.

'17.00, Sir,' said Sanford. 'You wanted a shake.'

Swinging his legs off his bunk Cunningham said, 'Thanks, Cox'n. Yes, I wanted to have a word over the main broadcast.'

'All ready for you, Sir,' Sanford replied and disappeared back into the control room, with Cunningham close on his heels.

Cunningham moved towards the raised search periscope and Ramsay, who was the PO of the watch, stood back to make way for him. Spending less than two minutes on an all-round look, Cunningham then handed the periscope back to Ramsay, saying, 'Can't see a bloody thing!' Reaching up for the main broadcast microphone, he steadied himself against the chart table and pressed the button. The usual metallic click was heard from all speakers throughout the boat. Gathering his thoughts and noisily clearing his throat, he began to speak.

'D'you hear there, all compartments? This is the captain speaking. I want to spend the next few minutes briefing you on our current situation, and to explain why we are back at sea a few days earlier than planned.' His tone was clear and measured. He paused briefly before continuing, 'No doubt many of you will have already made your minds up about what's going on, but now we're on our way, I can give you the authentic version.'

In the for'd mess White had just turned out of his bunk. He now sat on the mess table, bleary eyed, ham-like fists scratching the thick black mat of hair covering his bare chest. 'Yeah, yeah, we friggin' know. Just get on with it.'

'Firstly, under the circumstances, I make no apologies for the short-notice change to our programme.' Another pause, and they knew that back there in the control room he would probably be rubbing his chin now. 'But this is not a run-of-the-mill job!' Another pause. 'We're off on a search. One of our submarines is missing, and we're going to look for her, find her and hopefully bring her back with us. It seems there is a distinct possibility she may now be in the hands of the Russians!' Immediately the attention of every man on board was riveted towards the nearest speaker as Cunningham continued, '*Spearfish* has been operating in the Barents for the past few weeks. She is now well overdue with her surfacing signal. There could, of course, be a number of reasons for this, but time is going on and we can no longer leave anything to chance.' He again paused briefly, allowing his words to sink in. 'We are currently heading north and, assuming that the present situation remains unchanged, we shall continue north on the surface until we round the North Cape. Now I know that some of you may be feeling resentful about missing your weekend leave, and some of you may have had to change domestic plans at very short notice. Well, so be it! But for obvious reasons I could not tell you of this developing situation before now.' He cleared his throat before continuing, 'It seems that *Spearfish* may well be in serious trouble, and I'm sure that many of you, like myself, have got friends in her who may well be counting on people like us at this very moment. And we won't be letting them down! This may well be a false alarm; perhaps even just a communications problem. Let's pray that that's the case, but we can't leave anything to chance – I'm sure you'll understand that. We shall dive to catch our trim when we clear the Minches. After that we will continue north with all possible speed. I will brief you as and when necessary. That is all.' The microphone clicked off.

For a few brief seconds there was a complete silence in the for'd mess. They all looked at each other, with concern in their eyes. Yes, many of them had friends aboard *Spearfish*.

Deane, seated at the end of the table, was the first to speak. 'Yeah, well, it 'ad to be somethin' like this, didn't it? You only 'ad to put two an' two together. We all knew she was up there on a "sneakie", didn't we? Poor bastards! Let's just 'ope we meet up wiv 'em on the way up.'

'You never had a bloody clue, Dixie,' muttered Moore. 'Go on, admit it.'

'Do you think we'll be goin' up under the ice, then?' Samuels sounded excited.

Fred Steer gave him a withering look. 'Course we ain't, yuh little prat! What the 'ell would we be doin' that for? You ain't goin' to find nothing under the fuckin' ice.'

'An' 'ow would you know that then, Fred?' White, still perched on the mess table, had joined in the conversation. You're the friggin' expert all of a sudden, are yuh?'

'Well, they must think it's a possibility,' said Deane. 'The yanks 'ave been under, ain't they? Nautilus, weren't' it? And, let's face it, they've strengthened the fin, an' we've got all this extra warm gear: long johns an' such. You don't get them if you're goin' on a friggin' Med cruise, do yuh?'

'Yeah, that's right,' said Steer. 'They didn't put all that extra ironmongery and woodwork in the fin for fuck all, 'ave they?'

'Fred, my son,' said Deane with mock sincerity, 'you've obviously never seen a rampant whale.'

'Oh, I wouldn't say that,' chipped in Sam Conroy, the leading signalman. 'You didn't see that bird he was with the other night. God, the face on her! Gives me nightmares just thinking about it, 'an as for 'er legs, well, I reckon she could get a job in any dockyard kick startin' frigates.'

Amid the laughter, Steer's ruddy features turned even redder. 'Don't start off on that again. In any case, you don't 'ave to look at the mantelpiece while you're pokin' the fire, do yuh?'

Ignoring Steer, Deane continued, 'Them whales gets pretty 'orny up there where we're going. Must be the long winter nights wot does it.'

'Yeah, well,' said Spotty, with a seriously puzzled look on his face, 'I'd thought it were too cold fer that sort of thing up there!' Now the whole mess erupted in laughter.

Waiting for the laughter to drop, George Dagwood, another one of the torpedo men, volunteered, 'I was up there last year in *Thunderer*. We was on a sneakie like *Spearfish* is, an' I can tell you that them bastard Ruskies don't fuck about if they find you.'

'Bollocks!' scoffed White. 'Anyone would think we was at bleedin' war with 'em.'

'Well technically, I suppose, we are,' said Deane, 'but it ain't a proper war, is it? It's what they call a cold war, innit?'

'You can say that again,' muttered Allen, still shivering, and still dressed in his oilkins since coming off the bridge.

'Yeah, well, I know that, don't I.' White was trying to look serious. 'But they ain't goin' to take one of our boats out, are they? No more than we would take one of theirs out,' he grinned mischievously. 'Well, not on purpose, anyway.'

Now, at 17.15, Donovan had arrived back in the mess, still fully clad in oilskins, red-faced and shivering with cold. 'No tea wet, I suppose?' Then he sighted Samuels. 'Here, Spotty, ain't you supposed to be on watch?'

'Control room messenger, ain't I?' Samuels puffed out his chest.

'Then what the 'ell are you doin' in 'ere then, yuh loafing little sod?' This came from Allan.

Samuels disappeared aft towards the control room, and White turned to Donovan. 'Ain't you supposed to be on watch as well, Donno?'

'Yeah, but I just come down off the bridge, didn't I? I heard the news about *Spearfish*. Bit of a rum do, eh? An' I was hoping that there might be a brew on.'

White stood up and yawned. 'Right then, gents, let's 'ave a brew then. One volunteer to mash the tea, please.'

★ ★ ★ ★ ★

So that was it. The news had been broken. They were in the picture at last. Now they would take things as they came. But under that perpetual veneer of brashness, bravado and banter, each one of them was putting himself aboard *Spearfish*, and each one of them was promising himself that he would spare no effort to get this job done. No more questions would be asked. There was no more need for questions.

Donovan had come off watch at 18.00, and was now gratefully tucking into his supper: a mixed grill – one of his favourites, and it was good, very good. The coxswain and the two cooks had excelled themselves tonight, but he knew this wouldn't last. After the first few days at sea the fresh fruit and veg would be used up, and the bread, though still edible, would develop green patches. "Penicillin bread", they called it. Then they would resort to the freezer and the packeted and canned food: things like canned kidneys, bacon, tinned tomatoes and, of course, biscuits, with the cook occasionally baking bread if the circumstances permitted. This situation was, of course, inevitable and common to all boats on extended time at sea. But still, compared to other boats he'd been on, the victualling aboard *Sturgeon* was not bad at all. Coxswain Sanford took a great pride in his victualling expertise; and "Nosey" Parker, the leading cook, took a great pride in cooking these victuals. Donovan mopped up gravy with a piece of fresh bread, savouring the last mouthful. He was just starting to get warm again. He lit up a cigarette and rubbed the stubble on his chin.

White was looking at him quizzically. "Ow's the set comin' then, Donno?' He leaned closer, eying Donovan's cheeks. 'Not much 'appening yet then!'

'Oh, it'll be all right,' said Donovan. 'Just give it time.'

'Yeah, it'll need time all right,' White replied. 'But now, my dahling, you still got skin like the lee side of a mouse's dhoby bucket. If I was that way inclined, I'd give you a big kiss right now.'

Donovan grinned. 'I shouldn't if I were you, me old mate. We don't carry a dentist on board.'

Now Moore said, 'Where's that dopey little sod Samuels gone to wet the tea? Back to the after ends?'

'Give it a rest, Pony,' said Donovan. 'Just give the little bugger a chance. He pulls his weight.'

Now Samuels appeared again, carrying a fanny of tea.

★　★　★　★　★

Sturgeon had cleared the Minches and at precisely 20.00, Sanford was on the main broadcast microphone. 'Diving stations! Diving stations! Open up for diving. Uncotter main and auxiliary vents. Turn out the fore planes.' Within a minute, the accommodation spaces had become practically deserted as men hurried to their stations to prepare *Sturgeon* for her dive.

Donovan had followed Ramsay into the fore-ends and, together with five other torpedo men, started to prepare the compartment for diving. Ramsay picked up the clipboard carrying the diving checklist, and although they all knew the routine by heart, each man carried out the individual checks around the compartment in sequence, as instructed by Ramsay, who diligently ticked off each check or operation as it was completed. Muttering to himself, Ramsay scanned down through his list, carefully making sure that he had cross-ticked every item. Then, appearing satisfied, he looked up and called across to Donovan. 'You 'appy, Donno?'

Donovan raised a thumb in acknowledgement, and Ramsay reached up for the microphone. 'Control – Fore-ends. Fore-ends opened up for diving.'

From the control room, 'Roger, Fore-ends.' Now they would wait. Soon the first lieutenant would arrive, accompanied by "Jan" Thompson the outside

ERA, more commonly known as the "outside wrecker". Starting from the fore-ends, these two would then walk the length of the boat to check that *Sturgeon* was correctly opened up for diving.

They listened idly to the various reports coming from the rest of the boat over the main broadcast. Ramsay was sitting now. Having made himself comfortable on a bag of cotton waste near the watertight door, he intently scanned through a dog-eared and oil-stained instruction manual, which in reality he could have recited chapter and verse while blindfolded. Standing over the TI, Donovan engrossed himself in scratching white paint off a brass name tally with his knife, while softly whistling something tuneless between his teeth.

The other five clustered in front of the tubes, talking quietly, grabbing out at the storage rails for support whenever the deck, still continuously lifting and plummeting beneath their feet, gave an extra-fierce lunge. They had now changed into "steaming rig" – mostly old slacks or jeans and sloppy T shirts. They would live in these clothes for the rest of the trip.

Donovan looked towards Dagwood. 'Soon as the Jimmy's been through, George, you can fetch some spuds up, and the five of you can make a start on the peeling.' He turned to Ramsay with a wink and whispered, 'That'll take the wind out of their bloody sails!'

Morton climbed through the watertight door into the fore-ends, closely followed by ERA Thompson. 'Evening, TI, Donovan, gentlemen.'

Ramsay hauled himself to his feet. 'Evenin', Sir. Fore-ends opened up for diving.'

Although the compartment was brilliantly lit, Morton flashed his torch in every direction, while the outside wrecker struggled and squeezed into a succession of barely accessible places to check the many gauges and test the positions of various valves with his wheel spanner.

Finally satisfied, Morton nodded to Ramsay, 'Very good, TI,' and stepped back through the watertight hatch, with the wrecker close on his heels. Together they would now check every compartment in the boat.

The control room was now in red lighting, and Cunningham was at the search periscope. Slowly rotating in a clockwise direction, he had completed three sweeps and there was no traffic in sight, no visual lights and nothing on sonar or radar. He knew that out there was just an endless carpet of black rolling swell, mingling somewhere in the distance with a sky that, tonight, was without moon or stars. Thick low cloud had seen to that.

They would get this dive over, catch their trim, then surface again and be on their way. Cunningham was eager now, impatient to get this job over with. Finally Morton appeared at his side, his rounds complete.

'Submarine is opened up for diving, Sir.'

'Very good! Break the charge. Stop engines. Tell the officer of the watch to secure the bridge and come below.'

Morton moved over to the helm and, leaning over the helmsman, he called up the voice pipe to the bridge, 'Officer of the watch – First Lieutenant. From the captain, break the charge, secure the bridge, and come below.'

Now Morton positioned himself behind the two planesmen. He could hear the rattling and banging in the conning tower as the lookouts dropped from the lower hatch, binoculars swinging from their necks. He heard the upper hatch slam shut and the officer of the watch's voice shouting, 'Upper hatch shut and secured.'

Leading Signalman Conroy, who had been securing the Aldis lantern inside the conning tower, came tumbling through the lower hatch, closely followed by Bramwell the torpedo officer. Still red faced from the exertion of shutting the upper hatch, Bramwell reached up to shut the lower hatch. He again shouted loudly, 'Bridge cleared, Sir. Voice pipe cock shut. Tower secured. Both hatches shut and clipped!'

The helmsman shouted, 'Lower voice pipe cock shut, Sir!'

Without taking his eyes away from the search periscope, Cunningham called, 'Dive the submarine when you're ready, Number One. Go to 150 feet.'

'Dive the submarine when ready. Go to 150 feet, Sir!' Morton repeated the order. Nothing was left to the risk of misinterpretation in a submarine at sea. Now he was ready. 'Open one, two, four, six and seven main vents. Group up, half ahead together. Keep ten degrees bow down.'

They were diving in slow time. This was mainly for reasons of safety. This first dive after leaving harbour was known as a "trim dive" and always a bit of an unknown quantity. Its primary purpose was to check that *Sturgeon* was properly weighted and trimmed, so that when dived, her trim could be checked and adjusted if necessary, both fore, aft and laterally, to give her a perfect underwater balance. Morton had calculated the contents of water in each of her trim tanks yesterday, and the sardonic chief stoker Beresford, together with the "outside stoker", Dutchy Holland, had then adjusted *Sturgeon's* harbour trim by accurately measuring the contents of each internal trimming and compensating tank, before pumping or flooding as necessary to redistribute the water in the trim tanks to adjust her balance. It was a long and tedious job, and if they got it wrong *Sturgeon* could either sink like a stone when her main vents were opened or, conversely, she could refuse to dive at all.

Cunningham was by nature a cautious man, never knowingly taking unnecessary risks. He was also a realist. Being well acquainted with the laws of Sod, he knew that things didn't always happen quite as they should, and although he considered that a submarine's ability to dive very quickly was of paramount importance, with him it was as always safety first. Tonight *Sturgeon* would dive in slow time, but after this, all dives would be initiated as he preferred – off the second blast of the klaxon horn: "crash diving" as they called it in the American submarine epics, though this was a term seldom, if ever, used by British submariners.

At Morton's order, the outside wrecker, now stationed on the diving panel, had swung off the levers controlling the main vents and as the vents opened Cunningham, still at the search periscope, watched in the near-total darkness the white blasts of air mixed with water expelling from number one and two main ballast tanks' main vents, much like a multiple blow from a huge whale. Then, as the air in these tanks was replaced with water, the venting air and water stopped and *Sturgeon* began to dive, her casing now awash and the egg shape of the ASDIC dome perched up on the bow gradually disappearing under the rolling black surface. He braced himself against the sloping deck and pulled the periscope around in another 360-degree sweep. In this dark he couldn't see anything. Good! All clear. He continued to circle until the black sea water slopped over the periscope head. Then he stepped back and the periscope slithered quickly down into the darkness of the well.

Morton, Beresford and Holland had done their jobs well: the trim was good. *Sturgeon* was gliding downward at a steady ten degrees bow down, and a few minor corrections were all that would be required. Cunningham looked across to Morton. 'Well done, Hugh. Go to "watch diving" when you're ready. Catch your trim and we'll surface again as soon as you're happy with things, but remember, time is of the essence!'

'Thank you, Sir.' Morton knew exactly what Cunningham meant. He watched his captain leave the control room and go into the sound room, and turned back to the depth gauge. The needle was just passing 110 feet. 'Group down. Slow ahead together. Trim from for'd to aft.'

Sturgeon was nosing downward into the depths as though she, too, was glad to be again returning to her natural habitat. It was quiet in the control room now: just the occasional creak and groan of the hydroplanes, and the soft hum of the hydraulic pumps as they cut in to control the flow of the hydraulic oil – life blood into the veins of her control systems – while outside, there was the occasional hiss and gurgle as the last pockets of air trapped in her steel skirts finally released and made their way to the surface.

'Depth 150 feet, Sir.' Sanford spoke softly.

'Very good. Half ahead together.' Morton leaned over the two planesmen to reach for the ballast pump telegraph. 'Just a touch out of the after trim tank, I think. How does she feel, Cox'n?'

Sanford said, 'Pretty good, Sir. Just about spot on, I'd say.'

★　★　★　★　★

At 20.45 *Sturgeon* was again back on the surface. Now, with her trim dive completed and her systems checked, she could get down to the business that she was made for. She would remain in "patrol routine", opened up for diving, ready to dive at a moment's notice. But for the time being she would proceed on the surface transit in order to maintain as much charge in her batteries as possible. Now thrusting forward, and helped by the stern sea, she continued her course, while in her dimly lit accommodation spaces her people again sought the refuge of their bunks.

★　★　★　★　★

Cunningham lay fully clothed on his bunk. The meagre yellow glow from the bunk light above his head now provided the only lighting in these small, cramped quarters that were graced with the name of "captain's cabin". But this cabin was very much his refuge, his personal sanctuary, the nearest he could possibly get to solitude – one of the few privileges that his rank afforded aboard this tightly packed mass of machinery and manpower that was called *Sturgeon*. He had always appreciated any opportunity to indulge in periods of solitude. Apart from diving stations, and a few brief visits to the sonar office, he had been here on his bunk since early afternoon and had, by now, more than made up for any sleep lost during the past forty-eight hours. Now the time was 20.30 and, although his eyes were closed, he was not asleep, but just lying here, taking advantage of his sanctuary and thinking things through.

There was no particular pattern to his thinking, though, perhaps inevitably, the majority of his thoughts were concentrated around *Sturgeon*, *Spearfish* and the possible eventualities of the coming days or weeks. But he now felt completely at ease with the current situation and had come to terms with the events of the past four days. This was just another job.

Then his mind would stray to more personal things. He thought of Sarah and the boys. She would be overseeing their homework before preparing for bathtime, and then bed. He knew that she would be getting the inevitable moans of protest as bath and bedtime drew nearer. He opened his eyes to check the time: it was just coming up to 22.00. What sort of day had she had? And how had those two lads been behaving? They could be a bit of a handful at times, he knew that. It was always one of his regrets that he had not been able to spend more time with them as they had grown up. Sarah had in many ways been both mother and father to the boys for most of their childhood. He closed his eyes and sighed. Whatever sort of day it had been for Sarah, she would cope. She always did! He thought of the house back there at Harrow, and of all the jobs that he wanted to do but never seemed to find the time to get around to. Not surprising really. And the garden – he loved his garden. He was lucky: it was an unusually big garden for the area in which they lived. Gardening took him into a completely different world – a world of tranquillity, secluding him completely from the noise and bustle of people and traffic, but perhaps even more importantly, the world of submarines. Just thinking of his garden back there in north London gave him absolute release from the tension and anxiety that was his daily lot in his present world. Sarah shared his love of their garden, and in the spring they planned to completely redesign it. They would do it together, have big bonfires to clear the rubbish, and they would build a fishpond. They'd had always wanted a pond.

He again opened his eyes. Through the thin plywood of his cabin bulkhead he could hear the helmsman calling up to the officer of the watch on the bridge. Outside the pressure hull he could hear the sea rushing noisily past her sides. It sounded so close that he felt that he could reach out and touch it. It was still blowing a full force eight up there, and still deteriorating. He could feel it under his back. But young Morton would look after things. A very capable man was young Morton. Cunningham closed his eyes, again listening to the dull roar of the sea beside him, and the deep steady beat of the diesels back in the engine room. All was well.

Sturgeon had made good progress since surfacing after the trim dive. The following sea had helped her, and she had maintained a good ten knots average speed while at the same time keeping her batteries well charged.

Now, after a quick rap on the panelling outside his cabin door, the curtain was brushed open and Morton stepped in. He looked tired. 'There's a full gale blowing right up our arse, Sir, and it's getting worse. I'd say it was well on the way to storm force ten now.'

'Well, at least it's in our favour. I want to be around the North Cape as soon as possible so let's just hope that this weather stays up our arse! Keep the main batteries up though, Hugh.'

Morton nodded. 'Well, as I said, the glass is still falling, Sir; weather's going to get worse before it gets better.' As if to compound this statement he lurched on a particularly heavy roll and grabbed at a small bulkhead bookshelf for support. Then steadying himself, he said, 'I was thinking about those three passengers who are not now coming with us. Well, we've got our own divers anyway: Andrew Watson and Leading Seaman Donovan are both qualified, and the TI is pretty much on the ball where ordnance is concerned. And...' he flashed a broad smile towards Cunningham while releasing his grip on the bookshelf, 'I see you that you've brought along a copy of the English–Russian Language guide! That could come in handy. But in any case the PO tel has a good working knowledge of Russian!'

'Has he really?' Cunningham sounded genuinely surprised.

'Oh, yes, Sir. Apparently Simmonds joined up as a coder, not long before the end of the war.' He paused before adding, 'So when you think about it, Sir, the absence of our proposed passengers shouldn't cause us problems, anyway.'

'Well, let's just hope that we don't have to rely on Simmonds's special talents,' muttered Cunningham, 'and it will, of course, depend on how events turn out, but I don't really want to get that familiar with our Russian friends.' He glanced up at the ship's speed indicator and saw that *Sturgeon* was still making ten knots. 'Is there any chance of a bit more speed?'

Morton again staggered and made a grab for the bulkhead as *Sturgeon* corkscrewed viciously. 'Not much hope of that just yet, Sir, not if we want to keep floating the load.'

'Keep us on ten knots,' said Cunningham, 'and do whatever you can with the charge.'

★ ★ ★ ★ ★

Forward, in *Sturgeon's* accommodation spaces, those off watch were not having a happy time. Most had not managed to sleep at all – the weather had seen to that. It had needed all their concentration just to stay in their bunks, leave alone sleep. But at least those bunks had provided some sort of refuge.

'Keep still, you big black bastard!' Moore was certainly not a happy man.

'Is you talkin' to me, dahling?' White was awake too. He yawned and rubbed his eyes, studying the deck, which was now awash with a mixture of sea water, diesel oil and spilt tea. 'Jesus, look at the state of this friggin' deck. A man could 'ave a serious accident on that!'

Ignoring White, Moore looked around for Samuels. 'Spotty, where are you, yuh little bastard? Grab some rags an' 'elp me get this lot cleared up.'

White, now sitting on the edge of his bunk and with his feet on the table, scratched at the broad expanse of his hairy chest. Rough weather never seemed to affect him. 'Young Spots was up before you were mate, an' 'e ain't feelin' too chipper either, but the little bugger's still gone to wet the tea, so you lay off 'im a bit. Give the lad a break. Know what I mean?'

'Tea sounds good.' Coulson, still clad in his bleached blue boiler suit, had tumbled from his bunk and now sat expectantly at the table.

'Well, there's nowt fer you or anyone else till we get this shithole cleared up.' Now White was using his authority.

Among several others, Bell had now appeared. He, too, flopped down at the table next to Coulson, his face almost as pale as the table top. 'Fuck this fer a game of soldiers, eh!'

'Well, if it ain't our pissy-arsed oppo!' White looked gleefully at Bell. 'What's the matter then, Dinger, me old mate? Still not feelin' too spruce yet? Well, never mind, Ducky. P'raps you didn't realise we was goin' to sea, eh? And p'raps you forgot that all this green wet stuff we got outside can get a bit loppy from time to time.' He glared at the sullen faces of those now assembled around the table, revelling at their obvious misery while shaking his head from side to side in an overplayed gesture of disgust. He continued, 'I don't know, just look at you bastards! Bloody good kids in 'arbour, eh!' Then, realising that his banter was failing to hit home, he changed tack. 'Right then, let's 'ave sort of order in 'ere. All of you grab some rags from the fore-ends and get this friggin' deck an' passageway cleaned up. Then p'raps we can *all* 'ave a wet of tea.'

★　★　★　★　★

The control room was in red lighting but even in this light the shambles was easy to see. Sea water mixed with diesel and hydraulic oil slurped over the deck, turning it into a skidpan. Books and charts were sliding off the chart table, and the helmsman was fighting a constant battle to maintain his course as *Sturgeon* corkscrewed her way through the mountainous seas that still crashed relentlessly over her stern, sometimes threatening to completely overwhelm her. Now these seas were breaking over her bridge, flooding deluges of icy water down through the tower and into the "bird bath" – a temporarily rigged canvas container in the shape of a child's paddling pool – set in the deck at the foot of the tower ladder.

Cox'n Sanford was PO of the watch and was clearly fighting a losing battle against the shambolic state of the control room. He turned as Ramsay entered the control room. 'Christ, Gus, what a bloody night!'

'Who's on the bridge?'

'The Jimmy, God bless 'im. It's no picnic up there tonight and that's for sure.' Sanford lowered his voice. 'I reckon we'll be dived within the hour.'

'You could be right,' replied Ramsay, 'but it ain't no weather for snortin', and the old man wants to keep the battery on top line. Nah, in my opinion, for what it's worth, we'll be up 'ere for the rest of tonight and until we get to the North Cape, whether this bloody hooly keeps up or not!'

★　★　★　★　★

Sturgeon rounded the North Cape shortly after midnight on Friday, 6th November, just over five and a half days since leaving Faslane. She had made good time, but as she altered course to east by south-east, those helpful following seas now bore directly onto her starboard beam and her progress was slowed, and she still had 600 miles to go before reaching the Kola Inlet.

Then, to the grateful relief of everyone on board, and with a 600-mile transit to her allocated area, *Sturgeon* finally dived. Although dived, she stayed mainly at periscope depth, which was almost as uncomfortable as the surface transit from Faslane to the North Cape.

Both Cunningham and Morton had addressed the crew over the main broadcast system several times during the past few days, reiterating the need for every man to be fully on the ball and reminding them all of the need to be careful with stores and fresh water. Fresh water had already been rationed to a tooth clean and a face freshener each day. Any machinery usage was to be kept to an absolute minimum, and even then only used with permission of the officer of the watch. *Sturgeon* was now, to all intents and purposes, on a war patrol. Cunningham knew that this heavy beam sea would make for difficult snorting, but he needed to snort whenever the seas permitted, in order to keep her batteries as full as possible.

The hours of daylight had become increasingly short as *Sturgeon* had made her way north. Now any daylight lasted for barely ninety minutes, and even this could not be described as daylight. Days and nights were now almost as one, barely separated by the transience from a pitch-black darkness to a pale, greyish twilight. Small electric fires fitted in the accommodation spaces were the only form of heating in the boat and already condensation was becoming a very real problem. With large drops of icy water constantly dripping from unlagged pipes or uncovered patches of the pressure hull, many of the crew were now developing sore throats and head colds. The brief periods of snorting that they did manage in this sea helped to clear the air in the boat as well as provide a boost of charge into the main batteries, but to snort in any sort of light, as brief as it was, would almost certainly leave a vapour trail behind the snort exhaust mast, providing an immediate giveaway to any vigilant patrolling surface vessel or aircraft.

Absolute stealth was now the order of the day. On two occasions during the past forty-eight hours *Sturgeon* had been forced to go deep, firstly to avoid a Russian cruiser apparently exercising with two destroyers off the Norwegian coast about three miles to their south. Cunningham had recognised the cruiser as one of the improved "Kirov" class – possibly part of the Baltic Fleet. The destroyers were too far away to present a risk, but all the same he had taken *Sturgeon* to 300 feet and quietly continued eastward. On the second occasion they went deep after picking up fast-approaching aircraft rackets on their ECM mast while snorting during a heavy snowstorm. Morton was officer of the watch at the time and, though it seemed there had been little chance of detection, Cunningham had congratulated him for his prompt action. The seamen up in the for'd mess hadn't viewed this matter in the same light, as they had had to shut down the old Bell and Howell cinema projector in the middle of their twice-weekly movie.

Sturgeon was now averaging only seven knots. This transit was slow going. It had started to snow heavily. Then in just over three days since turning east, and still with heavy snow falling, *Sturgeon* had arrived at her first appointed destination, 100 miles north of the Kola Inlet, 69N – 40E. It was from here that she would begin her search.

★ ★ ★ ★ ★

Cunningham sat in his cabin and drained his second cup of coffee. Although he had spent most of the night awake, it had been a completely uneventful night but now the wind, still a strong southerly, was bringing with it a persistent blanket snowfall which, together with the short hours of daylight, was making any visual sighting almost impossible.

Sturgeon remained mainly at periscope depth, waiting, watching and listening. Outside his cabin the watch changeover had just taken place, forenoon watchmen being replaced by the afternoon watch. Everything seemed so normal that at this time it would be easy to forget the potential importance of his mission. He wondered just how long it would be before things started getting difficult. Turning his chair towards the small shelf, which acted as a desk, he resumed the report he'd started an hour or so earlier, then, pausing, he reached for another cigarette while listening to the light-hearted banter of the men passing outside his cabin. They seemed cheerful enough and, perhaps inevitably, the private parts of brass monkeys and polar bears' arseholes figured highly in the general conversation. Cunningham smiled to himself and turned back to his report.

And so the afternoon passed, with Cunningham catching up on various items of paperwork, while *Sturgeon* cruised slowly on a course of one-one-zero in an easterly direction. Then, on completion of each ninety-minute leg, she would turn and steer a reciprocal course westward. He wondered how many of these transits he would have to complete before the situation altered, that is, if it *did* alter. Specifically at this time, his orders were to patrol the approaches to the White Sea for forty-eight hours. If there was no contact after this time, he should then move north in a series of zigzag courses to continue the search.

Throughout the afternoon he made occasional short visits to the control room, checking the surrounding area through the search periscope, even though the relentless snowfall and lack of light reduced visibility down to yards. He also paid frequent visits to the sound room, just to satisfy himself that his long-range passive sonar was detecting and classifying where possible, and sending all contacts moving south to the plot in the control room.

Sturgeon was still on an east-west zigzag course in accordance with her orders, and even at fifty-eight feet was still corkscrewing viciously against the surge of the long sweeping rollers above her. To Bramwell, her torpedo officer, now standing behind the search periscope, it seemed that time was standing still. He had been on watch for less than an hour, and the heavy snow that had dogged them for the past three days had reduced to just the odd flurry, but again they were heading into a night of stygian blackness, with no moon or stars to cast even the slightest relief from this blackness. To all intents and purposes, Bramwell was entirely superfluous on the periscope. He was literally blind. *Sturgeon's* trim was not good and he was constantly employed in making adjustments.

Again he stood back from the periscope, rubbing his tired eyes and thinking of the events of the past few hours. Cunningham had gathered all the officers together in the wardroom at 17.00 to tell them the latest developments, but as yet he had no firm plan apart from this zigzag course northward in the hope of meeting the Russian. Well, how could he have a plan at this stage?

In Bramwell's opinion they would be bloody lucky to meet up with this Russian anyway. But he didn't voice that opinion to the old man. Furthermore, what could Cunningham do if they did find the Russian and he didn't want to play? Threaten him with torpedoes? This thought disturbed Bramwell. Oh, Christ, It'll be down to me then. He made a mental note to speak to the TI in the morning, and check that all routine maintenance on the weapons and the firing systems was up to date.

In spite of Bramwell's thinking, Cunningham had told them of his intended action during the 17.00 meeting in the wardroom, reiterating his sole aim, which was to meet up and intercept the Russian while it was still in international waters. After that there was no plan. Any action taken if or when they succeeded in meeting up with her would depend upon whether it was *Spearfish* under her tow and why, and then, of course, the Russian's response to handing her back to the care of *Sturgeon*.

'We must intercept her before they reach Russian territorial waters,' he had reiterated. 'It's as simple as that — well perhaps "simple" is the wrong choice of word in this case: there's an awful lot of sea room to cover and if we're going to catch this Russian we're going to need an awful lot of luck.' He paused, scratching his chin before continuing. 'But my guess is that she will have been moving towards us on a course south by south-west, roughly on a closing course to our own mean course. Depending on her speed and, bearing in mind the weather and the fact that she could be towing *Spearfish*, we could be in close contact within the next forty-eight hours. Much longer than that, then we can assume that we've missed her!'

★   ★   ★   ★   ★

Aboard *Otvashni*, Portrova was seated in his cabin, restlessly casting his eyes over a pile of official papers. *Otvashni* had been steaming south but, because of the heavy head seas, making very limited progress. Portrova was becoming increasingly frustrated with this progress. But for this head sea, he should have reached the White Sea by now. The door of his cabin banged twice.

'Come.' The door swung open and the doctor stepped inside.

Portrova looked up. 'Well, Doktar?'

'The young seaman, Comrad Kapitan. He has died!'

Portrova continued to survey the doctor with his impassive stare. 'So, now we have yet another account to settle with the British. You will inform Comrad Carlov of this. I want this man buried as soon as possible. Tell Carlov to send a signal to base saying that we are delayed by the weather and that we will again be stopping to bury one of our crewmen.'

'I will do this, Comrad Kapitan.' The doctor left, pulling the cabin door shut behind him.

★　★　★　★　★

Now *Sturgeon's* forty-eight hours of the zigzag search was up – more than up and, frustrated that this period had proved utterly fruitless, Cunningham, at 10.00 on Tuesday the 10th, gave the order to steer north. As well as frustration, he now felt worried. He knew that he could so easily have missed the Russian. She could well be south of him now, having slipped through his zigzag search net.

Then his luck finally arrived. At just after 15.00, while he lay on his bunk, there was a sharp rap on the woodwork and the curtain slid back to reveal Petty Officer Simmonds, the PO telegraphist.

Simmonds handed him a sheet of paper. ''Tis sorry I am to be interruptin'' you, Sir, but I've just picked this signal. Came in just two minutes since, so it did.' Despite living in Gosport since his late teens, Simmonds had never lost his thick Ulster brogue.

Cunningham took the signal from Simmonds and read it carefully, twice: 'From *Otvashni* to base. Weather very poor. Estimate arrival within three days. Will stop when convenient to bury dead crewman…'

Simmonds said, 'We lost it then, Sir. It'll be the bad weather, so it will. It was sent in Russian, so it was, but not in code. I've translated it to English as best I could.'

His mind now racing, Cunningham said, 'No, no, you've done very well to get this. Thank you, Simmonds. Thank you very much.'

Simmonds turned and left the cabin, and Cunningham called for Morton, who arrived within the minute. Morton read the signal and handed it back to Cunningham. 'Well, it seems that they're still up here and north of us after all, Sir. And pretty close. Seems they're pretty cocky as well, drafting a signal like that.'

Cunningham nodded. 'We'll make random checks with the radar as we move north, Hugh. Who knows, we might get lucky.'

From now on *Sturgeon* would continue the search using her long-range passive sonar, with the additional random use of radar for very short bursts of time not exceeding two minutes. Cunningham knew that to use any active search equipment for even such short periods as this would be risky even at this range, and he didn't like taking risks. But this risk could much reduce the chance of him of losing his prey. Now travelling north by north-east on a course of zero-three-zero, he turned *Sturgeon* through a full circle on every hour to check out any sonar blind spots.

★ ★ ★ ★ ★

Deane had now been relieved from his watch in the W/T office at 16.00 and now sat in the mess, enjoying a cup of tea. But the tea wasn't the reason for the secretive smile on his face as he waited in vain for someone to ask him for the latest buzz. Finally, tired of waiting, he could hold himself no longer. 'OK, you bastards. Who wants the latest buzz, then? Except that this aint a buzz; it's the real thing.' Now he had captured the attention of all those in the mess.

'Well, as you know, I just got off watch. Nothin' much was goin' on when Paddy Simmonds comes in, lookin' for one of his porn mags. Then right out of the blue we get this transmission. In Russian it was, but not coded. So Paddy grabs a pencil an' gets what he can of it. Then he got very excited and rushes off like a startled gazelle to the skipper's cabin with it. Seems that this signal has given us the position of *Spearfish!*'

'Then what the friggin' 'ell are we 'anging about here for? Why aint we going up there after 'er right now?' asked Steere.

'I don't know, do I?' returned Deane. Then, in an exaggeratedly upper-class tone, tinged with obvious sarcasm, he continued, 'In case you didn't know it, Fred, it's the old man who makes the tactical decisions on this boat, not me. He'll have a plan by now though; you can be sure of that.'

Steere glowered. 'I still reckon you're full of shit, Dixie.'

CHAPTER FOURTEEN

radley stirred uncomfortably on his white-painted iron cot in *Otvashni's* dimly lit sick berth. He looked at his watch, but the blurriness in his eyes, combining with the semi-darkness of his surroundings, meant he couldn't make out the time, and he certainly had no idea of the date. Some hours earlier the ship's doctor had given him another heavy sedative in an attempt to reduce his pain and give him sleep. Neither of these two objectives had been fully successful, though the pain in his head had by now reduced to a dull ache and he had, albeit briefly, flitted in and out of sleep during the past hour. Now he could feel a distinctive roll under his back, together with the fierce but regular lift and fall of *Otvashni's* bows. She must be headed south. But he had no notion of how long she'd had been underway.

He had made no further attempt to talk to Jackson. The deep, regular breathing coming from the nearby cot told him that the trawler captain was sleeping heavily. 'Sleep well, old chap,' Bradley muttered under his breath. 'You've got a rough time ahead of you, whatever happens!'

The sick berth door opened, and Bradley looked up at the large moon-faced white-clad sick berth attendant Yuri, who was now leaning over him and appeared to be beaming from ear to ear. Bradley stared back, filled with curiosity. The Russian muttered something in his native language then, still beaming, he raised both arms above his head to form an arch before pointing due south, his whole demeanour radiating intense excitement.

Then the penny finally dropped. Yuri was trying to tell him that they were on their way home. Bradley gave a half-hearted smile, and raised an arm to acknowledge the Russian's attempt at communicating. 'So we're going home! Your home maybe, my friend, but certainly not mine.'

Yuri turned to check the inert Jackson, looking down at him for a full half-minute. Then, apparently satisfied that he was still asleep, he disappeared through the sick berth door, still muttering excitedly to himself.

Bradley again closed his eyes and lay there thinking. It seemed that a forced visit to the Soviet Union, with all that may or may or not mean, was now inevitable, just a matter of time. Again he felt that now-familiar sense of absolute despair rising within him. Painfully, he pulled himself up in the cot and swung his legs over the side, where the grey canvas-covered deck immediately struck an intense cold into the soles of his bare feet. He realised, with some surprise, that except for his shoes and socks, he was still fully dressed. He reached up gingerly to feel his scalp. The hair on the left hand side of his head felt stiff and matted. He knew that this would be congealed blood, and the harsh stubble on his cheeks reminded him that he had not had the luxury of a shave since leaving *Spearfish*. Now his gently probing fingers carefully explored his aching neck and shoulders. The shoulders, neck and front of what was once an off-white submarine sweater felt stiff. Even in this dim lighting he could clearly see the dark stains that almost covered the sweater front – dried blood, his blood! 'Bloody hell,' he muttered to himself, 'you must have really upset someone!'

He looked across to the other cot. 'You awake, Skipper?' There was no reply. The deep breathing of the sleeping Jackson continued unabated.

Slowly, painfully, he pulled himself to his feet, clutching for support from the headrail of the cot with both hands. He was weak; he hadn't realised just how weak. He shut his eyes tightly to block out the dizziness, knowing that he was a hairsbreadth from collapse. With legs like putty, he clung doggedly to the headrail until the dizziness passed. Then he turned towards the sleeping Jackson. 'Come on, Skipper, wake up, for Christ's sake.' There was still no response from Jackson. Taking a deep breath, Bradley summoned all his strength and, letting go of the headrail, half walked and half fell towards Jackson's cot. 'Come on. Wake up, you bastard; we need to talk.'

At last Jackson stirred. 'Eh! Eh! Wassup? Oo the 'ell are you?' He opened his eyes and focussed on Bradley, who was now draped over his prone body. 'Get off me, will yuh!'

'Sorry, but we need to talk.'

Now Jackson was awake. Rubbing the sleep from his eyes, he yawned loudly. 'So we need to talk again, do we, Commander? Just as I was 'avin a really good dream, you want to talk, eh?'

'Just thought you might be interested to know that we're now on our way to Russia and, incidentally, to your firing squad; that is, unless we can do anything to change things in the meantime.'

'Yeh well, I'm gettin'to the stage where I really couldn't give a rat's arse about firin'squads, or owt else, for that matter.'Jackson yawned again. 'Anyway, you ain't goin'to get an easy time over this yourself, are yuh? Chances are that you'll end up with ten years in the salt mines. That's if they don't decide to put a bullet in you as well.' He sounded almost casual. 'So what was you thinkin'of doin'then, Commander? Capturing this friggin'barge an'takin'em all back to Blighty? Was that it?'

'Oh, for Christ's sake, pull yourself together, man,' Bradley snapped angrily. 'What I'm trying to say is that my surfacing signal will be so well overdue by now that all sorts of alarm bells will have been raised back home. Almost certainly some sort of search team will have been organised, whether it's an air search, a surface search, a submarine-based search, or maybe all three of those. But you can bet your boots that someone will come looking for us.'

'So?' Jackson was now listening a little more intently. 'Well, we did manage to get a signal off when you broke away from this friggin' Russian the first time. Given 'em your position an' all that.'

Bradley's eyes lit up. 'Did you just? So now you decide to tell me!'

'Sorry I didn't mention it before, Commander. Must 'ave forgot, what with all the excitement.'

Cunningham said, 'Never mind. I thank you now for what you did. That signal could make all the difference; it could even save your life.' He thought in silence for a few minutes before continuing, 'But even if they do locate us, we know that our friend Portrova is not likely to hand us and *Spearfish* back with a whimper. There would almost certainly be some sort of a confrontation, so you and I must do our bit to prepare for that.'

'*Our* bit?'

'Yes, *our* bit. We need to be ready. I've spent some time thinking about this, and I think we *could* do our bit if we're given the chance.'

'What, like? Spike their friggin' guns?' Jackson's tone was again derisive.

'Whatever it takes,' replied Bradley. 'A bit of sabotage wouldn't hurt, I suppose. We won't know till the time comes, but if it does come, then we must be ready to do something.'

Jackson now looked up into Bradley's face, studying his features closely. 'Yeh, well, it all sounds good, an' I know you mean well, my friend, but I reckon these bastards 'ave got you an' me well and truly by the short an' curlies. Anyway, with me tied up to this bed like a turkey on a spit waitin' fer Christmas, what the 'ell can I do about anything? I don't even know whether me legs work yet!'

'Well, there's only one way to find out.' Bradley pulled himself off Jackson's cot and slowly made his way to the cupboards at the forward end of the sick berth, where he began to open doors and drawers. Finally he found the scalpel he was looking for, and returned to the cot.

'I'm going to take you off your spit, Captain. Raise yourself as much as you can. I want to cut you free from underneath.'

Jackson arched his back, grunting with the pain and effort but rising to put almost two inches of space between his back and the mattress. 'Go on then, but just watch it on the downward roll. I don't want to see me liver and kidneys just yet.'

Bradley reached under the trawler skipper's arched back and began to saw away at the half-inch ropes that held him to the cot. Within minutes they were completely severed, and now, with Jackson relaxing back on the cot, Bradley turned his attention to the rope binding his knees.

Then Jackson was free, and already striving to move, but Bradley still lay over him, preventing any movement from the big trawlerman. 'Right,' he muttered, 'I've cut the ropes from under you so you can lie back on them and, apart from a complete inspection, no one will know the difference. Now, let's see how you are for movement.' He stood up and, stepping back, looked down on Jackson. 'We need to take this a bit at a time. Try your arms first. See how much movement you've got in them.'

Jackson grunted, but raised each arm in turn. 'It 'urts like 'ell, but there's still enough in 'em to choke a friggin Ruskie if one 'appens to drop by!'

'Good! Now let's see what you can do with your legs, but remember, there's a guard outside the door.'

Grimacing with pain, Jackson slowly raised each leg in turn. 'Christ, that 'urts even more, Commander, but don't you be worrying about me. If and when the time comes I'd crawl over broken glass to get at that bastard who sank my *Imogen* – you can be sure of that much.'

Bradley sighed with relief. 'Thank you, Captain Jackson. Keep the ends of your ropes underneath you, but exercise your arms and legs as often as you can. I'll be doing the same. We'll be ready if and when the time comes.' Carefully he wrapped the scalpel in some tissue that was lying beside the cot and, placing it in his shirt pocket, he slowly made his way towards one of the portholes on the starboard side. Lifting the deadlight, he stared through the thick glass. Outside it was completely dark. He could see nothing but the white tops of the nearest rollers passing away to *Otvashni*'s starboard side. Gently lowering the deadlight, he made his way back to his cot, gratefully sinking his body onto the mattress. He had done all that he could for the time being, yet still he was troubled. His only consolation was that everything now lay in the lap of fate. Matters were certainly outside of his control. He was sure that there would be some sort of search for *Spearfish*, and possibly a rescue attempt. But even if they did find them, would they be in time to do anything? He knew his government's policies on international relations all too well, and he doubted they would be prepared or permitted to face the Russians down until all other means, including exhaustive discussion and negotiation, had been used and had failed, by which time *Otvashni* and *Spearfish* would be inside Russian territorial waters. Then the political games would really begin. He lay there listening to Jackson, who was still grunting with the effort of repeatedly raising his legs to the vertical position, one after the other, until finally flopping them, exhausted, onto the cot mattress.

'God, this bloody well 'urts, Commander. I just 'ope I ain't doin' all this for nowt!' Again Jackson's arms began to rise alternately in slow, measured, and extreme effort.

Bradley allowed himself half a smile. 'You're doing well, Captain Jackson. Remember, it's your firing squad they're taking you back to, so keep with it. Both our lives may depend upon your fitness.' He waited for Jackson's reply, but there was none, just a series of grunts and moans as the trawler captain continued with his exercises. Now, after taking several deep breaths, Bradley started on those same exercises.

★   ★   ★   ★   ★

Cunningham now stood in the radar office. He still couldn't believe his luck in picking up that signal, and equally positive was the fact that no one senior to him would be able to dictate his actions now, no matter how or what subsequent events materialised.

His main concern now was what he should do when he made contact with this Russian. If there was no sign of *Spearfish* on her tow, should he just slip quietly away and resume his search elsewhere, or should he take the bull by the horns and question the Russian? Perhaps the first option might be the most sensible, but what a bloody waste of time this transit would then have been!

If it was *Spearfish* on the end of the Russian's towline, as he strongly suspected it would be, what would he do then? Well, he hadn't come all this way to do nothing; he would have to try to get her back. Obviously some diplomatic dialogue would be the first move. Maybe *Spearfish* was just a pain in the Russians' arse and they would be only too pleased to hand her over and be on their way. But could he be so lucky? No, if the Russians had indeed caught *Spearfish* red-handed, snooping in their operational areas, they would want to make the most of it. Politically they would want to squeeze the situation dry; they wouldn't just meekly turn her over at his request, no matter how diplomatic it was. There was even a strong possibility that they would try to add *Sturgeon* to their bag as well. He was going to have to deal with a potentially explosive situation. If he was sure of anything at this time, he was sure of that.

He had not slept well during the past days. Yawning heavily, he rubbed his tired eyes, knowing that, as much as he needed it, sleep for him would now be out of the question. In all his years he had never had to deal with a situation as potentially volatile as this. Under the current political climate he doubted that any possible spin-off from this incident could precipitate international military action, but if this wasn't handled properly there would certainly be sacrificial goats – there always were. He knew that if this happened, his would be one of the first heads to roll.

★　★　★　★　★

Aboard *Spearfish*, Strong crouched behind her bridge screen in a vain effort to find some respite from the bitter wind and driving snow, while at the same time wondering just what he was doing up here. The lookout, Able Seaman Dunn, crouched just a few feet behind him would no doubt be wondering the same thing. The two of them were alone on the bridge and, with the upper hatch of the conning tower securely shut to prevent flooding, they were to all intents and purposes cut off from those in the steel-walled circular world below them – a world to which the voice pipe between bridge and control room provided their only connection. They had no control over *Spearfish*'s speed or direction; she would travel at a course and a speed dictated by *Otvashni*. Both he and Dunn were, in effect, no more than lookouts.

Occasionally he raised his head above the bridge canopy to strain his eyes forward into a non-existent visibility; occasionally catching a brief sighting of *Otvashni*'s shaded stern light when it wasn't obliterated by the heavy seas, now, for the most part, covering her quarterdeck. This easterly sea was reaching heights of up to twenty feet and regularly crashed over the battered remains of twisted torn metal that had once been *Spearfish*'s fin.

'Aw, fer fuck's sake!' Dunn was brought to his knees by a particularly heavy deluge. Grasping at his safety harness, he hauled himself to his feet and shouted towards Strong, 'A joke's a friggin' joke, Sir, but this is gettin' to be a soddin' pantomime!'

Strong had long since ignored these regular outraged tirades from Dunn, and in spite of his own discomfort, concentrated his mind on the events that had developed aboard *Spearfish* since beginning their second forced journey south.

He had been more than a little surprised when Ravoski had been returned to *Spearfish*. Surely his Russian captain could not have been too happy with him when *Spearfish* had slipped the leash previously. In anyone's book Ravoski had failed completely in his previous assignment. Yes, Ravoski had taken command of *Spearfish* upon boarding her. But Strong had also expected that Ravoski would take a much closer interest in what was going on in *Spearfish* now. Instead, the Russian officer's attitude seemed one of almost studied complacency, indifference even. He had merely ordered the petty officer of the guard to take charge of the other guards and had then spent much of his time on his own in Bradley's cabin, allowing Strong full charge of the day-to-day running of the boat. But this was not the same gregarious Ravoski that Strong had known prior to *Spearfish*'s first capture. Ravoski had certainly changed. Maybe some of the other officers had not noticed the change, but Strong had. Since their first meeting he had taken to this mysterious Russian, and had almost come to regard him as a friend. This was substantiated by Ravoski's apparent compliance in their first escape from *Otvashni*; and with his subsequent willingness to fall in with all of Bradley's plans, Strong had really believed that Ravoski was indeed relying upon *Spearfish* as a means of defection from the Soviet Union, even though the Russian had never voiced this intention. But now circumstances had changed, and changed for the worse. Once more the man now down below in Bradley's cabin had become a complete enigma, and *Spearfish* was again heading under guard towards Russia, where she would no doubt be impounded, together with her whole crew, for a very long time. Bradley was a prisoner aboard a Russian warship and could stand trial for spying, resulting almost certainly in a lengthy prison sentence, or worse. And what, Strong wondered, would happen to the rest of them, and to *Spearfish*? What would happen when and if all this business finally became public? Then the shit really would hit the fan! And it wouldn't be just a case of a few red faces. Almost inevitably there would be huge international political turbulence – the Russians would see to that. No one was going to come out of this smelling of roses, except perhaps the Russians.

Immediately *Spearfish* had again been taken in tow, Ravoski ordered all torpedo-firing reservoirs be drained down and isolated, thus rendering her torpedo firing systems temporarily inoperative. Strong was fairly certain that this order had not come from Carlov, who knew nothing of submarines, so why would Ravoski have done this? While Carlov was still aboard, he and Ravoski had talked together, but they had spoken only in Russian, and these conversations had been brief and seemingly curt. Strong had quickly sensed that there was no love lost between them. Furthermore, Ravoski's ready smile and twinkling eyes had been completely absent during the past two days, and Strong had no doubt that the pistol holstered to Ravoski's waist was again fully loaded.

Crane had perhaps noticed the change in Ravoski more than any of the other officers, and had confided his thoughts to Strong whenever the opportunity occurred. 'I'm not so sure about our Russian friend after all, Oliver,' was his general message.

Strong knew that morale among his crew was haemorrhaging rapidly and was now at its lowest since *Spearfish's* patrol had begun. It was becoming increasingly frustrating to him that he could do little to change this. He had spent time, whenever the opportunity occurred, trying to explain the current situation and its possible outcome to groups of his men in their messes. But these opportunities were rare, and although Ravoski spent a lot of his time in Bradley's cabin, the guards and the young officer Gorski seemed to be putting their eyes and ears around everywhere. And he wasn't sure if any, or how many, of these would understand English. He thought probably none of them, but he couldn't be sure of that. But had Ravoski now simply reverted to his true self? He ducked instinctively as yet another icy torrent broke over his head, ignoring a further foul-mouthed outburst from the drenched Dunn, and even ignoring the freezing cascade that had almost taken his breath away. He was fast realising that he must remain focused upon what was probably the most unprecedented, the most unlikely, and the most dangerous situation that he could ever imagine himself to be in. There were so many doubts in his mind, so many questions to be answered. Somewhere there must be answers, and if there was going to be any chance of recovering control of *Spearfish*, it could well depend on him finding those answers. Time was running out fast!

* * * * *

Sturgeon continued her transit northward, while Cunningham, still in her radar office, continued to imagine all the scenarios that might develop if and when they and the Russian did meet up. Time was now becoming short, and he knew that if this Russian was indeed heading his way, it was highly possible that *Sturgeon* could make contact with her within the next few hours. Then, finally, he ordered the operator in front of him to activate radar for two minutes.

On the first sweep a contact appeared on the screen, bearing north-east and moving very slowly south. It was in fact a double contact: a smaller vessel stationed immediately astern of the larger one. This was all that Cunningham needed to know. 'Switch off the set,' he ordered.

He then returned to his cabin, where the fruits of his still-jumbled thought pattern began to crystallise into a defined plan. He would have to face this Russian head on; there was no realistic option on that point, so he would take the offensive from the outset. There would be no place for formal pleasantries or diplomacy in their meeting. He would simply tell them why he was here, and if they did have *Spearfish* in tow, then he would demand her release into his custody, using whatever threat was most appropriate. First though, he must have some means of backing up any of his demands. In spite of an increasingly aching throat he lit yet another cigarette. Being a heavy smoker, he was far less committed to imposing the "one all round" rule on a dived submarine than many other submarine commanders, and often treated himself to a sly one when in the confines of his cabin. Now stubbing out the remains of the cigarette, he rolled his legs off the bunk. He stretched and rolled his shoulders in a vain attempt to dispel the tension that had built up within him. But now this tension was mixed with a growing excitement. Pulling back the curtain at the entrance to his cabin, he called to the steward, who was standing by his sink outside the wardroom, 'Get Lieutenant Morton to come in and see me, would you please?'

Within a few minutes Morton had stepped into the cabin. 'You called, Sir?' Morton sounded slightly tetchy; it was obvious that the steward had just awakened him.

'Sorry to disturb you, Hugh, but this can't wait.' Cunningham's grey eyes studied his first lieutenant's sleep-swollen features. 'What sort of explosives are we carrying, if any?'

Morton fingered his blond locks, trying to comb them into some sort of order while he searched his memory. 'Well, I know that we've got at least two boxes of those anti-personnel charges. They were left over from that fleet exercise we did back in the Autumn of last year. Never did return those.' He looked apologetic. 'Should have, I suppose, though no one ever asked for them. Two boxes of ten – twenty charges in all, Sir. I suppose they're still all right – fit for use, I mean. Why do you ask, Sir?'

Cunningham ignored the question. 'Good! Anything else?'

'Well, I'll have to talk to the TI, Sir. I have a feeling that he might have a little bit of something tucked away.'

Cunningham fixed his hawk-like stare on Morton's puzzled face. 'Go and do that right now, Hugh.'

Morton disappeared. Reappearing some twenty minutes later, he again rapped on the woodwork outside his captain's cabin. Now fully awake, he had rinsed the sleep from his face, and his blond curls had obviously received the attention of a comb. 'Well, Sir,' he said, 'it looks like the TI does have one or two bits stored away for a rainy day. All recorded on the boat's ammunition inventory, I hasten to add.'

'Yes, yes. Well what exactly have we got?' Cunningham couldn't disguise his impatience.

'Plastic explosive, fuses, timers – all that sort of stuff.'

'How much? Would there be enough to damage a surface ship?'

'Well, Sir, to quote the TI, he's got enough explosive to blow the arse off anything that floats!'

'Good.' Cunningham looked thoughtful. 'Though I hope it doesn't come to blowing anyone's arse off – maybe just stir up her piles, eh? If we have to do anything, just disabling the Russian's steering gear and or her propulsion would be sufficient. Incidentally, what's happening with the weather up there now?'

'It's easing. Much less bumpy than it was, and getting better by the hour. But it's still snowing heavily.'

'What's the sea temperature?'

'Last reading was – I don't actually know offhand, but it was bloody cold! Why do you ask?' Morton was plainly puzzled by his captain's questions.

Cunningham again ignored Morton's question, his high freckled brow now wrinkled in thought. 'We've got two qualified divers aboard. Watson and Donovan. That's right, isn't it?'

'That's right, Sir.' Then he repeated his previous question. 'Why do you ask? What are you planning?'

'Is the TI familiar with these explosives he's been hoarding?'

'More than most. He's a bit of an expert in that field. But what's this all about?'

'And we know now that Petty Officer Simmonds has more than a fair grasp of the Russian language!'

'Yes, Sir, but what's all this about?'

Still ignoring Morton's questions Cunningham said, 'Arrange a meeting of the officers in the wardroom in twenty minutes from now. In the meanwhile I want to get one or two things just a little more straight in my mind, then I'll put you all in the picture.'

★ ★ ★ ★ ★

Exactly twenty minutes later Cunningham stepped into the crowded wardroom. They were all there with the exception of Heywood, who was officer of the watch in the control room. Now the steward was serving coffee.

They formed a tightly packed mass around the small table. All eyes turned expectantly towards their captain, who waited for the steward to finish the coffee and leave the wardroom before beginning to speak.

'Well, gentlemen, now it's down to business. You're all aware of the situation and what is required of us, and now I'm going to tell you how I plan to play it.' He looked around the table and saw that he had their undivided attention.

'According to that last signal, we're looking for a Russian "O" class destroyer.' He reached behind him and came up with a volume of *Jane's Fighting Ships*. Opening the heavy book to a page he had pre-marked, he slid it towards the centre of the table and placed a long bony finger on one of the monochrome photographs. 'There she is, chaps. She's very fast, well armed and potentially very dangerous!' He pushed the book around the table, giving each man a brief period to study the photograph while he continued to speak. 'The weather's improving, though it doesn't feel that way at the moment, but the sea's still coming up from the south. Ivan will now be steaming into it on a closing course to our own, or as near as dammit! So that factor alone should help to buy us some time! Yes, I'm banking that she's coming this way and hopefully with *Spearfish* in tow, though this, of course, will hang on the credibility of that original signal from the British trawler.' Pausing, he stroked his chin, seemingly deep in his own thought pattern, while his officers waited expectantly but not impatiently. They knew their captain too well for that.

'Then what, Sir? If we do make contact, I mean.' Morton posed the question on behalf of all of them.

'Well, first of all we discontinue this transit as from the end of this briefing.'

A look of complete astonishment flooded over the faces of his audience.

'Discontinue the transit, Sir?' Again it was Morton who spoke.

'That's what I said, Hugh.' Cunningham looked around the table, his piercing grey eyes resting on each face in turn. 'In my opinion there's not a great deal of point in us travelling much further north. We've hung our hats on the surmise that she is heading our way, and we're presently well into international waters, so why don't we just sit where we are and wait for her? Save our battery power, and let her come to us? Well, perhaps not exactly *sit* here. We'll do a series of fifty-mile transits east and west of our present position, which is about 44 east, 66 north. That should increase our chances of locating her. We'll be using passive sonar but going active on radar in occasional short bursts. It goes without saying that if we can keep our own noise to a minimum we'll stand a much lesser chance of her detecting us before we're ready. I want our meeting to be a complete surprise to her.' He stopped talking and looked around the table, watching for their response.

They were all nodding in agreement. 'Certainly makes sense, Sir,' said Morton. 'But if and when she does arrive, what's the plan of action then?'

Cunningham fixed a hawk-like gaze on his first lieutenant's face. 'Yes, well, now we get to the difficult bit. We can't expect her to welcome us with open arms – quite the opposite, I suspect. Once we locate her, we'll initially keep clear of her, let her pass to the south of us, then skirt around to the north and creep up on her tail! Who knows, they seem to have been a bit lax up to now, cocky even, as you said before, Hugh. So with a bit of luck she may well not be bothering to clear her stern arcs. If we can get close enough behind her without her knowing we're here, she won't be able to bring her heavy armament to bear – certainly not those after big guns: they won't be able to depress them enough to do us any harm. When we're close up her backside we'll surface, remaining trimmed down as far as possible. If *Spearfish* is with her then we'll get as close to the Russian's stern as we safely can, alongside *Spearfish*, or even closer if possible. I don't have to tell you that this will be more than dodgy, especially if there's any sort of sea running. We'll make sure it's properly dark before we make a move.' He permitted himself a brief wry grin as he looked around the table. 'To sum up, we'll get as close as we dare up Ivan's arse before declaring our presence and requesting her to stop.'

'Sounds OK in theory, Sir, but what if she refuses to stop?' asked Guy Bramwell. 'And what about any other bits of weaponry she might choose to use? She still could blow us clear out of the water if she wanted to!'

'As I've already said,' replied Cunningham, 'everything depends on us getting ourselves in the right position and taking her by surprise. There'll always be a risk with her armament but it's a risk we're going to have to take. I'm banking that under the circumstances she's not likely to take any immediate offensive action, and by the time she's recovered from the surprise of first sighting us, we shall have informed her that we have our bow tubes ready to fire, and we would use these torpedoes instantly should she fail to stop, alter her course, or move her guns.'

Bramwell visibly paled. 'You mean you would actually sink her, Sir?'

Cunningham noted his torpedo officer's use of the word 'you' as opposed to 'we', and again smiled wryly to himself. 'No, Guy, that's not what I'm saying. I'm saying that if we're in the right position, our threat to sink her should be all that's required, and hopefully she won't want to call our bluff.'

'Sounds like a good way of starting World War Three to me,' murmured May under his breath.

'But what then, Sir?' said Morton. 'It seems to me that they're not likely to cave in to any demands we may make – at least not for very long. Won't we have put ourselves into some sort of stand-off situation?'

'Yes, Hugh, you're right. But this won't be for long. While we're engaging the Russians in conversation, we'll slip our divers over the side and plant some bangers around her rudder and screws, and destroy her mobility. Hopefully *Spearfish* will by now have realised what's happening, and will be making her own escape arrangements.'

Watson shot a sharp glance towards Cunningham. 'Divers, Sir?'

'Yes Andrew, divers! You and Leading Seaman Donovan may well be called upon at this point to exercise your underwater skills, but I'll talk to you about that after this meeting.'

'Sounds exciting,' said Bramwell. Then seeing the look Watson gave him, immediately wished he hadn't spoken.

'Sounds bloody cold,' muttered May. 'I'm glad it ain't me that's goin' to get wet. An' it sounds bloody dangerous. An' what if *Spearfish* can't dive?'

'That's something we'll have to face when we get to it,' said Cunningham. 'We hope to be virtually alongside *Spearfish*, so we can get a full breakdown of her mechanical situation, but all the same, I *am* relying on her being able to dive.'

'Yeah, well,' muttered May, now in a louder voice, 'breakdown's probably the right word, an' if you ask me, she ain't goin' to be in any…!'

Now several others spoke all at once, voicing their doubts and drowning out the engineer officer's muttering.

'Gentlemen, please!' Cunningham barely resisted the urge to bring his fist down hard on the table, and his annoyance plainly echoed in the tone of his voice. Now there was quiet again. 'I know all this is very unusual, very different, but we're here to do an unusual and a different job, and if we have to fight fire with fire to get success, then that's what we'll do. The plan that I've outlined may well not work exactly in the way it's been presented, but it's the only one I've got that in my eyes stands any chance of success, and it's still only a plan. We all know that plans may change at very short notice, so we'll all have to react very quickly to any change as it happens. But above all else we must stay positive — you people must stay positive.' He paused, drawing a deep breath, again instinctively rubbing his chin while looking around the table and briefly studying the face of each officer in turn. 'If we can't make this work, gentlemen, then we'll probably end up accompanying *Spearfish* to Russia; and have no doubts when I say that that would be the better of two possible results if we fail!'

Morton said, 'Of course, Sir, you're basing your whole plan of action on the premise that it *is Spearfish* the Russian has got in tow. What if she's just towing one of her own?'

'Then the situation will certainly be potentially less volatile,' Cunningham replied. 'Instead of challenging them, we politely ask if they have seen her or have any news of *Spearfish*'s whereabouts — that's all we can do. But I for one am now convinced that they've got her. However, whether they've got her or not, they won't welcome our presence up here — I think we can bank on that. Are there any more questions? If so, let's have 'em now.' Cunningham waited. Of course they would have more questions, bloody hundreds of them, but he had just given them what amounted to orders, and these were, he hoped, completely clear. They wouldn't question his orders.

The officers remained silent, and Cunningham grunted, pulling himself to his feet. 'Thank you for your time, gentlemen.' Now his hawk-like features relaxed into what could pass as a fleeting smile. 'Just imagine the story you can tell to your grandchildren – in about thirty years from now, that is.' Then he stood and left the wardroom, closely followed by Morton.

Outside the wardroom Cunningham beckoned Morton into his cabin. 'Sit down, Hugh.' He swung his chair around for his first lieutenant's use, while he seated himself on his bunk and looked across at Morton. 'Well, there you have it. Now you know as much as I do. How do you think they took it?'

'Well, they're a bit wary, Sir, understandably, I'd say. But they'll be OK. They won't let you down.'

Cunningham sighed loudly. 'Wary, eh? That's one way of putting it, I suppose, but then, aren't we all? Wary, I mean.' He rubbed his jaw thoughtfully before continuing, 'We're heading towards what's potentially a very dangerous situation, Hugh, not only for ourselves, but on a national, or even an international scale. This one really calls for kid glove handling. Trouble is, there's no precedent for a situation like this – certainly nothing in the rule book.' He paused again. 'I wonder what my old friend Captain Richard Sterne would do if he were up here now in my shoes?'

'Well, I think it's pretty well known that he's not the world's greatest diplomat, Sir,' replied Morton. 'He'd probably have all tubes brought to the action state by now, then go in like a bull in a china shop!' Then, looking directly at Cunningham, he said, 'That bit about the torpedoes. Would we really use them?'

Cunningham returned Morton's earnest look and said, 'God, I hope not, Hugh, I really hope not. Things would have to have reached a pretty desperate situation before we resorted to that, but if needs must – well, we'll see. I would use them as a very last resort in order to save ourselves and *Spearfish* from possible destruction. No, a tactful and diplomatic approach must be our first move, and that's exactly what we'll try as our opening ploy. Any threats can follow. If a simple request for her to release *Spearfish* into our charge doesn't work, then we'll put our lads in the water and see if knocking her about a bit will change her mind. If we do have to use our torpedoes, then we've failed! And I'm not counting failure as an option, even though it seems a very real possibility at this stage. You'll keep that to yourself, won't you?' He stood up and stretched his long, thin frame before looking back down at Morton. 'Well I suppose I'd better bring my log up to date before the fun starts. Round up Ramsay, Donovan and Simmonds. I'll see them, together with Andrew Watson, in here in half an hour from now. I want you personally to brief each department on what we've talked about in there. Do this as soon as you can, and certainly within the next two hours. Make it clear that this is no exercise and everyone must be fully on the ball from now on.'

Morton said, 'Batteries and high-pressure air bottles are pretty much on top line, Sir, as long as we don't start thrashing about the ocean too much but, as you've already said, you intend to let them come to us. I'll organise those people you asked for to be here in half an hour.' He left the cabin, still feeling and looking slightly bewildered.

Sturgeon was now steering in repeated circles of one-mile diameter, very slowly, at periscope depth. Morton had been right: the weather had improved considerably. It had now moderated to a medium swell with an average wave height of no more than eight feet, and the snow had now stopped.

Now there was a tapping on Cunningham's cabin door. 'Come in, gentlemen,' he called, and his door curtain rolled back, revealing Watson, Ramsay, Donovan and Simmonds. It was a tight squeeze, but eventually all four were seated side by side on Cunningham's bunk, while he sat on his chair, facing them and said, 'Well, firstly, thank you for your time. I take it that by now you've been fully briefed by the first lieutenant?'

Ramsay, Simmonds and Donovan nodded, and Cunningham continued, 'Good. Well, now I've got the four of you in here to give you an extra briefing. You know the story, and you'll realise that your part in it may well prove critical – indeed the difference between success and failure. But although this situation has no precedent as far as I'm aware, this is not wartime, and what I am asking you to do is purely on a voluntary basis.'

Watson was the first of the three to speak. 'You said something earlier about hanging a few bangers on the Russian, Sir?'

'So I did,' said Cunningham. 'If necessary I want to immobilise her steering and propulsion. To do this I want you and Donovan to plant some explosive around her rudder and screws, and I want you, TI, to prepare sufficient explosive to do the job.' He looked pointedly at Ramsay. 'We don't need to blow the arse off her. Our aim will be merely to prevent her chasing us when we leave her, and that's all. The ship we're looking for is a destroyer: one of their "O" class, quite new by their standards, and heavily armed.'

'Oh, bloody 'ell.' Ramsay was making no attempt to conceal his feelings. 'Well. I'd already figured on this bein' my last friggin' trip anyway, Sir!'

Cunningham grinned to himself, knowing that if he got nothing else from Ramsay he would always get the truth. 'Well it's not all doom and gloom.' He leaned across to his book rack and pulled down the volume of *Jane's Fighting Ships*. Flicking through the pages until he found his marker, he passed the book over to the three men opposite.

'There's a picture of our target. As you can see, she's quite heavily armed, but I don't see that as an immediate problem.' He paused, waiting for their reaction, his left hand moving instinctively towards his chin for that familiar scratch. 'If we can take her by surprise and get close enough to her, she won't be able to depress those guns sufficiently to do us any damage.'

'We'll have to get very damn close then, Sir...' – Watson was shaking his head – '...both in order to avoid those guns and, equally, to minimise the time that Donovan and I are in the water. The sea temperature is very low. Could be a killer!'

'An' what about them torpedoes,' said Ramsay, still closely studying the picture. 'I see she's got nine tubes.'

'They'll be no problem as long as we position ourselves directly on her stern,' replied Cunningham. 'If we can do that we can avoid all her heavy fire. No, I think her torpedoes are the last thing we'll need to worry about.'

'And ours too, Sir,' Ramsay muttered. 'We can't fire 'em 'cos we'll be too close to set any time of run on 'em, an', even if we could, we'd probably blow our own bows off as well.'

'Yes, I fully appreciate that,' replied Cunningham, 'but, more to the point, will the Russians? This is all going to be one big bluff on our part and we've just got to pray that they fall for it.'

'An' their depth charges, Sir?' Ramsay was being persistent. 'An' what about her smaller guns? Hand weapons, even. I've seen men downed by a round from a sten gun before now! An' just a couple of machine gun bullets in our ballast tanks would give us big problems.'

'I don't think she'll resort to depth charges: they would have to be set so shallow she'd risk damaging herself. As for her other weapons, right down to small arms, well we'll just have to wait and see. Anyway, Gus, why so pessimistic?' Except for his officers, Cunningham rarely called any of his crew by their first name, and Ramsay hadn't missed this exception.

'Oh, just mentionin' all the possibilities, Sir, but I'll go along with yer plan whatever. I'm not trying to teach you to suck eggs, Sir.'

'Glad to hear it.' Cunningham disguised a smile then looked directly at Donovan, who had not yet spoken. 'How do you feel about all this, Donovan?'

Donovan looked his captain squarely in the eyes. 'To be perfectly honest, Sir, not too happy. For a start I'm not used to handling explosives and, furthermore, as Lieutenant Watson has already said, the sea temperature out there is low enough to kill a man within a very short time. I know that much.'

'Point taken.' Cunningham nodded and now looked towards Watson. 'And you, Andrew, what's your feeling?'

Watson looked uncomfortable. 'Well, Sir, as you know, I only qualified as a diver during the build period. I haven't got the diving experience of Donovan, but I have had some basic training with underwater explosives. As Donovan has said, our biggest problem will be sea temperature.' He paused, darting a sideways glance at Donovan's passive features, as if seeking some sort of backing. Then, shrugging his shoulders, he said, 'Nevertheless, I'm up for it. If this Russian is engaged in pinching one of our boats then I'd like nothing better than to blow her arse off! I'll go along with the plan, Sir.' Watson stopped, suddenly realising that he was perhaps sounding too enthusiastic, gung-ho almost. Then he continued, 'But it's definitely a job for two, Sir, and without wishing to place him in a corner, I would respect Donovan's decision on this one.'

'Thank you, Andrew.' Now Cunningham looked at both Watson and Donovan. 'I want you two to understand that what I'm asking you to do is not an order! If you decide that, for whatever reason, you are not prepared to do this, then I can assure you that no one will think the worse of you, least of all me. Looking at it from any angle, the job I'm asking you to do is very high risk, and you have the choice on whether you do it or not! If we were officially at war then, of course, things would be different: you certainly wouldn't have that choice. However, the fact remains that the crippling of the Russian destroyer will almost certainly be the key element in our plan if we are to retake *Spearfish*, and freeing *Spearfish* will mean nothing unless we prevent a subsequent chase, which, when you think about it, could lead not only to her rebagging *Spearfish*, but also taking us in as well.' He paused, again rubbing that long Punch-like jaw. 'All this is, of course, dependent on the fact that our Soviet friend has actually got *Spearfish* with her and we catch her red-handed, so to speak. But if *Spearfish* is with her, then you can be certain that she's being escorted back to Russia, where her captain, and probably her crew, will be facing very long prison sentences, and if—'

'Count me in, Sir! I'll do it, albeit against my better judgement.' Donovan slammed the "Jane's" shut and passed it back to Cunningham, who replaced it in his book rack while trying to conceal a sigh of relief.

'Thank you, the both of you.' Now Cunningham turned his attention to Gus Ramsay. 'Right, TI, the first lieutenant tells me that you might possibly have a little store of fireworks stashed away!'

'Sounds like I've got enough for what you want, Sir. We've got a few anti-personnel charges as well, but they ain't goin' to do much more than make a noise and kill off a few fish, maybe.'

Cunningham nodded. 'Yes, but they may help towards causing panic and confusion if nothing else. What I really want is just to take out her rudder and her screws.'

Gus took on a thoughtful expression and Cunningham could see that he was really enjoying his moment. 'Well yes, I 'ave got a little something that could look after that for you. I got some plastic, an' wiv the right amount of that stuff put in the proper place, we could hit her as hard as you want.'

'Well, as I've already said, I don't want to sink her, only cripple her,' replied Cunningham, 'and as for the proper place for these charges, I was thinking about her propeller shaft "A" brackets for a start. Take them away and her shafts would be virtually useless. She would never risk turning her screws. As for the steering, surely the best thing would be to simply blow her rudder off?'

Ramsay nodded. 'Sounds like good sense to me, Sir.'

'But can you be sure of the right amount of explosive to do the job? Not enough to do any more damage than disable her sufficiently to stop her giving chase when we break away.'

'You just leave that to me, Sir.' Ramsay sounded confident. 'What sort of fuse do you want? Timing, I mean.'

Cunningham looked at the two divers. 'What do you say, gentlemen? Ten minutes? Would that be enough? I want to keep it as short as possible.'

'Well, that should do, Sir,' replied Watson. As long as we're close enough, ten minutes should give us time to clear the water once the bombs are in place, but I'm not sure how the water temperature will affect us. They tell me you can't predict this. Anyway, if I am going to freeze to death I'd much sooner it happened while I was in one piece! What do you say, Donovan?'

'Ten minutes should be enough, Sir. If we're in the water much longer than that, I doubt we'll get back out anyway.'

'Make it so then, TI. Ten minutes on the charges.'

'Ten minutes it is, Sir. But remember, it ain't no exact science.' He looked at the two divers. 'You two 'ad better keep yer 'ands over yer balls on the way back!'

Cunningham smiled to himself. 'Are there any more questions?' If there were more, he didn't wait to hear them. Instead he continued, 'I will, of course, be keeping you all completely in the picture from now on in, and I'll let you know right away should there be any changes to our plan. Right...' he looked up at the bulkhead clock, 'I think that must be all for now. TI, I want you to start making up the bombs right away, if you will; and you two...' – he motioned towards Watson and Donovan – '...it might be an idea if you give your diving gear a thorough checkout; make sure everything is on top line.' Now he turned to Simmonds. 'Sorry, Simmonds, you must be feeling a little left out by now, but since I now understand that you have a fairly good knowledge of the Russian language, that may well come in handy. I want you to be ready if I need to call upon this, so you will be standing by from the time the plan is put into action.'

'To be sure I will, Sir,' replied Simmonds. 'I can do any translating required, so I can.'

Cunningham now turned back to Watson and Donovan. 'Are you both happy with the state of your diving gear?'

'It was all checked and serviced by the base staff before we left, Sir,' said Watson.

'Then check it again, Andrew. We'll take no chances. After you've done that, get your heads down. Take yourselves out of the watch bill, all four of you. You'll need as much sleep as you can get.'

The four volunteers rose from the bunk and made their way forward, while Cunningham walked out into the control room.

★ ★ ★ ★ ★

After their meeting with Cunningham, Watson and Donovan went straight to the fore-ends, where for the next hour they carried out a very thorough check on all their diving gear. Ramsay was with them.

'Well, there you go then. Who would have thought it, eh? Me last trip to sea in this bloody sewer pipe, an' me first bit of real excitement in years!' Ramsay had been a shallow water diver himself in his younger days and was more than ready to offer his assistance and advice.

'Yeah well, it might seem exciting to you, Gus,' muttered Donovan, 'but to me it's goin' to be bloody cold, an' more than just a bit iffy in other ways as well.'

Donovan's remark didn't even penetrate Gus's thinking. 'Right then, if all's well with the gear, bottles, torches an' all the rest of yer stuff, you better go an' get yer 'eads down. I'm out of the watch bill too, so I'll shake you whenever things start 'appening. In the meanwhile I'll be making up a few fireworks. What did the old man say? Go careful – was that it? Yeh, well, Russians – I've shit 'em! Oh, by the way, I've got something for you, gents.' Ramsay reached down to produce a thin nylon rope, dark blue in colour, roughly ten foot in length, and with a loop at either end. 'It's going to be bloody cold down there – you already know that – an' it's goin' to be bloody dark as well. Chances are you won't be able to see more than a yard or so in front you,

291

even with a torch. This is a two-man job, so you must stick together. When you go over the side, use this! I'd like to see you *both* come back, even if,' – he shot a quick glance in Watson's direction – 'you both give me the shits at times! Now bugger off, the pair of you, an' like the skipper said, get yer 'eads down an' let me sort out the technical bits. I'll be givin' each of you two lumps of explosive fer strappin' to her "A" brackets, and some more to knock out her rudder. There'll be a single detonator for each pair, an' the timer will be set for ten minutes. To start it you just turn the knob through ninety degrees clockwise. But then, I'll be tellin' you all this again before you go.' He grinned to himself. 'Even you should be able to manage that, Donno! As I said before though, it ain't an exact science, so you better get yer arses out of the water toot sweet once you've set them timers.'

Donovan sighed. 'OK, Gus, O bloody K! You just make sure you don't blow the fore-ends off this bastard while you're playing with your bombs!'

It was 23.00 before Donovan returned to the forward mess, and sat for a while, drinking a mug of tea. White, knowing the situation, said, 'You all right then, Donno?'

For a while Donovan didn't answer, and then he said, 'The skipper wants me to take a cold bath.'

'Yeh, I know,' White replied, 'but then there you go, me old mate. That's the price of fame, or so they tell me.'

Now Deane wandered into the mess, having just been relieved in the radio office. 'I don't suppose you bastards 'ave left any tea in the pot?' Then he turned to Donovan. 'Seems like they're askin' you to get in the water then, Donno.'

As tired as he was, and probably for the first time in many days, Donovan felt like talking. He needed to talk. 'Well, you two might as well know, there's a sprog on the way. Shoulda told you before, I suppose. Don't know why I didn't. It's due in about a fortnight, so whatever you two pricks might think, I'm going to be a dad!'

White held out his hand. 'I figured as much, Donno. I thought you was 'iding something from us. You ain't bin yer usual self lately.' He looked towards Deane for confirmation. 'So, it's a sprog, is it? Good to 'ear it. I was beginnin' to think you 'ad sawdust bollocks!'

Deane said, 'Bloody 'ell, Donno, you old bastard. Can I be a godparent then?'

'An' me?' said White.

'Yeah, well, I suppose it all depends on what happens tomorrow, won't it?' Donovan knew that now he was being deliberately open, leading, asking their opinions, and he felt guilty. Was he making more of this than he should? But both White and Deane had immediately cottoned on to his thoughts.

'Christ, Donno!' said Deane, 'You ain't worried about what may 'appen tomorrow, are yuh? Even if we do catch up with them friggin' Russians, an' even if they 'ave got *Spearfish* wiv 'em, they ain't about to risk some sort of major incident, are they? Nah, mate, I doubt you'll even get yer feet wet. They'll be just trying to pull a fast bastard. You know what I mean? Seein' what they can get away with. What do you reckon, Knocker?'

'Yep,' Knocker nodded in agreement, 'I'd even bet your tot on it.'

Donovan looked dubious. 'Well, the old man don't seem to be thinkin' that way, and I guess he should know what's likely to develop.'

'It's all guesswork, innit, my son, and the end of the day it's all one big friggin' game to them bastards up there an' our bastards down 'ere!' White was studying Donovan's face, noting the worry. 'Of course the old man's got to stay one step ahead and consider all possibilities, you know, be prepared for the worst scenario an' all that shit. That's what they say in the wardroom, ain't it? But then, 'e is the skipper, an' that's what 'e gets paid for: bein' one step in front of them bastards up there.'

'Well, I hope you're right,' said Donovan, obviously still not convinced. 'Andy Watson's up for this, but I don't know about him. He seems a bit too keen for my liking, bit of a cowboy, maybe? All this could turn out to be a bit nasty. I should know by now never to volunteer for anything, especially something like this.' He turned and looked at both White and Deane. 'D'you know, I think I might well have shit in my own nest over this one, chaps!'

'Nah, you'll be all right, my son,' said Deane. 'By this time tomorrow we could be sittin' 'ere like we are now, an' you'll be full of Knocker's tot, an' it'll all 'ave bin a bit of a giggle. Now go and get yer 'ead down. That was what the old man said, didn't he?

'Yeh, me too,' said White, finishing the last of his tea. 'I got the friggin' mornin'. Can't stay up all night nattering to you bastards.'

Samuels, who had been sitting quietly sipping his tea and mopping up the conversation, said, 'I'd do it for you, Donno. I ain't got no missus or kids, but I ain't got no training either, 'ave I? Good news about the sprog though, innit?'

'Thanks, Spots, I appreciate that.' Donovan stood up and went towards his bunk, but he didn't sleep well that night. Lying with his eyes wide open in the darkness, he listened to the middle watchmen closing up, and tried in vain to distance himself from their muttered conversation as they brushed past his bunk curtain. He was still awake when the morning watch turned out at 03.45, and he was still thinking of June and the baby that was due in about two weeks from now. His baby, their baby. He wanted this baby so badly, for both of them – they wanted a family. Now he knew that the way things were, his baby may well be born before *Sturgeon* got back to Scotland, if she ever got back to Scotland. He had imagined receiving some sort of news when they arrived alongside – news that would precipitate his immediate departure for London. But since his visit to Cunningham's cabin, things were no longer that clear cut, and his mind again began to wrestle with what he was being asked to do. He knew that if this situation developed, then his life would be on the line. But the old man was no fool, and in his own rational and calm way had made it quite clear to both Donovan and Watson what the risks were, and it was clear to Donovan that this was exactly what it might come to. Even if they did manage to free *Spearfish* from the Russian, it would all be pretty pointless unless the Russian could be prevented from taking up the chase. No, the old man was right: this was the plan, and this is what surely had to happen. In the darkness he reached up and ran his fingers over the photograph of June. Now, possibly for the first time in his life, Thomas Donovan felt a distinct dread, a real fear, not for himself, but for everything he had lived and planned for since he and June had first met. He had always harboured a secret feeling that his life with June was becoming too good to be true. Someone, something, was bound to come along and ruin everything – that was the way of things in his experience – and now it seemed that these fears could well come into fruition within the next few hours. Would he ever see June again? Would he ever hold his newborn baby? Sod the Navy! Sod submarine service! And sod the bloody Russians! He turned over and buried his head into his pillow, knowing that sleep wouldn't come.

Meanwhile, back in the wardroom, Watson slept like a baby.

CHAPTER FIFTEEN

Shortly after 07.30 Cunningham was awakened by the control room messenger. He had slept well, and it had taken several rough shakes of his shoulder from the messenger to bring him out of this sleep. Now he shot bolt upright in his bunk, blinking into the fierce white fluorescent light that now invaded his cabin. 'Eh, what?' He rubbed his sleep-filled eyes and tried to gather his thoughts.

'Sound room's got a contact, Sir. They think it's the Russian destroyer.'

'They do, do they?' Now fully awake, Cunningham tumbled from his bunk. Brushing aside the startled messenger, he leapt across the passageway into the semi-darkness of the sonar office, where White and Bell were now closed up, White listening intently to a headset, while Bell studied the erratic movement of two pen recorders on the set in front of him. Sensing Bradley's presence, White turned and removed his headset, while Bell continued to study the movement of the pens as they jerked across the paper chart in front of him.

'I reckon we got a good contact, Sir.' White sounded excited. 'About twenty-four miles to the north-east, only making about four knots, an' if she keeps comin' the way she is now, an' we stay on position, she'll pass about three miles astern of us at a range of about three miles off our starboard in about six hours from now. Twin screws, but it sounds like one's got a bit missing out of it.'

Bradley took the headphones from White and held one receiver to his left ear. Stroking his jaw, he listened intently for almost two minutes. It was a destroyer, all right. He'd listened to this type of HE so many times before, and even though the signature of this contact sounded slightly different, he had little doubt that it would be a destroyer. Almost certainly a Russian. But was it *his* Russian? Still rubbing his chin, he handed the headset back to White and nodded, 'Well done, chaps. Very well done! Keep on it. I'll be in the control room. Let me know immediately there's any change.'

Back in the control room he spoke quietly to Heywood, who was the officer of the watch. Explaining the new developments, he said, 'Let's have a quick burst on the radar. Then take her down to 150 feet and steer a closing course. We might as well meet up with her a bit further north – give ourselves a bit more distance from the mainland. Raise the radar mast. I'll be in the radar office for a couple of minutes.'

Just two sweeps of radar aerial confirmed his thinking. He watched the screen intently. Yes, there it was. The screen confirmed what White had told him. Contact range was twenty-four miles and was on a closing course to *Sturgeon*. This screen also told him that the contact was made up of two individual parts. 'Right,' he muttered, 'that's good enough for me; it has to be them! He patted the operator on the shoulder and said, 'Well done. Switch off and secure the set.' Then, back in the control room, he ordered the radar mast to be lowered. 'Switch off all unnecessary lighting and machinery and pass the word: no noise throughout the boat. We'll go to action stations at 08.30.'

The forenoon watchmen had been shaken at 07.15; and now at 08.00, having breakfasted, they took up their watch keeping positions. The men they relieved were eager to fill them in on the current situation. In the sound room White had declined a relief, simply sending Bell forward to fetch him a cup of coffee and something between two slices of bread. He had made up his mind that he would stay in the sound room now until, in his words, 'this bloody carnival' was over!

The time was 09.00. During the past hour Cunningham had made many visits to the sound room to assure himself that the situation was progressing satisfactorily. Now back in the control room, he again studied the chart. Marking *Sturgeon*'s exact position, he drew a pencil line for a distance equating to 24 at a bearing of zero-four-zero, then fringed this with two more lines at five degrees either side of his first line. The control room messenger came up behind him. 'Coffee, Sir?'

'I'd rather have a large brandy!' Cunningham was finding it difficult to suppress his excitement. 'But yes, please, I'll have a coffee.' Then Morton had appeared at his side. 'Come to my cabin, Hugh, and I'll bring you up to date.'

In his cabin, over yet another cup of coffee, Cunningham fully outlined the situation to Morton. 'So it looks like the first phase of your plan is about to begin, Sir.'

'Yes, I am rather banking on this being the contact we came up here to find,' replied Cunningham. 'We'll stay at this depth for a while, and keep a speed of three knots. That should half our closing time. Meanwhile, I want no noise and minimal movement throughout the boat.'

Just after 10.30 White reported from the sound room that the sea strength was decreasing and the contact was still on her original course. Bradley, after making some quick calculations, established that with his own speed at three knots and the contact speed of five, if nothing changed in the meantime they should pass at about three miles off *Sturgeon's* starboard side at between 13.30 and 14.30.

Cunningham's judgement proved correct. The contact passed down *Sturgeon's* starboard at 14.10, at a distance of three miles.

In the control room Cunningham said to Morton, 'Stay where you are, Hugh. Let her get five miles to the south of us, and then we'll go down to 300 feet and swing around to pick up her tail. Keep everyone closed up and I want absolute silence in the boat from now on in. Let's hope we can give her a nasty surprise. Oh, and pass the word: "one all round". Could be the last one for a while!'

Immediately cigarettes and lighters were produced and a thick pall of smoke rose over the grateful smokers, polluting even more the already stale air in the boat. Cunningham went to his cabin and, flopping onto his bunk, lit his own cigarette and tried to gather his thoughts. Now he again went into the sound room, where White reported the contact just over five miles to their south-east.

Cunningham ordered Morton to bring *Sturgeon* to 200 feet, come around to a course of one-four-five, and maintain a speed of eight knots. Now he was tracking his target, and calculated that if the Russian remained on her present course and speed, he would be looking at her stern in about two and a half to three hours from now.

The time was now 15.00 and although the sea state had dropped considerably, for some reason the Russian had slowed to just fewer than two knots, and was now barely one mile dead ahead. Cunningham had brought *Sturgeon* to periscope depth. Raising the attack periscope, he searched carefully for his target which, by his reckoning, should now be dead ahead. It was quite dark up there and that was good, and it was again snowing heavily. He could see nothing. 'Nothing in sight. Can't see a bloody thing!' He stepped back from the periscope. 'Dip and raise. Sonar – Control. Report all contacts.'

White's coarse scouse tones immediately came back over the intercom, 'Control – Sound Room. Contact bearing dead ahead, distance 1200 yards.'

'Roger, sound room.' Now the attack periscope was up again and Cunningham's left eye was glued to its monocular lens. 'Still snowing like hell, but at least the sea state's still dropping. That'll be useful – I hope. Slow down a smidgen, Hugh; we don't want our bows wedged up her duck run just yet. Bloody ice. Dip and raise attack.'

Slowly, cautiously, *Sturgeon* crept forward, guided and now utterly reliant upon the expertise of White in the sound room. Then at 16.00 White's voice again came over the sonar room intercom. 'Control – Sound Room. Target is stopped!'

Cunningham leapt for the periscope as it again emerged from the well. 'Still can't see a bloody thing up there.' He couldn't hide his disappointment. 'Just water, snow, and bloody dark!'

Again from the sound room, 'Repeat, target has stopped.'

Cunningham glanced at the clock. 'Roger, Sound Room.' His heart sank. He felt a bitter mixture of anger, disappointment and frustration welling up inside of him. He turned to the circle of faces now watching him intently in the dark red lighting of the control room.

'It looks like they've detected us, chaps! I can't think of any other reason for them to stop. So,' he mused, 'it looks like the bastards weren't asleep after all – at least not all of them. Oh, well, I guess it's shit or bust now. We'll continue with our plan.'

★ ★ ★ ★ ★

Portrova wiped the remains of his meal from his mouth with the back of his hand. As almost always, it had been a sparse meal, this time of cabbage and stewed meat. Portrova smoked and drank far more than he ate. Reaching for a cigarette, he lit up before slumping back into his chair with a loud belch. He was not tired. He had slept soundly since early this morning, leaving *Otvashni* under the control of his first officer, Carlov. The sea had dropped considerably now though it was again snowing heavily. He told Carlov to carry out the delayed burial of the young seaman at 16.00.

He needed a drink. Pulling open a drawer in the grey-painted steel locker beside his chair, he produced a half-full bottle of vodka, together with a glass. Filling the glass to its brim, he raised it towards the plain-looking woman in the photograph beside his bunk. 'To you, my Anna.' He downed the drink in one massive gulp and then poured another. He felt satisfied, content. He knew that soon this task would be over. Soon *Otvashni* would again be in Russian territorial waters, and he, Alexci Portrova, would be able to hand the Britishers over to the authorities. Drawing heavily on his Sobranie, he began to reflect upon the events of the past days.

It was clear to him that in spite of all that had happened, he had won. Yes, there would be many questions to answer when *Otvashni* finally reached her destination and, no doubt, many recriminations. They would try to make him look the fool. But no matter, he would have delivered the latest class of British submarine to his masters in Moscow. Surely they must applaud him for that. He took another gulp of vodka, emptying the glass. Now he would go and visit this Britisher in the sick berth. Perhaps now, Commander Bradley would be ready to answer his questions.

★ ★ ★ ★ ★

Again on his feet, Bradley was peering through the starboard porthole of *Otvashni*'s sick berth, while Jackson still lay in his cot, snoring, completely drained by the constant exercising Bradley had forced him into over the past days. The two of them were alone, but still with a guard stationed just outside the door. He turned quickly, taken by surprise as the door of the sick berth opened behind him. The white-coated doctor stepped over the coaming, closely followed by Portrova and Yuri.

Portrova strolled forward towards Bradley. 'Ah, Commander, it is good to see that you are on your feet again. I trust you are well?' His tone was again overtly smug, patronising.

Bradley quickly recovered his thoughts. 'Not well, Captain, but yes, recovering, despite the efforts of you and your tame gorillas.'

Portrova shrugged and turned to the doctor and Yuri. 'You may go, Dimitry. I wish to speak to the commander in confidence.'

The doctor and Yuri left, pulling the door shut behind them, and Portrova turned towards Bradley, still with his patronising approach. 'Why not return to your bed, Commander? It is good to see you up again but you must be very tired and we still have much to talk about. Our doktar tells me that you will be fully fit very soon. This is good, *da*?' Now his tone hardened. 'Shortly we will be committing yet another of my comrads to the deep! Murdered by your people!'

'If you're talking about that little KGB shit, then he deserved everything he got! In fact, I'm surprised he lived as long as he did,' hissed Bradley. 'I'm sorry to hear about your other man with the head wound, but perhaps you, too, may spare a thought for Lieutenant Commander Cannings.' Then, raising his hands in a gesture of dismissal, he continued, 'And as for you, Portrova, you can go to hell. I've said all I'm going to say to you!'

'Come, come, my friend. I understand how you feel, but if you persist in this way then you sentence yourself to a long term of imprisonment at the very least. Why not just admit that you were spying? We are both men of the sea. Let the politicians do as they will: we are nothing more than pawns in their game of chess. They care nothing of us. You know this as I do. We do what we are told, do we not, *da*? But you, Commander, can put an end to this regrettable affair quickly and quietly. You will please trust me. I know how these things work.'

'I wouldn't trust you as far as I could throw you and, as I said before, you can go to hell!'

Portrova sighed. 'You are not being helpful, Commander.' He glanced towards the still-snoring Jackson. 'Your friend there, the trawler captain. He is a pig! Would you not agree? He sleeps now, but he will pay for his actions. He will be shot! But you, Commander, once we have repaired the unfortunate damage to your vessel, could be on your way back to your United Kingdom where, together with your crew, you could again enjoy your beautiful English countryside. You must think about this.'

Bradley scowled but said nothing.

Portrova's eyes clouded with ill-concealed anger. Stepping back from Bradley he hissed, 'Very well, Commander, as you wish! You still have time to reconsider your position. We will talk again later.' He turned and strode towards the door. Pulling the door open, he called in the doctor and his assistant, who had been waiting in the flat outside. 'You have done well with this Britisher, Comrad Doktar, but it would seem that he is now well enough to cause me more trouble.' He fastened his sloe-black eyes on the doctor. 'He must never be left without a guard outside of this door! Are our people ready for the burial?'

★ ★ ★ ★ ★

Now, at 17.00, Portrova was again slumped in his bridge chair, his frame already covered in a thick blanket of snow. Seemingly oblivious to the biting cold, he smoked a cigarette while staring ahead into the swirling snow. A hand shook his right arm. He turned up and looked into the face of the ship's doctor.

'*Da*, Comrad Doktar, what is it?'

'You asked me to prepare our comrad for committal, Kapitan. This I have done. He is now ready.' The doctor spoke in a low, patently pious tone. But there was no sign of piety in Portrova's reply.

Stubbing out his cigarette, he said, 'So our little friend is ready to meet his maker, *da?*' He pulled up his cuff to look at his watch. 'This is good. I will now stop the ship. You will arrange with Comrad Carlov to conduct a short service. No more than five minutes. I want no delay!'

'You will not attend, Comrad Kapitan?' The doctor looked surprised.

'*Nyet!*' Portrova was clearly agitated. 'Go now, Doktar. Comrad Carlov will preside over things. I want all men off watch gathered on the upper deck immediately. You have little time, and we have to do what we have to do.' He slumped back into his chair, again groping for his cigarette case. Then he turned and called after the departing doctor. 'Be sure you warn Comrad Ravoski before we stop. I want no collisions.'

★ ★ ★ ★ ★

Aboard *Spearfish*, Murray was officer of the watch and now alone. It had been agreed with Ravoski that there was no point in having more than one person on the bridge under the present circumstances, but that person had to be an officer. Heavy snow had been falling non-stop since noon, and a thick mantle of crisp white covered both the bridge and Murray, and it was very dark. Looking ahead of *Spearfish*'s bow, he could see the stern light of the Russian, but little else. *Otvashni* had shortened the tow down to twenty-five yards during the afternoon, and now it had remained for the most part bar-taut. The wind had now dropped almost to nothing, and the black swell beneath *Spearfish* seldom reached peaks of more that four feet. Murray leaned towards the voice pipe. 'Bridge – Helm. What speed are we making?'

'Just two knots, Sir,' came the helmsman's reply. 'Permission to relieve the lookout, Sir.'

'What bloody lookout? For Christ's sake, buck up.' This was an uncharacteristic outburst from Murray, who now drew back from the voice pipe and muttered under his breath, 'God's socks, are we all going bloody barmy?'

The strain of the past few days especially, had been telling on all *Spearfish's* officers, and the frustration of not knowing what to expect did nothing to help. Murray was no exception to this. Gone now was that laid back casual attitude that had so much impressed the men in *Spearfish*. He, like everyone else, was now ready to snap the head off anyone for the least possible reason. They had all watched these Soviet guards, coarse and brutal, continuously striding through the boat on the constant lookout for trouble. More than one of *Spearfish's* crew had suffered at their hands. A wrong look was all it needed to be knocked to their knees with a gun and then often followed by a vicious kicking. Even more aggravating was the fact that Ravoski made no attempt to control them.

It was so different from before. Before, the guards, though sullen and not sure of their exact role, had been guided by Ravoski, who had then been completely friendly towards the crew. But now, these guards were openly threatening, bullying, and there were twice as many of them. The senior of the guards, a petty officer, had proved himself to be a singularly vicious character. No more the passive, almost apologetic smiles and grunts, or the friendly banter which, although they didn't understand, they went along with anyway. These guards were now in complete control, and they knew it.

Murray cowered beneath the bridge coaming, looking for whatever shelter the wrecked bridge could now provide. He wondered morosely what was in store for him and the others, and how his captain was faring aboard the Russian destroyer in front of him. To him, all this now felt like a very bad dream. Then the dream was suddenly broken!

He sensed it at first, rather than seeing it. Raising his head above the bridge coaming, the glaring white light from *Otvashni's* signal lantern dazzled him even through the blanketing snow. What the hell does she want now? But he could read signals and the message from the Russian's signal lantern quite plainly. There was more to come. He leaned towards the bridge voice pipe,

'Control room – Bridge. The Russian officer Ravoski and the first lieutenant are required on the bridge at the rush, and shake the signalman as well.'

Within three minutes Strong and Ravoski were on the bridge. Ravoski watched *Otvashni*'s blinking signal lantern, and then he reached for the megaphone and called her. He spoke in Russian. The conversation was short, and Strong didn't understand a word of it. Then Ravoski lowered his megaphone and turned to Strong. '*Otvashni* is about to make a short stop. They are going to bury one of my comrades! We will need to watch our tow, *da*? You will turn your motor astern if the wire becomes slack. It will be a short stop.'

★ ★ ★ ★ ★

Otvashni had now come to a stop, with *Spearfish* holding a gap of some twenty-five yards from her stern. Aboard *Sturgeon*, Cunningham, with his left eye still glued to his attack periscope, could hardly believe that he had got this near to her without being challenged. Surely they must have known that he was here? At last he could now see something and he now breathed a sigh of deep relief. He'd brought *Sturgeon* around in a sweeping arc. Now she was facing south-west, no more than sixty yards directly off the Russian's stern. He tried to hide both the tension and the excitement in his voice. 'Watch your depth, Number One, keep fifty-eight feet and slow down a smidgeon; we don't want to nudge her up the backside – at least not just yet anyway. Load the forward and after SSEs with red grenades and bring all bow tubes to the action state. Lieutenant Watson and Leading Seaman Donovan, report to the control room.'

Cunningham kept his attack periscope up slightly longer this time, as usual giving a running commentary on everything he saw. 'Yes, it's a Russian "O" class all right, and she's towing one of our "S" boats. It's got to be *Spearfish*. Her fin looks a bit different. Looks like she may have had a nasty accident. Either that or she's taken one hell of a pounding from the Ruskies. There's hardly anything left of her fin. They're both stopped.' He stood back from the periscope, flipping up its handles as the periscope slid down into its well. The time was now 17.07. 'OK, Hugh, pass the word though the boat: from now on be prepared for anything! Up attack. We'll have another quick look at 'em, then we'll try to sidle up on to *Spearfish*'s port side.'

This was going to be a very risky operation. Even though the sea state had dropped considerably, to put *Sturgeon* where he intended to put her was certainly not good submarine practice and could well be a recipe for complete disaster. Even a slight sideways drift to starboard could cause severe damage to the ballast tanks of both boats – enough to make them unable to dive.

Watson and Donovan, both now in wet suits and carrying flippers and air bottles, were standing under the lower hatch of the conning tower together with the second cox'n, the signalman and two of the casing party. From the attack periscope Cunningham now looked towards them.

'You two OK?'

It was Watson who replied. Trying to look cheerful, he raised a thumb and grinned ruefully, not realising that his captain couldn't possibly see his pale anxious face in the dull red lighting. 'As OK as can be expected, Sir.'

Cunningham said, 'Right, then, when we get to the surface I want you up on the casing right away, get yourselves around to the port after side of the fin and stay out of sight of both the Russian and *Spearfish*. The second cox'n will help you over the side, if and when I give the order.'

Turning back to the attack periscope, he called to Morton, 'Hold your course and speed, Hugh, and bring her up slowly, I want the casing just clear of the water, but no more.' Stealing a further quick glance towards *Spearfish*, he could see that she was high in the water, and he could tell by the absence of exhaust that she was not running her engines. 'Ye gods!' he muttered. 'Would you look at that fin! Mutilated! It looks like she's been mauled by a bloody panzer tank or something similar. There's someone on her bridge. Can't see who, though. Depth now?'

'Fifty-five feet,' called Morton.

Cunningham turned his periscope back to survey *Otvashni*'s quarterdeck. 'No sign of movement on the Russian either,' he muttered. 'They must be all asleep up there.' Then he pulled back from the periscope. Again in the dimness of the control room the astonishment on his face was hidden, but not so in his voice. 'They've got a large group of men mustered down her port side. Can't see how many. What the hell's going on? Stop both, Oliver. Slow astern together; we'll be up her arse in a second or two!' Immediately, *Sturgeon* began to sink. Still at the attack periscope, Cunningham called, 'Right, gentlemen, let's get this show on the road. Fire the forward and after SSEs. Oh, and get Petty Officer Ramsay and Petty Officer Simmonds to the control room at the rush.'

He waited, listening for the familiar sound of the discharging SSEs. Then, receiving confirmation that both had been fired, he turned to Hugh Morton. 'OK, Hugh, take us up there.'

Morton gave the order for a two-second blow on main ballast, and even that was more than what was required, but the low-pressure blower would have been far too noisy. *Sturgeon* was moving upward. Cunningham took a deep breath. God, but he was taking a risk! All it needed was just one thing to go wrong now and they would be finished. It would all be his fault, of course. He would be judged by his seniors back in the UK as "putting his vessel at risk" though at this moment that was the least of his concerns. Yes, of course he was putting *Sturgeon* and her crew at risk, and the same went for *Spearfish* – just one collision could sink them both. That was the worst possible scenario, but a very real one. He was also risking the complete failure of this rescue operation, with the possibility of *Sturgeon* ending up on the Russian's towline, alongside *Spearfish*. Again he wiped his sweat-drenched face with the back of his hand as he focused his eye into the lens of the attack periscope. Now the time for this sort of thinking was over. Within seconds *Sturgeon* was on the surface, and right where Cunningham had wanted her – just off *Spearfish's* port side. He turned to Heywood. 'Get on the search periscope, Chris, and keep a damn good watch on our position. I want to hold us alongside *Spearfish's* port beam at a distance of no more than about eight yards, and that'll take a lot of concentration! You've got the con 'til I get to the bridge. Watch the Russian in front as well. Hugh, you and the signalman and the divers, follow me. Open the lower hatch.'

★ ★ ★ ★ ★

Portrova had resettled himself into his bridge chair, waiting impatiently for the burial service now taking place on the upper deck to be concluded. The off-watch men stood down there on the port side of the upper deck in three ranks, bare-headed in the falling snow, while Kapitan Lieutenant Sergei Carlov read out some appropriate words. Then the canvas-lashed bundle of what once had been the young seaman was slid over the side, and it plummeted downward into the freezing black water.

At exactly the same time that the canvas bundle met the water, Carlov and his men looked upward in complete astonishment as, almost in a salute to their dead comrades, the two red grenades from *Sturgeon* hurtled skyward not twenty-five yards from *Otvashni*'s stern.

Portrova too, had seen the flares. Now he watched in utter shock as the last falling embers from the grenades melted into the darkness of the sea. His watch officer and two lookouts were still staring upward in complete puzzlement.

'It must be the British submarine, Comrad Kapitan. She must have released flares,' was all the watch officer could offer.

Cursing loudly, Portrova rushed to the port bridge wing and stared aft into the driving snow, convinced that *Spearfish* was making yet another bid for freedom. What he saw again caused his jaw to drop in sheer astonishment. There were now two submarines behind *Otvashni*, side by side, each showing a full set of navigation lights. Portrova's jaw dropped even further as an amplified voice from the submarine on the port side of his stern carried clearly across the wind towards him.

'Do you hear there, the Soviet warship? I require you to remain where you are! Do not restart your engines.'

Portrova grabbed the megaphone from its stowage and raised it to his face. 'Who are you?'

I am Lieutenant Commander James Cunningham, commanding officer of Her Majesty's Submarine *Sturgeon*. Who are you?'

Portrova scowled in sheer disbelief. Yet another Britisher! He could hardly speak. 'I am Kapitan Alexci Portrova, commander of this ship.'

'Captain Portrova, I order you not to move your ship.'

'On what authority do you make this order?'

'You have a British submarine in tow against her will.'

'This is nonsense, Commander. As you can see, the submarine we have in tow is badly damaged. We are escorting her to port in order that she may be given some temporary repairs before proceeding south. Wait, I will come to my quarterdeck.'

Portrova turned to his watch officer. 'Train both searchlights on the vessels astern of us. I will stay in contact with you from the quarterdeck phone. You will do exactly as I say! Bring the ship to battle stations. Use word of mouth only. I want no unnecessary noise or movement but you will tell me immediately the ship is ready for action.' Then, passing his megaphone to one of the bridge lookouts, he grunted, 'Come! You will come with me. Bring this with you.'

Portrova now stood on his quarterdeck, one gloved hand holding a megaphone, the other gripping *Otvashni*'s stern rail, thus steadying himself against the rise and fall of the deck beneath his feet. Beside him stood the two seamen who had followed him from the bridge, and Lieutenant Bassisty.

On the bridge of *Sturgeon*, Cunningham and his colleagues were suddenly blinded by the twin spears of white light as the destroyer's searchlights were switched on. Cunningham felt naked, exposed and suddenly very vulnerable.

Portrova raised the megaphone, directing it towards *Sturgeon*'s bridge. 'Now, Commander, I can see you. Now we can talk, *da*? What is it that you want?'

'I want *Spearfish* to be released to me, and I want a clear passage to escort her home to the United Kingdom.'

'*Spearfish* is in my custody, Commander, and I intend her to remain so!' Portrova paused, wiping ice from his mouth onto the sleeve of his coat. 'She has been spying in Soviet territorial waters. She is under arrest! I will not turn her over to you. You will please bear off before I am forced to take action against you.'

'You appear to speak very good English, Captain, so you will understand me when I tell that I have all my bow torpedoes ready to fire. You are proposing an act of aggression, piracy even. I am quite prepared to sink you if you refuse to co-operate with my requests!'

'Yes, Commander, I speak good English. But what you request is not possible.' Portrova was thinking hard, playing for time, waiting for the message from his watch officer on the bridge to tell him that *Otvashni*'s gun crews were at their stations. But already he was realising that this new submarine had all the advantages. She was too close under his after guns for him to bring them to bear, and too close for him to loose depth charges without risking serious damage to his own ship and, of course, to his prize, *Spearfish*. This Commander Cunningham was plainly no fool; he had planned this meeting well, and had made it plain from the outset that he would be prepared to use his torpedoes if necessary. But was he bluffing? Had he been given permission to do this?

Now Portrova lowered his megaphone and muttered, 'Well, Commander, let us see.' Then, almost as an afterthought, he again raised his megaphone and called, 'So, Commander, you would risk committing our countries to war over one damaged submarine, to whom we were trying to give assistance?' Already he was realising that again he had been negligent in not anticipating a situation such as this. Of course the British would have been looking for their missing submarine. But how did they find her? Was it luck or intelligence? And were there more of these British around?

'And a sunken destroyer – your destroyer, your ship, Captain Portrova.' Cunningham's reply came clearly through the snow, firm, decisive. 'I say again, do not make any attempt to move your ship!'

* * * * *

Puzzled at why *Otvashni* appeared to have stopped, Bradley had climbed from his cot and had been peering through the sick berth porthole when *Sturgeon* fired her red grenades. Although he didn't see either of the flares, their red glow reflected momentarily over the frosted glass of the port, and that was enough for him. He knew exactly what they were. He leaned over the cot and shook the still mound that was Jackson. 'Come on, Skipper, wake up. Something's going on up there. I don't know what but I've just seen a red grenade. At least, I'm fairly sure that's what it was.' He shook the mound that was Jackson again, even harder this time. 'Oh for Christ's sake, wake up, will you?' Then he realised that in the semi-darkness, Jackson's eyes were wide open and staring up him.

'Easy, Commander, take it easy. You got an injured man 'ere. You do know that, don't yuh?'

'Yes, of course. Sorry, Skipper, but I'm sure something's up. This may be the break we've been waiting for. Come on, man, get on your feet.'

Jackson threw off his blanket and sat up. 'Ee, Laddie, I bin awake on and off fer quite a while now, an' what's more, I was listening to your conversation with that Ruskie bastard. Thought it better to let 'im think I was still asleep. He really don't like me very much, does he!' Then he said, 'Christ, what I'd give fer me pipe an' a plug of baccy right now.'

'Never mind your bloody pipe,' Bradley hissed. 'He wants to see you shot, and if you don't bloody well pull your finger out that's just what's going to happen.'

'OK, OK, lead on, McDuff,' Jackson grunted. 'Yeah, I saw the red glow as well. Didn't realise what it was, though.'

'Well, as you've no doubt noticed, at the moment we're stopped, and something seems to be going on out there, though I don't know why or what.' Bradley pulled Jackson to his feet. Now, from outside in the passageway, he could hear the sound of many running footsteps, loud excited voices and heavily booted feet clambering up the steel ladder to the upper deck. He waited until this passed and it became quiet once more, while Jackson quietly limbered up in the semi-darkness.

'I'm pretty sure they were red grenades,' said Bradley. 'They came from aft and I believe they were fired from a submarine, one of ours, but not *Spearfish*! If I'm right then someone's up here to take us back. I told you they would, didn't I? They'll have seen *Spearfish*, and they've come to take her back. And now they've deliberately exposed themselves to the Russians. Christ, what a bloody risk they're taking!'

'Yeah, yeah, I know that, but what about us?'

Bradley sat down on Jackson's cot. 'I reckon this could be that one and only chance I was talking about earlier. So we've got to lend a hand in things. A spot of diversion and disruption will do, I think. But, first things first: we need to find out exactly what's happening. I need to take a quick look around. There's a guard posted outside our door, and he's armed. Go and stand behind the door and when I get him in here, you nobble him, but don't make too much noise over it.'

'Oh, sure, Commander,' replied Jackson. 'Might as well get shot fer a sheep as a friggin' lamb, eh?' But all the same, he hauled himself painfully across to stand behind the door.

Now Bradley started thinking aloud. 'If it was me in that boat, I would put her bows as close as possible under the Russian's stern – that way she'd be safe from the after guns – and I believe that's just what she's done.'

'So 'ow does he get *your* boat free then, Commander, considerin' she's likely got 'alf the bleedin' Russian navy aboard 'er at the moment?'

'I don't know the answer to that,' replied Bradley. 'Some sensible persuasive dialogue, perhaps?'

'Dialogue my arse,' scoffed Jackson. 'That black-muzzled Ruskie bastard's got us an' your friggin boat by the bollocks, you know that, an' he'll 'ang onto us both. Why the 'ell shouldn't he?'

'Well, I suppose he could be slightly concerned about taking a Mk 8 torpedo up his stern glands,' replied Bradley.

'They wouldn't dare,' snorted Jackson.

'Well, for our sake I hope you're right,' muttered Bradley. 'You may not have realised it, but I can tell you that here in this sick bay we're only a few yards from the quarterdeck ourselves!'

Now, from outside in the passageway came the sound of more hurrying footsteps and more garbled Russian talk. Both men listened anxiously until this had passed. 'Sounds like they're preparing for some sort of action,' muttered Jackson. 'Right then, Commander, tha's not short on guts, I'll give thee that much. I'm with you. What's the game plan?'

'We'll get our guard in here first, and put him out of action. Then I'll go outside and have a quick look around – see if I can make any sense of what's going on. Then I'll be back and we'll go from there! But first things first: let's sort out this bloody guard. We'll have to get him in here. You ready for this?'

'Ready aye ready, Cap'n, Sir.' Jackson gave a mock salute but now, as he stood behind the door, his voice was barely a whispered croak.

'Well, I just hope you are, for both our sakes,' muttered Bradley. 'Don't kill him though, not unless you have to.' Reaching into his pocket, he carefully withdrew the scalpel that he'd found in one of the sick bay drawers earlier. Carefully unwrapping it, he now balled it into his fist and then banged loudly on the sick berth door.

At first there was no response from the guard, who was seated in the flat outside the sick berth door. Having just watched the flurry of action as his comrades had rushed up from the deck below him heading to their battle stations, he had wondered what was going on. But he'd been given his orders and, in accordance with those orders, he would remain on guard outside this door until relieved. He knew better than to disobey orders, or even to question them, but still this banging from inside the sick berth door continued, and he could hear the muffled voice of the Englishman on the other side of the door. At last he reluctantly rose from his chair and, raising the single door clip, pushed the door open wide before stepping through into the gloom of the sick berth.

Bradley positioned himself about six feet back from the now-open door. The guard paused momentarily as he entered, his eyes becoming adjusted to the relative darkness. Then, seeing Bradley's shape in front of him, he stepped towards him, grunting and making jerking movements with his submachine-gun, urging Bradley to step back. But Bradley didn't step back; instead he took a deliberate step forward. The guard looked confused, alarmed. Then the door behind him slammed shut and Jackson grasped him, one forearm locked around his neck in a vice-like grip, his other arm around the guard's chest in an unbreakable bear hug. The guard dropped his weapon, eyes bulging, features already turning blue. Bradley picked up the submachine-gun and without any hesitation clubbed the guard hard on the side of his head with the butt. Jackson let go his grip and the guard dropped to the deck and lay motionless.

'Christ, Commander, remind me not to upset you in future,' muttered Jackson, his voice a mixture of surprise and respect.

Bradley was now kneeling beside the prone Russian, searching for a pulse. He looked up despairingly at Jackson. 'I did say not to kill him unless you had to!'

'Well, you're the one what 'it 'im, an' you didn't fuck about, did you, Commander! What a whack that was! If that young fella don't wake up with a very bad 'eadache then I don't know who will. An' just look at 'im, Commander. He's nobbut a lad.'

'Well, let's both hope he enjoys a nice long sleep. Anyway, if I'd left it much longer you'd have strangled him.' Bradley was still searching for a pulse in the Russian's neck. 'Ah, I've got something. He's not dead.' He stood up. 'Thank God for that!'

'Can't say I give a shit either way myself,' muttered Jackson. He raised a bandaged left arm. 'Look. Me arm's started bleeding again. All down to that bastard.'

Bradley climbed to his feet. 'Never mind that. Come on! Help me get him into my bunk. Get his coat off first.'

Together they removed the guard's topcoat, dragged him across the deck and flopped him into Bradley's bunk. Using the ropes that had previously bound Jackson, they tied the Russian's hands and feet and strapped him firmly to the bunk. Bradley rifled through some drawers and finally came up with a roll of medical tape. Then, packing a wad of rolled-up bandage between the Russian's slack jaws, he squeezed the jaws together and applied a treble strip of tape firmly over his mouth before pulling the blanket up to cover all but the guard's hair, which was, by happy coincidence, the same straw colour as his own.

The whole business of capturing the guard from his entrance into the sick berth to getting him into the bunk had taken less than four minutes, but Bradley was now completely exhausted. Then, together they sat on Jackson's cot, with Bradley frantically trying to catch his breath and gather his thoughts while Jackson continued to moan about his bleeding arms.

Standing again, Bradley pulled on the Russian guard's coat, which fitted him almost perfectly but stank of stale sweat and tobacco. Then, picking up the flat black sailor's cap, he adjusted it on his head, using the bulkhead mirror. Turning to the still-muttering Jackson he asked, 'How do I look, then?'

'Just like a bloody Ivan!' replied Jackson.

'Good.' Picking up the guard's gun, Bradley examined it closely. 'Looks like one of their older type guns to me. Still bloody lethal though. Must weigh getting on for ten pounds. Hang on, there's some marks on the butt.' He rubbed the side of the butt with his sleeve. 'PPSh 41, whatever that means.' He tapped the long curved magazine. 'I reckon she's fully loaded.'

'An' I reckon I'd feel a lot safer if you would put the bloody thing down. You don't know how to use it and nor do I!'

Bradley shot a sharp look towards Jackson, but laid the weapon carefully on the bunk. 'Now listen carefully: we're only going to get one chance at this, so we'd better get it right first time. The first thing we've got to do is to get up there on deck and find out exactly what's going on. I think it would be better if I had a quick look on my own to start with. You get back into your bunk, cover up well, and wait for me.' He motioned towards the gun. 'Here, hide this under your blanket but try not to shoot yourself. If anyone comes in, be asleep! I won't be long.'

'Suits me.' Jackson lay back in his bunk, tucked the machine gun into his side, and pulled the blanket up to his neck. Then, looking up at Bradley, he added, 'Watch yerself, Laddie. I'm beginning to like you.'

Bradley gave Jackson a very exaggerated wink, then turned and made for the door. Carefully easing the door open, he looked up and down the now deserted and dimly lit sick berth flat. Stepping carefully over the coaming, he pulled the door shut behind him, securing it by its single clip. Then he made his way forward towards another watertight door, which he assumed would take him onto the destroyer's upper deck. Already he was sweating profusely. To his left was a large open hatch in the deck, from which a ladder led down at forty-five degrees to the flat below. He paused to peer briefly downward into this brilliantly lit flat. From somewhere down there he could hear a radio playing loudly. He also hear the hum of running machinery. Ah well, he thought, might as well have a quick look down there first. Slowly, step by step, he eased himself down the steel ladder onto the deck of the flat. Standing stock still, he looked about him, hardly daring to breathe.

Behind him was a partially open steel door from which white light flooded into the flat. This was where the music was coming from. Must be one of their messes, he thought. Hope there's no one still in there. Directly in front of him was another partially open door, through which came the noise of running machinery. He moved forward carefully and, peering through the gap in the doorway, he realised that he was looking into some sort of machinery space combined with an electrical switchboard. The compartment was deserted. He stepped through the doorway and scanned the neat rows of different sized but equally well-polished brass and copper knife switches in front of him. Each one was topped by a small, coloured indicator lamp. Moving towards the end of the compartment, he could see a gyrocompass. It was very much like the compass aboard *Spearfish* – a large black bowl with a clear plastic top, through which he could see the quivering azimuth ring held level in its gimballed supports. 'Well well,' he muttered to himself. 'Looks like the compass room and main electrical switchboard. I'll bear this place in mind.'

He turned and made his way slowly, carefully, back up the ladder. Reaching the top, he looked at his watch. It was just five minutes since he had left the sick berth. Wondering fleetingly what Jackson was doing right now, he headed forward towards the door to the upper deck. Although this door was fitted with six securing clips, only one was keeping it shut. This door opened outwards. Carefully lifting the clip, he eased the door open.

He had told himself before he left the sick berth that he was prepared for just about any eventuality, but even as he stepped onto *Otvashni*'s upper deck, he realised that he wasn't. Even with the Russian guard's heavy coat the sudden intense cold of that late arctic afternoon robbed him of his breath. He gagged, fighting to breathe, while instinctively covering his mouth with his hand to muffle any noise. It was snowing heavily, but then he knew that it would be, and now, as he stepped over the coaming of the watertight door, the cold lancing up through his legs rudely reminded him that he was still in his stockinged feet; he had no shoes on. Wincing against what was now very real pain in his feet, he looked around. He had memorised *Otvashni*'s upper deck layout well from his volume of "Jane's". God knows, he'd had enough time to do this since that first fateful meeting. Now, as he emerged from the deckhouse containing the sick berth, he was standing aft of *Otvashni*'s after set of triple torpedo tubes, while aft of the deckhouse behind him was *Otvashni*'s stern 5.1 inch twin gun mounting. The upper deck was well lit but this was not the usual upper deck lighting of a destroyer at sea – this light was glaring, harsh. It came from *Otvashni*'s bridge-mounted port and starboard searchlights. He ducked low into the shadow provided by the torpedo tubes, but this light was not directed towards him or towards the upper deck – it was directed towards an area directly astern of *Otvashni*.

Nudging his way aft around the starboard side of the sick berth flat, he reached the shelter of the after gun, where he waited, watched and listened. He could hear movement inside the turret, and realised that *Otvashni*'s crew must be closed up at action stations. Then, with a loud whine, both gun barrels suddenly swung upward as one to an angle of some forty-five degrees, then depressed to their lowest point, just about parallel with the quarterdeck. Startled by the noise and sudden movement of the gun, Bradley dropped flat and began to crawl around the starboard side of the turret, using all the shadow he could find.

Now he was looking directly at four men standing at the destroyer's stern rail, bathed in the brilliance of the searchlights behind them. Three were holding weapons, but there was no mistaking the bear-like figure that held the megaphone. 'Aha, Kapitan Alexci Portrova,' Bradley grunted to himself, 'I could finish you now, but that wouldn't solve our problem and, in any case, I didn't bring that bloody gun. Portrova, you are a very lucky man!'

★ ★ ★ ★ ★

Strong now stood beside Murray on *Spearfish*'s bridge. Behind them stood Ravoski. Murray said, 'Bloody hell, it's *Sturgeon*, Sir!'

Strong could hardly believe his eyes. The signal lantern aboard the boat, now not more than ten yards off their port beam, again started to flash. 'Quick, Ross, give me the Aldis.' Now Strong started to answer *Sturgeon*'s questions.

Ravoski waited for a full three minutes before reaching out and taking the signal lantern from Strong's hands. Then placing a reassuring hand on Strong's shoulder, he said, 'Come, my friend. Together we will now go below. I too have been waiting for this submarine. She is British, *da*? Your comrads! They want you back, eh? Well, we shall see.'

On *Sturgeon*'s bridge the signalman had received the message from Strong, which had then been continued by Murray. Turning to Cunningham, he said, 'Seems like she's got ten guards and two Russian officers aboard her, Sir, an' it looks like she's being taken somewhere she don't really want to go. All her masts are out of action except for her attack periscope, and she's got no propulsion on her starboard side. She's able to dive, but not to more than 250 feet. Her main vents have been locked off and the Russians have the keys. Her CO is a prisoner aboard the destroyer, and she's being towed to… Sorry, Sir, that's all I've got. She broke off. Nothing else.'

'Well, at least that answers a whole lot of questions,' replied Cunningham. 'Well done, Bunts. Keep a good eye on her; we may get more from her yet. I'll look after the destroyer.'

★ ★ ★ ★ ★

Aboard *Spearfish*, Ravoski gently nudged Strong towards the bridge ladder. 'Come, Oliver, my friend. The situation has changed, so we too must change. We must plan what to do. Your watch officer will look after things up here.' Strong knew that Ravoski wasn't inviting him to go below, he was ordering him!

Together they made their way down to the control room – Strong first, Ravoski following. On their arrival in the control room Strong noted that the young officer Gorski was manning the attack periscope, training it alternately between *Spearfish*'s port beam and her bow. He would also be watching both *Sturgeon* and the stern of *Otvashni*. Gorski's eye did not move from the periscope eyepiece, and Strong wondered fleetingly why he had not come to the bridge with Ravoski. Had Ravoski ordered him not to? Ravoski again nudged him, his voice barely more than a whisper. 'Come, Oliver, we must talk. We will use your kapitan's cabin.'

Strong entered the cabin first, and turned to face Ravoski. 'You say that we must make plans, Viktor. What exactly do you mean by that?' He was once more searching for that sparkle in Ravoski's eyes, desperately looking for some clue as to what this Russian was really thinking. But still there was no sparkle in those eyes, no clues.

Ravoski simply said, 'We must wait now, Oliver. We must see how things develop between my kapitan in *Otvashni* and your friends on this other submarine, and then perhaps we too will make a plan, *da*?'

Strong could no longer control his exasperation. Knowing that he really had nothing to lose, he threw caution to the wind. 'Tell me, Viktor,' his voice was a hoarse whisper, 'I need to know one way or the other. Are you with us or are you against us? Because I just don't bloody well know! And at the moment I just can't trust you.' Ravoski showed no reaction to Strong's outburst, simply studying the lieutenant's agitated features with what appeared to be calm indifference. Then suddenly, that long-absent smile once more lit his bearded face, and the twinkle returned to his eyes. 'I mean you no harm, my friend. You must trust me. But we will wait.' As if to illustrate his point he reached up and removed the ushanka from his head and, throwing it down on the desk beside him, he slumped into Bradley's chair.

Strong was again struck with this man's faultless English. It was hard to believe that he was having a conversation with a Russian. 'But where does this leave me? Or, perhaps more to the point, *Spearfish*? You'd better have a bloody good story, because if you haven't, then one way or another someone's going to get a very bloody nose!'

Ravoski's face remained impassive. 'May I say to you, Lietenent Strong, a bloody nose is the least of our worries at this time, be it yours or mine.'

★ ★ ★ ★ ★

The snow had again stopped, but standing on *Otvashni*'s quarterdeck Portrova hadn't even noticed this and was becoming more frustrated by the minute. To him it now seemed that the commander of this new submarine had the advantage over him and he cursed himself viciously for again allowing himself to be taken by such complete surprise, leaving him unable to take any sort of evasive action, and with his main armament completely useless at this short range. Even though something was telling him that this man Cunningham was bluffing about using his torpedoes, could he afford to call that bluff? After all, he had pushed this whole situation to breaking point – it was all his doing. No, he would wait. He would ride out this frustration. At this time matters were merely at an impasse. Things could easily change, and when they did...

'Captain Portrova, I am waiting for your answer!' Cunningham's strident tones over his megaphone snapped Portrova sharply out of his thoughts. He lifted his megaphone in reply.

'Is my ship not still stopped, Commander?'

'But you moved your gun barrels. I warned you not to. I will give you fifteen minutes to slip the tow wire on *Spearfish*, Captain Portrova. You will also lower one of your boats and collect your men from *Spearfish*. Failure to comply with these instructions within the next fifteen minutes will give me no alternative but to take offensive action against your ship.' Cunningham spoke slowly, clearly, emphatically.

Portrova again raised his megaphone. 'Armed aggression, Commander? Come, we both know there is a line which we would both hesitate to cross!'

'You have already crossed that line, Portrova.' Cunningham's reply was immediate and unfaltering. 'But be that as it may, I, too, will not hesitate to cross that line if you force my hand. You may be assured of that!' Then turning quickly to Morton, he hissed, 'We're getting nowhere fast, Hugh.

Pass the word: get the divers in the water and those bloody charges under the Russian's screws, now.'

Portrova grunted, but made no attempt to reply to Cunningham's warning. Instead he turned to one of the men at his side. 'Call the bridge: send Kapitan Lieutenant Carlov down here, but do not make any attempt to move our ship or our guns unless I order it directly.'

Still lying prone on the starboard side of the after turret, Bradley breathed a slow sigh of satisfaction. So James Cunningham, his old CO, had come to the rescue. That bloody old warhorse had come all the way up here to dig him out of the dirt. The sense of satisfaction he had felt now changed to a mixture of humiliation and shame. Where would all this end? 'Ah well,' he breathed, 'at least things are looking a bit more even at the moment. Maybe we can give you a bit of a hand, James.' Looking at his watch, he saw that it had been over twenty minutes since he'd left the sanctuary of the sick berth. Still crawling, he began to make his way back.

Jackson still lay on his bunk, the thick woollen blanket pulled well up to his neck. To him, the past twenty minutes had seemed more like twenty hours and now his mind was buzzing. Where's the young bugger got to? Let's hope he's not out there playing some sort of heroics. Maybe I should never have let the little sod go out there on his own; he's most likely cocked everything up by now. The Russian guard in Bradley's bunk groaned loudly. 'An' you can keep quiet as well,' he muttered, 'unless tha wants another smack.' Then at last came the sound that he had been waiting for: a muffled bang on the steel door. Jackson breathed a sigh of silent relief. 'Come in, Commander, and for Christ's sake be quick about it.' The door opened and Bradley stepped inside.

'Tha took tha's bloody time, didn't thee?' But the relief was plain in Jackson's voice.

'Sorry, old chum.' Bradley closed the door quietly behind him. 'But there's a lot going on out there.' He moved across to where the Russian guard lay and again felt for a pulse. 'Good! At least this one's still with us. Don't want to kill more than we have to. Not good for international relations!'

'Never mind that bastard,' retorted Jackson. 'What's 'appening out there? I bin shittin' clump blocks in 'ere, fer Christ's sakes.'

321

'Yes, I can imagine you have.' Bradley sat down on the edge of Jackson's bunk. 'And, as I've already said, I'm sorry.' He almost felt tempted to pat Jackson's furrowed brow, suddenly realising that he was becoming very attached to this coarse but refreshingly honest Yorkshire trawler captain, whose only sin was to have been in the wrong place at the wrong time. Then he told Jackson everything that he'd seen and heard during the past twenty minutes, right down to the last detail.

Jackson listened intently, then looked up at the clock on the bulkhead. 'Aye well, it figures. Sounds like we've got some sort of stand-off, but from what you say this won't go on for ever. They're testing each other – your people and them bastards. I know what their game is – I've read the friggin papers same as you 'ave – but believe me, Laddie, I wouldn't trust these Russians as far as I could throw 'em. Any road, you know that I'm with you all the way. Just tell me what to do.'

Bradley said, 'Well, first of all, let's try and sort out this bloody machine gun; it's beginning to look like we may need it.'

Jackson groped under his blanket and passed the weapon to Cunningham, who again examined it. He pushed in a latch that appeared to hold the magazine and the magazine dropped into his hand. It was fully loaded. 'Looks to be about seven-millimetre rounds. Don't know how many but enough to do some damage anyway.' He snapped the magazine back in place and pulled back on another small catch. 'And this must be the safety. It's cocked and ready to fire now.' He carefully slid the safety catch back on and said, 'Well, that all looks pretty straightforward. Now the plan is to cause some sort of diversion, upset the Russians in any way that we can and—'

The door of the sick berth now swung open and in stepped Yuri. Now wearing a heavy black topcoat over his whites, together with a seaman's hat which made him look even more incongruous; he too was obviously at action stations.

Jackson was still lying in his bunk, with Bradley sat beside him. Both were taken completely by surprise. The big Russian, suspecting nothing, simply raised a hand to acknowledge the two men. Then, on seeing Bradley in a Russian coat and with a weapon in his hands, a look of dismay slowly spread across his flat features.

Bradley moved very quickly. 'Sorry, Yuri.' He bounded across the deck and flailing the weapon like a club, brought the butt down hard on the Russian's skull. With a low moan, Yuri fell to the deck and lay still.

Jackson pulled back his blanket and climbed painfully from his bunk. 'Ee, Lad, tha's getting' good at smackin' Ivans.'

'Never mind that,' snapped Bradley. 'Here, help me take his coat off and get him into your bunk.' Together they manhandled the bulky frame of Yuri into the bunk, and secured him in the same way as they had the other sleeping Russian. Bradley indicated towards Yuri's coat. 'Here, you'd better put that on, and you'd better try his boots as well. He's about your size. Then follow me.'

★　★　★　★　★

Donovan and Watson had lowered themselves on to the port ballast tank at the after end of *Sturgeon*'s bridge. Already they winced as the bitter cold water washed over their legs. Now, with masks and goggles in place, they were ready to go. They looked at each other in the darkness and, for the final time, tested the six yards of rope that Gus Ramsay had provided to join them – Watson's left arm to Donovan's right. Then the second cox'n leaned over to tap Watson on the shoulder, and as one, Donovan and Watson slid down into the freezing black waters of the Barents.

★　★　★　★　★

At the same time as the two divers from *Sturgeon* entered the water, Bradley and Jackson stepped cautiously through the door into the deserted flat outside the sick berth. With Bradley now clutching the submachine-gun, they made their way forward towards the outer door. Bradley signalled to Jackson, 'Hold up a minute, Skipper. I think perhaps I'll just start the ball rolling.' Dropping quickly down the ladder at his side, he stepped into the switchboard room. Ignoring the strident alarm bell, he toppled the compass by smashing the butt of his gun into its control panel. 'That's you fixed,' he muttered. 'Let's hope that you're the only decent compass they've got.' Turning back to the switchboard, he quickly began to pull out the copper knife switches one by one, starting with the biggest switches first and trying to ignore the blue and yellow sparks that now arced across the switchboard with each pull. Then he heard machinery stopping. The lights went out and the gyro alarm went silent. Now he was in utter darkness, as indeed was the whole of *Otvashni*. Feeling his way back up the ladder, he rejoined the waiting Jackson and together they stepped out on to the upper deck.

★　★　★　★　★

Kapitan Lieutenant Carlov arrived on *Otvashni*'s quarterdeck to stand next to Portrova just as all her lights went out – first the two searchlights and then the whole of her upper deck lighting. Now *Otvashni*'s stern, upper deck and her upper works were in complete darkness. Not for the first time that day, Portrova was taken by complete surprise.

★　★　★　★　★

On the bridge of *Sturgeon*, Cunningham too was taken by surprise. This was something he hadn't expected. 'What the hell's she playing at?' He muttered. 'Come on, signalman, shine your lantern on her arse; I need to see what's happening.' He raised his megaphone again, directing it towards the shadowy figures on the Russian's stern. 'Ahoy, the Russian. Your fifteen minutes are up. This is no time for games. Have you lowered your boat as requested?'

In the darkness Portrova gripped the stern rail in defiance. 'No boat will be lowered, Englishman, until I give the order!'

From the port side of *Otvashni*'s after gun turret, Bradley released the safety catch on his weapon, pointing the barrel skyward, and fired five rounds into the night. Now he stepped forward onto the quarterdeck.

'Do what the man says, Captain Portrova. Give the order for a boat to be lowered or, so help me, I'll cut you in two and, believe me, I'll enjoy doing it!' He pointed his gun at the two guards standing beside Portrova. 'You two, drop your guns, now!' Although the two guards had no idea of what Bradley had said, they obeyed him instantly.

Stunned, both Portrova and Carlov faced Bradley. Then, recovering some degree of composure, Portrova hissed, 'So, Commander Bradley, is it now you who gives the orders aboard my ship?' His voice was defiant, but he was obviously still in complete shock.

'You're damn right it is, yuh Russian prick!' Jackson stepped forward and, gathering up the seamen's guns he threw one over the stern and cocked the other. 'Just gimme the nod an' I'll be obliged to do fer the pair of yuh. It'll be my pleasure, make no mistake about—'

Then Carlov made his move. In the darkness he had slipped the button off the holster at his waist, and as he drew his pistol only the night hid his snarl of contempt. 'It is you who will drop your weapons, British pigs, or you will surely die.'

But Jackson did not drop his newly acquired weapon. Not trusting his expertise with it he instead threw it directly at Carlov's head before launching himself at the tall Russian officer. Taken completely by surprise, Carlov had barely cleared his pistol from its holster before Jackson had smothered him in a vice-like bear hug. 'So you want to play rough, eh. Well, that's fine by me.' Jackson tightened his grip. 'I'll break yer friggin' back, yuh Ruskie bastard.'

Now Carlov was gasping for breath, but Jackson was relentless, unstoppable. 'Sink my *Imogen*, would yuh? Kill my boys? Well 'ere's one for you then, yuh Russian bastard. Go to hell!' He gave a final squeeze and broke Carlov's back.

Bradley had kept his gun on Portrova. 'You all right, Captain Jackson?'

Jackson casually flipped the dead Russian officer over the stern rail. 'An' why wouldn't I be, Commander? That bastard didn't do me arms much good though! They're burnin' like hell again.'

During the last few minutes the only light on *Otvashni*'s quarterdeck had been provided by *Sturgeon*'s and *Spearfish*'s signal lamps, and Cunningham had witnessed this drama as it had unfolded. Now Bradley called out towards *Sturgeon*'s bridge through cupped hands. 'This is Nigel Bradley, CO of *Spearfish*. Is that you, James?'

Cunningham, ever cautious, bawled his reply through his megaphone, 'Can't see you very well! What's your wife's name?'

'Sue.' Perplexed, Bradley replied instantly. 'Christ, don't you start buggering me about, James; I've had just about enough of this lately.'

Ignoring this, Cunningham again bawled, 'I think we've all had enough of this lately. Tell me, Nigel Bradley, who got very wet at your paying-off party in *Thunderer*?'

'The sodding navigator did! He fell off the plank on his way inboard. I got wet too because I was pissed enough to go in and pull the silly bugger out!'

'What was his name?'

Bradley was now becoming irritated. 'Bill Jessup.'

'AKA?' Cunningham was taking no chances.

'Oh, for heaven's sake! Silly Billy Jessup!'

'Nice to see you again, Nigel; we'd just about given up on you.'

Bradley breathed a sigh of relief and turned to Portrova, 'Get a boat into the water now! Give the order, Captain Portrova.'

Portrova shrugged. Turning to the seaman standing at his side with the telephone, he said, 'Tell the watch officer to lower a boat.' He still couldn't believe what was happening: he had just watched his first officer die in front of his eyes, and now this Britisher was giving him orders. How could things have changed so quickly?

Now the telephone calls started to come. The first was a frantic call from his watch officer on the bridge. 'Kapitan, we have no power, our guns will not train, and we have no compass. What are your orders?'

Portrova snatched the telephone. 'Wait, I will—'

He never finished the sentence, and he certainly never heard the explosions that threw him across *Otvashni*'s quarterdeck.

Bradley and Jackson were caught equally by surprise, though Bradley was aware of at least four separate explosions under him before they were all sprawled, semi-conscious, across the quarterdeck – Bradley, Jackson, the two seamen and Portrova.

Portrova was the first to regain his feet, immediately staggering forward into the darkness towards his bridge, while Bradley rose unsteadily to his knees and groped for his gun. 'What the bloody hell was that? Are you OK, Skipper?'

'Aye, Laddie, I'm still with you,' croaked Jackson, now also on his feet. 'What now, Commander?'

'My guess is that this ship has just lost its propulsion,' Bradley muttered, 'but we've still got one or two jobs to do yet.' Both of the Russian seamen had now risen to their knees and Bradley calmly, methodically, clubbed them over the head with the butt of his weapon.

Jackson winced. 'Jesus, Commander, like I said before, you don't fuck about, do you! What now?'

'We need to put all their sensors out of action before they can restore power, particularly their radio gear, otherwise we'll have the whole of the bloody Northern Fleet down on us before we know it.'

Together Bradley and Jackson made their way forward towards the starboard side ladder at the break of the fo'c'sle. *Otvashni*'s upper deck was still in pitch blackness and completely deserted. She was at battle stations, but there were no active signs of her crew. Bradley knew that by now they would be completely confused and looking for some sort of leadership. This was the order of things in the Russian navy. Without leadership the lower ranks would do nothing. Still he could hear the constant hoot of sound-powered telephones, and he smiled to himself. Oh, yes, they were confused all right. Now, behind them on the port side of the upper deck, they could hear the noises of Russian seamen preparing to lower a motor boat. They continued to stumble for'd in the darkness until they at last reached the starboard side ladder at the break of the fo'c'sle and almost fell over the inert body of Portrova.

Bradley leaned over Portrova, feeling for a pulse. 'Is 'e dead?' asked Jackson.

'No, he's not dead. Looks more like he's collapsed. Heart attack, maybe? Or else he's taken a bad fall and knocked himself out. Can't tell.'

'More's the pity,' muttered Jackson.

'No, we need this man alive,' Bradley retorted in a loud whisper. 'He may well be our ticket out of here, and he'll be no bloody use to us if he's dead!'

Now Portrova groaned. Opening his eyes, he looked up into the darkness at Bradley's face. His voice was weak, barely a whisper. 'So, Commander Bradley, you and your friends have taken my ship, *da*?'

'No, Captain Portrova,' Bradley spat, 'not yet we haven't, and in any case I never wanted your bloody ship in the first place. All I wanted was my own ship back – you know that! Now get on your feet. I've not finished with you yet.'

Together Jackson and Bradley hauled Portrova to his feet, holding him upright between them.

'Right then, Captain,' growled Bradley, 'first things first – I need to look at your wireless office.'

Portrova staggered, still barely able to stand. 'I will show you nothing!'

Now Jackson grabbed Portrova by his hair. Jerking the Russian's head up, he hissed, 'You'll do as the man says, Laddie, or I'll do fer you right now!'

Together they half pushed, half dragged Portrova up the ladder onto the fo'c'sle, and pushed him through the watertight door into a passageway, which was now dimly lit by two emergency lanterns. 'Wireless office – now!' snapped Bradley.

Portrova looked fleetingly towards a grey steel door, and that short glance was enough for Bradley. 'You ready for this, Skipper?' Without waiting for a reply from Jackson he swung the door open and pushed Portrova inside. Portrova stumbled and fell flat on his face in front of the two startled wireless operators. Bradley knelt beside him and pressed the muzzle of his gun hard into the Russian captain's neck. Looking up at Jackson, he said, 'I think their radio equipment needs some slight adjustment, Captain Jackson.'

Jackson needed no second bidding. With the butt of his gun, he proceeded to wreck all three transmitters, together with all other equipment that looked in any way technical. Then, grinning malevolently, he turned to the two cowering operators and, again raising his gun butt, he floored the first one with a single blow to the head. It took two blows to down the second man.

Jackson looked down on the unconscious men, one of them very young with a mop of blond hair now patched with blood. 'Jesus, this one's nobbut a boy either!'

Bradley again dragged Portrova to his feet. 'Well now, Captain Portrova, your ship is in a bit of a state, don't you think? No leadership. No radio. No lighting. No compass and, to top it all, I think, no propulsion and maybe no steerage. Now, how do you like playing with the big boys? Perhaps you may care to remember that your ship is now in much the same state as you left mine just a few days back? There is a saying in my country: "What goes around, comes around". I don't suppose you've heard that one, though.'

Bradley knew that he was gloating, and he was enjoying it. 'Well, come along, let's have a look in your sonar and radar offices; they might benefit from our attention as well, don't you think?' Some ten minutes later, having now also totally wrecked *Otvashni*'s sonar and radar equipment, Bradley and Jackson, still holding up Portrova, were back on the upper deck. 'Captain Portrova, you look as though you could do with some fresh air. Shall we go and find a boat?' Bradley jammed his gun hard into Portrova's back and nudged him forward.

CHAPTER SIXTEEN

After entering the water Watson and Donovan kicked down to twenty feet before turning forward and making their way along the port side of *Sturgeon*'s keel, towards the stern of *Otvashni*. The bitter cold of the water penetrated their wet suits within seconds. At first, the surface water above them was lit with the glow from *Otvashni*'s twin searchlights, but as they neared her stern this light was gone, and they were in total darkness. With Ramsay's rope linking them together, and now using their torches, they kicked strongly towards their target, both trying to ignore the intense cold. Already Donovan was breathing heavily on his air bottles. He knew that Watson would be doing the same.

Then they were under the Russian destroyer. Clearing her stationary propellers, they headed forward towards her shafts, immediately locating the "A" brackets which supported each shaft, and began to secure their packs of explosive – one to each leg of each "A" bracket, and then another pack to each side of the rudder. Donovan worked on the starboard side while Watson worked on the port.

Finishing first, Donovan flashed his torch beam through the murky water in the direction of Watson and got an answering flash. Watson had finished. Donovan gave a further double flash, which again Watson returned. These were previously agreed signals. Together they pressed the buttons to start the timers, and then kicked strongly backward, away from the destroyer's stern. Donovan checked his watch and estimated they had less than four minutes to clear the water, and that was only if Gus Ramsay had got the timers right.

Swimming hard, Donovan sensed that the rope still attached to his right arm had become suddenly tight. Turning in the water, he again shone his torch towards where Watson should be, and pulled hard on the rope. Now Watson was beside him, but no longer swimming. He was motionless, inert in the water, and slowly sinking. Donovan could feel himself being dragged downward with Watson's weight. Again he checked his watch: less than three minutes maximum. He knew that it was almost certainly the cold that had beaten his partner. He also knew that this cold was now telling on him. He turned onto his back and, reaching out, closed his left arm around Watson's neck while kicking towards the surface, knowing that neither of them would survive if they were still in the water when the charges under *Otvashni*'s stern detonated.

The two divers broke surface between *Spearfish* and *Sturgeon*, just off *Sturgeon*'s lowered starboard fore plane. *Sturgeon*'s second cox'n Petty Officer Mitchell and two others were waiting for them, eagerly searching the dark rolling surface for the first sign of their return. Donovan was completely drained – there was no strength within him. Now, within some twenty feet of *Sturgeon*'s bow, miraculously, he grabbed the first line thrown and together the three men on her for'd casing hauled both him and Watson clear of the water.

Now flopped on *Sturgeon*'s forward casing, Donovan looked up at the faces above him. Feebly nudging the inert Watson, he gasped, 'Get 'im below, will yuh? Get 'im warm, 'cos 'e'll bloody well croak if you don't.' Then he too lost consciousness, not even hearing the charges now exploding under *Otvashni*'s stern.

★ ★ ★ ★ ★

Murray and the signalman had remained on *Spearfish*'s bridge when Ravoski had ushered Strong below, and for the past fifteen minutes had watched and listened, fascinated at the drama unfolding between *Sturgeon* and *Otvashni*, seeing all the lights on the destroyer suddenly go out and put it into complete darkness. Beside him the signalman directed his signal lantern onto *Otvashni's* darkened stern, boosting the light coming from *Sturgeon's* lantern. Murray had heard the rattle of gunfire and had seen some sort of brief tussle between two men on *Otvashni's* quarterdeck, after which he thought he saw a man falling over the stern rail. The signalman had then directed the beam of his lantern into the sea around *Otvashni's* stern but there was no sign of anyone in the water. Murray was becoming increasingly angry and confused. What the hell were Strong and Ravoski doing below? They should be up here now with him!

Now there was a shout on his starboard port bow, and the signalman's lantern beam picked out two men in the water. Murray studied them. Could they be divers? Some two minutes later these two swimmers were being hauled aboard *Sturgeon's* starboard fore plane. Watching this, Murray was puzzled. 'What the hell's going on out there, Bunts?'

'Search me, Sir,' replied the signalman, 'but whatever it is I think that—' He never got to finish his sentence. The explosion under *Otvashni* must have lifted her stern at least three feet out of the water.

'Jesus Christ! That's it then!' Murray leaned towards the voice pipe. 'Bridge – Helm. Get the first lieutenant up here at the rush!'

★   ★   ★   ★   ★

On *Sturgeon's* bridge Cunningham, too, was taken aback at the ferocity of the explosions under the Russian's stern. He had certainly not expected a result quite as spectacular as this.

'Bloody hell, TI,' he muttered to himself. 'I only asked you to disable her propulsion and steering gear.' He watched anxiously as *Otvashni's* stern now fell heavily back into the water. She appeared to settle on an even keel and with no immediate signs of serious damage. Breathing a sigh of relief, he continued to watch her carefully for a full three minutes. No, she was not about to sink.

★   ★   ★   ★   ★

Still below in Bradley's cabin, Strong seated himself on the chair by Bradley's desk and waved a hand towards his captain's bunk. 'Make yourself comfortable, Viktor. Use the bunk.' Already he was begrudging this time away from *Spearfish*'s bridge. He needed to be there, to know what was happening, but he consoled himself with the knowledge that Ross Murray was up there and would call him immediately there was any change in the situation.

It was cold in the cabin, and though they had removed their hats, both men kept their coats on. Then from his seat on the bunk, Ravoski delved a hand into the side pocket of his leather coat. 'Would you mind if I smoked, Oliver? I know that you do not smoke yourself.'

'Go ahead,' replied Strong. Then he added, 'I didn't realise you smoked.'

'Just now and again – a little self-indulgence, perhaps. That and your English chocolate. I must confess that I have a great liking for your chocolate.' His hand now emerged from the pocket, holding a packet of cigarettes, and Strong was surprised to see that they were Players Navy Cut. Ravoski now patted his other pocket, obviously searching for a lighter.

Strong pulled open the drawer of Bradley's desk. 'Might have something in here,' he said. Now fumbling around in the drawer he drew a sharp intake of breath as he felt his fingertips brushing against the hard butt of Bradley's Parabellum. Then he located a box of matches, which he threw across to Ravoski.

Ravoski lit his cigarette. Strong's mind was in turmoil. He almost wished that he hadn't found that gun. Was the bloody thing loaded? Could he use it on Viktor? Would he need to? And if he did, just what would he gain? No, he would wait and see how things developed. There was time yet, and the pistol would be his fallback, his plan B, even though as yet he had no plan A!

Ravoski blew a large cloud of smoke into the bunk and coughed. Smiling apologetically, he cleared his throat and said, 'Believe me, Oliver, these are my only vices and even these are very occasional.'

Strong was both puzzled and irritated. Sod his vices! Where was all this small talk leading? Already he was running out of patience, knowing that he should be up on his bridge and not sitting here listening to the ramblings of this aging Russian. His reply was sharp, plainly showing impatience. 'Well,

I suppose we're all entitled to a few vices, as long as they don't cause harm to anyone else.' Meanwhile his mind was saying, 'As far as I'm concerned you can either set yourself on fire with your bloody fags or give yourself a heart attack through eating too much chocolate; maybe that would do us all a favour!' But now his voice again said, 'I see you're smoking British.'

Ravoski flicked non-existent ash towards the deck. 'We all have our personal preferences, do we not? This brand of cigarettes, or as you British call them, "fags", have always been a favourite of mine.' He settled back on the bunk and again drew deeply on his cigarette before continuing. 'Oliver, my friend, lately I have put you through many trials, but I think you are a good man and so now I will be honest with you – not only because I like you as a man, but also because I may need to use you if the occasion arises. For this, I make no apologies.'

Strong was now listening carefully, watching the Russian's eyes as he spoke. For some inexplicable reason he still felt that he could trust this man. 'All right, Viktor, tell me about it.'

Ravoski took another deep draw on his cigarette and again coughed loudly. Then he said, 'Three years ago, and very much against my will at that time, I was sent to Britain as a spy.' He paused, watching Strong's face closely. 'Yes, Oliver, I work for the KGB, and still do. I cannot change this fact. Even though initially I had no choice in this matter, I am one of their many agents. Because of my technical background and my ability to speak fluent English, I was placed in your country ostensibly as a civilian naval design engineer and given a position in your Cammel Lairds ship building yard at Birkenhead. I had all the qualifications, but there were obviously – how is it you say? – strings pulled to arrange this placement. In the event I spent many hours in the planning and initial construction of this very vessel and that is why, my friend, I know *Spearfish* from stem to stern. But this does not change the fact that I was, and, alas, still am, a spy!'

Ravoski paused and looked hard into Strong's eyes, almost as if searching for some sign of understanding before continuing, 'But I must confess that I was not a good spy. My heart was not in what I was being asked to do by my masters in the Kremlin. I was given the telephone number of my controller, who had been placed in Liverpool, and my orders were to report to this man twice weekly…' Ravoski leaned over, stubbed out his cigarette on the heel of his boot, and then looked around for somewhere to place the butt. Strong used his boot to nudge Bradley's empty wastepaper bin towards the Russian, who continued, '…though I never met him in person.'

Ravoski paused for at least half a minute, as though contemplating what to say next. Then again he looked Strong directly in the eye. 'I had not been in your country for long, Oliver, when I began to realise how different and how much better things were in England from the life that I had known in Russia. Naturally I made these comparisons: the lifestyle, the people, the food, the housing and, possibly the most important of all, the freedom – oh yes, the freedom. I began to make friends, many friends, good friends. I enjoyed both my work and my new lifestyle.' He smiled fleetingly. 'And I became very fond of your Guinness and your fish and chips.' Again he paused, looking down at his boots before continuing in a lower tone. 'If it were possible I would very much like to return to that life.' He paused again, now looking up directly into Strong's eyes. Then, raising both hands in a clear gesture of dismissal, he said, 'But I digress, my friend. I only tell you of these things in order that you may understand the reasons for any subsequent action that I may have to take.'

'No, no, please carry on,' Strong blurted, watching the Russian even more intently.

Ravoski nodded, a weariness now clouding his eyes. 'So, Oliver, your friends are now here to release you, and hopefully bring this debacle to an end. This is good for you, but of course they may yet fail. Please listen carefully, Oliver. I mean you and your countrymen no harm. What I tell you now is between ourselves, *da*? But I feel that I must – how is it you say in your navy? – clear my yardarm. If your friends in this new submarine succeed in releasing you then I, too, will be your friend. But if they fail, and Kapitan Portrova finally succeeds in taking you to my mother country, then I must be your enemy. Is that clear? At this time I must have nothing to lose. If your vessel does not escape, then, unlike your captain, you and your crew will not be detained for very long – of this I am sure. But in that event all that I have said to you, my friend, counts for nothing. You understand me, *da*? Yes, I would like to have sanctuary in your country, Oliver. I will be seeking diplomatic immunity, and this – well, shall we call it an unfortunate incident? – might give me the opportunity to do so. But I must be on the winning side, you understand? I do not wish to risk the wrath of my countrymen at this time.'

Strong was slowly realising that he was not surprised by what Ravoski was saying. He had known all along that there was something very different about this man. He too now coughed, hoping that it didn't sound like a nervous cough. 'Well, I suppose that's fair enough. You've said your piece. At least we both now know where we stand. Even though my future and that of *Spearfish*'s appear to be in the lap of the gods at the moment, it looks like you've got yourself into a pretty bombproof situation.' Again he pushed a hand inside Bradley's desk drawer, knowing that his captain was partial to chocolate. And yes, his fingers closed over something that he knew was chocolate. He also knew that there were still about two dozen bars in the steward's refrigerator. They were Bradley's substitute for cigarettes. Deliberately ignoring the Parabellum under his groping fingers, he produced a bar of milk chocolate, now slightly soft but still fully edible. He threw it towards Ravoski. 'There, indulge yourself, Viktor!'

The sudden move took Ravoski by surprise, but still he caught the chocolate.

'So what you're telling me, Viktor, is that you're aspiring to be a double agent?'

'No, Oliver, you are wrong. It is not a question of being a double agent. You must listen to what I say. Both you and I now know the story from both sides, yes? But I will never betray my country.' He sighed deeply and began to remove the wrapping from the chocolate. 'Oliver, I am becoming an old man, and I wish to live in your country as a free man, no strings attached, you understand? How is it you say? I prefer to bat for the winning side. But what I have told you means nothing unless we can break away from the destroyer. I can help you with that, or at least make your escape less difficult. Then I will be happy to accompany you to Britain and to seek asylum. Why do you think that I allowed your captain to break away from *Otvashni* before, even though, in the event, that escape attempt proved futile? But this was mainly because your Commander Bradley was not ready. Now your captain is a prisoner and so is this boat, together with all aboard her.'

Strong nodded. 'But now we've got a bit of back-up, and it looks like your captain's not going to get it all his own way after all!'

Ravoski smiled wearily. 'Do you know, Oliver, I really think that I am now too old for this business. Who do you think might have summoned this back-up that you talk about? Do you not think it strange that your friends have appeared so quickly in this exact place?'

It was becoming increasingly clear to Strong that Ravoski must be listened to. He knew now that this officer could well tip the balance between the success and failure of *Spearfish*'s escape, and that if and when push came to shove, Ravoski could well be his biggest asset. But then, even after this conversation, could he really trust the man? Too much had happened over the past days, too many changes. But already he knew that if this whole business was to reach any sort of satisfactory conclusion, he would need to put the past few days behind him and place his trust in this Russian. In any case there was time yet. He would wait, and he would think things through. There was no point in going off half cocked. Now he realised that he was sweating profusely, he reached into his anorak pocket for a handkerchief and wiped his brow as he again studied the Russian's features. 'But can I trust you, Viktor?'

'Do you have a choice, Oliver?'

'No, I don't think I do. Whatever happens, you hold all the cards – at the moment, that is.'

Ravoski smiled to himself. Apparently relaxed, he continued to unwrap his chocolate.

Then it happened. The explosions forward of *Spearfish*'s hull shook her almost as much as they had shaken *Otvashni*. Strong heard the helmsman's urgent call over the main broadcast. 'First lieutenant to the bridge at the rush!'

Strong leapt for the curtained doorway, closely followed by Ravoski. They almost collided with the Starshl Lieutenant Gorski, who had left the attack periscope and was rushing towards them from the control room as Strong was leaping up the ladder into the conning tower. Gorski was plainly shaken. 'Our ship, Comrad, she is exploding!' He spoke in Russian, but the panic in his voice was plainly obvious to all around him.

Ravoski grabbed the periscope and, for a full minute, carefully surveyed *Otvashni*. Then standing back from the periscope, he turned to Gorski, again speaking in Russian, 'She is not sinking. You will return to the periscope, Lieutenant, and keep watch. Make sure that all the guards are alerted. I will be on the bridge.'

★   ★   ★   ★   ★

Bradley and Jackson were still on the port side of her upper deck, under the break of her fo'c'sle, when *Otvashni*'s upper deck lighting suddenly came on. Between them they held the still-protesting Russian down. Now Jackson clamped a hand over Portrova's mouth and held him face down on the deck

'Oh, Christ!' muttered Bradley, 'They've been back to the switchboard and restored power; we'll wait here for a moment.' Now he shrugged out of the heavy watch-coat he had "borrowed" from the sick berth guard, preferring to endure the freezing cold than the rancid odour of this coat.

Jackson had kept Yuri's coat on. 'Yeh, well, only too glad of the rest myself, Commander. Bit tiring, all this sabotage!' replied the irascible Jackson. 'This 'ere 'Ivan's no friggin' lightweight, is 'e? 'E's what I would call a fat bastard!'

Thankfully the upper deck lighting was not overly intrusive, just forming small pools of white light at regular intervals along each deckhouse structure but still leaving plenty of dark shadow along the upper deck.

Bradley rose carefully to his knees, listening intently for any sign of movement, while Jackson lay flat and still, his hand clamped tightly over Portrova's mouth. Bradley wondered whether the starboard motor boat was yet in the water. He could hear voices and assumed that these would be from the boat-lowering party, who would by now be awaiting further orders. Then *Otvashni*'s main searchlights flashed on, again casting their combined bright white light down on the after half of her upper deck and on the two submarines behind her.

'Blast!' Bradley cursed his luck and dropped down close to Jackson. In barely more than a whisper he said, 'We need to take that motor boat, so we'll have to get over to the starboard side. I don't know how many men will be there but we'll try to surprise 'em. Whether they let us take the boat will depend upon how much love they have for their captain.' Then he nodded towards Portrova. 'Roll him over but keep his mouth covered.'

Jackson grunted and rolled Portrova over until the Russian captain looked up directly into his face. Bradley whispered, 'Now listen carefully, Captain. We can either do this the hard way, or we can make things easy. It's up to you. But you should know that if you cause me problems then I will kill you, have no doubt about that. Captain Jackson and I are going to borrow your motor boat, and then we are going back to my submarine. You will come with us! What was it you said to me earlier? Be your guest? Well, now I'll be the host! I think you know that my colleague aboard the other British submarine is fully prepared to sink your ship if necessary, and you should also know that if me and Captain Jackson die, then we would consider that preferable to rotting in one of your stinking labour camps!' Bradley's voice was a muted hiss. 'Do you understand me? Nod your head if you do.' Portrova's eyes were beginning to bulge and Bradley suddenly realised that Jackson's huge hand was slowly suffocating him. Now Portrova nodded his head violently, and Bradley reached down and removed Jackson's hand from his mouth.

Portrova gagged, and gasped in large mouthfuls of air. Then, finally breathing normally, he fastened his sloe-black hate-filled eyes on Bradley and grated, 'For the sake of my ship and my men I will do as you ask. But I will hunt you down, Commander Bradley. I will take you back to Russia, where you will pay for the crimes that you have committed this day, and you may have no doubts of that!'

'Bollocks,' muttered Jackson and hauled Portrova to his feet. 'Listen to me, yuh Russian prick. You already got me lined up fer a firing squad so I ain't really got a lot to look forward to,'ave I? What's more, I don't really give a shit anyway! All I want to do is to take you down first, then I'll rest easy.' He jammed the muzzle of his gun hard into the Russian's back. 'I gotta lot of bullets in 'ere, an' each one of em's got your name on it, so be warned.' Portrova, now upright, looked hard at the big trawler captain, and he knew that this man was not speaking empty words.

'OK,' Bradley whispered, 'might as well get the show on the road, but be prepared for anything, Captain Jackson' – he nodded towards the scowling Portrova –'especially where this bastard's concerned!' Slowly they made their way aft, with Jackson constantly prodding his gun into Portrova's back. Now low to the deck, almost crawling to evade the glare from the searchlights, the trio finally reached *Otvashni*'s after torpedo tube mounting, where the voices of the group of men on the starboard side were much louder.

Bradley cautiously raised his head above the bank of three tubes now trained fore and aft. He could count at least ten men standing at the starboard side rail looking down at the motor boat, which was now in the water. Bassisty was the officer in charge, and appeared to be awaiting further instructions from the bridge. He was speaking loudly into a sound-powered telephone fitted to the deck housing. There was no mistaking the confusion and panic in his voice. It was plain that the support he was getting from his colleagues on the bridge was of little or no help to him.

Slamming back the telephone handset into its waterproof housing, Bassisty turned and dismissed eight of the boat-lowering party, who quickly disappeared for'd. Bradley noted that the remaining two seamen were the ones carrying submachine-guns, and that Bassisty carried a holstered pistol on his belt. He lowered his head and turned to speak to Jackson. Then, without warning, the ear-splitting shriek of the *Otvashni*'s siren blotted out his hearing and his thinking. Three ear-splitting blasts from somewhere near the top of *Ottvashni*'s forward funnel warned him that that at last someone had taken charge of the ship. His run of luck was fast coming to an end. Now things could get really difficult. He cleared his ears, heard loud voices and heavily booted feet running along the upper deck, and knew that this period of grace was now over. Oh well, he thought, we've had a bloody good innings up to now.

Crouching beside Jackson, who was now kneeling on Portrova's stomach and holding one hand again over the Russian's mouth, he whispered, 'There's a boat in the water, Skipper, and as you can hear, the Ruskies have finally realised what's happening. We've got to make a move now or we'll never get away. Forget the boat though: too dangerous now. We'll have to swim for it.

D'you fancy a swim? They tell me the water's lovely up here at this time of the year. Very refreshing.'

In the darkness Jackson leered up at Bradley. 'Ready when you are, Commander. Could do with a bit of a cool down.' He slapped Portrova's head. 'An' if things don't turn out right I'll be drownin' this bastard anyway, yuh can be sure of that!'

Portrova moaned, and Bradley continued, 'The snag is there's two submachine-guns and a pistol out there.' He looked at the two Russian seamen still standing at the ship's side. 'If those two stay together, with a bit of luck we'll take 'em with us when we go. If we move quickly enough we'll be on them before they know what's hit 'em, but the young officer with the pistol is worrying me. He won't hesitate to finish us if he can.'

'What about when we 'it's the water then?' Jackson whispered, 'always assuming we're still alive, that is.'

'Well, we've got our friend here,' – Bradley motioned towards Portrova – 'and I'm assuming they'll want to keep him alive. If we can keep him close, they may not risk shooting at us. Are you a strong swimmer?'

'Better than most,' whispered Jackson. 'An' you? What about you? 'Ows your swimmin'? I don't want to be 'oldin' the two of yuh up!'

'Oh, I'll do my best,' Bradley nodded. 'Don't forget the water's going to be bloody cold, but if we can keep a hold on Portrova and handle this properly, then he'll be our ticket out of all of this.'

'So, what now?' Jackson asked.

'Well, when the time comes, you and I will get rough with these people on deck,' whispered Bradley. 'There's only three of them at the moment so we'll move quickly. You up for this?'

'You bet your sweet arse I am,' whispered Jackson, his hand still clamped firmly over Portrova's mouth. 'Just give me the word.' Then frowning, he said, 'But me arms an' me legs is givin' me gip an' that's fer sure.' Again, with his free hand he slapped the struggling Portrova hard on the side of his head. 'Christ, when I think about this – where's it all goin' to end? I only came up 'ere to catch some cod!' Yet again he slapped the struggling Portrova, before reaching for his weapon. 'Keep still, you Ruskie bastard, or I'll do for you right now!'

Ignoring Jackson, Bradley again raised his head over the torpedo tubes, his heart pounding. Now it really was "shit or bust". Bassisty, standing beside the upper deck telephone, was obviously still awaiting further orders from the bridge and stamping his feet on the iron deck, either because of the cold or his growing frustration. The two armed seamen standing together at the rail appeared to be totally relaxed, making conversation with the crew of the motor boat in the water below them.

Bradley whispered to Jackson, 'I'll take the man on the telephone, and I'll keep this blighter with me.' He nudged the still-grunting Portrova hard in the ribs with his elbow while at the same time forcing his left hand over the Russian's mouth to replace Jackson's grip. 'You get rid of those other two. Don't be too fussy about it – any way you can. Take 'em over the side with you if you like, but you'll have to surprise them or you'll be a dead man!'

Jackson nodded in the darkness, and Bradley took three deep breaths, trying desperately to calm the relentless pounding inside his chest. Then realising that this was a completely futile exercise, he shouted, 'Right, Captain Jackson, go get 'em!'

Jackson obeyed instantaneously. Flinging himself forward, he covered the five yards from the shadow of the tubes to the ship's rail in seconds. The two seamen at the rail turned, startled at Bradley's shout, but they hadn't stood a chance. Jackson was on them. Grasping both by their necks, he hauled them into his chest in a bear hug and, with a crushing, suffocating, and relentless pressure, and seemingly oblivious to their flailing arms and to the pain as their booted legs beat against his already throbbing shins, he strangled the life out of them.

Bassisty, still manning the telephone, was also taken completely by surprise. Swinging around, he fumbled frantically with the flap of the pistol holster on his belt. Now Bradley stepped forward, pushing Portrova in front of him, his left hand still clamped around the Russian captain's mouth, and his right gripping the trigger of the cocked submachine-gun.

But Bradley had severely underestimated both the determination and the strength of Portrova, and as they lurched from the shadow of the torpedo tubes he stumbled over a ringbolt on the deck. Thrown off balance, he momentarily relaxed his grip on Portrova.

This was all the Russian captain needed. With a bellow of pent-up rage Portrova swivelled around and with his left fist landed a wild but heavy blow to the side of Bradley's head. Stunned, Bradley fell to his knees, while Portrova threw himself towards Bassisty, who, still in a state of bewildered panic, had now managed to clear his pistol from its holster.

Portrova snarled. 'Your gun, Comrad, give me your gun.' Bassisty did not hesitate, and thrust his pistol into his captain's outstretched hand. In a single movement Portrova turned and fired at Bradley, who, still on his knees, had now raised his machine gun to point it roughly in Portrova's direction. But the Russian was faster. His first shot sliced through Bradley's left shoulder, the hammer-like blow of the bullet spinning him around and throwing him heavily onto his back. Bradley felt no pain at this time, but was conscious of an all-consuming grey mist spreading over his squirming body like a murky blanket, and he knew that he was fast losing consciousness.

Grunting with satisfaction, Portrova shifted his aim towards Jackson, who was still slowly throttling the life from the two seamen at the rail. Portrova's second shot shattered the flailing leg of the man held in Jackson's left arm, causing the legs to then flail even more, splashing blood and bone fragments over the deck. But there were no screams; this man was already nearly dead from strangulation.

Portrova's third shot slammed full into Jackson's broad back. The force of the bullet pushed Jackson forward, but he still didn't release his death grip on the two men in his arms. He turned his head and roared something unintelligible towards Portrova, then choking in his own blood and already semi-conscious, he toppled, almost in slow motion over the guardrail. Even before he hit the water Jackson was as dead as the two men still clamped firmly in his arms.

Fighting the grey mist in front of his eyes, Bradley had now risen to his knees, his right hand scrabbling on the deck in search of his machine gun, while trying to ignore the searing pain in his left shoulder. Although Portrova and Bassisty were little more the ten feet from him, in his pain-misted eyes they now appeared as floating "will o' the wisp" like shadows, dancing in the white glare of the searchlight.

Portrova had now swung back to face Bradley. Uttering a savage snarl of hatred, he fired two more shots in quick succession, but these were hurried shots. The first slammed into the deck at Bradley's right side and ricocheted aft into the darkness. Bradley felt the wind of the second bullet as it skimmed by his left ear and slammed into the destroyer's superstructure before it, too, whined off into the darkness.

Steadying himself against the deckhouse, Portrova took four steps towards the crouching Bradley. Now they were almost within arm's length of each other and Bradley could sense the hate in the Russian's eyes – a hate even more apparent in the guttural snarl that came from the bear-like figure. 'And so now *your* time to die has come, Commander! You will die for what you have done to my ship on this night. It could have been so different, but you and your friends have chosen not to make it so, and you must die for this. It is my regret that you can only die once!' Again raising his pistol, he took careful aim and tightened his finger on the trigger, while Bradley's right hand finally located the Russian submachine-gun.

Portrova was startled by the dull click of his pistol's hammer. Again he pulled the trigger, but again the same dull click. His gun was empty. Cursing, he threw it aside and leapt towards Bradley, who had now managed to raise the submachine-gun with his right arm and pull the trigger. This time there was no dull click. Bradley's weapon was set to automatic and the force of the fire almost jerked the weapon out of his hand as it barked out its stream of bullets. He had little or no control of the weapon, but still he kept his finger firmly pressed on its trigger.

Portrova was in mid air as the first stream of bullets from Bradley's weapon scythed through both his legs. He screamed and landed flat on his belly, writhing in agony alongside Bradley, whose weapon continued to bark out a constant stream of fire into the night. Now Bassisty too, reeled backward and crumpled to the deck. The hail of Bradley's bullets had literally cut him in two.

Bradley finally released his grip on the trigger, and the noise stopped. Then he heard footsteps, heavy footsteps. Russians were coming from both the bridge and from aft on the upper deck. He must move now. He fired a short burst both forward and aft along the upper deck and the footsteps stopped. Grunting with satisfaction, he turned forward and again squeezed the trigger. His vision was clearer now and this time he was aiming at the eye of the starboard bridge searchlight. One quick burst and the searchlight exploded into blackness.

At his side Portrova was still writhing and cursing, partly in English, but mostly in Russian. Bradley glanced at his watch. It was less than two minutes since Jackson had grabbed the two seamen and the shooting had started.

He rolled over and clamped his right arm over the Russian's neck. Now his own pain had returned in full measure. A red-hot knife blade was twisting and probing into his shoulder; it was absolute hell. He fought off the urge to scream, knowing that he must hang on to consciousness at all costs. Leaning over the Russian, he spoke directly into his ear.

'Listen to me, Portrova. You can either die here with me on your own ship within the next few seconds, or we can take our chances together. But either way, you will die before me!' To emphasise this point, he pressed the barrel of his weapon hard into the Russian's stomach.

Portrova gasped and spat a mixture of sputum and blood directly into Bradley's face. 'English pig. It is you who will die for this. Whatever happens to me, my men will kill you.' He spat again. 'That, I promise.'

Bradley spat back into the Portrova's face. He couldn't resist the temptation. Then he leaned even closer to the Russian's ear and hissed, 'Brave words, Captain, but you don't really want to die yet, do you? Well, whether you like it or not, I'm not staying aboard your bloody ship any longer – and neither are you! You're my ticket out of here. But first, I'm afraid you're going to have to get a bit wet. In fact, we both are.' Then he realised that Portrova was no longer hearing him. The Russian had lost consciousness.

So much for the staying power of the Russian bear! Bradley mustered every ounce of his remaining strength to haul himself upright. The pain in his left shoulder was almost unbearable and he knew that it was only adrenalin keeping him going now. Dropping the machine gun, he gripped the inert Portrova by the collar and lunged towards the rail. 'Come on then, Captain, let's see how well you swim!'

Together Bradley and Portrova went over the rail, just as the first of *Otvashni*'s machine gun crews opened fire. The party from aft had opened fire first, sending a stream of fire forward along the upper deck, forcing their fellow crewmen from for'd to dive for cover. Then together, the two parties concentrated on firing into the sea, randomly, almost hitting their own motor boat until a panic order from the bridge stopped them.

Landing in the sea not five yards astern of the Russian motor boat, Bradley immediately sank. He had no control over this. Having already released his grip on Portrova and now with arms and legs flailing desperately, he continued downward. Then he was again on the surface, with just enough time to cough out another lungful of water and frantically replace it with a gulp of air before once more sinking. Fleetingly he recalled the old adage of coming up three times before you go down for ever, and he hoped that it was true. Then he found himself on the surface again. This time he intended to stay there. The icy cold of the water had put new life into him, and although it chilled him to the bone and made his breathing difficult, it had also numbed the pain in his shoulder.

The initial shock on hitting the water had left him. Now he floated on his back, treading water and gathering his thoughts, at the same time clearing his eyes from the stinging salt while coughing up solid streams of sea water from a searing throat, and he thanked God that the waves now breaking over his head were no more than two feet high. Rising with each successive peak, he could see that the Russian motor boat had now cast off from *Otvashni*'s port side and was no more than ten yards forward of him, its crew shouting to each other in the darkness, searching with boathooks to locate anyone in the water, but without success. He kicked hard away from *Otvashni*'s stern, distancing himself even further from the confusion around her starboard side.

Then he felt something bump hard against his shoulder, his injured shoulder. Resisting the urge to scream with the pain, he rolled over to stare into the open-mouthed features of Portrova. He was not struggling, he'd given up struggling. Still unconscious, Portrova was again sinking beneath the dark restless surface of the Barents, those pallid, coarse features again becoming invisible under the swell. Bradley realised that the Russian captain was still wearing his heavy leather watch-coat and God knows what else beneath.

Hooking his good arm around Portrova's neck, he hauled the Russian's face clear of the water. Even in the freezing windswept darkness of this night he could sense that Portrova was very near death. Ignoring the pain of his shoulder wound, which now seemed to be consuming the whole of his upper torso, he continued the struggle to keep Portrova's waterlogged body afloat knowing that without this man, a true version of events over the past weeks would be so much more difficult to prove. He had long since accepted that his own career was almost certainly over, but Strong and the rest of them didn't deserve to answer for the fiasco that he'd created. The truth, if properly corroborated by Portrova, would almost certainly exonerate his officers and crew from any blame. He gasped, coughing up gouts of bitter salt water. 'Come on… you bastard,' he muttered, 'don't you… die… on me now. You've got a bloody… story to tell… before you go.' Tightening his grip on the Russian's neck, he again kicked out, driving himself towards the two British submarines.

★   ★   ★   ★   ★

Cunningham, together with Morton, had remained on *Sturgeon*'s bridge since they had surfaced astern of *Otvashni*. But now that the gunfire on *Otvashni*'s upper deck had stopped, Morton had gone below to see to the divers. Some five minutes later he returned to the bridge. Keen and alert as ever, he wedged himself between the signalman and his captain. 'So what's the latest, Sir?' Then, without waiting for his captain to reply, he calmly proceeded to issue Cunningham with his own situation update.

'I'm afraid that Andrew seems to be in a bit of a state. We've done all that we can for him. Hypothermia, I think – God only knows. Just hope he'll pull through! The cox'n's keeping a good eye on him. You know, brandy, warm blankets and all that. He should be all right. Donovan seems perfectly fit though.'

Cunningham grunted. Barely acknowledging his first lieutenant's words, he continued to gaze forward at the Russian destroyer. Now scowling, he turned and looked directly at Morton. 'You do realise, Hugh, that we're still into some sort of a bloody impasse situation here. We don't really know exactly what's happening but they can't move, and neither can we. If we move from here the buggers have got enough firepower to blow us out of the water – us and *Spearfish* as well! If we give those Russians the opportunity of using their weaponry, and I don't just mean their guns, they won't hesitate to attack us now that we've fired the first shots, as it were. No, there's got to be another way. Perhaps some more meaningful dialogue might do the trick.' Again he turned his gaze forward, shrugging his shoulders almost dismissively. 'See if you can organise some more coffee, Hugh; I've a feeling this is going to be a long night. And keep everyone below on their toes, because whatever is about to occur won't be planned, and I very much doubt that any warnings will be issued!'

CHAPTER SEVENTEEN

With her electrical power fully restored, *Otvashni*'s upper deck was again well lit, and amplified by the beam of the bridge port searchlight. Cunningham had speculated that his explosives would have put her propulsion and steering gear out of action, but whether they had, was still only speculation. Just how badly had he hurt *Otvashni* with those charges? To his mind she was still a very dangerous animal and in truth he had no real appreciation of exactly what was going on aboard her right now. But he did know that both *Sturgeon* and *Spearfish* were still extremely vulnerable. Perhaps more to the point, what was that young bugger Bradley doing at this time? Was he dead? Or was he, even now, causing more mayhem aboard the Russian? Brushing the salty rime from his tired eyes he again raised his glasses and made yet another sweep of the Russian destroyer's stern and upper deck. Surely by now, something should be happening. But then again, perhaps they weren't getting orders. He remembered what many of his colleagues had said in the past: 'Russian forces, without leadership, are nothing! Chickens with their heads cut off. Bloody peasants, most of 'em!'

Well, that may be so, but he wasn't about to prove this theory, though as far as he could see at this time there was no evidence of any leadership aboard the Russian. By now there should have been some sort of response from *Otvashni*, whether by small gunfire, signal or spoken word. So where was her captain – this bloody Portrova fellow? What was he doing right now? He wished that he could see more clearly, but the constant glare from that bloody searchlight blurred his vision. This was becoming quite surreal; *Otvashni* was like a ghost ship. Surely there must be someone up there on that bridge, someone in control?

He thought back to his first sighting of Bradley on *Otvashni*'s quarterdeck. He had certainly seemed to be on top of the game then. But surely Bradley, as a one-man army, couldn't have overcome the lot of them? Not the whole bloody ship's company. But then again the Bradley that he knew would never have put himself in this situation in the first place.

Then at least half a dozen men had appeared on the starboard side midships section of the destroyer's upper deck. Cunningham didn't count them, but he could see that they were lowering a boat. 'Ah well,' he muttered to the signalman beside him. 'Looks like the bastards are finally after a parley!'

'Looks that way, Sir.' The signalman continued to scan the area around *Sturgeon* with his six-inch Aldis. 'I bloody well 'ope so anyway. Christ, but it's cold up 'ere!'

Cunningham suddenly realised that there had been no word or movement from the two lookouts standing behind him in each corner at the rear of the bridge. He called back to them, 'Are you two all right?'

One of the lookouts mumbled something unintelligible under his breath, while the other, in an overtly facetious tone, shouted forward, 'Marvellous, Sir; wouldn't 'ave missed all this for the world, Sir!' In the darkness, Cunningham smiled to himself and turned to resume his study of *Otvashni*'s port upper deck. Situation normal. Bloody jokers, what would we do without 'em?

Morton was by now on his way below to the control room when he heard Cunningham's voice over the helmsman's voice pipe. 'Bridge – Helm. This is the captain. Tell the first lieutenant that the Russian has launched a boat. Looks like something may be starting to happen.'

Within a minute Morton had reappeared beside Cunningham. The Russian motor boat was now in the water, manned by four men. Cunningham could now see only two men on *Otvashni*'s upper deck. They were leaning over the starboard guard rail immediately over the boat which, although now fully in the water, was still secured to the ship's side. Ah well, he thought, we'll give 'em a few minutes to get their act together and with a bit of luck we'll hear what they've got to say for themselves.

Then, without warning, the small arms fire had started. Cunningham and Morton ducked instinctively, but soon realised that the shooting was contained within *Otvashni*. After the first single shot there was a brief pause. Seconds later a further shot rang out, closely followed by a third. Now, through his glasses, Cunningham watched body-sized bundles topple over the guard rail and land in the water just aft of the motor boat. He didn't know how many – possibly two, maybe three. It had all happened so quickly. He turned to Morton. 'Well at last something's ha—'

Before he could finish, a further short burst of gunfire erupted on *Otvashni's* upper deck. Then there was silence – a very brief silence – now quickly followed by a continued staccato of harsh fire from some sort of machine gun or automatic weapon. Sparks glinted into the night sky as bullets ricocheted off the destroyer's upperworks. Then the starboard searchlight exploded into darkness and there was silence – complete silence. This whole episode was over in less than two minutes.

'What the hell was all that about?' Cunningham turned to Morton, searching for some sort of answer.

Morton said what his captain was thinking. 'Well, they're obviously not shooting themselves up, are they, Sir? It looks to me like Bradley could be throwing a tantrum. D'you think that's a possibility?'

'Oh, it's a possibility all right, but at this stage I'm beginning to think that anything might be bloody possible! You could well be right, Hugh, and this may be what we've been waiting for.' He turned to the signalman. 'Bunts, make to *Spearfish*: Are you in a position to take my orders?'

* * * * *

Strong now stood, together with Ravoski and Murray, on *Spearfish's* bridge, Strong still breathing heavily with the effort of his headlong rush up the conning tower ladder. They had read Cunningham's signal but, being still exposed to the harsh white light from *Otvashni*'s searchlight, they could see very little forward of them. Murray had reported the earlier sound of small arms fire aboard her, and *Sturgeon*, being just a few yards off *Spearfish*'s port side, was still as large as life.

Strong looked enquiringly towards Ravoski's hooded features and spoke in a low clear voice. 'Well, Viktor, you've laid out your position quite clearly. Now you can see ours. So I guess it's your call now!'

For a moment Ravoski was completely silent. Then he turned towards Strong and let out a long deep sigh. 'So, you and I, Oliver – it looks like we shall be friends after all, *da?*'

Strong let out an equally long sigh, but his was one of overwhelming relief. Ravoski had made his decision. 'Yes, most certainly!'

Now *Sturgeon*'s lamp flashed again: 'Be ready to act upon my command. Watch me and stand by.'

Cunningham looked behind him towards the two lookouts. 'And that goes for you two as well!' Now he turned back to Morton. 'Go below, Hugh, and give everyone a brief of the current situation. Use main broadcast, but I want everyone on the ball, standing by for anything.' In the darkness he stroked his chin, musing to himself aloud. 'Well, you know what I mean. We'll have to be ready for anything. I just hope that *Spearfish* can—'

He never finished his sentence; his words were drowned out by the signalman behind him. 'Captain, Sir, look! There's someone in the water, about five yards off our starboard bow!'

'Bloody hell, so there is!' Cunningham turned and shouted down to Morton, who was, again, half way down the bridge ladder. 'Hugh, get the second cox'n and three hands onto the for'd casing at the rush. Tell 'em to stand by to fish some bodies out of the water.'

'Now,' he muttered to himself, 'what the hell's going on here?' Training his glasses into the dark water towards the area the signalman had indicated, he muttered, 'Yes, I can see something. Well done, Bunts.' Straining his tired eyes, he could now see lighter splashes of water. Someone was swimming out there. Now he strained his ears as well as his eyes. Yes, he was definitely hearing something other than the sound of the sea slapping against *Sturgeon*'s ballast tanks. He was now hearing cries coming from this sea: broken, weak, but definitely human cries for help.

Below him, Second Cox'n Mitchell, together with a party of three seamen carrying ropes and buoyancy rings, again made their way forward towards *Sturgeon*'s bow. Mitchell lowered himself onto the starboard fore plane and called up to the seamen above him, 'Pass down the ropes, an' tell the old man there's two of 'em in the water. Sounds like one's a Brit!' One of the seamen made his way aft, shouting this information to Cunningham on the bridge.

Cunningham shouted back, 'Good. Get them inboard as quick as you can.' He felt a shiver of excitement run through him. Was this Bradley? Now below him he could hear Morton's voice on the main broadcast system, saying exactly what he had told him to say. Looking forward to *Sturgeon*'s bow, he could see that Mitchell had already retrieved one of the bodies from the water, laying it across the fore plane before passing it up to the waiting arms of the seamen above him. Now he turned back to peer into the darkness, searching for the other swimmer. Even in the meagre light provided by the signalman's lantern, he could see that the second man in the water was now in dire straits. Mitchell had thrown a line in his direction but the swimmer was obviously too weak to reach for it and was floating face upward, almost submerged, and slowly drifting away from *Sturgeon*. Suddenly Cunningham was convinced that this swimmer was Bradley.

Then Mitchell stood upright on the fore plane. Peeling off his oilskins and kicking off his heavy sea boots, he secured one end of the line firmly around his waist before shouting to the men on the casing above him. 'Bloody 'ell. Do I 'ave to do everything around 'ere? Just 'ang on to the other end of this line an' stand by to pull me in.' Throwing himself into the icy black water, he struck out towards the second swimmer.

Cunningham called to the signalman, 'Don't lose them. For Christ's sake keep that lamp on them,' though knowing as he spoke, the signalman's lantern would be gifting any sniper aboard the Russian's upper deck.

Mitchell had now reached the second swimmer and grabbed him by the neck while shouting hoarsely for his men to pull him back towards *Sturgeon*.

Then, at last, both the swimmers, together with Mitchell, were lying face down, exhausted, on the forward casing.

Still on his bridge, Cunningham pondered for a moment, studying the sea state. Then he leaned forward and shouted down the voice pipe, 'Helm – Bridge. This is the Captain. Ask the first lieutenant to open the accommodation space hatch and provide hands to help all those on the casing to come below.'

On the casing, Bradley stopped coughing and pulled himself up onto his knees, groaning at the searing pain in his shoulder. Mitchell, once more back on his feet, was removing the line around his waist before handing it to one of his seamen.

Bradley too, now climbed unsteadily to his feet. Looking at Mitchell, he said, 'Nice night for a swim, but thanks anyway for pulling me out. Bradley, CO of *Spearfish*.'

Mitchell said, 'The pleasure was all mine, Sir. Mitchell, second cox'n, *Sturgeon*.'

'And this miserable piece of shit,' muttered Bradley, jabbing a foot into the still-inert Portrova lying at his feet, 'is Captain Portrova of the Russian destroyer, and the cause of all my problems. I want him kept alive if possible.'

Mitchell looked down at the sodden heap that was Portrova. 'Might not be too lucky there. 'E don't look too 'ealthy to me, Sir. In fact, it looks like 'e may 'ave gone already.'

From the bridge, Cunningham's voice called sharply over the loudhailer, 'Is that you, Nigel?'

Bradley took a few faltering steps towards the bridge fin. 'It is, Sir! Permission to come aboard, please?'

'Who've you got with you?'

'The Russian destroyer captain – more dead than alive, I'm afraid!'

'Better get him below, yourself too, before you end up over the side again. I'll be down as soon as I can.'

Bradley raised his good arm and walked back to Mitchell, who was now kneeling over Portrova.

Mitchell said, 'He was trying to say something, Sir.'

Then, almost as though he knew they were discussing him, Portrova groaned loudly and stirred. Bradley too, leaned over him and said to Mitchell, 'Turn him onto his back; I need to see this bastard's face.'

As Mitchell rolled him onto his back, Portrova again groaned loudly. In the beam of the bridge signal lantern Bradley could see the Russian's eyes flickering wildly before opening fully to stare at the faces above him. He began to speak, his voice weak at first, then becoming stronger, but still in a mixture of Russian and English. Most of what he said was making no sense at all to Bradley or Mitchell, who were listening hard to catch the little they could.

'It is finished, Gregori... I can do no more. Again I am saved... These accursed Britishers. But I would be with you, my friend... You will know that I have repaid my debt, have I not?' Then his eyes closing, he again faded into silence.

Mitchell said, 'Is 'e gone, Sir?'

Bradley pushed his fingers under the Russian's collar, feeling for a pulse. 'No, he's still with us, though I suspect not for much longer.'

Behind them the accommodation space hatch sprang open with a loud metallic clunk. Four seamen emerged, dragging up a Neil Robinson stretcher, and unrolled it beside the Russian.

'Get him below as quick as you can,' said Bradley. 'Get him warm and try not to damage him any more. I want him alive.'

The unconscious Portrova was quickly secured into the stretcher before being carefully lowered through the hatch into the waiting hands of men below, who carried him aft to the wardroom. Mitchell turned to Bradley. 'Your turn now, Sir. Can you manage this ladder? 'Ere, I'll 'elp you.' He held Bradley's uninjured shoulder tightly and guided him into the hatch well, then shouted down the hatch, 'Under below, stand by to receive one naval officer. Watch 'im though; 'e's got a bad wound.'

With the help of Mitchell, Bradley lowered himself down the vertical ladder into the accommodation space, where he screwed up his eyes at the unaccustomed dazzle of white lighting as willing hands half guided, half carried him, aft to the wardroom.

★　★　★　★　★

'Aw, fer fuck's sake! 'Ow many more times?' Samuels had been standing under the open fore hatch of *Sturgeon*, armed with a bucket and mop. He had only just finished mopping up the last deluge of sea water that had flooded down as the hatch had been open for the two divers. Now he was about to start all over again.

Moore had by now climbed the ladder. Pulling the hatch shut, he secured the clip before dropping down beside Samuels. 'Stop yer moaning and just get on with it, yuh little shit!'

They had carried Portrova aft, where Morton had directed them to lay him on the wardroom table, and Cox'n Sanford had carefully unbuckled the straps of the stretcher, and opened it out under the prone Russian. Morton now stood next to him. Someone had placed a pillow under Portrova's head.

Sanford muttered, 'Looks like he's taken bullets in both his legs, Sir. Pretty badly shot up by the looks of it! We'll have to get these boots off before I can get a good look though, so let's just hope the poor bugger stays unconscious.'

One by one the cox'n eased the heavy black leather sea boots from the Russian. There was no easy way of doing this. Sanford gritted his teeth, but Portrova remained unconscious. Then, with the boots finally off, he began to carefully cut away the Russian's trouser legs with a pair of large scissors. This too, took some time – first the oilskins, then the thick serge trousers – before finally exposing Portrova's bare legs. Sanford gave a low whistle and looked towards Morton. 'Jesus, Sir, look at the state of 'em! Not sure I can do a lot for this poor sod.'

Bradley now pushed his way into the wardroom. 'Hello, Hugh, nice to see you again.'

Morton smiled broadly and shook Bradley's hand vigorously. 'That must be the understatement of the decade, Sir. Welcome aboard.' He indicated towards Portrova. 'Your Russian friend here is in a bad way. Doubt we can do much for him.'

Bradley nodded and tried to answer, but now he started to shiver uncontrollably, his legs starting to buckle at the knees. Morton grabbed out, with both hands clutching Bradley's shoulders, and Bradley groaned in pain. Now for the first time Morton noticed Bradley's left arm, the sleeve of which was soaked in oozing black blood, and those puce grey features told him the rest of the story. 'It doesn't look like you've come out of this completely unharmed yourself, Sir.' He called to one of the men standing by the door. 'Here, lend a hand. Get him to the captain's bunk.'

Bradley lay stretched full length on Cunningham's bunk and took several deep breaths before pulling himself up on his good arm to address Morton. 'Took a pistol bullet in the left shoulder, Hugh, compliments of that bastard lying in there on the table. Don't know how bad it is, but it hurts like hell. I could really murder a large brandy. Any chance?'

'I'm sure we can bend the rules a bit on this occasion.' Morton called for the steward and within minutes Bradley was clutching a large brandy, which he studied carefully before downing it in one. Then he said, 'God, but I needed that. Is James coming down?'

'He'll be down shortly. He hasn't left the bridge since we caught up with you. I'll go up and relieve him in a moment. You just rest up as best you can for now. I'll get the cox'n to come and have a look at your arm.'

Sanford, still in the wardroom, having finished examining Portrova's legs, now called to Morton as he left the captain's cabin. 'There really isn't much we can do for this fellow, Sir. He needs expert medical treatment. All that I can do is to try and stop the bleeding, clean him up and give him some pain relief. He's had a jab of morphine but he needs a proper doctor. Surely they must have some sort of doctor on his ship?'

'I expect they will have, Cox'n, but for now you've done the best you can. Strap him back in the stretcher and put him on a bunk. It'll be up to the captain to decide what we do with him. As soon as you've finished with him, have a look at Lieutenant Commander Bradley. I'm going to the bridge.'

Morton again stood beside his captain on *Sturgeon*'s bridge. The forward casing had now been cleared and secured. Cunningham was listening carefully to what Morton had to say while at the same time studying the destroyer's upper deck and bridge with a signal lamp and keeping a watchful eye on the Russian motor boat still heading towards them, now about ten yards for'd of their bow. Cunningham raised his megaphone and shouted, 'Ahoy, the motor boat. You will stop and remain where you are.' The motor boat stopped as instructed.

Cunningham turned to Morton, 'Well, Hugh, how does this put us? We've got her captain, so I would say this gives us a position of some advantage, wouldn't you? They obviously want their captain back; in fact it looks like they may be coming for him even as we speak. All good negotiating stuff, eh? Well, as far as I'm concerned they can bloody well have him. Perhaps he'll be the key to breaking this bloody stalemate we seem to have got ourselves into. Perhaps we can do some horse trading, eh?' He turned forward again, raising his glasses to once again scan the Russian ship and the stationary motor boat. 'Keep your light on them, Hugh; I don't want them to start playing silly buggers again! I'd better get below and have a word with Bradley. You stay here and make sure that motor boat keeps its distance for now. Get a half a dozen armed men on the casing right away. Keep 'em in the shelter of the fin and be ready for anything. Call me if you have any doubts. Bradley's wounded, you say?' He was already climbing down the fin ladder.

Morton shouted after him, 'Shot in the left upper arm or shoulder, Sir. Don't know how bad it is but the cox'n should be looking at him by now. It looks like he's really been through the mill though, Sir.' Morton realised that his last sentence had sounded like a plea to Cunningham to go easy on Bradley. He sighed loudly to himself and raised his glasses to study the destroyer and the now-stationary motor boat, knowing that he shouldn't be worried. Cunningham would approach this matter in his usual measured way.

★ ★ ★ ★ ★

Bradley winced as Sanford, armed with large scissors, carefully started to cut off the left arm of the sleeve of Bradley's uniform jacket at the shoulder. 'Sorry, Sir,' muttered Sanford, 'got to let the dog see the rabbit. Your painkiller should be kicking in soon, anyway.'

Before starting with the scissors Sanford had injected Bradley's good arm with a large shot of morphine. 'The problem is that you've got so much dried blood around your wound, it's sticking your sleeve to your arm'. Now he removed the jacket. 'I'll be gentle as a lamb,' he grinned, starting to snip away at the sleeve, 'but I'm afraid that you ain't going to be wearing this jacket on divisions again, Sir.'

'Divisions, eh!' Bradley muttered. 'If and when we get back to the UK I very much doubt I'll be needing this jacket, or any other bloody uniform jacket, come to that! No, Cox'n, I've a feeling it'll be "Harry Tweeders" and a bowler hat for me.'

Sanford raised his eyebrows but said nothing. He was long enough in the tooth to know that conversations like this should be nipped in the bud.

At last the sleeve was cut through, and now Sanford gently snipped off the shirtsleeve. Bradley bit his lip in an attempt to stifle a moan of agony, while Sanford tutted and clucked like a mother hen. 'There, that's the worst bit over. I'll soak your shirtsleeve in warm water before I attempt to remove it. How's the pain now?'

'Bloody awful,' Bradley grimaced though gritted teeth.

The curtain to the cabin jerked open and Cunningham stepped in. 'How's he doing, Cox'n?'

'Oh, I think he'll live, Sir. You'll be wanting to talk, so perhaps if I could just soak his sleeve and come back later?'

'Yes, do that.' Cunningham's tone was terse, and hearing it, Bradley winced yet again, but this time the wince was not induced by pain.

Sanford, kneeling beside the bunk, soaked warm water into Bradley's blood-blackened shirtsleeve. Then looking up at Cunningham, he said, 'I don't think this wound is life threatening, Sir. I reckon the round has gone straight through his arm but he'll be in a lot of pain until the morphine takes charge.' He looked back down at Bradley, studying his pallid features, and could see that those features were already markedly more relaxed. The morphine was taking an effect. Standing up, he again turned to Cunningham, 'I can't really do any more till I've got his shirt off and had a good look, Sir. You'll be having a lot to talk about, but I doubt you'll get much sense out of the patient for a while yet. Anyway, shout if you need me.' He picked up his bowl, bandages and scissors, and left the cabin.

Cunningham pulled his chair across to the bunk and sat down. Bradley's eyes were again closed. Was he asleep? Cunningham studied the face of the man on the bunk for a full two minutes, loath to wake him, but there were questions to be asked, the answers to which would almost certainly decide the nature of his immediate plans. He coughed loudly, and cleared his throat. Bradley's eyes flickered open and centred on the hawk-like features of the man seated at his side.

'Hello, James, good to see you again!' Bradley's voice was surprisingly strong and clear. Cunningham made no reply, merely grunting and massaging his chin as though in deep thought.

Bradley's pale features hardened. 'So it's hard talk and recrimination time, eh?'

Cunningham remained silent, still stroking his chin, considering how he should approach this conversation. Then he said, 'I'm glad to see you, Nigel, and yes, we do need to talk, but any hard talk and recrimination, as you put it, can wait till we get back to Faslane. You will know that you're in for a bumpy ride – nothing can change that – so I sincerely hope for your sake that you've got a good story. How's that arm feeling?'

'Not too bad, actually. Throbs a bit, but I think the morphine's working now. Would you help me up? I'd rather be sitting.'

'You're sure? I don't want you keeling over on me.' Cunningham carefully helped Bradley up until he was sitting on the bunk, with his feet on the deck.

'That's better, thanks.'

'Well – you know what I've got to ask next! What the hell went wrong?'

'It was entirely my own fault. Last day of the patrol. Russian "Hotel" class missile launch. Got too close, far too bloody close. Took a chance which didn't pay off! Two Russian destroyers, one behind the other. Never saw the second until it was too late. Took the top off the fin together with everything else except the attack periscope. Then the bastards depth charged us. I went deep – as it happens, too bloody deep. I almost lost her, James. Port stern gland blew in, flooded the shaft space. Then we hit the bottom and wrote off the starboard screw. In spite of what had happened I had to get our boffin Toby Cannings, who was badly injured, medical help, so I had to trust the Russians.' He grinned wryly. 'Wrongly, as it turned out. Waited on the bottom till I judged it to be safe, then blew to the surface, slap bang in between those two bloody Russian destroyers. The bastards had been up there waiting for us.' Bradley paused and looked up at Cunningham. 'It *was* my fault, James – all of this is down to me and my bloody stupidity. I just wasn't on the ball. Too bloody anxious to get those pictures. None of this needed to have happened. Men have died, James, some of them good men. Toby was the first to go.'

'Toby's dead?'

'It was during the first attack. Oh, Christ, what am I going to do?' Bradley felt the hot tears running down his cheeks and he didn't care. 'I've fucked up everything!' Now he covered his eyes with his right hand and began sobbing, quietly but uncontrollably.

Cunningham sat back, seeing that the man seated in front of him was at the end of his tether. Once again that hand went up to his chin, thinking, digesting what he had heard. Then he leaned forward and placed his hand on Bradley's shuddering shoulder. His voice was quiet, reassuring. 'You've been through a lot, Nigel. The important thing is that you and *Spearfish* are still here. In that sense you've been lucky.'

Bradley looked up, rubbing his eyes. Suddenly his voice was loud, strong, filled with anger. 'Lucky, you say? The hell I'm lucky!' He lifted his left arm, wincing as he did so. 'You don't yet know the half of it. I'd have been luckier if those bastards had put this bullet through my brain!' He stopped and leaned back against the bulkhead, exhausted by his outburst. 'I'm sorry. Didn't mean to shout, but there's much more happened since, and most of it is still sinking in.'

Cunningham nodded. 'Of course, and we'll have plenty of time to talk later. Oliver Strong has already the information on the state of your boat.'

'You've seen the state of the fin. The only mast left up there is the attack periscope. Most of the sonar is out of action as well and we've got a fuel oil leak from three starboard main ballast. I wouldn't be surprised if more problems have come to light since. Oh, and by the way, there'll be at least one Russian officer aboard her, maybe more, together with a number of armed Ruskie seamen – don't know how many. I'm not sure about one of the officers though, a senior engineer who appears to be a "Jack of all trades" regarding submarines. This guy was instrumental in enabling us to make our first break, but more about that later. Let's just say that he may be on our side. I think he wants to defect!'

'Well, that's as may be,' muttered Cunningham, 'but the rest is not exactly encouraging news. However, we're going to make the best of a bad job. Now, what about that destroyer? I think my chaps have taken away her screws and possibly her rudder, and at the moment we're too close up her arse to let her use any sort of heavy armament, but what about the rest of her stuff? Wireless and all that?'

'Nothing much of that left working. Me and a good friend saw to that before I invited her captain in for a swim!' Bradley's eyes again clouded over. 'My good friend didn't make it, by the way. He died while getting me out of the shit.' Again he felt tears running down his cheeks. He rubbed his eyes again then blurted out, 'Oh my God, there's so much that you don't know, so much that I have to answer for, and look at me now – a complete bloody wreck!'

Cunningham studied the face in front of him, a face contorted in misery, and he knew that this man was fast letting the end go. This man who had been his first lieutenant in *Trojan* not so long before. This bright, efficient young Lieutenant, with a self-assurance approaching cockiness at times. Many of his peers had judged him as being arrogant, but never Cunningham. Between them there was a mutual liking and with this came a mutual respect, and as far as he was concerned this respect still existed.

Cunningham grunted. 'As I said before, there'll be plenty of time for recriminations if and when we get back to the UK. In the meantime, we've got work to do – or rather I have. I want you to stay here in my cabin, get some sleep, and don't come out. The cox'n and the steward will look after you.' He sniffed and eyed the empty glass on his desk. 'Have another brandy. I'll send the cox'n in again to sort out that arm.' He rose from his chair and stepped out of the cabin, calling for Cox'n Sanford.

Cunningham now went for'd to gaze down at the prone figure of Portrova, who was still enshrouded in a Neil Robertson stretcher and lying in one of the seamen's bottom bunks. The bottom end of the stretcher was soaked in blood and Portrova had again lapsed into unconsciousness. Cunningham knelt on the deck and leaned over him, studying in the pale glow of the bunk light what little he could see of the Russian's coarse features. 'So,' he breathed, 'you're the chap who's been causing me all this bloody trouble!'

Then Cox'n Sanford appeared beside him. 'Can't do much more for him, Sir. Too much blood loss. His only chance is back aboard his own ship, where they should have a qualified doctor. He might even need an amputation, so I hope they've got a good one. Risk of gangrene, you know.'

Still studying Portrova's face, Cunningham said, 'Back to his ship is just where he'll be going if I can sort out some sort of truce with the Russians. But you've done the best you can, Cox'n. In fact you've done a bloody good job! Now go back and see if you can do some more for Lieutenant Commander Bradley.'

Sanford nodded and then said, 'By the way, Sir, I'm a bit concerned over Lieutenant Watson. He's got a hell of a fever: temperature well over the ton and he's having difficulties with his breathing. I suspect he may be developing pneumonia, that's if he hasn't already got it.'

'Do whatever you can for him, and keep me in the picture.' Cunningham frowned, stood up and walked quickly back to the control room, where the navigating officer was on the search periscope. 'All quiet, Chris?'

'There's nothing much happening up there, Sir. They still have their motor boat standing off our bows, and Hugh's making sure they keep their distance, but apart from that, nothing. Still all quiet on the destroyer as well, Sir.'

The calm before the storm? Cunningham wondered. Then he said, 'Well, so far, so good. Arrange a relief for the first lieutenant, will you? Better get Guy up there. I need to have a chat with Hugh as soon as possible. I'll be in the wardroom. Now what do I have to do to get a cup of coffee around here? Where's that steward?'

Some five minutes later, although *Sturgeon* was still closed up at "action stations", both Cunningham and Morton were seated on their own in the wardroom. The steward, who had just finished sponging Portrova's blood from the table, had arrived at the door with two steaming cups of coffee. Cunningham put the cup to his mouth, then shied back. 'Bloody hell, that's hot!'

Morton grinned to himself, satisfied to clutch his cup in both hands in an attempt to thaw out his freezing fingers. 'And it's bloody cold up there, Sir.'

'Time of the year, Hugh, time of the year.' Cunningham gingerly patted his scalded lips. 'The cox'n tells me Andrew's in a bit of a bad way – he suspects pneumonia! He's been doped up and wrapped up warm, so let's just hope he'll sweat it out of his system.'

'Christ,' muttered Morton, 'I knew he was bad, but pneumonia? Poor old Andrew. That's all we need.'

Cunningham had another cautious sip of his coffee. 'Donovan all right?'

'Seems to be, Sir.'

Cunningham grunted and took another sip of his coffee. 'Good. Well, Hugh, it looks like we've got some work to do!'

'You've got a plan, Sir?'

'I don't know whether you could call it a plan, exactly. It's all a bit loose at the moment but it's the nearest that I can get to any breakaway procedure at this time, and we can't leave things as they are, can we?' Cunningham was again stroking his chin. 'I've just had a chat with Nigel, and from the information he's given me it appears that we may have a fighting chance of getting both ourselves and *Spearfish* out of this bloody mess. So let's sum up the situation as we think it is. We here in *Sturgeon* are in top form, ready for anything. Right?'

'Well, yes, Sir, of course.' Morton was glad to agree with his captain. 'But,' he added, 'the men have been closed up at action stations for a long time now. Their normal routine is shot to buggery and some will be very tired.'

'We're all bloody tired,' muttered Cunningham, 'but we're just going to stay on the ball for a bit longer yet.' He raised his coffee cup and, ignoring its heat, drained it in one. 'So, let's have a quick appraisal of our current situation, eh! Feel free to interrupt with any questions you may have.'

Morton grinned to himself. This was typical of the old man, but he'd never known Cunningham to make a wrong decision yet. Again Cunningham's thin fingers were gently massaging the sides of that long aquiline nose – a sign that he was in deep concentration. He would say nothing – just sit and listen to his captain.

Cunningham stopped rubbing his nose and began, 'We and *Spearfish* are virtually wedged under the Russian's arse. She can't bring her heavy guns to bear, and she can't use her torpedoes or her depth charges. As long as we stay where we are, fire from her small arms is our biggest worry and we don't want to do anything to start that off: a burst from a machine gun could open up our ballast tanks like a can opener! We believe we've taken away her propulsion and steering – at least I hope we have, because everything is going to depend on that. Nigel tells me that he's wrecked their W/T and all their other sensors, and I believe him. So at this time we can consider our destroyer to be pretty much a lame duck. Furthermore, our own sensors are telling us that there's no other traffic in the near vicinity.' He paused, searching his side pockets for cigarettes. Selecting one, he placed it between his lips and began a further search for a lighter. After patting all his pockets in turn, he finally produced his faithful American Zippo and lit up. Now drawing deeply on his cigarette, he studied the face of his first lieutenant. 'Any questions so far, Hugh?'

Morton shook his head, so Cunningham continued, 'Our ace card at the moment is that we now have her captain! Even though we don't particularly want him, and though we know the bastard's almost dead, I'm hoping they'll want him back. So at least we've got something to barter with, eh?' He paused. 'And then there's *Spearfish*. OK, we've got Nigel back, but I don't think he can take any more, so effectively he's out of our reckoning. *Spearfish* has been pretty badly knocked about but she's by no means finished yet. She has a limited diving capability and propulsion on one side only. She's no sensors to speak of and only her attack periscope is in working order. She also has a leak in one of her external fuel tanks, which is not good, and in addition to this she's got a party of armed Russians on board. You're still with me, Hugh?'

'Yes, Sir… Go on.'

'So you can see then, perhaps we should be playing these bastards at their own game. The only reason they want *Spearfish*, and possibly now ourselves as an unexpected bonus, is political. You know, propaganda – that's what it seems to be all about these days. So just think how they might react to the thought of us accusing them of piracy on the high seas? That's going to put this cold war, or whatever you care to call it, into overdrive! I'm no expert in these things, but I don't think either they or us are ready for that just yet. Let's face it, they know what we're doing up in these waters as well as we know what they do around the UK. Frankly I'm surprised that they've suddenly chosen to sour the situation.'

Morton nodded, but sensed that Cunningham was now rambling on a bit. 'Well, they probably took exception to us horning in on one of their first ballistic nuclear launch trials. And your plan, Sir…?'

'Is there any more coffee?'

Morton pulled aside the door curtains and called to the control room messenger, who was standing by the wheel. 'Find the steward and get some more coffee for the captain.'

The curtains brushed open and the steward laid another pot of steaming coffee on the table. Morton thanked him and then turned back to Cunningham.

Cunningham grunted and poured himself a fresh coffee before pushing the pot over to Morton. 'Nigel seems to think that one of the Russian officers now aboard her is looking to defect to the west. That could come in handy, don't you think? We should also remind them again of the vulnerability of their present situation i.e. that we could, between us, dive and sink them with torpedoes.'

Morton, thinking for a moment, said, 'I'm really not sure, Sir. From what I've heard of the Russian navy they're either fanatics or peasants, doing just what there're told to do. This is a really big beast we're talking about. She could do us an awful lot of damage if things went wrong, or if indeed she isn't quite the lame duck that we think she is.'

Cunningham nodded. 'Exactly, but I still think that with a bit of meaningful negotiation we can come to some sort of agreement. I know that's what the bowler hats back in Whitehall will want, so that's what we'll aim for. But we've got to act quickly while it's still dark up there and, more importantly, a relatively calm sea. If our plan fails then we'll resort to plan B!'

'Plan B, Sir?'

Cunningham's hawk-like features relaxed into what passed for a grin. He shrugged his shoulders. 'There is no plan B, Hugh, but I do need to speak to whoever may now be in charge of the Russian. Their first officer, perhaps?'

'Their first officer is dead, Sir. Nigel told me that when we hauled him aboard, and, so it seems, are many others. It would appear that between them and us, there's going to be quite an extensive casualty list.'

'Hugh, all I want is for those people left in charge aboard the destroyer to think that they're in a no-win situation and succumb to their common sense. But listen to me: at this time they *have* to believe that their bloody destroyer is crippled and that we have the upper hand.'

'So where do we go from here?'

'Well, first of all we'll get that bloody motor boat alongside and hopefully have a meaningful powwow with whoever's in charge.' Now Cunningham focused his piercing grey eyes directly on Morton. 'I reckon that, all things being equal, we've been very lucky up to now, and it's going to be largely down to you and me to see that things stay that way.'

Morton finished his coffee, and then said, 'So, assuming our powwow is successful and they let us go, we've still got a long way to transit before we get to safe waters – off the Norwegian coast, I mean. And with *Spearfish* being a bit of a lame duck, do you really think we'll make it that far unchallenged?'

'I can't look into the future, but I'm banking on the fact that the destroyer will have to look for some sort of help, and with no wireless that's going to be a bit of a problem for them, but it will give us time. Also I'm thinking that they won't now want to turn this little drama into an international crisis. Yes, they would have been quite happy to take *Spearfish* in, and ourselves as well, but only if they could make political capital of it. However, with the situation they're facing now, again I'm banking that they won't want to push their luck any further. They won't want red faces any more than we do. We have to believe Bradley when he tells us about taking out their radio equipment.

Without communications, or, indeed, propulsion and steerage, she'll be the lame duck. No, with a bit of luck I think we stand a good chance of getting a useful head start before any sort of balloon goes up.'

'Sorry, Sir, I'm certainly not trying to pick holes in your thinking, but you've already said that *Spearfish* has only got drive on one side, and she can't go deep.' Morton paused and looked questioningly at his captain. 'So what can she do? Six knots at the most while floating the load? The North Cape is at least 600 miles to the south-west, and it's going to take us some time before reaching the North Cape and safe waters – five days if we're lucky.' He paused and looked at Cunningham. 'Do you really think the Ruskies will give us that space?'

'Yes, well, as far as any transit to the west is concerned, surfaced or otherwise, you've come up with roughly the same figures as me. As to whether we'll be left to get on with it, your guess is as good as mine. Yes, I know it can only be a matter of time before they come looking for her, and yes, we don't know where the nearest Russian unit is! But, d'you know, I've got a feeling in my water that these Russians have had a gutful of us! The ball's not in their court any more. This may now be publicity they'll want to avoid. They may well be glad to see the back of us.'

Morton said, 'I hope you're right, I really do.' Then he said, 'What about towing her? Wouldn't that give us a few extra knots, maybe?'

'Yes, it probably would, but I think that the risks associated with towing may, in this case, outweigh the advantages. No, I think we'd be more useful as her escort. We can watch out for her, and take any necessary action to protect her, while at the same time we'll both be able to dive quickly enough to avoid any trouble that may come our way. We could arrange for a tow later, from one of our own ships, but we'll think about that when the time comes.' Now he straightened up and folded both arms in front of him. 'Well, that's the general plan, Hugh, and I want to get things rolling as soon as possible! The longer we hang about now, the more chance there'll be of losing any advantage we may have! But first of all I need to go up and have a chat with Strong aboard *Spearfish*. You'd better make another general broadcast to let our people know what's happening and what's likely to be happening. I want everyone closed up properly at their diving station and fully on the ball. We aren't going to get a second chance if this goes wrong. When you're happy, come up and join me on the bridge.'

Now on *Sturgeon*'s bridge once again, Cunningham nodded to Bramwell. 'All quiet, Guy?'

'Nothing much to report, Sir. All quiet on the destroyer. Her boat's still standing off, and *Spearfish* is keeping in good station.'

'Good.' Cunningham surveyed the whole scene through his binoculars. Satisfied, he said to Bramwell, 'You can go below now, Guy. Hugh will be up here shortly. Get yourself a cup of coffee and something to eat.'

Bramwell needed no further bidding. With a brief 'Thank you, Sir' he disappeared down the fin ladder. This left only the lookout and the signalman on the bridge with Cunningham, who was now studying the figures on *Spearfish*'s crumpled bridge.

★ ★ ★ ★ ★

Strong now turned to Ravoski and half whispered, 'Right, Viktor, are you still with me?'

'I am, Oliver.' Even now, in this darkness, Strong could sense that enigmatic smile on Ravoski's face.

Within a few minutes a panting Murray arrived on the bridge, where there was now hardly enough room for him to stand.

Ravoski started back down below immediately, while Strong rapidly briefed Murray on what he intended to do. 'Keep in touch with *Sturgeon*, Ross, and for Christ's sake don't let that bloody Russian motor boat come any closer.' Murray nodded in the affirmative and Strong turned to make his way down the ladder to the control room.

As he landed in the conning tower well, Strong saw that the young Lieutenant Gorski was still peering through the attack periscope. Ravoski had moved across to stand by the chart table. There was no sign of the Russian guards.

Strong nodded briefly towards Ravoski and then went directly into Bradley's cabin, where he opened the desk drawer and groped for the Parabellum. Checking that it was still fully loaded, he slid it deep into the right-hand pocket of his coat. Already his stomach was beginning to churn. Now, sitting in Bradley's chair, he took several deep breaths, searching in vain for some sort of composure. Then he returned to the control room to stand beside Ravoski. 'You're going to have to help me out here, Viktor, you know that, don't you!' His voice was low, secretive. He could feel the tremble in his voice.

Ravoski, on the other hand, replied in a normal voice. He spoke openly in English, though Gorski was no more than three feet away from him. 'You have your pistol in your pocket, Oliver?'

'Yes.'

'This is good, but it must stay in your pocket!' He looked into Strong's face. 'You must let me take care of my men. I would like to do this without bloodshed and I am sure that you would like this too, *da*? They speak no English but they will trust me. I am their senior officer.'

'You have a plan?'

'I will simply give some orders. You will cover me, but do nothing unless there is trouble.' Then he stepped forward and patted Gorski on the shoulder. Speaking in Russian, he said, 'You have been doing a good job, Comrad Lieutenant. Maybe one day you too would like to serve in submarines, *da*?'

Gorski stepped back from the periscope. '*Da*, Comrad Kapitan Lieutenant, I think I would like this. Perhaps I could then damage these Britishers, and some Americans too?'

Ravoski continued to pat the young officer's shoulder. 'Yes, yes my friend, I am sure this will happen one day.' But now he looked solemn. 'These Britishers have caused much damage to our ship. She now has no propulsion and no steerage. Also her radar has been wrecked, and they have taken our kapitan prisoner. Our first officer has been killed, together with many others. We dare not risk this other submarine sinking *Otvashni*, for that is what they have declared they will do.'

'But Comrad, do you say we should surrender to these Britishers?' Gorski's features darkened, defiant, angry. Strong sensed trouble, and he buried his right hand deeply into his coat pocket, gripping the butt of the Parabellum.

Ravoski said, 'It is a situation that none of us would have wished for, Comrad, but there are many political issues involved. We, alas, have to work to the will of our masters. I think, Comrad Lieutenant, that we must accept the situation as it is.' Ravoski looked sad but resolute. 'We can do no more at this time; you must understand this, Comrad. We have lost many of our men; we must not lose more. But firstly we must recover our kapitan.' Ravoski removed his hand from Gorski's shoulder. 'We must bring all our guards to this control room, Comrad Lieutenant. You will then give them orders to disarm, and then we must board our motor boat and return to *Otvashni*. Do not be concerned, Comrad Gorski; you have done your job well and we will live to fight another day – you may depend upon that.'

Now Ravoski reached for the main broadcast microphone above his head. Speaking in Russian and in short, terse tones he said, 'This is Kapitan Lieutenant Ravoski. All guards will come to the control room.' He replaced the microphone and turned to Gorski. 'Comrad Gorski, you will explain the situation to our men, and then get them onto the fore-casing, where they will be collected by our motor boat! They must leave their weapons here.'

Within a few minutes all eight guards appeared in the control room, some having been called from their bunks and still wiping sleep from tired eyes, but all listening to Gorski as he explained their situation. Finally, when Gorski ordered them to lay down their weapons, five of the guards obeyed, laying their weapons on the deck, where they were immediately picked up by the control room watch keepers. But the remaining three more senior guards looked questioningly towards Ravoski, confused, sensing that something was not right. Ravoski, leaning nonchalantly against the chart table, said, 'This is not a good day, my friends, but if we wish to save our ship and our kapitan, you must do as you are instructed. There will be other times, but now you must do as Comrad Gorski says.' The remaining three now laid down their weapons and Ravoski continued, 'Now, Comrad Gorski, you will lead these men up to the deck, where they will be picked up by our motor boat. But first, my friend, you also must give me your pistol. The Britishers have said that there must be no arms carried during your repatriation to *Otvashni*. I, too, have to comply with this.'

Without a word, Gorski pulled his pistol from his belt and handed it to Ravoski. Then all eight guards, together with Gorski, were herded up the conning tower ladder and onto the forward casing.

Ye gods, Strong thought, this man should be playing at the Old Vic. He breathed a long sigh of genuine relief, and Ravoski said, 'See, my friend, that was not so difficult, eh? You should send at least three of your men to guard them until we can transfer them. Now we two will go back to the bridge and supervise the safe return of my men to their ship, *da*?'

★   ★   ★   ★   ★

On *Sturgeon*'s bridge the lookout reported to Bradley, 'Seems to be some more movement on *Spearfish*'s bridge, Sir, and there's men on her forward casing.'

Cunningham trained his glasses on *Spearfish* and watched as nine figures emerged from her fin to stand huddled in a group on the casing. Then three more men carrying Lanchesters emerged from her fin and appeared to be standing guard over this group. In the signalman's lantern Cunningham could see that the men in the huddle were clearly Russian, and the three armed men British. He picked up his megaphone and called towards *Spearfish*'s bridge.

'Is that you, Lieutenant Strong?'

'It is, Sir. I have Kapitan Leitenant Ravoski up here with me. We have our nine other Russian guests under guard on the casing, awaiting transfer back to their ship.'

'Well done! Wait as you are for further orders.' Cunningham lowered his megaphone and muttered under his breath, 'Bloody well done! How the hell did he manage that?' Then again raising his megaphone, he called towards the motor boat still standing off his bows, 'Ahoy, the motor boat. Does anyone speak English?'

From the stern of the motor boat a lone figure stood up, his leather coat and black ushanka indicating that he was some sort of officer. '*Da*. I speak a little English. I am Leitenant Maronoff. What do you want?' His voice held a tone of defiance which Cunningham didn't miss.

'Bring your boat around to the starboard side of the other submarine and take off nine of your crewmen.' Cunningham paused and lowered his megaphone, hoping that he had been understood.

The Russian officer called back in very fragmented English, 'You will wait, please.' Then he sat back down in the stern sheets of his boat.

Cunningham felt annoyance building up inside of him. 'Wait be damned. Cheeky sod.' Then he called down the voice pipe, 'Helm – Bridge. Ask Lieutenant Morton to come to the bridge.' Then stamping his numbed feet, more through impatience than the effect of the bitter cold, he turned his megaphone back towards the motor boat. 'Ahoy, the motor boat. You will obey my last order, immediately!'

The officer in the boat again stood, and again called back, 'You will wait!' But this time he remained standing.

Now Morton stood beside Cunningham.

Cunningham said, 'Glad to see you, Hugh. Everything ready for action down below?'

'All closed up and ready for anything, Sir.'

'Good. I'm having a bit of a problem with this bloody motor boat at the moment. The bastards don't seem in a hurry to co-operate.' Again he raised his megaphone. 'You will do as I have instructed – now. If you do not co-operate, nine of your comrades will drown and we will take your captain with us. Also you may give us no choice other than to sink your ship.' Then, turning to Morton, he said, 'Get two more seamen up here on the casing with Lanchesters, Hugh, just in case the boat's crew or anyone else aboard the destroyer decides to play silly buggers.'

The officer in the boat again called, 'You will wait.' He then appeared to be speaking into some sort of telephone.

'Obviously he's asking for advice from the destroyer,' Morton volunteered.

'I'll give him some bloody advice if he doesn't pull his finger out. We can't afford to wait here for much longer.' Cunningham's agitation was plain to see. 'If necessary, *Spearfish* can get 'em all back down below and take them back to the UK with her! And that goes for us and Captain what's his bloody name. I had hoped that it wouldn't come to that, though.'

Then, as though being a party to Cunningham's thoughts, the Russian officer again called from the motor boat, 'Ahoy, the Britisher, we will do as you ask. We want no further violence!'

'I will trust you.' Cunningham was relieved but still wary. 'But be assured that if there is any more shooting, we will destroy both you and your ship. When you have taken your men from the other submarine, you will return to my port side and pick up your captain!'

'I will do as you say,' replied the Russian.

Now the motor boat's engine spluttered into life and she made her way towards *Spearfish*'s starboard side. Cunningham turned towards *Spearfish* and yelled, 'Cut your tow, but keep your present station.'

★ ★ ★ ★ ★

Strong and Ravoski leaned over the starboard side of *Spearfish*'s bridge, watching the approach of the motor boat. Strong had already prepared two engine room artificers, together with *his* second cox'n, to be ready to cut the tow wire. Now they were up on *Spearfish*'s bow doing just that, while Strong used the voice pipe to order the port main motor movements necessary to keep station.

The Russian motor boat bumped alongside *Spearfish*'s starboard ballast tanks, and lines were thrown to the men waiting on her casing. Two seamen took charge of the lines and held the boat steady as one by one the nine Russians slid down the tanks and were pulled into the boat. Not a word was spoken. The signalman on *Spearfish*'s bridge continued to train his Aldis lantern on the motor boat as the lines were thrown back and she pulled away in a wide turn, back around *Spearfish*'s stern, to make her way towards *Sturgeon*.

On *Spearfish*'s bridge, Ravoski turned to Strong and said, 'This is good, Oliver.'

'Good so far,' replied Strong, 'but let's save any congratulations till later, eh.' Now the second cox'n came aft on the casing and called up to Strong, 'Tow wire's gone, Sir.'

'Very good,' shouted Strong. 'All hands below, now.'

With the Russian boat now approaching *Sturgeon*'s port side, Cunningham called down the voice pipe to open the fore hatch and get the Russian captain onto the casing, together with the full casing party.

Again *Sturgeon*'s accommodation space hatch clunked open, and once again Able Seaman Samuels, who had opened it, cursed roundly as a deluge of freezing water landed on his shoulders. Then he was pushed aside as six more seamen, together with Petty Officer Mitchell, climbed up the vertical ladder to the casing.

Portrova was strapped firmly into the Neil Robinson stretcher. Now conscious, despite the liberal doses of morphine supplied by the coxswain, he moaned with pain as his stretcher bearers stood the stretcher on its end before hauling it carefully up through the hatchway.

Bradley, still lying on Cunningham's bunk, had realised what was happening, and climbing from his bunk, he draped a heavy coat over his shoulders and walked forward to follow the stretcher through to the fore hatch. With the stretcher finally settled on the casing, he knelt and shone a torch directly onto the pallid features of Portrova.

Portrova's eyes remained closed, but then, almost as though he could sense the presence of Bradley, he spoke, his voice little more than a strained whisper.

'So, Commander Bradley. All this has been for nothing, *da*? And is it that now we will again go our separate ways? Yes, I think it is.' He paused momentarily, gulping for air. 'But you should know, Commander, that I bear you no ill will. It would seem that I have lost and you have won. But such is life, *da*? If I live, I will suffer the consequences of my failure, and this holds no fear for me. But you should know, Commander, the events of the past weeks have very little to do with you, or your reason for being here. These were events ordained many years ago, and you and your crew are – how is it you Britishers say – the fall guys? I was saved from the sea by Britishers many years ago, but those Britishers were not as you. For you, Commander Bradley,

I now have respect, and this is not just because you appear to have saved my life, but because you are a man of honour. Both of your vessels will leave this area with no interference from my ship. You will go, and we will go. Then this business will be over, *da*? We will never meet again.'

Portrova closed his eyes, but now seemed to be struggling to pull his right hand from the confining straps of the stretcher. 'I would shake your hand, Commander, but it seems that I am confined. However, I wish you well.' Again he lapsed into unconsciousness. Bradley was glad that he had resisted the urge to interrupt him. This whole business had all been so tragically futile. He reached down and placed a hand upon Portrova's shoulder and again felt hot tears running down his cheeks. Whether this was the culmination of the stress built up over the past weeks, or this new empathy he felt for this man who just hours ago had been his mortal enemy, he didn't know and now he really didn't care.

The Russian motor boat was bumping alongside *Sturgeon*'s port ballast tanks. Two seamen, now shouldering their Lanchesters, caught the lines that were thrown and held her steady. Four more seamen, under the watchful eyes of Mitchell and Bradley, lowered the stretcher carefully over the side and into the boat.

Cunningham called from the bridge, 'Ahoy, the motor boat. We have returned your men and your captain! You will now return to your ship, but you should know that any attempt at further action will result in your destruction. Please advise your senior officer of this. My two submarines will shortly break away. We expect no opposition!'

The leather coated officer standing in the stern of the motor boat replied, 'Ahoy, the Britisher. You may now go. We do not intend further action, but where is Kapitan Lieutenant Ravoski? Is he not to be returned to us?'

'Ravoski will be held until we reach the United Kingdom. You will understand that this incident has many political connotations. He will be returned in good health in the course of time. Do you understand me?'

'*Da*, I understand you, Kapitan. I will now give your message to my senior officers.'

The motor boat sheered away, heading back towards the port side of *Otvashni*, with the young Russian officer now crouched in its stern sheets, again speaking on his telephone. Cunningham scratched his chin and pondered the situation. Could this really be so easy? Then he turned to Morton. 'D'you know, Hugh, I think we're going to be all right after all. I'm betting those buggers have had enough of us – well, we'll soon see! Stand by to dive whenever *Spearfish* is ready. It'll be a stern dive. Go below and get things ready, will you.'

Morton disappeared below and Cunningham again picked up his megaphone and shouted across to *Spearfish*, 'We've got rid of our gash! Are you opened up for diving and ready to go?'

Strong shouted back, 'Affirmative, Sir. Ready whenever you say, but you know our limitations!'

'Clear your bridge and watch me through your attack. Dive when I dive. Dive astern with as much power as you can muster. Go to ninety feet and come around on a starboard arc to a course of two-five-zero. I'll be taking a port arc. Try not to bump into me! Stay on that course for four hours, then come to periscope depth and look for me! I'll be looking for you! Understood?'

'Affirmative, Sir. Clearing my bridge now.'

Cunningham watched carefully until all the heads had disappeared from *Spearfish*'s battered bridge, and then he turned to watch the Russian motor boat pulling up to the starboard side of *Otvashni*. At long last *Otvashni*'s remaining searchlight went out, leaving the two submarines in almost total darkness. The effect of this was startling to Cunningham. It seemed to him that they'd been bathed in a relentless light beam for hours. Now he found it difficult to adjust his vision to this darkness. Was this a good sign, or a portent of yet more trouble? Well, he wasn't about to hang around and find out! He turned to the signalman and the lookout behind him. 'Clear the bridge!'

In the control room Morton was on the search periscope, keeping an eye both on *Otvashni* in front of him and *Spearfish* on his starboard beam. Cunningham pressed the klaxon button twice, and ordered, 'Go 200 feet, Hugh!' Then he took over the periscope, while Morton moved across to stand behind the planesmen. Taking one last look through the periscope, Cunningham stood back and snapped up its handles. 'Down all masts.'

Sturgeon's stern dipped as she began to drive astern. Cunningham called to Morton, 'When you reach 200 feet, go to half ahead together, turn through a port arc, come around to two-five-zero and maintain a speed of ten knots. Keep closed up at "diving stations".'

Then he strode forward into the sound room, where White and Bell were closed up in front of their active sonar sets. Cunningham said, 'Keep a good look out for any contacts, especially *Spearfish*. She'll be running at ninety feet, on a course parallel to ours. You can't mistake her; she's running on one motor.'

'I've got her now, Sir.' White was concentrating on the screen in front of him. 'She's just coming down to ninety feet and moving away to starboard. Range is about 100 yards and increasing.'

'So far, so good,' breathed Cunningham. 'Keep a good eye on her; we don't want any underwater bumps at this stage of the game. Report to me when she's steering two-five-zero.' He turned and stepped through the sound room door while calling quite unnecessarily over his shoulder, 'Oh, and report any other contacts within fifteen thousand yards!'

★   ★   ★   ★   ★

The time that it had taken *Sturgeon* and *Spearfish* to journey west to the North Cape seemed endless – sometimes dived, sometimes snorting, and at times on the surface. This was a tense time both for Cunningham, whose *Sturgeon* was now playing the role of "mother hen", and for *Spearfish*, where Strong was now back in command and sharing the same experiences.

After the first two days of the transit Cunningham had decided to use his radar whenever possible, and on two occasions they had gone deep on picking up distant rackets. But there had been no other interruptions. Both Cunningham and Strong had found it hard to believe this apparent good fortune, and on rounding the North Cape Cunningham sent a surfacing signal, to which he added, almost as an afterthought, that the operation had been a success. Both boats then set a course towards the UK, knowing that they still had a 1500-mile transit to Faslane. Cunningham had calculated that if the weather remained fair, as it presently was, and there were no interruptions, this transit, allowing for *Spearfish's* speed restrictions, would take somewhere in the region of eleven days.

Cunningham now had the time for many in-depth conversations with Bradley and slowly but surely he pieced together the story of *Spearfish's* capture, but he was deeply concerned.

Bradley was not in good shape, either mentally or physically. The events of the past weeks had taken everything from him: confidence, spirit, maybe even his soul. In truth, he was a broken man. He repeatedly asked himself what had been the reason for all this. Since *Spearfish* had set out from Portsmouth all those weeks ago, what had he achieved? The answer to this was nothing, absolutely nothing! In truth, his only achievement had been to leave a sickening trail of death and destruction. Now he had purposely isolated himself in Cunningham's cabin, eating, drinking or sleeping very little, and talking only to Cunningham.

Another of Cunningham's major concerns was the condition of Watson, who had been unable to move from his bunk since being pulled from the water up there in the Barents. Sanford again confirmed his fears that Watson had developed full-blown pneumonia. Watson was in a very bad way, drifting in and out of a shallow, feverish sleep which sometimes lasted for just moments, or sometimes for hours at a time. Sleep during which he continuously babbled, sometimes loudly but more often than not in a low, barely audible mumble, and always incoherent. Sanford spent many hours at his side, and when not able to be there, had detailed the steward to take his place. Cunningham too was a regular visitor, but there was little any of them could do apart from keeping an extra blanket in place over Watson's sleeping bag and cooling his sweating brow with cold towels.

Sanford told Cunningham, 'This'll only go one of two ways now. I've given him all the drugs we've got, but if his fever doesn't break soon we're going to lose him! He's pretty much out of it for most of the time – rambling a lot, you know? Can't really make out what he's on about but the generators keep cropping up. Chief EA Arnold has been with him for a lot of the time and he can't make any more sense out of it than I can. He is in a very bad way though, Sir. I don't want to be a prophet of doom but I'm beginning to think he won't make it.'

'Generators, eh?' Cunningham replied. 'Well, that at least makes some sense. He's had a lot on his mind since we left Faslane.' Now he felt strong twinges of guilt: had he put too much stress on Andrew Watson over those bloody generators?

Sanford's prophecy was right. Three days after *Sturgeon* had altered course to the south-west, Watson gave up his fight for life. Total sadness and despondency now hung over all those in *Sturgeon* – a sadness which now completely eclipsed the jubilation of their recent success. Cunningham was mortified.

★ ★ ★ ★ ★

Aboard *Spearfish* Strong was a satisfied man, though the news of the latest death aboard *Sturgeon* had caused him sorrow and regret. But as *Spearfish's* acting captain he had done all that could be expected of him. He had taken himself out of the watch bill, which allowed him to spend many long hours in conversation with Ravoski, and with each day's passing, his liking for this elderly Russian increased. Viktor was in many ways a character not unlike Toby Cannings – garrulous, completely open and often very amusing. Again he was a firm favourite with *Spearfish's* crew. But perhaps pointedly, in all their conversations Ravoski never once raised the subject of what was going to happen to him when *Spearfish* reached base, and Strong was glad of this.

The weather remained favourable and on reaching the Shetlands Cunningham sent a further signal requesting a tow for *Spearfish* for the remainder of the transit to Faslane. The Admiralty sent the tug *Hauler* to take *Spearfish* in tow.

★ ★ ★ ★ ★

Now *Sturgeon* was reducing speed prior to passing through the Rhu narrows, while *Spearfish* was still on tow in the Minches, continuing to make steady progress south. Cunningham stood on *Sturgeon's* bridge, with Morton beside him. Again there was that group of families and friends welcoming them, waving from the water's edge on their starboard side.

Morton said, 'How the hell did these people know that we would be here today? Seems like security's not so tight after all, Sir!'

Cunningham, with his glasses still trained to starboard, smiled wryly and muttered, 'Ah well, such is life!' Then he turned his gaze to the port side, and didn't fail to miss the sharp glint of sunlight reflected from either a binocular glass or a camera lens, up there in those rugged gorse- and heather-covered hills.

EPILOGUE

The passage from the Barents back to Faslane was the last time that Lieutenant Commander Nigel Bradley would ever go to sea in a submarine. At a Board of Enquiry held aboard the depot ship HMS *Adamant* in late January of 1960, he was recommended to face a court martial, which subsequently found him guilty of hazarding *Spearfish* and the lives of her crew. He was immediately relieved of command and sent on indefinite leave to fully recover from his wounds. On his return from this leave he was returned to general service, where he served for almost twelve months as the first lieutenant of a frigate before, thoroughly disillusioned, he resigned his commission. Then, in the autumn of 1962, together with his family he emigrated to Australia, where he worked in the newspaper industry until his death thirty years later.

Cunningham was also called to a Board of Enquiry on the same criteria as Bradley. This Board was duly dismissed, and Cunningham continued his command of *Sturgeon* for a further six months. Promoted to commander in the late summer of 1960, he was appointed commander SM1 based in HMS *Dolphin*. He received an OBE in the New Year's honours list of January 1961, though there was no mention of the incident in the Barents within this citation. Retiring with the rank of captain in 1975, and now a widower, he spends his days still in his house at Harrow, tending his beloved garden and fish pond. Now, at the age of eighty-seven, he still takes an active interest in the submarine service.

Both Strong and Morton went on to command conventional submarines before continuing their individual careers in the nuclear submarine programme, where both eventually gained commands of nuclear-powered submarines, with Strong eventually rising to the rank of rear admiral.

Viktor Ravoski was granted diplomatic immunity on his arrival back in the UK and, soon after this, British citizenship. Working as an interpreter for the British government for three years before taking up a career in teaching, he died of a heart attack in the autumn of 1978, remaining a firm friend of Strong until the time of his death.

Leading Seaman Thomas Donovan continued in the submarine service, retiring as a CPO submarine coxswain at the age of forty, and becoming a London postman. Having four married sons, he still lives in London with his wife June and is still in regular contact with his old friend Dixie Deane.

"Knocker" White, rated Petty Officer White in the January of 1960, met an untimely end while still serving in *Sturgeon*. On a bright sunny July morning of that year, while riding his beloved Norton Dominator to work, he was killed instantaneously in a head-on collision with an MoD truck on the narrow twisting road between Helensburgh and the Faslane submarine base. The Norton was a total write-off.

Petty Officer "Gus" Ramsay retired from the service early in 1960, and took up a job in the Ministry of Defence torpedo maintenance organisation at Gosport. He did not live long to enjoy his naval pension, dying of a severe stroke in the summer of 1961.

The destroyer *Otvashni* was eventually located by the Russians and towed back to Archangel. Kapitan Alexci Portrova had his left leg amputated shortly after his arrival back in Russia. This operation saved his life but he was never forgiven by his masters at the Kremlin for his part in what they too referred to as "The Barents Incident". While still recovering from surgery, Portrova was called before a tribunal, where he was summarily stripped of his rank and dismissed from the service. Within months he had become a full-blown alcoholic recluse, existing in a sleazy bedsit somewhere in the suburbs of Moscow, where in the summer of 1962 his partially decomposed and fly-infested body was found hanging from a beam. The pathologist confirmed that he had been reunited with his beloved Anna some two months earlier.